For anyone who has ever felt displaced.

NOWHERE, MISSISSIPPI

JEFF FRANTAL
PAUL MUNRO

NOWHERE, MISSISSIPPI

JEFF FRANTAL

PAUL MUNRO

ISBN 978-1-941907-59-7

ISBN 978-1-941907-60-3

Published by Firebrand Publishing

CONTENTS

FOREWORD

PAUL MUNRO

Back in February of 2018, my good friend, Jeff Frantal, asked if I would help him write a memoir of his teenage years. I told him I didn't know the first thing about writing a memoir, as I had only written fiction before. However, the project intrigued me for a number of reasons. These were not your average teenage years, you understand. Not even close.

When a troubled, young Jeff was thirteen years-old, his father shipped him off to a Southern Baptist boys home, 400 miles from Atlanta, in a place called Eastabuchie, Mississippi.

Easta-where?

Imagine a backwoods hellhole in the middle of nowhere, hence the title of the novel.

Jeff was fond of recounting all of the wild memories from his time there. He had a bottomless pit of stories, ranging from harrowing to hilarious, and often a blend of both. I eagerly lapped them up. For as long as I have known him, Jeff has been a captivating storyteller. But how could I help him tell *his* story in a way that truly captured his experiences? I had no idea, and neither did he, but we went for it anyway.

As we stumbled our way through the process, our ideas evolved into something beyond a memoir. We gathered some of Jeff's most outlandish stories and began weaving a fictional narrative around them, bringing a crazy cast of misfits to life along the way. From there, we brought you to Nowhere, Mississippi. A place where the names have been changed and liberties have been taken, but the essence of Jeff's story remains. The people. The place. The past.

THE MIDDLE OF NOWHERE

Sunday, April 1, 1990 - Day 1

I wish I could scream into a mic and let everything pour out of me, but there's no one who cares to listen. No one gives two shits about me anymore. That could be the album title of my life right now. It's a heavy metal soundtrack that has turned my mind into a mosh pit. And how could it not be? I'm a month shy of getting my driver's license, and I have to spend the next ninety days in a Mississippi boys home.

My mood darkens as I gaze out the passenger side window of the rental car. Beyond the glass, a redneck dystopia flashes by like an endless movie reel of pine trees and trailers. So, this is Nowhere, Mississippi, huh? Of course, it is! This place is one step from *Deliverance*, and I'm not talking about that crappy Christian metal band either.

"Dad really pulled out all the stops this time, didn't he?" I lean back in the seat and crack my knuckles. "He should've just sent me to juvie like the judge said. At least I'd be back in Atlanta instead of being dumped here with a bunch of inbreds playing banjos!"

I glance over at Joyce, my dad's insufferable secretary. He was "too busy" to bring me himself, of course, so he sent the next worst person imaginable.

"We've been through this, Will," she mumbles in her unbearable nasal tones. "Your father is only trying to do what's best for you."

"What's best for me, or what's best for *him*?"

Joyce sighs. "What's best for everyone, I suppose."

I snort out a scornful laugh and shake my head. "I guess I'm talking to you like you actually care. How stupid of me! I'll tell you one thing for sure, though. Mom would never approve of this. She would be furious! She would…"

A tear trickles down my cheek before I have a chance to blink it back. I wipe it away, trying to ignore the look of pity in Joyce's eyes. She reaches out a consoling hand and draws it back as I flinch away from her touch. Joyce frowns and pulls the car over to the side of the road. She checks her cheap perm in the rearview mirror and turns to look at me.

"Listen, sweetie," she says. "I know how tough it's been since your mother's accident." I blink back another tear. "But none of that is your father's fault. He's struggling just as much and he's been struggling with everything that's going on with you. So, if you can't accept the blame for landing yourself in this situation, then at least try to accept the situation you're in." Joyce sighs again. "And the situation we're in right now is that we're lost."

No shit! She's driven back and forth along the same goddamn

road for the last twenty minutes, too stupid to follow the directions and too timid to stop and ask the local hicks for help.

"*You're* the one who's lost," I tell her.

"Well, you could try being more helpful, Will. I've already told you what we're looking for. The young man I spoke with on the phone said the driveway is about a quarter mile past the fire tire. You could help me by looking for one."

"Well, since I have no idea what a fire tire is, how the hell am I supposed to know what to look for? You're sure that's what he said?"

"For the hundredth time, yes! That's exactly what he said. I wrote it down right here in the directions." Joyce waves the piece of paper as though I haven't seen her constantly checking it.

"But you didn't ask him what a fire tire is? What have you been looking for this whole time? Some flaming tire on the side of the road with an arrow pointing the way? There's got to be a sign for this place somewhere. What's it called again? Victory Bridge or something?"

"Victory Ridge. And, no, the man said they don't have a sign. That's why he told me to look for the fire tire."

"They don't have a sign? Even that homeless guy outside the airport had a sign. What kind of dump are you dropping me off at? You should just drive us back to Hattiesburg, so we can call Dad and tell him this is a huge mistake."

Joyce adjusts her glasses again and squints at the directions as if she must have missed something the first few hundred times she read them.

"I'll just have to stop somewhere and ask," she mutters. "The next place we see, I suppose."

The next place we see is a dirt lot with three trailers stacked side by side that look like they've been duct-taped together. A horde of animals, dogs, chickens, and goats roam around a junk-littered yard. I'm about to suggest the next place we see, but Joyce is already pulling off of the road.

The chickens scatter and the dogs break into a barking frenzy as they charge toward the car. One leaps at Joyce's window as she parks, and she flinches away with a yelp. She looks on the verge of turning the hell around when the front door of the middle trailer flies open.

A pale, shirtless man emerges and shouts something at the dogs. They bound off toward him, following behind as he marches our way. Joyce rolls down her window.

"Y'all ain't from the CPS, is ya?" the man yells.

Joyce clears her throat and fixes her best fake smile. "No, sir, we're not. We're just…"

"The hell y'all want then? This here's private property, understand? This ain't no turnaround spot."

"Y-yes, sir. I understand that," Joyce stammers. "We're sorry to intrude like this, but we're a little lost and we're hoping someone could point us in the right direction."

The man hawks and spits loose a long stream of brown saliva on the ground between his feet and the car.

"What y'all lookin' for?" he asks.

"Well, the directions I was given aren't very clear. I was told to look for a…"

"Don't care what ya was told, lady. Jus' tell me what y'all are lookin' for and quit wastin' my time."

"We're looking for a place called Victory Ridge."

The man leans down to peer past Joyce, his attention now firmly fixed on me.

"That where you're goin', boy?" he says, flashing a grotesque grin with more gaps than brown teeth. I force myself to nod, and his grin widens. "Went an' got in some hot water, didn't ya? Gotta go live with all them other troubled boys. Well, it's 'bout to get a whole lot hotter in there for ya, boy." He laughs, and my stomach lurches and twists.

"Sir," Joyce squeaks, "would you mind telling us how to find this place?"

The man hawks another glob of spit on the ground. "The driveway's right over there." He points behind us, across the street toward a small road we must have passed a half-dozen times.

"Thank you!" Joyce says, already shifting into gear, but the man's attention is still focused on me.

"Brother Bennett's gonna set ya straight, boy," he calls out as Joyce reverses toward the main road. "He's gonna rid ya of all them demons."

"Oh my God!" Joyce cries out. "That was absolutely terrifying!"

My sentiments exactly.

———

THE CREEPY HICK'S words echo inside my head as Joyce steers us onto the driveway across the road. *Brother Bennett* is the name my dad mentioned. "A man of firm discipline and faith," he explained as he informed me of my fate. "Those are the things you need the most right now, son. This is the best option you've got."

The best option for him, more like. Dad wasn't looking for a way to rid me of demons. He was just looking for a way to rid himself of me. Out of sight, out of mind. That's why he vetoed juvie. Dekalb Youth Detention Center would be far too close to home. At least I would still be in civilization, though.

"Be thankful you aren't getting locked up with all those inner city kids," Dad told me. "You'd wind up straight back in the system, just like them. Brother Bennett has his own way of doing things. He's a man who gets results."

Dad must have mentioned this a dozen times during that conversation, along with Brother Bennett being a "big man" who knows how to handle himself. Good for him! I honestly don't care how big and intimidating he is. He's still only one guy. What is he going to do that someone hasn't already tried?

I lean forward in my seat as our low-budget rental car rattles along the potholed driveway. Columns of densely packed pines border both sides of the road, blocking out any view of where we are heading. After a couple of winding turns, the trees give way to a wide, green clearing in the woods. The driveway stretches out in front of us, curving up the side of a grassy ridge with a long red-brick building on top.

As we make our way toward the hill, we pass between two fields. The one to our left is a bumpy mess of turf and dirt. Patches of grass are streaked with white paint as if someone was trying to line a football field. The area to our right looked pretty much the same except for three shabby-looking trailers near the foot of the hill and a couple of pickup trucks parked alongside.

"You've got to be kidding!" I glance from side to side as we begin our ascent up the ridge. "*This* is where he sent me?"

My eyes follow the wall of pine trees surrounding the property. I wasn't expecting a giant barbed-wire fence like the detention center, but this is supposed to be a school for delinquent kids for crying out loud! I've seen more security at a Chuck E. Cheese! It's basically a straight shot through the woods back to the main road.

Even Joyce squints around skeptically, but her eyes light up as we reach the crest of the hill. "Look right there, Will! Some boys are out playing basketball." She points toward a gravel lot beside the building. Sure enough, a couple of guys are shooting hoops against a wooden backboard that's nailed to a power line post.

"See now?" Joyce chirps at me. "You can be outside playing sports just like them. That's not so bad, is it?"

I swallow my response as our tires crunch across the gravel, and the boys' heads swivel our direction. They pause their game and turn around to stare at us. I size them up while Joyce rolls to a stop, next to a rickety wooden porch on the side of the building. They're both around my age, possibly a year or two older. As a spectacle, however, the pair could not look more unalike.

One is a slim African American dude in a pair of gold and purple Lakers shorts, bouncing the basketball between his legs as he watches us. The other guy is an oversized white kid who looks like he eats every meal at Golden Corral. He folds his arms across the front of his sweat-drenched t-shirt, pinching his flushed face into a scowl.

Once again, the creepy hick's words return to haunt me. *"Went an' got in some hot water, didn't ya? Gotta go live with all them other troubled boys. Well, it's 'bout to get a whole lot hotter in there for ya, boy."*

Shut up! I tell him, wiping the beads of sweat from my forehead.

Glancing around, I spy more troubled boys leering at us from the porch. Others emerge from the side door of the building, jockeying for a view. I scan the crowd of unsavory faces. Most of their expressions brim with curiosity. The rest watch on with callous indifference. Either way, this doesn't feel like a welcome wagon.

Joyce clears her throat and peers at me through her thick-rimmed glasses. "It's time, Will." She reaches down and unbuckles her seatbelt. "We need to get this over with."

The back of my neck prickles with heat. "*Oh yeah?* I'm pretty sure it's you who needs to get this over with, Joyce. That's why Dad sent you, isn't it? 'A good dentist always keeps his hands clean,' as he likes to say."

Joyce's forehead wrinkles in a frown. "I'm here because he asked me to help."

"To help dump me in this shithole of a place? Wow, what a saint you are! I hope you feel good about yourself." I stare at my lap for a second and look back up at her. "You can still do the right thing, though. Just help me talk to my dad. We could ask to use their phone. Please, that's all I'm asking!"

I gaze at Joyce imploringly, but all she does is tut and roll her eyes. "We've been through this, Will. I don't know how many times I have to tell you. Your father said no phone calls. He was very clear about that."

I wilt into my seat with a sigh, and her expression softens. "Listen, sweetie, this isn't something you can avoid, okay? We're here, and this is happening. I need to get you inside and sign your paperwork, or I'm going to miss my flight home. Your father needs me back in the office tomorrow."

"I'm sure he does," I mutter through clenched teeth. "I guess we shouldn't waste anymore time then, huh? We need to make sure you get back to service my dad again."

I relish the wounded look in Joyce's eyes and the flicker of resentment that follows. She purses her lips and stares at me in disgust.

"I think that man back there was right," she says, with a tremble in her voice. "Maybe there are demons inside you."

She grips the handle of the car door and shoves it open, stepping out onto the gravel and slamming it shut behind her. Good riddance! If being ditched here means I don't have to look at her stupid face again, then so be it.

I cross my arms and stare at the dashboard, trying to ignore the rabble outside and the anxiety knotting in my stomach. My eyes linger on the empty ignition, and I fight back a scream. But even if Joyce had left the keys, I wouldn't know where the hell to go. Anywhere but here, I guess.

None of that matters now, though. Sitting alone inside the car, I feel the final dregs of hope filter out of me. I might be lost in the middle of *Nowhere*, but I can remember when my life was very different. I can remember what it was like before everything changed.

THE DEVIL IN DENIM

The week before my mom's accident, I made the middle school honor roll for the second year running. Mom made a fuss about it as usual. A trip to Perimeter Mall for a shopping spree at Spencer's and a pit stop at Orange Julius, in the food court afterward. She sat there, fretting over the length of my jeans while I sucked down my Cream Supreme.

"We really need to get you some new clothes," she said to me, and I groaned, thinking she is about to drag me around Macy's again. "Don't worry, honey." Her wide smile was always reassuring. "At the rate you're sprouting, there's no way we're shopping here. I'll pick you up a few things next week when I'm at the outlets with The Girls."

The Girls were my mom's best friends, Margerie, Margaret, and Diane. I remember standing in our driveway the following Saturday, watching Mom lower her tall, thin frame into Margaret's station wagon. As they pulled away, she rolled down the window and waved at me from the passenger seat.

"Throw your dirty clothes in the laundry while I'm gone," she called out. "You've worn that same t-shirt for the past four days!"

Those were the last words she ever said to me.

———

I HAVE LOST count of how many days I've worn the t-shirt I'm wearing now, though. It is a black *Reign in Blood* Slayer tee that's too badass to take off. That aside, the rest of my gear is pretty standard, just a pair of pale blue Levis and some Chuck Taylor high-tops. Compared to the guys who have gathered outside on the porch, I look like I've arrived for a photo shoot. They're all dressed in the same drab uniform, basically a plain t-shirt of some kind, with shorts or khaki pants.

Drawing a deep breath, I wipe my sweaty palms on my jeans and unbuckle my seatbelt. Being gawked at by a bunch of goons isn't my idea of a good time. It beats being baked alive in this car, though. I'm only making a bigger scene by sitting here, anyway. As *Metallica* would say, it's time to "Jump in the Fire."

I take another long breath and reach out to open the door. My hand stops halfway to the handle as I glimpse a flurry of movement to my left and turn toward the porch. All of the boys who had formed an audience are now clearing out in all directions. They peer back at me as they vacate the porch, but there's haste in their steps as if something spurred them on their way.

As I try to locate Joyce, someone taps on the window next to me. I jerk back around with a gasp, but it isn't my dad's charming secretary who's standing outside the door. A tall, middle-aged man in a black cowboy hat leans down and peers at me through the glass. My pulse pounding, I roll down the window.

"William Douglas?" The man's drawl is deep and thick. I nod as his dark brown eyes look me over. "My name's Brother Bennett. Welcome to Victory Ridge, son. It's time to get out the car now."

I fumble with the handle and ease the door open. Brother Bennett backs up a few steps, rising to his full height again as I step out onto the gravel lot. Other than his hat and a pair of brown leather boots, he's dressed from neck to feet in blue denim. The sleeves of his shirt are sheared off, exposing broad shoulders and a pair of burly arms.

Dad is right enough, I guess. Brother Bennett's size is nothing to sneeze at. He's easily six-two or six-three, several inches taller than I am. It is not like he's jacked like an American Gladiator or anything, though. Standing in front of me with his hands on his hips, he looks more like John Wayne than Hulk Hogan.

"My dad said you're a big man," I tell him. "But you ain't so big."

Someone gasps, and I spy Joyce standing a few yards behind Brother Bennett with her hand over her mouth. Brother Bennett glances back at her and turns his attention toward me again. Narrowing his eyes, he folds his bare arms across his chest.

"There ain't no man bigger than God, son. Round here, it's best you remember that. Now get your things and come with me. It's time to get ourselves acquainted." His mouth slants into a tight-lipped smile, and an icy tingle shoots up my spine.

I swallow the dry lump in my throat and turn around. As I shuffle toward the rear of the car, Joyce scurries past me to pop the trunk.

"You don't make things easy on yourself, do you?" she whispers while I reach inside to grab my suitcase. "Try to be polite, for goodness sake!"

She turns and marches up to Brother Bennett. "My apologies for not introducing myself properly. I'm Joyce O'Malley. I work for Will's father. He mentioned there was some paperwork I needed to sign."

"Yes, ma'am," Brother Bennett says, shaking her hand. "My wife, Tammy, has all that ready for you. We were expecting y'all a couple of hours ago."

Joyce clears her throat. "Yes, I'm sorry about that. We had trouble with the directions. I was told to look for a fire tire of some kind."

"Fire tower," Brother Bennett drawls like he's drinking his words.

Joyce blinks at him. "Excuse me?"

"Fire tower," he repeats and points back toward the main road, where a tall wooden pylon with a small cabin at the top rises above the pines. "That ol' tower right there's the tallest structure in the whole county. So, seeing as it's just a quarter-mile from the end of this driveway, we figure it shouldn't be hard for folks to find. But maybe y'all were looking for something else."

Joyce's cheeks burn red. "How silly of me," she mumbles and peers down at her watch. "Well, I hate to be rude, Brother Bennett, but I do have a flight to catch. I'd like to sign Will's paperwork and get going if you don't mind."

"Yes, ma'am. We can do that right now. Follow me to The Dorm over there and let's find Ms. Tammy." Brother Bennett turns to regard me, his eyes lingering on the old leather suitcase on the gravel by my feet. "Come along, William," he says. "I'm gonna sit you in my office while I get Miss Joyce here taken care of."

He waits for me to pick up my case and turns toward the red-brick building behind us. The Dorm, as he calls it, is basically a wide single-story ranch with a black shingled roof and a row of small, square windows along the side. It isn't much to look at, but it's the first building I've seen without wheels in the past couple of hours.

Joyce and I follow Brother Bennett as he ambles over to the wooden porch where the boys had gathered. My bicep burns as I carry my suitcase up the steps, and I consider what's inside it, from the life I left behind. Other than a few required items, Dad said I could take what I wanted as long as it fit in this bag, which seemed like an easy choice at first.

I stuffed it pile high with my favorite band tees—Metallica, Anthrax, Slayer, Megadeath, Suicidal Tendencies, and The Cult. I also crammed in a carton of Camel Filters I pressured Dad into buying me, and there was no way I was leaving my Discman behind. However, deciding which CDs to bring proved far more painful than I imagined.

I shift the suitcase to my other hand and trail Brother Bennett to the porch-side entrance of The Dorm.

"Our front offices are just through here," he says and pulls open the door for us.

Joyce and I step past him into a long, stuffy hallway with white cinderblock walls. A fluorescent light buzzes on the ceiling, fluttering from bright to dim, and the floor is covered with a crappy gray carpet that reeks of Pine-Sol and piss. And I thought the outside was depressing!

Brother Bennett joins us inside and pulls the door shut behind him. "I bought this property back in '83 when it was just an abandoned ol' boys home," he explains, and begins leading us down the hall. "We did her up as good as we could and built a schoolhouse out back, a few years ago."

His drawl drifts into the background as we pass an alcove with a worn-out couch against the wall. I stop and stare at the phone mounted beside it. The cord is plugged in, but the numbered dial is completely missing. How the hell is anyone supposed to use it?

"Everything alright, William?" I jerk around as Brother Bennett appears beside me. He gestures toward the couch. "We use this room for phone privileges, but new boys like you get none until you've been here three months. That's the rule."

Three months? Well, I guess I won't be trying to call home on a numberless phone then. I consider reminding him that I'll be out of here in 90 days, but I bite my tongue and follow him up the hallway again.

Brother Bennett pauses at a closed door several yards ahead and digs his hand in his pocket. He pulls out a set of keys, jingles through them, and fits one in the lock.

"Go on in and take a seat, William." He clicks open the door and waves me inside. "Put that bag of yours by my desk."

As I step through the threshold of Brother Bennett's office, gusts of cool air sweep across my face, soothing my sweaty skin. I didn't feel the slightest draft in the muggy hallway, but at least they have A/C in the rooms. That will be a lifesaver for sure.

The office itself is pretty small. A large, wooden desk occupies most of the room. Its surface is neat and orderly, just a short stack of ledgers, a blue fountain pen, and a black telephone that actually has a dial. A wooden cross hangs on the back wall, along with a framed photograph of President George H.W. Bush and about a half-dozen plaques with Bible verses on them.

I set my bag down beside the desk and turn around to face the doorway. Brother Bennett watches me from the hallway. His gaze shifts to the chair facing his desk and back to me again. I take the hint and sit myself down.

Brother Bennett nods approvingly. "I'm gonna walk Miss Joyce down the hall for a minute. When I get back, I expect to find you right where you are. Is that clear, son?" His dark eyes bore into me as he waits for my response.

"Got it," I mumble, and turn away to face the desk.

"'*Got it*' ain't the answer I'm looking for, boy!" Brother Bennett's voice lashes out like a whip, and I jerk back around. He glares at me beneath the rim of his cowboy hat. "It's either 'yes, sir' or 'no, sir.' Round here, our boys learn to speak with respect. Do I make myself clear?"

I glimpse Joyce behind him, wide-eyed as she watches on. "Yes, sir," I say, returning my gaze to Brother Bennett.

"I'm glad we have an understanding, William," he remarks gruffly. "That sure makes things a whole lot easier for both of us." He turns to Joyce, whose forehead wrinkles as her gaze flits from me to him. "I apologize for the holdup, ma'am. Now let's get you down to Ms. Tammy."

Brother Bennett steps out of view, and Joyce shoots me another tense look before following him. I sit staring at the doorway and the empty corridor behind it. He didn't even bother to shut me in. He just left the door wide open, like it's some kind of test to see if I'll stay put.

I consider my options. I could take my chance and bolt for it right now, head through the woods to the main road. What then, though? I'll just be a fugitive trying to get out of *Nowhere*, with nowhere to go, no one to run to, and no idea where the hell I'm going. There's no way I'm knocking on anyone's trailer either, not after our last encounter. My best bet would be the rental car. I've taken enough driver's education to joyride my way out of this place, but the keys are in Joyce's purse.

I'm still brooding over my meager options when Brother Bennett returns to his office. He closes the door after him and strides over to the chair behind his desk.

"I'm afraid I have to keep our conversation short today, William," he says, lowering himself into the chair. "I've got another meeting to attend up in Ellisville."

Brother Bennett removes his cowboy hat and places it on the desk in front of him. Flecks of gray speckle his dark brown hair, and rows of wrinkles line his forehead. Leaning back in his seat, he clasps his hands upon his lap and studies me.

"I know what you're thinking, son." He raises one of his large leather boots and rests it on the desk beside his hat. "Boys like you ain't no stranger to sitting in someone's office. But this ain't the same ol' lecture you're used to hearing, and I ain't like those other men who sat across the desk. So listen real good to what I tell you. Understand?"

I try to swallow, but my throat feels like it's withered shut. "Yes, sir," I reply croakily.

"Good." Brother Bennett cracks his knuckles. "You're gonna need open ears and a closed mouth 'round here, son. I expect my boys to do what they're told when I tell 'em. The sooner you learn that, the less reminding you'll get. And we've got more than a few ways of teaching y'all the rules."

He sits up and leans forward onto the desk. "This ain't like other places, William. I do things differently. There ain't no locks on y'all's rooms, and there ain't no fences 'round this property. Some boys get the wrong idea when they show up. But there ain't nowhere to hide from me 'round here, son. I know these parts better than you know yourself, so don't even think about running. Do I make myself clear?"

"Yes, sir," I answer as swiftly as possible.

Brother Bennett turns his wrist and peers at his watch. "One last thing before I go," he says, and reaches down to open his desk drawer. He lifts out a thick, black Bible and sets it on the desk between us.

"This is the good ol' King James. The one true book." He stares at it reverently and slides it gently toward me. "This is your path to a better life, William. Through the teachings of Jesus and accepting Him as Lord. Go ahead and take it. It's yours to study and care for."

What the hell? I consider asking him if he's serious, but there's not the slightest hint of humor on his face. As I reach out to pick it up, someone knocks twice on the door.

"Come in," Brother Bennett calls out and rises from his chair.

The door swings open and two older boys saunter into the office.

"This young man is Shane Hogan." Brother Bennett gestures to the tallest, a lean skinhead who doesn't even bother to acknowledge me. Eyeing the huge pair of steel-capped Doc Martin's he's wearing and the dent in his nose, I make a mental note not to mess with him.

The other kid is stockier, with cropped brown hair and a rash of acne across his cheeks. "And this is Donald Molloy." He scowls as Brother Bennett introduces him, and I'm guessing, like me, he prefers to go by a different name. And when I'm introduced as William instead of Will, I suppress a cringe of my own.

"I need y'all to keep an eye on him," Brother Bennett informs them. "Make sure he learns how things are done 'round here. And make sure he knows what's not done."

He turns to me. "We'll finish our conversation on another day, William. Until then, I'm leaving you in trusted hands."

And with that, Brother Bennett strides out of his office, closing the door shut behind him.

LOSING MY SHIT

A tense silence fills the room as the clomp of Brother Bennett's boots fades along the hallway. The two older boys stare at me sourly. I try my best to appear untroubled, but I can't help squirming in my seat a little.

"So..." I say, and pause to clear my throat. "I actually go by Will, not William. Just so you know."

"Does it look like we give a shit?" The kid called Donald sneers at me. "But just so *you* know, I go by Molloy, not Donald. Got it?"

I return his stare for a few seconds and look away. "Sure," I mutter. "Anything else I need to know?"

"Yeah, shut your mouth and open your bag." The skinhead, Shane, folds his arms across his chest. He nods toward my suitcase on the floor beside Brother Bennett's desk.

"Huh?" My forehead wrinkles in a frown. "Why?"

"So we can check it, dumbass!" Molloy snaps. "Just do what he says and hurry up about it."

I rise tentatively from the chair, picturing the carton of Camel Filters stuffed inside my case.

"What do you need to check it for?" I ask, as my stomach knots with dread.

Shane stifles a yawn. "Stuff you ain't allowed, obviously," he mumbles.

"What, like weapons or something?" I reach down and hoist my old suitcase onto the desk. "Don't worry, I left my AK-47 at home this time."

"Very funny, dipshit." Molloy jabs a finger in my chest. "I guess you should've left that joke of a t-shirt at home, too. This is the last time you'll be wearing it."

"Wait, what?" My face flushes with panic. "What's that supposed to mean? What's the problem with my t-shirt?"

"Enough with the questions!" Shane barks. "Just open up the bag."

Sweat beads on my forehead as I reach out and unzip my suitcase. Shane and Molloy's eyes widen as they spy the carton of smokes sitting on top. They exchange a wordless glance, and I know without question that I'll never see those Camel Filters again. The question remains, though—how much of my shit am I about to lose?

"You ain't allowed any of this shit." Shane hits me with the news I'm anticipating, but it pummels me nonetheless.

"Not even my music?" I watch on helplessly as he pulls out my stack of CDs and sets them aside on the desk, along with my Discman. "You've gotta be kidding!"

"Does it look like I'm kidding?" Shane eyes me coldly. "No music allowed. That's the rule."

I knew I should've called Dad's bluff about bringing whatever I wanted. It sounded too good to be true, but I wasn't about to argue. I'm sure Dad counted on that, of course. There's no way I'm losing my favorite CDs without putting up a fight, though.

"How can there be a rule against music?" I ask, folding my arms defiantly. "That makes no sense if you ask me."

"Good thing no one's asking you then." Molloy flips through my CD collection and snorts. "This crap barely counts as music, anyway," he mutters, dumping them back on the desk.

My cheeks burn. "I'm serious! I wanna know why I can't keep my shit! What's so bad about a few CDs?"

"Let me explain something, new boy." Shane steps forward and looms over me. "We don't make the rules around here. We just make sure you follow them. You ain't allowed music 'cause Brother Bennett thinks it's sinful. You've got an issue with that, you take it up with him. Be my guest."

"He thinks it's *sinful*?" I shake my head in stubborn disbelief. "Well, I think that's ridiculous!"

"Newsflash, dumbass!" Molloy waves his hand in my face. "No one cares what you think."

My chest heaves as anger seethes through me. "This is such bullshit! I thought this was America, not the goddamn Soviet Union for Christ's sake!"

Shane's hand darts out and grabs me around the neck in a chokehold. "Listen real good, new boy," he growls. "We don't take the Lord's name in vain around here. Not ever. You hear me?"

"Ye...yes," I sputter as my eyes flood with water.

Shane releases his grip, and I gasp in a few frantic breaths.

"You good?" he asks, patting me casually on the shoulder.

"What do *you* think?" I croak, and curse myself for sounding so pathetic.

Shane responds with an apathetic shrug. "Better than a round of licks from Brother Bennett. You slip up in front of him, he'll paddle your ass so hard you'll be too sore to sleep."

"You're kidding me, right? There's no way that's legal." I squint at him, searching for a sign that he's messing with me.

Shane and Molloy look at one another and chuckle. "You're in Nowhere, Mississippi, dumbass. No one knows and no one cares."

I'm starting to realize that more than ever.

I sigh and stare longingly at my CDs. "Could I at least keep a few of them?" Of the ten I chose to bring with me, it's the thought of losing The Holy Trinity that agonizes me most. My top three albums of all time: *Sonic Temple* by The Cult, *Peace Sells...but Who's Buying?* by Megadeth, and, of course, one of the greatest albums ever made, Metallica's *...And Justice for All*.

Shane shakes his head. "You ain't keeping any of them," he says, with firm finality. "Anything to do with music stays here. The t-shirts too."

My shoulders slump, and as my rage shrinks away, I feel too fatigued to fight anymore.

"What about the smokes?" I mumble.

Shane's eyes narrow into a scowl, and he grabs me by the collar of my shirt. "What smokes?"

4

STUCK LIKE CHUCK

After a final lingering look at my possessions, Shane and Molloy lead me out of Brother Bennett's office. My suitcase feels significantly lighter now, and I feel even emptier.

"Where are we going?" I ask, as we enter the hallway.

"Back to our room so we can change and get ready," Shane explains. "And where we go, you go. Got it?"

"Got it," I say. "What are we getting ready for?"

"Evening service."

"Wait, we're going to church?"

"Well done, genius."

I glance down at the Bible I'm carrying. My "gift" from Brother Bennett. His so-called "path to a better life." I guess it shouldn't surprise me that going to church is part of the deal, but I'm struggling to remember the last time I set foot in one. Before Mom's accident, most likely.

"So, church on a Sunday night, huh?" I say. "I'm guessing that's normal around here."

"Better get used to it, new boy." Molloy glances my way as I follow him along the hall. "Better get used to going on Sunday mornings, too. And every Wednesday after dinner."

Three times a week! My stomach swirls like it's trying to churn my insides into butter. I do my best to ignore it, trailing Shane and Molloy into a small dining hall at the center of The Dorm. Four long, wooden tables, with benches on either side, sit empty in the middle of the room. Our footsteps creak across the floorboards as we pass by a service window in the wall that leads into a cramped-looking kitchen.

Reaching the opposite side of the dining hall, we enter another narrow hallway that echoes with the din of voices and laughter. The air is thick and sticky, heavy with the smell of stale sweat. A boy darts out of the doorway in front of us, followed by another kid who chases him into the room across the hall. My eyes widen as I realize the doors are missing from both rooms. All that remains are tiny holes in the doorframe, where the hinges have been removed. Okay, so no dial on the phone and no doors on the bedrooms. Nothing weird about that, right? The rooms themselves look identical—four neatly made bunk beds, concrete floors, and a small square window in the cinderblock wall. Stick some metal bars between the doorway and you'd call it a cell.

As we reach the second set of doorways, an outbreak of laughter tugs at my attention. In the room to my right, a group of Latino boys huddle on the floor, playing Uno. One of them spots me gawking and glares at me. I make a swift return to minding my own business and follow Shane and Molloy down to the far end of the hallway.

"This is *our* room." Shane pauses outside the last doorway

and turns to face me. "You'll bunk with me and Molloy until Brother Bennett says otherwise. Got it?"

"Got it," I say, and step inside after him.

"This bunk's mine." Shane points at the stack of beds to his left. "Molloy's over there. You get the bunk beside his. Just keep your shit in your own space and keep the hell out of ours. Touch anything that isn't yours, and I'll stomp your hands until your fingers snap. Understood?"

"Understood."

———

FOR THE NEXT half-hour or so, Shane and Molloy go about their business as though I'm not there, hushing their conversations now and again when they don't want me to hear. At first, I'm fine with being ignored, but now it's starting to piss me off. But the moment I open my mouth, I'm told to shut it again and get ready for church.

Apparently, this involves wearing a tie, which I neglected packing. Unfortunately, this means I have to borrow Molloy's spare one, which looks like a thin strip of my grandmother's curtains. On top of that, the only dress shirt I have on this journey—which I'm pretty sure was by mistake—is an off-white button-down I outgrew a couple of years ago. I can barely squeeze my arms inside the sleeves, and my shoulders feel like they'll burst through the seams.

Making matters worse, unlike Brother Bennett's office with its constant stream of cool air, there's no AC inside the bedrooms. The air is so stiflingly humid it feels like I'm sitting in a sauna, making my shirt feel even tighter as it clings to my sweaty skin. And to add insult to injury, my stomach feels like it's being whisked by a knife.

I try to distract myself by eavesdropping on Shane and Molloy and nearly gag as they shower themselves in cheap cologne. I sit on my assigned bunk while they prep and preen, talking shit about guys I don't know yet and arguing about sports. Soon though, their focus shifts to one thing and one thing only—church chicks.

"So, what did she say after you said that?" Molloy asks, holding up a small mirror to inspect his nostrils.

"She said she had someone in mind," Shane replies.

"One of her friends?"

"Well, yeah, I would assume so, genius."

"Might not be, though. Might just be some random chick she knows. Just because she said 'she has someone in mind,' doesn't mean it's one of her friends."

"What the hell does it matter, Molloy? You asked me to ask, and that's what I did, so quit busting my balls about it. C'mon, new boy. It's time to go."

A couple of minutes later, the three of us exit the dorm and cross the gravel lot toward a rickety green bus at the top of the driveway. Its engine groans and rattles as we approach, and a short, round man in a crumpled blue suit stands outside the door holding a clipboard. He is probably a decade younger than Brother Bennett, with a shiny bald head and a scruffy goatee. We wait while he checks the kids in front of us off his list.

"This the new boy?" The man squints at me as I shuffle forward.

"Yes, sir," Shane responds.

"Does he play?"

Shane shrugs. "I've no idea, sir. You'll have to ask him."

And with that, he and Molloy step past him onto the bus. I stand there, wondering if I should do the same while the odd, middle-aged man inspects me like a workhorse.

"You're a good build for a catcher," he mutters.

"Excuse me?"

"Excuse me, *sir!*" he barks. "Round here you keep your manners in check, or we start dishin' out licks. You understand me?"

"Yes, sir," I say. "Sorry, sir."

"That's more like it, son," he says. "You can call me 'sir,' or you can call me Brother James. Now, what can *I* call *you*?"

"Will Douglas, sir."

"*Wrong!*" he yells, and a speck of spit lands on my cheek. "I can call you anything I want to, boy. Anything at all."

He cackles, and I catch a whiff of his breath, which reeks of Listerine and booze, a stench that reminds me of my dad. Brother James grins at me, flashing yellowed rows of teeth, and I have to fight back a wave of nausea.

"You like baseball, Will Douglas?" he asks, oblivious to the fact I nearly hurled on his shoes.

"Um...yes, sir."

"Who ya root for then?"

"The Braves, sir."

"The Braves? Ha!" Brother James scoffs. "Hell, the Braves ain't had a player worth watchin' since Hank Aaron, and that's a fact."

I inhale a deep breath and ease it out, feeling the queasiness subside.

"Well, I am from Atlanta, sir, and we do have Dale Murphy, so...."

Brother James's face twists in disgust. "Boy, you musta got dropped on your head. Are you tellin' me Dale Murphy is as good a ball player as Hank Aaron was?"

Nope. No, sir, I am definitely not. But I let my silence answer that question.

Brother James grunts his approval. "That's what I thought. Dale Murphy couldn't lace Hank Aaron's spikes. Wouldn't know how to. That's a fact."

He squints at his watch and mutters "shit" under his breath. "Get your ass on the bus and find a seat!" he says, shoving me toward the bus door. "We shoulda left five minutes ago, but you got me yappin' and now we're runnin' late again."

I hurry up the steps as Brother James scrambles into the driver seat. He shifts into drive and stomps on the gas before I have a chance to grab hold of something, and I nearly topple onto the lap of one of the Uno players from earlier. He glares at me and growls something in Spanish that spurs me on my way.

My stomach spasms as I stagger down the aisle in search of a seat. I spy one midway down and hurry toward it. A guy lounges back in the window seat with eyes shut. I recognize him as the black kid I saw playing basketball when I first arrived, now wearing khakis in place of his Lakers shorts. He startles as I slump down next to him with a sigh.

"Cool if I sit here?" I ask.

His expression softens as he peers at me. "For sure," he says. "It's all yours, new boy."

"Thanks." I lean back and close my eyes, inhaling slow, deep breaths. The cramping in my guts is almost too much to bear, and I can't stop myself from grimacing anymore.

"You okay, my man?" asks the kid next to me.

"Yeah, I'm fine," I lie, trying to mask the strain in my voice. "I'm just not in the mood for church. It's not really my thing if you know what I mean."

A wide smile spreads across his face, etching dimples into his cheeks. "It ain't my kinda thing either. But you wanna keep that quiet round here, bro. My name's Angelo."

He extends his hand and I reach and shake it.

"Will," I tell him.

"Well, welcome to paradise, Will. What do you make of your first ride on The Booger?"

"I'm not sure I follow." I say, using my confusion to hide another grimace.

"This big, green piece of junk we're sitting in." Angelo gestures a hand towards the front of the bus, where Brother James is crooning out some hillbilly country song as he taps his fingers on the steering wheel. "We call her The Booger. For obvious reasons."

"I get it. Very clever," I mutter.

"So what's your story, man?" Angelo asks. "What got you shipped off to Nowhere?"

"My dad did," I grunt.

He chuckles. "Yeah, you and half the guys here, bro, but I'm asking how you earned the ticket, not who paid for it. What did you do?"

My guts twinge yet again, but I focus on my breathing. *What did I do?* Nothing that deserves this. I open my mouth to answer, but all I can do is shake my head.

"It's all good, man," Angelo says. "I ain't trying to get in your business or nothing. Forget about it. How long you here for?"

I try to clear my throat and find I have to cough to do so.

"Ninety days," I rasp.

Angelo's thick brows arch upwards. "Ninety days? That's it?" I nod, and he shakes his head. "That's crazy, man! No one's stayed less than eighteen months since I've been around. You must have done some small-time shit to get a weak-ass sentence like that. No wonder you don't want to talk about it. Did you draw some dicks on the bathroom stall at school or something?"

Laughter erupts out of him as I wince my way through another painful spasm.

"You sure you're okay, bro? 'Cause you really don't look good."

I open my mouth to speak, but as the wave of nausea recedes, another one hits even harder. I double over in my seat and clutch my stomach, sweat pouring out of me. The world blurs and swirls and all sounds merge into static. As my entire stomach convulses, I lean over into the aisle and heave everything that's been stewing inside of me onto the floor of The Booger.

———

MY EPISODE TRIGGERS A MIXED REACTION, overall. For many of the boys, I am crowned a hero for the night.

"No church! Three cheers for Chuck!" are the chants, while Brother James turns the bus around and floors it back to Victory Ridge.

Those closest to my mess find it far less amusing, however.

They begin a chant of their own. "Yucky Chuck! Chuck needs yucked!"

And so it is that before nearly everyone on the bus has a chance to learn my actual name, I'm given a new one—Upchuck. By the time we arrive back at The Dorm, Upchuck is shortened to Chuck, and now I am stuck with that.

As I lie awake in the pitch-black bedroom, sweating on the thin, shabby mattress, I feel stuck in every sense of the word. Stuck in my head. Stuck in the past. Trapped in memories that are impossible to escape.

I'm back in the darkness of my own bedroom. The door creaks open and my father shakes me awake. There has been an accident, he tells me, but Mom is fine. There is nothing to worry about. I should go back to sleep and he will take my sister, Candy, and me to go see her in the morning.

But when I wake up the next morning, Dad is nowhere to be found. I find our next-door neighbor, a close family friend sitting at our kitchen table with a cup of coffee and a face so grave and pale I mistake him for a ghost. His bottom lip quivers as he delivers the news through sobs and tears. The news that Mom is far from fine. The news that Mom won't be coming home for dinner ever again.

That was December 15, 1988, the day I lost my mother. But today, April 1st of 1990, April Fool's Day to boot, it feels like I've lost everything else as well.

5

BALL-CHECKED BEFORE BREAKFAST

Monday, April 2, 1990 - Day 2

I spring upright on the bunk, my hands darting between my legs as my eyes flood with daylight and tears. Howling laughter echoes out around me. All I can do is slump back on my mattress and roll onto my side as a sickening pain spreads from my groin to my stomach.

"Rise and shine, Chuck. Quit playing with your nuts and get up. We've got shit to do!"

Peering through wet, bleary eyes, I make out Molloy's thuggish mug sneering down at me. The grimness of my reality floods back to me, sobering my mind in an instant. Yesterday feels like a bad dream, but my nightmare in Nowhere is only just beginning.

"What the hell was that?" I rasp, relieved that my voice doesn't sound like I've inhaled a canister of helium.

Molloy's grin widens. "That was your morning wake-up call, dumbass. If you don't get up before we do, you get ball-checked."

"Add that to the list of shit you need to learn today," Shane chimes in, leaning down to scrub one of his huge Doc Martens with black polish.

I take note of several thick scars etched across his shaved head. My mom once told me that every scar tells a story, the scars we see and the scars we don't. I wonder how many stories Shane has to tell, and which one landed him in this place.

"I have a cousin in Wisconsin who's a skinhead," I tell him.

Shane stops scrubbing and peers up at me, his forehead wrinkling. "Yeah? What type?"

There are *types*? Shit! "Just the regular type, I think. You know, shaved head, big boots, a generally pissed-off attitude." I chuckle, but Shane just stares at me silently. "So...what type are you?"

"The type that can't stand ignorant people. Now, get up and get dressed. Me and Molloy gotta get breakfast ready, which means we've gotta take you with us."

"We're going to the kitchen?" I ask, slipping down from my bunk.

"Where else would you make breakfast, dumbass?" Molloy replies.

"Our job is kitchen help," Shane explains. "We help Ms. Tammy fix all the meals. Which means we're there to work. Which means *you* need to keep your trap shut and stay out of our way."

"Understood," I say, while throwing on some clothes. "Who's Ms. Tammy?"

"Brother Bennett's wife. Make sure you stay out of her way

also. If she says anything to you, the only words you say back are 'Yes, ma'am, Ms. Tammy,' or 'No, ma'am, Ms. Tammy.'"

A few minutes later, we're marching down the hallway to the kitchen. Shane pulls a set of keys from his back pocket when we reach the door. He unlocks it and enters the dingy room, flipping a switch on the wall. Lights flicker on, illuminating a square room with a large grill in the middle. Sinks and counters line the walls on one side, and a couple of rusty, old ovens line the other.

"So, will this be my job too?" I ask, glancing around.

Molloy snorts. "Yeah, right. Kitchen help is the best job going. Only the senior kids get chosen. New boys start on kitchen crew. The shittiest job."

"Why's that exactly?"

"You'll see."

Shane pulls out his keys again as he walks towards a door on the opposite side of the kitchen. I move to follow him, but he tenses up.

"Where are *you* going, new boy?" he says, fitting a key into the lock. "I'm the only one around here who's allowed in this pantry, so you need to back off. Got that?"

I raise my hands as I retreat a few steps. "Got it. Sorry."

"Good. See that freezer over there?" Shane points towards the far side of the kitchen, and I nod. "I'd go sit your ass on that until we're done, if I were you."

I nod again and follow Shane's advice. Satisfied, he enters the pantry, and Molloy lifts a large pot out from under one of the counters. He sets it down in the nearest sink, flips on the faucet, and starts filling it with water. A few moments later, Shane reemerges with a large, blue box in his hands.

"What is that?" I ask, as he carries it over to the sink and plops it down on the side.

"Breakfast," he mutters, opening a flap on the top of the box.

Lifting it up, he tips it over the pot until a white powdery substance spills out into the running water.

My face twists in disgust. "You're kidding, right? What the heck is that stuff?"

"Does it look like he's kidding?" Molloy snaps.

"It looks like he's pouring baby powder into a pot of water," I say. "How is that breakfast?"

"What's wrong?" Shane smirks at me. "You don't like milk with your cereal?"

"That's *milk?*" My voice cracks with surprise.

"Powdered milk, dumbass." Molloy turns off the faucet. "Brother Bennett believes in stretching his dollars."

He and Shane snicker, and I'm left to watch and wait while they finish prepping for "breakfast."

Once the bowls of generic cornflakes are lined up next to the pot of "milk," Ms. Tammy shows up to inspect everything. Squat and doughy, with a large bun of gray-brown hair, she clucks about the kitchen like a chicken, chirping and drawling as she reviews everything Shane and Molloy have done.

"Now, y'all boys made sure to update my inventory, didn't y'all?" she asks, as her beady brown eyes dart back and forth between the two of them.

"Yes, ma'am, Ms. Tammy," the pair respond.

"And y'all double-checked it like I told y'all?"

"Yes, ma'am, Ms. Tammy."

After Ms. Tammy waddles off, Molloy unlocks two hatches on the wall, separating the kitchen and the dining hall. He lifts up the serving window and the clamor of voices floods through the opening. I watch from my perch on the freezer as service begins. Shane dips the ladle into the pot and pours lumpy, white liquid onto each bowl of cornflakes. Molloy hands them out as the line goes by.

Once the last person picks up their breakfast, Shane tells me to fix myself a bowl. I'm allowed to eat in the dining hall but have to head straight back to the kitchen as soon as I'm done. I pour some stale-looking cornflakes, add a splash of translucent powdered milk, and carry my pathetic excuse for a breakfast into the dining hall.

Most of the boys have already finished eating by the time I enter, so finding a near-empty table is easy enough. Digging my spoon into the cereal, I stir it around absentmindedly, trying to ignore the growling in my belly. I'm not sure I can hold down a breakfast covered in fake milk right now.

I scoop up a few flakes and crunch them down. Yep, definitely stale, but moist enough to chew up and swallow. Well, barely. After a couple of mouthfuls, I decide against another one and set down my spoon.

"Tastes like crap, don't it?" says a voice nearby.

I look up to find the kid I sat next to on the bus, standing there with his tray. He sets it on the table opposite mine and settles onto the bench across from me. My face burns as I recall barfing right in front of him, but his dimpled smile is far from mocking.

"You'll dig the breakfast on Saturdays, though," he tells me. "Ms. Tammy makes some mean cathead biscuits."

I stare at him blankly, scouring my brain for his name. "Angelo, right?" I mutter, with an air of relief.

"That's right," he says. "And you're Will. But I guess I'm the only one calling you that anymore."

I sigh and stare at my cereal, wondering if I should apologize for nearly puking all over him.

Angelo clears his throat. "Listen, man. You can't let some stupid nickname get you down. You'll get called worse things than 'Chuck' while you're here. You can trust me on that. Besides, you're only here for like nine months or something, right?"

I shake my head. "Ninety days."

"Oh yeah, that's right!" Angelo slaps his hand on the table and chuckles. "Mr. Ninety Days!"

This twangs a nerve. "So how long are *you* here for then?"

"How *long*?" Angelo raises his thick, dark brows. "Dude, I've been stuck in this shithole for nearly three years."

Three years! A cold chill spreads across my skin. "Is it like that for most of the guys here?"

Angelo shrugs. "Yeah, I guess so. Usually it's two or three years. Some of them are in and out in eighteen months, but there are a few Lifers here too."

"Lifers?"

"Guys who're here until they graduate," Angelo explains. "Like your shadow, Molloy, over there. He was here before me, and he'll be here after I'm gone. You can bet your ass on that. He's got nowhere to go."

"Damn! And I thought ninety days sounded like a lifetime. I mean, it's still ninety days too long if you ask me, but..."

"Nah, ninety days ain't nothing, man. Just keep your head down, and you'll roll out of here in no time. Trust me, I know how things work around this place. The good news is you'll be working with me on kitchen crew right after this, so I can give you the boys home 101."

Free advice and a friendly face? It seems too good to be true in a place like this, but everything about Angelo feels unquestionably genuine. Although, when people tell me to trust them, they have a habit of being full of shit.

6

____

KITCHEN CREW

"So what happens on kitchen crew?" I ask Angelo, as I dump mushy cornflakes into the trash can. "Molloy said it's the shittiest job, but that was about it."

"Well, it doesn't come with the same perks as kitchen help, that's for sure. Basically, we clean up whatever mess they make. I mean, if this place made any sense, then bathroom cleanup would be the shittiest job going, but they don't have Ms. Tammy inspecting their work three times a day. No one ever bothers to inspect their work. That ain't how it goes for kitchen crew, though."

"Sounds great," I mumble. "I guess I'd better get back to the kitchen."

"I'm right behind you," he says. "I'm gonna round up the rest of the crew."

I nod and hurry across the dining hall toward the kitchen door. When I enter, I'm met with a sight that stops me in my tracks. Shane and Molloy sit on the counter with an open box of

Golden Grahams between them and a gallon of whole milk. Real milk!

"What the...?" I stare wide-eyed at the scene before me.

Shane holds his finger to his lips. "Like Molloy told you, kitchen help is the best job going." He tips his bowl to show me the leftover milk, and then dumps it on the floor in front of me.

Molloy does the same. "Have fun on kitchen crew, dumbass."

They toss their bowls into the sink full of dishes, and Shane returns the "real" food to the pantry and locks it up again.

"We'll be back for you," he tells me, as Angelo and two other boys enter the kitchen, and then he and Molloy saunter out into the hallway.

Angelo and the other two boys stare around the room at the mess as if it's perfectly normal. The sinks are stuffed with dirty pots and piled high with bowls, spoons, and cups. The countertops are littered with cornflakes, and the floor, of course, is now sticky with real milk.

"Alright, let's get to work." Angelo claps his hands together. He turns to the other two boys, who look like polar opposites. I recognize one as the huge Neanderthal of a boy that Angelo was shooting hoops with yesterday. The other is a scrawny, rat-faced kid, who looks like he's used to being trodden on.

"Oaf, you're on counters and appliances," Angelo tells the big one. "Roach does the floors. I'll wash and Will can dry."

"You need to make sure ol' Chuck knows what's what," the kid called Oaf informs him gruffly, scowling at me with his beady brown eyes. "I ain't takin' licks for no new boy."

"You worry about your job, and I'll worry about mine, okay? I'll tell Will what he needs to know." Angelo stares at Oaf, who grudgingly turns and walks off.

"I don't think he likes me very much," I whisper.

"Who, Oaf?" Angelo glances at me and grins. "Don't take it personally, bro. Oaf doesn't like anyone, including himself. He's just shit-scared of licks is all. And if one of us messes up, that's what happens. We *all* get licks. That's why we gotta make sure everything's spotless before Ms. Tammy comes round. She checks everything we touch. *Everything.* If you half-ass something, she'll spot it a mile away. Just remember that, okay?"

"You got it," I say. "No problem."

I follow Angelo over to the sink and grab a drying towel as he starts to scrub one of the pots. The scraggy runt that Angelo referred to as Roach walks by with a bucket of water and a mop. Behind him, Oaf sprays down one of the countertops while mumbling one of the chants about me from yesterday. *"Yucky Chuck. Chuck get yucked."*

"So what the hell does 'get yucked' mean?" I ask, as Angelo passes me a dripping wet pot to dry.

"It means you get a yucking from one of the adults. They slap you around, throw you to the floor and drag you back up and shit. They basically do that over and over again until they've made a good enough example of you."

I stop drying and stare at him. "Are you messing with me?"

"I wish I was."

"Hold on," I say, "is that better or worse than getting licks?"

Angelo squints at me as if I'm an idiot. "You *do not* want to get yucked, Will. Licks are gonna happen whether you like it or not. How bad they are depends on what you did and who's giving them. But yuckings are a whole different level, man. You'll understand when you see one. Just keep your head down and make sure you're not on the receiving end. Trust me on that, bro."

I stare at the dirty dishwater, listening to the steady trickle of the faucet. I'm sure Angelo means well, but keeping my head down is never easy for me, and I'm not ready to fully trust him yet, either. However, the thought of Brother Bennett slapping me around prickles my skin.

"So," I say, eager to change the subject, "I thought kitchen crew was the new kids' job. That's what Molloy said, anyway. So how come *you're* still doing it?"

Angelo turns to me and raises his eyebrows. "Why do you *think*?"

I gaze back at him blankly. "I don't know. As a punishment or something?"

Dipping his hands back into the soapy dishwater, Angelo frowns scornfully. "Yeah, it's punishment for being Black."

"Oh," I mumble, as heat spreads across my cheeks. "Sorry, I..."

"Don't worry about it," Angelo blurts as I fumble for words, but I can't help feeling twinges of guilt as we work side-by-side in silence

I remember the time I got into a brawl with a Black kid at school, named Julius. It was during a seventh-grade field trip to Woodruff Arts Center, although I can't recall how or why it started. Anyway, I lost. Badly.

When my mom came by the school to pick me up, she was absolutely appalled. Not by the state of my bloodied face, but by the disgraceful word her darling son had used in the aftermath. I'll never forget how ashamed she was, and the shame that made me feel. I've lost count of how many times I've heard that word since I arrived here, though.

"So what's your story, Will?" Angelo asks, ending our silence.

"My *story*?"

"Yeah, you know what I'm talking about." He wrings out his rag and glances my way. "None of us came here on vacation, bro. You're in *Nowhere* for a reason, just like me and everybody else. You tell your story. I tell mine. That's how it goes around here."

"Alright," I say, wondering where to begin and how much to divulge.

"Just start with where you're from," Angelo suggests, as though reading my mind.

"Okay." I clear my throat as he hands me a stack of dripping wet bowls. "I'm from Atlanta."

"A city boy, huh? Same. Is it rough out there?"

"Well, we live in the suburbs, so not really."

"Ah, so you were a bored, rich boy looking for trouble." Angelo smirks at me, and my face flushes. "Just messing with you, man. What happened?"

"Just some stupid shit, mostly. Fights and stuff. That sort of thing. Then I got expelled from school again."

"What for?"

I puff out a sigh. "For 'possessing a deadly weapon on school property.' That's what the principal told my dad. Someone ratted me out for having a switchblade in my locker. It wasn't like I was carrying it around or anything. I wasn't even the one who brought it to school. This older kid traded it to me for my skateboard."

"That's some bad luck right there, I guess."

"Tell me about it. My dad grounded me for two months, and I

had a ticket to see Metallica that weekend. There was no way I was gonna miss that, though."

I grin mischievously, and Angelo chuckles. "Okay," he says, "I like where this is going. So you snuck out? Your dad didn't take away your ticket?"

"He didn't know about it," I explain. "He didn't even know there was a concert. He found out later that night when the cops called, though."

"Oh shit!" Angelo stops scrubbing and tilts his head to look at me. "You got arrested?"

I lower my eyes and nod. "Yep."

"At the show?"

I sigh and nod my head again. "I stole a t-shirt from the merch stand."

Angelo erupts with laughter. "That's some stupid-ass shit, man!"

"Yeah, thanks. I'm aware of that," I say, allowing myself to chuckle. "At least I waited until after the show. It would've sucked way worse if I'd missed seeing Metallica."

"I suppose that's one way of looking at it." Angelo turns back to the sink and starts washing some spoons. "So I'm guessing your dad flipped out and sent you off here, huh?"

"Pretty much. The judge sentenced me to ninety days in juvie, and then my asshole dad convinced him to transfer the sentence."

"Well, juvie ain't no joke from what I hear," Angelo says. "But Victory Ridge is a whole different type of Hell."

"So how did *you* end up here?" I ask, seizing my chance to step out of the spotlight. "Where's home for you?"

Angelo shoots me a dimpled grin. "I'm from sunny Los Angeles, baby! Born and raised."

Well, that explains the Lakers shorts. "And I thought I was far from home. They don't have places like this in California?"

"They got places like this across the whole damn country, bro." Angelo explains. "But my stepdad wanted the courts to send me as far away as possible. And at the time, I wanted to get as far away from *him* as I possibly could. I thought he was actually gonna kill me. Like, for real."

"Damn, Angelo!" I stop drying to give him my full attention. "What did you do to piss him off so much?"

"Everything I could think of, bro." Angelo's brown eyes gleam devilishly. "That guy's the biggest piece of shit I know. He did drive a badass car, though. A souped-up '88 Impala, midnight blue with shiny chrome rims. He was an asshole to my mom, but he loved that car more than anything, used to wax it down every damn day. But, guess what, I was the last person who ever got to drive it."

"You *stole* it?"

Angelo's smile broadens. "Took that baby for a ride down the coast one night, windows down and the stereo cranked up. Then I lit the biggest bonfire Redondo Beach has ever seen."

"Holy shit!" I crack up laughing. "You torched your stepdad's car?"

"Yep." Angelo chuckles softly. "I ain't gonna lie. It felt kinda awesome at the time, but look where it got me, man. I was only thirteen back then, but my stepdad pressed charges. Arson and grand theft auto. The rest is history."

"Well, your story's way more interesting than mine," I admit.

"What happens when you go back to L.A., though? Aren't you worried about what your stepdad will do?"

"He's my ex-stepdad now." Angelo's mouth twitches into a smirk. "My mom finally left his sorry ass after I got sent off here. I'll never understand what she saw in him, but at least she has my baby sister. She's the only good thing that came out of that relationship."

Angelo sighs and his shoulders sag. "But I haven't even met her yet," he mutters. "I wasn't there when she came into the world. I wasn't there for my mom, and I still can't be there for either of them. So what I did back then doesn't feel awesome anymore, you know. All I feel right now is regret. I guess that's what this place really teaches you."

GETTING SCHOOLED

All I feel right now is regret. Angelo's words echo through my head while Ms. Tammy prowls around the kitchen, inspecting our work. I've certainly got my own regrets. Running my mouth about the stupid switchblade in my locker is high on the list. And I should've ditched Joyce at the airport in Atlanta before we boarded our flight yesterday. Too late now, though.

After several minutes of fussing around the kitchen, Ms. Tammy grudgingly approves our cleaning job. "Alright now, y'all. It's time to get y'all's butts to school," she squawks, waving her arms to hurry us out of the kitchen. "And don't dally this time. Y'all go straight to the schoolhouse."

I lean toward Angelo as we walk to the door. "Is this like actual school? Like with actual classes and teachers and stuff?"

Angelo shakes his head. "Not even close, bro. It's way more boring and an even bigger waste of time. But it's easy. You'll see what I mean."

I open my mouth to ask another question, but as we step out

of the kitchen and into the hallway, Shane and Molloy are standing there waiting for me. I stop in front of them while Angelo, Oaf, and Roach head on without me.

"Have fun?" Molloy asks, sneering at me as he leans against the cinderblock wall.

"Yeah, I had a blast, thanks," I say, fixing a fake smile to match the sarcasm in my voice. "Can't wait to go to school next!"

Shane shoots me a deadpan stare. "This way."

He walks into the dining hall, and I follow him with Molloy at my heels. We head out of the back doors into the muggy morning and cut across the lawn toward a small, red building that looks like a mini version of The Dorm.

I spy Angelo and Oaf up ahead, Roach trailing behind them like a shunned mutt. We enter the schoolhouse a minute after they do, stepping into a rectangular one-story room that looks as plain and ugly as The Dorm. Except for the furniture, that is. Desks are mounted against three of the walls, and each is separated from the next by a plastic divider.

The majority of them are occupied. Boys hunch over their desks filling out workbooks of some kind. Others mill around a table in the corner, rummaging through tubs full of different-colored books and supplies. The room is silent, except for the occasional murmur of hushed voices and the scratch of pencils on paper.

As I glance around, I realize I'm now standing alone in the middle of the room. Shane and Molloy must have walked off and left me while I was staring. Good riddance, but they could've told me what to do at least.

"Psst!"

I swivel toward the sound and there's Angelo, standing beside a couple of empty desks. He waves me over to him.

"I saved you a spot over here," he whispers.

"Thanks," I whisper back. "But what the heck am I supposed to do?"

"You need to check in with Brother James real quick, so he can tell you." Angelo chuckles. "Don't be surprised if it doesn't make sense. He always makes it sound complicated, but it's as easy as copying answers from a book. Literally."

My eyes roam the room, but Brother James is nowhere to be seen. "Where is he?"

"Over there." Angelo points at a wooden desk on the far side of the schoolhouse. Someone lounges back behind it with their feet propped up, reading a newspaper.

Angelo nudges me that way, and I shuffle over to the desk and clear my throat. "Excuse me, sir."

Brother James crumples his newspaper shut and scowls at me. "You need something, boy?"

"Uh, yes, sir. I was told to check in with you."

His scowl morphs into a sneer. "Well, if it ain't ol' boy Chuck again. You made a hell of a mess on my bus, son."

"Yes, sir," I mutter. "I'm really sorry about that. I...I wasn't feeling too good."

"I don't give a damn how you was feeling, boy! You blow chunks like that again, you're getting licks whether you're feeling good or not." Brother James swings his feet down from the desk and leans forward. "And don't ever interrupt me when I'm reading the sports section, either. You see me reading, you sit and wait till I'm done. Understand?"

"Yes, sir," I say swiftly. "Sorry for interrupting. I just don't know what I'm supposed to do, and I was hoping you could help me."

Brother James scratches his beard. "Fine," he says. "But listen good and don't ask no questions. I'm only gonna explain this once."

And so he does.

"You were right," I whisper to Angelo as I sit down at the desk next to him. "That made no sense whatsoever. He said I need to read, answer, and check everything, and then take my test. But he never told me what I should read, answer, check, and take a test on. He just said to start where I'm supposed to. What the hell does that mean?"

Angelo chuckles from behind the divider and stands up from his desk. "Follow me."

He leads me over to the supply table and starts rummaging through the tubs. "You need four booklets, one for each subject. What grade are you in?"

"Tenth."

"Here," he says, "this should work." He hands me a tattered blue booklet with *Mathematics Grade 10* written across the top, another for Bible history, one for English, and one for science. "Finish the first two lessons in each of those, and then I'll show you where the answer sheets are so you can check it."

"*I* check it?"

Angelo smirks. "Yes, Will. *You* check it. Think about it."

And I do. If I'm the one checking, like Angelo already said, this will be as easy as copying answers from a book. Literally. But as I flip open the first booklet, I realize it's even easier than that. Checking my work will be a painless formality. Because in every section of the booklet, the answers have been written and erased so many times they're imprinted on each page.

After figuring out how to hack the system, I finish up so quickly that I feel self-conscious about turning in my work. Everyone else, including Angelo, is still hunched over their desk, working away. A few are even fully slumped over, one of them softly snoring.

I lean back and chuckle about some of the crap I've read today. It's crazy how much religious bullshit can be squeezed into everything and anything, including math problems about miracles. My Earth Science booklet wins out overall, though, but I guess that shouldn't come as a surprise. It's crammed with all kinds of fascinating facts!

For example, did you know that God got pissed off with the people he created in his own image and decided to drown them all in forty-days-worth of rain? Yep, that's in my science book! You see, the only reason animals still exist today is that this mad bastard called Noah built a ship big enough to save every species on Earth. He did it all by himself and somehow managed to stop the lions and tigers from eating all the other animals! I mean, if that's not *mind-blowingly* miraculous, I don't know what is.

After spending a short while in my head, I decide it's not a place I want to be right now. I search around the schoolhouse for a clock, but there is none to be found. Stretching out a yawn, I consider asking Brother James if I can go use the bathroom, but he's still hidden behind his precious sports section. Something else catches my attention, however. A bookcase on the wall behind me.

I lurch to my feet and stride over to inspect it. Though it's pitiful to admit, the thought of reading a book feels like an oasis in the Sahara right now. However, the mirage fades as I realize the shelves contain nothing more than some Bibles, several worn copies of Reader's Digest, and a set of old encyclopedias. Better than nothing, I guess.

My eyes roam the spines of the encyclopedias and settle upon the "M-N" edition. I slide it out and return to my desk, eyeing Brother James for any signs of disapproval, but he remains engrossed in his paper. Quite the read today, it seems.

Setting the heavy encyclopedia down on my desk, I blow off a layer of dust from its cover. I consider looking up my favorite genre of music, Metal, or my favorite band, Metallica. But by the look of this thing, it must have been printed back in the Dark Ages. I inspect the inside cover, and sure enough, it was published in 1972.

I decide to look up Mississippi instead, but as I flip through the pages, I find that one of them is missing. Someone has torn it out. I check the number of the previous page and scan the index until I find the missing one.

Mississippi, Road Map with Counties (p.217)

What the hell? Why would someone tear out a road map? And then it hits me. Better for Brother Bennett that no one knows their way out of Nowhere.

This sparks my curiosity, and I return the "M" edition to the shelf and select the "A" volume. I search the index for the Alabama road map, but when I flip to the designated page, all that remains is a torn edge of paper. After checking two more volumes, I confirm that the Louisiana and Tennessee maps have suffered the same fate. These guys aren't messing around.

"Alright then, y'all," Brother James announces while neatly folding his newspaper. "I'm callin' it for today. Y'all get changed and get your butts down to the field in fifteen minutes. We gotta get goin' before those afternoon storms roll in."

This news is met with several cheers. Chairs scrape against the floor as everyone rises from their desks at the same time.

"What's happening?" I ask Angelo, as I follow him toward the pack of boys jostling to turn in their work.

"School's over," he says.

"*Already?* What time is it?"

Angelo checks his watch. "Just after 10."

"Is this normal?"

Angelo chuckles. "I wouldn't use the word 'normal' for anything around here, man. But Brother James has a habit of ditching school, especially this time of year. Spring training is on the go, so baseball season's right around the corner. The guy's a baseball nut if you haven't figured that out already."

"So we're ditching school to play baseball?"

"Yeah, pretty much. But don't worry if it ain't your thing. There's about thirty kids here in total, so they won't make you play unless they're short on numbers. You can always chill out on the hill instead. That's where I'll be."

"Not a Dodgers fan, huh?"

"I'm Dodgers all the way, man," Angelo says. "I just ain't a fan of getting thrown at every time I'm at the plate."

"Yeah, that doesn't sound like much fun," I mutter, as I notice Shane and Molloy waiting for me by the schoolhouse door. "I'll probably sit this one out, too."

8

PICKING SIDES

My watchdogs lead me back to their room in The Dorm and tell me to get changed for baseball. I'm still not planning to play, but Shane informs me it's the only time we're allowed to wear shorts, whether you're playing or not. The rest of the time, shorts are considered sinful, just like everything else that's good.

Sinful or not, my Nike athletic shorts are a welcome relief from the Khaki pants, which keep sticking to my legs in the brutal humidity. It might only be April, but it's as steamy as mid-July in Atlanta. "The air you wear," my mom used to call it. But in Nowhere, Mississippi, it feels like the air wears you.

With our legs now bare and sinful, the three of us head back outside and join the line of boys marching like ants down the ridge toward the ballfield.

"I hate baseball season," Molloy grumbles. "I hate Brother James and his stupid Cincinnati Reds. I hope they shit the bed early this year, so I can watch him suffer again."

Shane rolls his eyes. "Okay, we get it, Molloy. You're a crappy baseball player, and I shouldn't pick you anymore."

"What?" Molloy has the audacity to look aggrieved. "You wouldn't?"

"No?" Shane smirks at him. "Maybe I'll pick Chuck first today instead."

Molloy glares at me like this is my fault somehow.

"Don't worry," I say. "I'm not playing."

"Really?" Shane glances at me with raised brows. "I had you pegged as a ball player."

"Used to be," I tell him. "I quit playing a couple of seasons ago."

"You hear that, Shane?" Molloy chimes in. "You don't want this dumbass on your team. He's a quitter. Me, I'm a winner."

Shane chuckles. "You sure are, Donny-boy. A winner all the way."

Molloy grins, seemingly oblivious to Shane's sarcastic tone. He pats me on the shoulder as we reach the field. "Have fun sitting with the losers, Chuck," he says, pointing toward the hill where I spot Angelo and several others sitting on the grass. "I guess that's where you belong."

I start up the hill as he and Shane take off toward the dirt infield, where the majority of the boys are moping around in small groups. Brother James paces back and forth between them, counting their numbers. I climb past the other "losers" until I reach Angelo at the top of the ridge. He lounges back with his hands behind his head, wearing a white t-shirt and his Lakers shorts.

"What's up, Will?" He greets me with a dimpled smile. "Welcome to the nosebleeds."

"No kidding," I say, panting as I plop down beside him and take in the view.

My eyes roam the horizon of pine trees that surround the property, idling on the wooden fire tower that pokes out amongst them. Down below us, the divisions between the boys are more obvious to see.

"You can learn a lot from watching up here," Angelo says, as though reading my mind. "Like how everyone sticks to their own group. Those are the Texas Boys over there." He points to a cluster of boys on one side of the infield. "Those guys are the Cali Kids, and that's the Cuban Crew across from them. Then you've got the Trusted Boys, like Shane and Molloy. They're basically Bennett's puppets if you haven't figured that out yet."

"Yeah, what's the deal with that?" I ask, staring down at them as they stand chatting with the other older kids. "What's in it for them?"

"$75 a week."

My eyes widen. "He *pays* them?"

"Well, most of the time, yeah. Bennett relies on them to keep things running when he's not around, which is pretty often. But they get a ton of other privileges too. And they're allowed to go on dates and drive into Hattiesburg on the weekends. Sometimes they even get sent to New Orleans to pick someone up from the airport."

I raise my eyebrows. That's a whole lot better than I imagined. I guess selling your soul to Brother Bennett makes life here a lot more tolerable. The thought makes me shiver, though.

"What about you and Oaf and that other kid?" I ask, stretching back on the grass. "Are you guys your own group?"

"The rest of us are basically loners," Angelo says, and points down at the field. "Looks like they're finally picking teams. Although, it's kinda pointless at this point. Everyone knows who's gonna pick who already."

I notice Shane and another kid standing apart from the crowd like captains. "Do they always pick the guys from their own group or something?"

Angelo shakes his head. "Not exactly. Groups matter, but when it comes to sports, winning matters way more. Plus, the winning team gets to shower first, which means a few of them might get hot water. Just watch, though. Shane will pick Molloy first, and Benny will pick Lucas."

"So, is Benny a Trusted Boy, too?" I watch Shane select Molloy, just like Angelo said.

"Yeah, but Benny mostly rolls with the Cuban Crew. That's why he always picks Lucas first. That's his bro from Miami. The other Trusted Boys are Trent." He points out a tall, chubby kid with a mop of blond hair. "And the kid with the mullet over there, that's Jerry."

The captains finish their selections, and the teams appear to be a fairly even mix of the groups, despite all of the Cuban Crew being on Benny's team. Shane's team fields first, and it's Shane himself who steps to the mound. He warms up by fizzing a few fastballs into the catcher, one of the Texas Boys called Taz.

"Shane's got one hell of an arm!" I say, as Taz takes off his mitt to massage his hand after catching a few heaters.

"Yeah, Shane ain't your average ballplayer, bro. He lost his shot at a scholarship when he got sent here. Dude should be playing college ball next year, but he managed to mess things up for himself, just like the rest of us."

"What happened?"

"Some kind of skinhead gang fight. His crew against some other guys. A dude came at him with a knife and Shane beat the shit out of him, is how he tells it. Stomped him with those big ass boots of his and left the guy paralyzed from the neck down."

"Damn!" Despite the incessant heat, I shiver once again. "So, basically, I'm bunking with a complete psychopath. Is that what you're trying to tell me?"

Angelo laughs. "I figured you knew that already. But look on the bright side, bro. Shane ain't your average ballplayer, but he ain't your average skinhead either. You ever heard of a SHARP before?" I shake my head. "It stands for Skinheads Against Racial Prejudice. So that skinhead he banged up was a whole different kind if you get what I'm saying. That's why no one says shit to me when Shane's around. Not since the first day he got here."

"Did he stomp someone out for being racist?"

"Hell yeah, he did," Angelo says, with a smirk of satisfaction. "Dragged his ass to the showers and knocked him out cold."

"Damn! That's pretty badass actually!"

"Yeah, Molloy ain't the brightest, but he learned a real good lesson that day. He hasn't even tried to mess with me since then."

"Wait a second..." I sit up and squint at him. "It was Molloy he knocked out?"

Angelo chuckles. "Weird how things turn out sometimes, huh?"

"Yeah," I say, peering down the ridge at Shane and then over at Molloy. "And things just keep getting weirder."

The baseball game begins with Shane striking out the first two hitters with his first six pitches. Pretty impressive, but despite being the leadoff hitters, it looks like they're swinging out of hope instead of skill. However, the next batter catches my attention with his first practice swing. Perfect form.

"Who's this dude?" I ask Angelo.

"That's Ol' Trippy," he says. "The kid can hit, but other than that, he's basically a nobody."

With his first pitch, Shane tempts him with a nasty curveball, but Ol' Trippy watches it all the way. *Ball one.* Taz tosses the ball back to Shane, who winds up again. This time he tries a fastball. Ol' Trippy swings and cracks the ball into left field.

"Damn!" I say. "So what's his story?"

"Dude's just a messed-up druggy, man," Angelo explains. "He did way too much acid for way too long. Now he has these crazy flashbacks, like full on fits and shit. Spazzing out on the floor and pissing himself. It's scary to watch, bro! And all kinds of things can set him off. Flashing lights, loud noises, you never really know. The dude should be on meds, but he's not."

Ol' Trippy makes it to second base, and the next batter runs him in with a two-run homer. Even from up here, I can see the crimson shade of Shane's face.

"Damn! Shane ain't used to giving up hits like this," Angelo tells me. "And getting lit up by a Roach makes it even more embarrassing."

I watch Shane fume on the mound while the batter trots around third and jogs toward home plate. "So the guy who just homered is a Roach, like that little, smelly kid on kitchen crew?"

Angelo sits up and stifles a yawn. "Yeah, that's Stankass Lou. He's a good ball player, but he's as unclean as they come. Sometimes we call him P.U. Lou, as well. It depends. But his real name is Louis Marshall. He's a Lifer, like Molloy."

An hour or so later, the game concludes with a rare victory

for Benny's team, ending Shane's impressive winning streak of twenty-three games. This sparks wild celebrations amongst the winning side, which carry into the dorms, souring Shane's mood even more.

I make myself as silent and invisible as possible for the remainder of the day. After night rolls in and the lights go out, I lie on my bunk, staring up at the dark ceiling and listening to the muffled shrill of the cicadas outside. A strange sense of relief settles within me. I am relieved that I only have to make it through a few months in this place, instead of a few years.

9

SHADY BUSINESS

Wednesday, April 4 - Day 4

'*One day at a time.*' Dad had a habit of saying that after Mom's accident, as if it would help me make sense of why everything had stopped making sense anymore. It certainly hits home now, though. Yesterday was a repeat of Monday and today has gone pretty much the same.

I sat in the kitchen while Shane and Molloy fixed breakfast and cleaned up afterwards with the rest of the kitchen crew. After that, it was off to school again until Brother James finished with his sports section and sent us back to The Dorm to change for baseball.

If it weren't for Angelo's company, I might be tempted to play. He's a wealth of knowledge when it comes to learning how things work in this circus of a shitshow. And he invited me to bunk in his room whenever I get off Watch, which will hopefully be sooner rather than later.

For the meantime, I'm on my best behavior around Shane and Molloy, in the hope they'll spread the word to Brother Bennett. I've sat around their room for the past few hours, bored out of my skull while they pretend I don't exist, and I haven't bothered them even once. I'm going to now, though, despite it being crappy timing. I have to for the sake of my own sanity.

I approach with caution as Shane shuffles a deck of Uno cards to begin another game. Neither he nor Molloy are in particularly pleasant moods now. A front of heavy thunderstorms resulted in afternoon sports being canceled, and we've all been stuck inside the sweaty dorms since lunch.

"Would it be okay if I went to a different room for a while?" I ask them.

Shane continues shuffling the deck as though he didn't hear me. Molloy shakes his head, seemingly too caught up in his own grievances.

"I bet he only agreed to play football today because he knew it was gonna storm," Molloy grumbles as Shane deals out the first cards.

"Of course, he did, you idiot!" Shane chuckles. "How many times are you gonna fall for it? Brother James obsesses over the forecast the moment spring season starts. You should know that by now."

I clear my throat. "Could I please go to a different room for a while?"

This time Shane actually turns to look at me. "Which one?"

"Angelo's."

Molloy snickers. "That asswipe? Go ahead. Have fun with your boyfriend. If you ain't back here before we have to fix dinner, I'm telling Brother James you snuck away."

"You know what?" Shane chimes in. "I heard Brother Bennett's supposed to be back before church. How about we tell *him* instead? I'm sure he wouldn't mind breaking you in with a few licks." This hammers his point home effectively, and I nod my compliance before leaving the room.

I haven't seen Brother Bennett since our chat in his office a few days ago. No one's mentioned where he is or what he's doing. No one seems to know. The only adults around are his son, Robbie, and Brother James, as well as Ms. Tammy, of course. Brother James and Robbie are far from formidable, especially in comparison with Brother Bennett. In fact, neither are particularly intimidating when you remove him from the equation.

Brother James can be hostile, sure, but he's also too lazy to give a shit half of the time. Apparently, he passes out with a bottle most evenings, too. As for Robbie—well, Robbie is about as simple as they come.

I seriously thought he was one of us the first couple of days. He only looks a few years older than me and tries to shoot the shit with the Trusted Boys, even though he stutters like Rain Man. Since I found out he's actually twenty-two and Brother Bennett's only son, I've started seeing him through a whole new lens.

Knocking on the frame of Angelo's doorway, I'm answered with a word that rhymes with Chuck, followed by a harshly enunciated "off."

"It's a pleasure to see you too, Oaf," I reply, stepping inside.

Oaf's face puckers into a scowl, and I turn my attention to Angelo, who lounges on his bunk reading a letter.

"Who's that from?" I ask.

He glances over at me as if he just realized I'm there. "Hey, what's up, Will? Just reading a letter from my mom."

"Everything good back in LA?"

"Yeah, man. My mom just started a new job. More money and way better hours." Angelo sits up and swings his legs down the side of the bunk. "Shane and Molloy finally let you loose for a minute, huh?"

"Just for a little while. I can hang out here as long as I'm back before they leave to fix dinner."

"Well, this room's closed, Chuck," Oaf blurts out. "So how about you find a different one to hang out in?"

"Whatever, Oaf." Angelo fires back. "I've got seniority here, not you. You don't like that, you're the one who needs to find a different room, bro."

The entire bunk creaks as Oaf heaves himself upright on his mattress and swings his tree-trunk legs to the floor. He stands up, stretching himself to his full height as he glares between Angelo and me.

"I'm going to take a shit," he announces. "That's the only reason I'm leaving."

Oaf turns and lumbers out of the room, trumpeting a fart as he enters the hallway. Angelo and I crack up laughing.

"And that, ladies and gentleman, is why we call him Big Dumb Oaf." Angelo chuckles away, stowing his letter under his pillow.

"He definitely lives up to his nickname," I say, hopping up onto one of the spare bunks. "Hey, there's something I've been meaning to ask you."

"Ask away, bro."

"Okay, so what's the deal with Brother Bennett? I thought he ran this place, but he's pretty much been gone since I got here. Shane said he's supposed to be back before church, but where the hell's he been for the past three days?"

Angelo shrugs his shoulders. "Bennett might run this place, but he runs a shitload of side hustles too. Dude's always looking for new ways to make money. So I ain't sure where he's been, but I bet that's what he was doing. And Bennett's shady business deals usually involve us, so we'll find out more soon enough, I guess."

"What do you mean they 'involve us'?"

Angelo sighs. "We're free labor, bro. You'll see what I mean before too long, trust me. But it usually involves a big-ass field and a day of hard labor under the sun. Don't expect to get paid for doing it either."

I shake my head. "This place is way shittier than I imagined. No wonder they keep new kids on Watch in case they run for it. It's starting to sound like my safest bet at this point."

"Oh yeah!" Angelo raises his eyebrows. "How far do you think you'd get? The last kid who tried made it a mile down the road before Bennett picked him up. The kid before him didn't even make it off the property. I can think of four other boys who made a run for it since I got here. Bennett brought back every single one of them. But maybe you'll have better luck than they did, bro. What do you think?"

My mind flashes back to the missing maps in those ancient encyclopedias. Even if I did make a run for it, I'd have no idea where I was going, nor how to get there if I did.

10

───────────

METALLICA GIRL

After a delightful meal of what can best be described as noodles and ketchup, we're greeted by the return of Brother Bennett. A familiar sense of dread seeps back into the air as he issues out a few stern reminders about our conduct during tonight's service. He warns us he'll be watching closely and tells us to change for church.

Compared to last time, getting ready is a breeze. This is mainly thanks to Angelo, who lets me borrow a shirt that actually fits. He also lends me a nicer tie than Molloy's shitty, home-made embarrassment, which still has a few puke stains on it from last Sunday.

When it's time to go, I head outside with Shane and Molloy, who are absorbed in a conversation about some girl called Brandy. As we board The Booger, I brace myself for the residual stench of my vomit, but the bus smells exactly as it looks and feels: grimy and humid. Unlike last time, there are still plenty of seats available, but I head down the aisle toward the spot where I first met Angelo. Just like before, there he is, lounging back in the window seat.

"How's your stomach feeling?" he asks as I ease down next to him.

"It feels full of whatever that was we just ate," I tell him. "But I think I should be able to keep it down for now."

I smile at him, but he just stares at me with furrowed brows.

"Bro, you're messing with me and you feel fine, right?"

Chuckling, I pat him on the shoulder. "Of course, I'm messing with you. Dude, by the time dinner rolled around I was so freaking hungry that it's mind over matter at this point. I'll keep it down by sheer willpower if I have to. Promise."

Moments later, Brother James starts The Booger on its way. Brother Bennett follows behind us in his beat-up, old truck, along with Ms. Tammy, and their son, Robbie. After driving along the state highway for about twenty minutes, we enter a small city, which Angelo informs me is Hattiesburg, the place I flew into last Sunday.

The airport must have been on the outskirts, though, because I never saw any of this on the way to Victory Ridge with Joyce. Not that there's much to see, really. There's no discernable skyline, no unique features or architecture to speak of; it's just a small, plain, shitty-looking city.

Several turns later, we pull up to Center Baptist Church, a fairly modest red-bricked box with a white spire and cross pointing toward the sky. The parking lot is already crammed with cars and churchgoers file between the traffic, holding the whole process up even more.

Eventually, Brother James finds a space large enough to accommodate our death trap of a ride, which backfires a gunshot-worthy fart as it shudders to a stop. I file off behind Angelo, planning to stay close and snag a seat next to him. But as I hop off the bus, Shane and Molloy are standing there waiting for me, and I resign myself to their unpleasant company once again.

A MUSTY SMELL turns my stomach as we enter the church. The smell of old things. Old carpet, old books, and old people. It's the type of odor that clings to your clothes, skin, and hair. I follow Shane and Molloy into the sanctuary, which is about as basic as you could imagine. Rows of wooden pews separate a central walkway that leads down to the pulpit, where a huge wooden cross hangs on the wall.

"This way." Molloy grabs me by the arm and shoves me toward one of the pews. "Slide in."

I do as I'm told, and he and Shane slide in after me.

"Do you see them?" Molloy mutters, as he scans the room. "Are they here yet?"

"No idea," Shane replies. "Not that it makes a difference anyway. We're stuck here with Chuck."

"It don't need two of us to watch him." Molloy says, still glancing around. "One of us could still go sit with them."

Sean glares at him. "Let me guess. You're offering to stay here while I spend the next hour hitting on chicks? Is that what you're saying?"

Molloy seals his lips and turns to stare at the entrance of the sanctuary again. I glance around as well, taking note of where the other rejects from Victory Ridge are seated. Most of them occupy the three pews behind us. I spy Angelo a couple of rows back, gazing blankly into space. Brother James sits at the end of the same pew, his eyelids drooping. He snaps them open again and shakes his head to wake himself up.

Ahead of us, two rows from the front, the tall, broad frame of Brother Bennett slides along the pew with Ms Tammy and Robbie. He's dressed in a black suit with a white shirt and a bolo string tie, carrying his cowboy hat in his hands. I notice Trent and Jerry, two of his Trusted Boys, sitting a few rows behind him with a group of local teens.

"How come they don't have to sit with us?" I point them out to Shane, who takes one glance and shrugs.

"Older boys can sit where they want as long as Brother Bennett trusts them enough."

"Yeah, and we'd be doing the same if we weren't stuck with your sorry ass," Molloy chimes in.

I consider telling him I'm not thrilled with the current situation either, but Molloy's already peering back toward the entrance again. "They're here!" he gasps suddenly, and Shane and I swivel around at once.

Three teenage girls, all of whom look about sixteen or seventeen, tread down the walkway together. Two of them are short, blond, and fairly cute, but the third girl has my stomach doing backflips. She's tall and pale with dark hair tied into a tight bun on top of her head, and when it comes to looks, she is quite literally head and shoulders above the other two girls. Judging by her sullen expression and the way she tugs at her ankle-length skirt, she would rather be anywhere but here, too.

"I can't believe they're hanging out with the giant lesbian again," I hear Molloy mutter.

"Are you talking about the tall brunette?" I ask him.

"Obviously, dumbass."

"How do you know she's a lesbian?"

"How do I *know*?" Molloy scowls at me. "Because it's freaking obvious, okay? The other girls round here go wild for us, but that chick won't give us a second look. She's a lesbian. She even told me so herself."

"She told you she's a lesbian?" I ask.

"Yep, pretty much. She said it right to my face. 'I'm not interested in guys.' Those were her exact words."

Shane snorts out laughter.

"What!?" Molloy scowls at him, his cheeks flushing.

"Yeah, her exact words to a point, you mean." Shane smirks at him. "You left off the part where she said 'like you.' I was right there when she said it, assbag. She said, 'I'm not interested in guys like *you*.' And you just stood there all cherry red with your mouth wide open."

Shane chuckles, and despite the ominous look Molloy throws my way, I can't help joining him. The thought of this chick roasting Molloy like that makes me all the more intrigued. I turn around for another peek at her and find all three of the girls staring in our direction. The tall one and I lock eyes for a moment, and I drop my gaze.

My heart stampedes inside my chest. When I check back a few moments later, the girls are parting ways. The two blonds slip into a pew on the other side of the church, and the tall girl slides in beside an older woman who greets her with a warm smile, presumably her mother.

Before Mom's accident, we would go to church as a family every once in a while. My parents would joke that we were

"CEOs"(Christmas and Easter Only). I never particularly cared for the services, but we went so infrequently that I never complained too much. And now I'm stuck without a choice. Three days a week for the next ninety days.

The service begins with a droning hymn. Shane and Molloy join in half-heartedly, but it's not one I'm familiar with. In fact, it sounds as though it's being chanted instead of sung, which makes it all the more *soul-suckingly* depressing. The songs I remember from church were pretty uplifting, but this is clearly not that kind of church. They have an albino Jesus for crying out loud.

After suffering through several more hymns, an old, wrinkly, bald guy with glasses hogs the podium and drones out some announcements. I zone in and out of listening. More out than in. And he's soon replaced by an even crustier-looking dude with a few wispy strands of white hair swept across his blotchy head.

The old preacher grips the pulpit with his frail hands, as though he might keel over at any moment. And he just might. A strong gust of wind would blow him off the stage. He begins waffling on in a soft monotonous drawl, the kind that lulls you into sleep. And soon enough, my eyelids start fluttering shut.

Until the old bastard starts screaming that is! Not like a man of God. Not like he's beseeching the Heavens. Screaming like a man possessed by a schizophrenic demon as he pounds his bony fist on the pulpit.

"Y'ALL NEED TO LISTEN TO WHAT THE GOOD BOOK SAYS!"

Well, I'm awake and listening now!

"HELL AND DAMNATION..."

Yeah, no joke. I'm living in it.

"HELLFIRE..."

Fire tire?

"SINNERS REPENT..."

So you say, but I was told sorry wouldn't cut it anymore.

After several minutes of manic ranting, the old preacher appears to have finally worn himself out and reverts back to a mind-numbing drone. I distract myself by flipping through a few of the small books that are stacked in the compartment along the back of the pew. There's a whole selection of them, most of which are written like informative pamphlets offering advice on being a good Christian and Baptist. In addition to that, though, there are these cringeworthy, twisted comics about the evils of homosexuality and alcohol and drugs. The weird can always get weirder, I guess.

The service eventually crawls to an end, and all of us are called to the altar to accept Jesus or repent being an awful human. I would prefer to pass on both, but when it comes time for our row to rise, Shane and Molloy usher me along to the front. We make our way up the aisle afterward, and they ditch me at the top of the walkway to talk to the two blond girls that came in with the tall brunette. I'm instructed to sit in a nearby pew and wait.

I take a seat, slump back, and fold my arms across my chest, fighting the temptation to prop my feet on the pew in front. The girlish giggling behind me and Molloy's grunting laughter make me grind my teeth with annoyance. But then I spy her walking up the aisle behind her mother. Walking right my way.

I watch as she draws closer and closer, her eyes lowered toward the Bible in her hands. A few deafening heartbeats later, and she's right next to me, passing by the pew. Something white falls from her Bible and lands on the floor beside her feet. She strides on, oblivious, and I lurch to my feet.

At first glance, it looks like a folded piece of white paper, but as I stoop down to scoop it up, I recognize it instantly. My jaw drops, and I stare after her as she continues up the aisle. She just dropped the cassette sleeve from Metallica's ...*AND JUSTICE FOR ALL* album. My all-time favorite album!

"Hey," I call out, scrambling up the aisle past a few disgruntled churchgoers. "Hey, is this yours?"

The girl heads toward the main doors, showing no signs of having heard me. Either that, or she's choosing to ignore me. Either way, I follow after her. This clearly isn't the wisest choice given my circumstances, but I let my impulses steer me, excusing myself as I squeeze past several people to catch up.

"Excuse me," I say, tapping her lightly on the shoulder. "I think you dropped something."

She startles and swivels around. Piercing, pale blue eyes lock on to me, and I find myself frozen in place, holding the cassette sleeve out toward her.

"You...you dropped this," I somehow manage to mumble.

Her eyes widen as she stares at the cassette sleeve. She darts out a hand, snatching it from my grasp and stuffs it back in her Bible. Glancing around nervously, she turns to leave, takes a half-step, and pauses to look back at me.

"Thank you," she whispers and then hurries off toward the exit.

"What did you give her?" asks a voice from behind me.

I spin around to find Shane glaring at me, Molloy a few steps behind him.

"Don't try saying you didn't," Shane growls. "I saw you give her something. What was it?"

"One of those little 'Going to Hell' books from the pew. She dropped it when she walked by."

The lie comes quickly, and I'm impressed by its quality. Judging by the shift in Shane's demeanor, it seems to have worked.

Molloy sneers at me. "Whatever, Chuck. If it was a book about how not to be a lesbian, you might actually have a chance. Let's go, dumbass. Back to The Booger."

11

THE LINEUP

Despite the doom and gloom of church, the mood on board The Booger is on the verge of party mode as the last few stragglers climb the steps. The boys in the back row stomp out a beat while the rest of the bus belts out several different songs at once, competing to be the loudest. As the volume amps up, Brother Bennett steps aboard, with a scowl etched into his face.

"ENOUGH!" he hollers. "Y'ALL AIN'T HERE FOR A GOOD TIME!"

Silence falls on everyone in the bus, and we all seem to shrink into our seats as Brother Bennett glares at us.

"It seems some of y'all ain't too good at listening. What did I say about talking in church? What did I tell y'all?" He glances around, but no one responds. "Oh, now y'all got nothing to say. How about that? Sounds like it's time for an old-fashioned reminder of the rules."

He turns to face Brother James, who stands a few feet behind him. "It's gonna be a quiet ride back, Brother James. These boys are all talked-out. I'd appreciate you telling me if you hear one peep out of them. Cause if he does…" Brother Bennett raises his voice again, directing his attention back to us. "Y'all are in for the worst lineup I've ever given. Do I make myself clear?"

"Yes, sir," we all utter at once.

We ride back to Nowhere in silence, except for the occasional cough and the strained rumbling of The Booger as she rattles along the road. As soon as we arrive at Victory Ridge, we're all sent straight to the dining hall. Brother Bennett awaits us, his mood even darker than before. His stuttering son, Robbie, stands beside him. He glances up at his father with nervous anticipation as we enter the room.

"I didn't tell y'all to sit," Brother Bennett says coldly, as several boys slide onto one of the benches and lurch to their feet again.

He folds his arms across his chest and glares around the room at us. An ominous dread creeps into me. I spy Angelo standing on the opposite side of the dining hall. I'm desperate to know what's about to happen here, but even if he was standing next to me right now, it would be too risky to ask him.

"Some of y'all's behavior in the house of the Lord makes me sick to my stomach." Brother Bennett's deep drawl resonates around the dining hall. "The disrespect y'all showed will not be repeated and it will not go unpunished." He turns to Robbie. "Fetch me my paddle, son."

Robbie jolts to attention. "Yes, Daddy!" he says, already scurrying toward the office hallway. "I'll b-be right back."

Holy shit! Someone's about to get licks. Who did he catch talking during the service? I glance around the room at the other boys. A few of their expressions match my own, but most seem fairly indifferent. All except for Oaf, I notice. He shuffles his enormous, tugboat feet around like he's ready to run for it. Was it him? God, I hope so!

The wooden paddle that Robbie returns with a few moments later is larger than I imagined. He presents it to his father like it's some kind of sacred relic.

"Line up," Brother Bennett orders as he grips the handle of the paddle and taps it against his free hand.

I glance around to see who's lining up. To my shock, I realize that everyone is. I catch Angelo's eye as he and the other boys move to form a line through the middle of the hall. He waves me over.

"What the hell's happening?" I whisper, as I shuffle in next to him. "How come we're all getting licks?"

"Like I told you," Angelo says, "licks are gonna happen no matter what. Just chill, okay? Watch what Oaf does and make sure you don't do the same thing."

I look down the line and find Oaf sticking out like an ugly, sore thumb, practically squirming in his spot. Judging by where Brother Bennett has positioned himself to start, Oaf is sixth in line for licks. Shane appears to be first, but looks completely at ease even though Brother Bennett looms right behind him.

"Whatever you do," Angelo whispers, "don't flinch. It's worse that way. Trust me."

I watch as Shane bends over and places his hand on the table in front of him. His expression remains unfazed. Brother Bennett winds up a swing and connects with a sickening smack. Shane doesn't even grimace. He just repositions his feet for the next lick.

Shane receives three in total, as does Molloy and then Benny. They all take their licks without complaint as Brother Bennett moves up the line. By the time it's Oaf's turn to assume the position, his shirt is drenched with sweat. His arms and legs quiver as he bends over and grips the edge of the table. A few of the boys chuckle, but one look from Brother Bennett silences them.

As Brother Bennett reels back the paddle and swings, my eyes are glued to Big Dumb Oaf. Just before the point of impact, Oaf flinches and arches backward. As a result, instead of striking him on the pads of his huge ass, Brother Bennett cracks him right on the small of his back. Oaf howls and crumples to his knees, tears flooding down his crimson face.

"Get up!" Brother Bennett growls, and Oaf whimpers his way back to his feet.

His final two licks aren't any prettier, and even though Oaf's by far the most toxic guy I've met here, I'm grateful that I don't have to watch him take another one.

When my turn arrives, my heart is hammering, but I take a deep breath and try my best to mimic Shane's approach instead of Oaf's. I bend over and keep myself as still as possible, clenching my jaw to brace myself for impact. The first lick knocks the breath right out of me. A stinging pain spreads across my ass, and I have to stop myself from reaching back to rub it. My final two licks are no different, and my butt cheeks sear with throbbing pain as Brother Bennett moves on to his next victim.

When all is said and done and we're sent off to bed, I'm told more than once that I took my first licks like a champ. They hurt like hell, but what doesn't, I guess? And though I make sure to thank Angelo for the advice, it's really Big Dumb Oaf who deserves the praise. So here's to you, Oaf. Thanks for being such a bitch at taking licks.

12

PEACH FUZZ

Monday, April 9 - Day 9

"Happy Opening Day, boys!" A giddy Brother James greets Angelo and me at the schoolhouse door. He looks like he's dressed for church, wearing a red tie dotted with tiny white C's. "Well, it ain't gonna be too happy for y'all Braves and Dodgers fans, but my Redlegs are gonna be something this year. Mark my words. I smell a pennant in the air." He flares his nostrils like he's inhaling a sweet scent, and we hurry past him into the schoolhouse.

Once all the boys are gathered inside, we become Brother James's captive audience for the next twenty minutes as he declares his adoration for all things Cincinnati Reds. This digresses into a rant about Pete Rose, which breaks off as Brother Bennett pokes his head inside to tell him he's leaving for Jackson. Fortunately for us, the interruption knocks Brother James out of his stride. He sends us off to start our work, but the moment Brother Bennett pulls away in his truck—in recognition of Opening Day—Brother James declares that school is over before it's even begun.

"Not a bad start to the day, huh?" I say to Angelo, but then I spy Shane and Molloy waiting for me by the schoolhouse doors again. "Actually, I take that back. This means I'm stuck with those assholes for four extra hours."

"Don't worry, man," Angelo says. "Shouldn't be too much longer."

As it turns out, Angelo is right. Shane and Molloy aren't here to escort me anywhere. A new kid arrives this afternoon, I'm informed. "You're off Watch. Pack your shit and find another room."

"This day just keeps getting better!" I tell Angelo as we walk across the field toward The Dorm. "I wonder what's gonna happen next? Maybe the Reds will whip the Astros so bad that Brother James cancels school every day until they lose."

Angelo chuckles. "As crazy as that sounds, I wouldn't put it past him, bro."

Neither Shane nor Molloy are in their room when I enter, which is another stroke of luck. I stuff my things into my suitcase and hightail it over to Angelo's room, only to find the giant frame of Big Dumb Oaf barring the doorway. He glances down at my suitcase and prods me in the chest with one of his grubby, fat fingers.

"Where do you think *you're* going?"

"Into my room," I tell him.

"*Your* room? Says who?"

"Says Angelo, actually."

Oaf puckers up his face. "I don't like this," he growls. "I don't like your stupid, smug face."

"Anything else you want to tell me?" I say, standing my ground. "Maybe something I don't already know."

Oaf sneers. "You think you're so smart, don't you, Chuck?" I suppress the urge to tell him I'm most certainly smarter than he is. "But you're not that smart at all. You're just a smartass little bitch that I could crush like a bug."

"Everything good here?" a voice asks from down the hall.

I turn to find Trent and Jerry walking our way. Oaf drops his finger from my chest, his cheeks flushed. He glares at me for a moment, and then he turns and lumbers over to his bunk.

———

WE'RE HALF-WAY through a lunch of bologna sandwiches on stale white bread when Benny bursts into the dining room.

"He's here!" he announces. "A car's coming up the drive right now."

Benches scrape against the wooden floor as everyone abandons their lunches to flock outside for a glimpse of the newest member of Victory Ridge. Angelo and I find ourselves at the back of the crowd. By the time we make it outside, the porch is swarming with boys all jostling for position as an old, silver station wagon crests the ridge of the driveway.

As it turns onto the gravel lot, memories of my own arrival nine days ago flood back to me. Sitting alone inside the car, a sweaty, anxious mess with a crowd of delinquents leering at me. But this kid just hops out of the car the moment it stops. Short and scrawny, with a scruff of rusty hair, he looks like he was bred for guys like Big Dumb Oaf to snack on. That said, he just stretches his arms and stares around at everyone without a hint of trepidation.

A haggard man in overalls and a gaunt woman with waist-length hair exit the car and join him in the driveway. Brother James, looking abnormally professional in his Opening Day attire, emerges from the main building with Brother Robbie at his heel.

"All y'all boys need to clear out now," Brother James hollers.

And what Brother James hollers, Robbie always repeats.

"Y-y'all c-clear out!" he yells, cupping his hands around his mouth while Brother James ushers the new boy and his family toward the porch-side door. Just like Brother Bennett did to me nine days ago.

———

THE NEXT TIME I see the new kid he's standing in the kitchen after dinner, getting the lowdown from Angelo about kitchen crew. As it turns out, he's from my home state of Georgia. A place called Harlem, which I associate with an entirely different state. A place he describes as "backwoods and backward," so he must feel right at home here in the bowels of *Backwards*, Mississippi.

Unfortunately for the new boy, whose real name is Clyde Jackson, he arrived sporting the most pitiful excuse for a mustache I've ever seen. It's basically a mix of blond and orange fluff that looks like a sickly caterpillar. But, perhaps, most unfortunately, he's incredibly proud of it. So proud that he felt justified in telling Shane and Molloy he'd bite the fingers of anyone who tried to shave it off.

The problem for Clyde, however, is that no one except the Brothers and the so-called Trusted Boys are allowed to grow facial hair. No exceptions. Except, Clyde didn't take too kindly to hearing this, and told Shane and Molloy to pass his threat along. A task they eagerly completed.

Brother Bennett came for Clyde towards the end of cleanup duty. I wasn't sure what was about to happen, but I felt a profound sense of relief. Relief that I was no longer the new kid. Relief that I wasn't the one in Clyde's shoes.

The rest of the kitchen crew was ordered to leave the room, so I didn't hear Clyde's response when Brother Bennett asked him to explain why he still hadn't shaved. But I did hear the *smack* that followed, and the grunt from Clyde that followed after that.

By the time we're lining up for our cold showers, Clyde Jackson is no more. The skinny, little hick from Harlem, Georgia, is now known as Peaches. A name that will stick longer than the pathetic little strip of peach fuzz he once held so dear.

13

THE YUCKING OF ALVARO PÉREZ

Monday, April 16 - Day 16

A new prisoner arrived yesterday: Alvaro Pérez, another Cuban kid from Miami. Alvaro is the type of guy who makes you feel inferior the instant you see him. He's tall, tanned, and muscled like a Greek god, with a chiseled jaw and long, thick black hair that falls midway down his back.

After watching Peaches lose his stache last week, it was no surprise to learn that long hair like Alvaro's is forbidden here too. It's a rule even the Trusted Boys have to follow. Apparently, according to the laws and logic of Brother Bennett, boys having long hair is unchristian. Yes, even though Jesus wore it that way.

However, just like Peaches, Alvaro had his own opinions on the matter. In fact, he spent the majority of breakfast spouting them off for all to hear. No one would be getting near his precious locks, he declared. Just let them try. He wouldn't be responsible for what happened to them if they did. That was the gist of it, at least, but despite Alvaro's bravado, his Cuban comrades exchanged worried glances. Alvaro may have been a badass back in Miami, but he doesn't know shit about how things work here in Nowhere.

Now as breakfast comes to an end and I head to the kitchen for cleanup, the rumors are already circulating. At some point today, whether Alvaro likes it or not, that impressive mane of his will be getting the chop.

The anticipation is a welcome distraction from a sink full of dirty dishes, but Alvaro's fate isn't the only piece of news being passed around. Today, we're all going to be pawns in one of Brother Bennett's notorious money-making schemes. Angelo's mood soured the instant we were told, but I can't help feeling curious. I mean, it can't be any worse than sitting around in the schoolhouse filling out work packets all morning.

"I ain't in the mood for this shit," Angelo mutters, as he picks up a tray of clean silverware. "I'm sick of being Bennett's field slave whenever he wants to make a few extra bucks. We've gotta bust our asses all day in the heat, and he gets to pocket all the money for himself!"

"I guess Jesus just turns a blind eye to that kind of stuff, huh?" I say.

"Hell, I ain't blind to it," Peaches, the newest member of kitchen crew, chimes in. "That's one hundred percent profit right there. I mean, I know it ain't right and all, but who wouldn't want a deal like that?"

"Are you fucking serious, Peach?" Angelo shakes his head and glares at him. "That's some messed-up shit to say, bro! Three dudes got heat stroke from digging ditches last summer. Does that sound like a good deal to you?"

Peaches frowns and dips his mop in the bucket. "Guess not," he mutters, as he rinses it out again.

We resume our cleaning in awkward silence, but several minutes later, Angelo starts snickering while he's drying off the bowls I just washed.

"What's funny?" I ask him.

"Just thinking about one of Bennett's schemes from a couple of years ago," he says, wearing a devilish grin. "It was a complete disaster, but at least it didn't involve us. We just sat back and watched it all fall apart. It was perfect, man! Just pure poetry."

"You gonna jerk off about it or tell us what happened?" Peaches asks, and we all chuckle.

"Okay, so Bennett disappeared for a few days like usual, right?" Angelo begins. "When he showed up again, he had a purebred female Dalmation with him. Apparently, some guy he knew owned a purebred male, so they were planning to breed them and then sell off the puppies. The dog didn't come cheap, though. I ain't sure how much he paid, but I know he dropped some serious cash. 'Cause he sold Ms. Tammy's Jeep the day he came back, and the next morning that dog was getting fucked behind his trailer. He just stood there watching it all too, the sick bastard."

I frown in disgust. "What the hell, dude! That's some sick shit! So did the dog have any puppies?"

Angelo beams with satisfaction. "Oh yeah, she definitely had puppies, but I never got to see them. None of us did."

"Why not? Did he sell them off the second they were born or something?"

"Nah, Bennett never saw those puppies either, bro. The bitch broke out of his trailer one night, and no one ever saw her again." Angelo cracks up laughing.

"I don't get what's so funny," Peaches says.

"Yeah, same," I agree.

"No, no, no..." Angelo pulls himself together. "You guys don't understand. Bennett was obsessed with this dog, man. He treated her like royalty. Fed her leftovers from his own table and shit — hotdogs, meatloaf, steak, whatever he had. That dog ate better than we did. And the more pregnant she got, the more he spoiled her. He was practically licking his lips at the thought of all the money she was gonna make him.

"The morning after she escaped, Bennett lost his shit completely. He was convinced someone must've stolen her and had us line up outside his office to be interrogated. When it was clear we had nothing to do with it, we spent the next few days searching through the woods for her and putting up posters by the road. A $200 reward for anyone who found her, which is pennies when you think about how much someone could get for selling her and the puppies for themselves. But Bennett was beyond desperate."

Angelo smiles and lets out a soft sigh. "It felt good to see him so defeated. It was a reminder that he isn't invincible. That he's just a human being, and he can hurt inside too, you know."

"You know what, Angelo?" I tell him. "That might be the best story I've heard in a long time.

———

THE NEXT STORY I hear is far less amusing. We're being bussed over to a field a few miles away to build a fence around the entire perimeter, in the sweltering heat. Apparently, Brother Bennett's latest money-making scheme involves a half-dozen cows. Calves, technically. Buy them young and small, fatten them up, sell them on, and the skies will rain hundred dollar bills. Just like the Dalmatian.

A couple of the boys groaned when Brother Bennett announced this, and now he's working himself into a tirade.

"Not one of y'all knows the first thing about hard work!" he informs us. "Y'all just wanna stand around and complain! Well, that ain't happening today, boys. Today's a day for giving back." He raises his arm and points towards the blazing sun. "'Commit thy works unto the Lord, and thy thoughts will be established.'"

He glances around as though inviting us to challenge him. When no one does, he nods his approval. "Now get on that bus and get busy. I need that fence up before noon. I've got another job for y'all after this one."

About fifteen minutes later, Brother James turns The Booger down a narrow dirt road and parks by the side of a large, dusty field dotted with coarse patches of grass. He splits us into two groups. One is tasked with digging holes around the perimeter of the field and hammering in fence posts. The other has to unroll the bundles of barbed wire, string them around the posts, and fasten them securely.

Angelo and I are in the barbed wire group, which seems like the least exerting of the two jobs. However, under a blistering heat like this, nobody's a winner. The Mississippi sun feels like it's perpetually pissed off, and I can't say I blame it.

As I soon discover, this is the type of work that will drain you in even the coolest of climates. Finish one area, move to the next. Repeat the grueling process. No breaks. No water. By the time we've attached the last section of barbed wire, my mouth is so parched that my lips are cracked.

After a short trip back to Victory Ridge, we line up behind The Dorm and take turns drinking from the hose. Shane and Molloy serve us "Mississippi Brunch" for lunch, which turns out to be a slice of bologna served on the palm of my hand, and a fist-full of chips. I devour it all without a fuss, but our break is far too brief.

"D-Daddy says y'all need to hurry down to his trailer r-right now," a flush-faced Robbie runs up and informs us.

"You've got to be kidding me!" Angelo's face twists into scowl. "What the hell does he want now?"

As it turns out, it's more about what Ms. Tammy wants, not Brother Bennett, but the answer to Angelo's question does nothing to sweeten his mood.

"She wants a new deck for their trailer, huh?" he grumbles as we're assigned into groups again. "And we're the ones who have to build it, of course."

"And she wants one that's big enough for a swing," I add. "I doubt there's a swing that's big enough for her ass, though!"

"Keep your voice down!" Angelo nods toward Robbie, who's standing several yards away.

Fortunately for us, we're assigned to the group that gets to break down the old deck before the other group has to build the new one. The prospect of destroying something that belongs to Brother Bennett puts a grin back on Angelo's face. Peaches is in our group, too, along with the Cuban Crew and their new messiah, Alvaro, who keeps lifting up his shirt to check his abs every few minutes.

Molloy, Trent, and Jerry, are the only other boys of note.

Unless you count Robbie, that is. He's supposed to be our supervisor, but he's more focused on trying to be one of the guys and failing miserably as usual. Every time he attempts to be funny, he glances at Alvaro to check his response, which makes me wonder if he was told to keep an eye on him.

In fact, Robbie seems particularly wary of Alvaro, and who can blame him? He looks like a twig in comparison. A simpleton like Robbie won't intimidate a guy like Alvaro Pérez. Better luck getting him to like you, which seems to be Robbie's strategy. No that it's working, however. Alvaro has the strained look of someone who has other things on his mind. Something he's chewing on.

Once our brief break is over, we start on our second backbreaking job of the day. Angelo and I take turns with a sledgehammer, and despite the heat, demolishing Brother Bennett's deck is a blast to begin with. We hoist the hammer above our heads and smash it down with as much force as we can muster, enjoying the satisfying crack as the wood splits apart.

We start switching out more frequently before long, though. My shoulders ache in protest each time I raise the sledgehammer, and the palms of my hands are chafed raw and blistered. Just like earlier, no one offers us water. No refreshments are on hand. No snacks. No bandaids. That shit doesn't happen here.

Once the deck is dismantled into several piles of broken lumber, we're finally allowed another break. We line up in front of the hose on the outside of the trailer and are given ten seconds each to quench our thirsts. A couple of boys break off to throw around a football in the adjacent field. The rest of us, the intelligent ones, relax in the shade before it's time to haul the busted-up deck over to the woods.

Angelo, Peaches, and I lounge back on the hillside, our bodies baked and leaden from exhaustion. No one says a word. Everyone else is the same. The Cuban Crew are sprawled out in silence. Only Alvaro is sitting up. He stares off toward the trailer, running his fingers through his perfect long hair while he watches the other group hammer the new deck together.

A few yards above him, Molloy, Trent, and Jerry are stretched out on the grass with their hands behind their heads. I notice Robbie lazing alongside them with his eyes shut, clearly in need of rest despite not lifting a finger to help. I guess he learned that from his Daddy.

Several blissful minutes pass until the sound of Ms. Tammy's squawky voice has us moving again. Alvaro is first to lurch to his feet, but he's puffed out like he's ready to brawl instead of work. His gaze follows Ms. Tammy as she waddles about, scrutinizing the building crew's work.

"There's that fat whore again!" Alvaro blurts out for all to hear. "The one that said I gotta cut my hair. Yo, if that bitch comes near me, I'm gonna punch her fat fucking face in!"

Everyone falls silent. Just the knock of hammers and the shrill drone of cicadas fill the air. My mouth hangs open. HOLY SHIT! Did he really just say that? I glance at Angelo, and over at Peaches, but their eyes and everyone else's are firmly fixed on Ms. Tammy's son. Judging by the shade of Robbie's face, there's no doubt he just heard the same thing we did.

First of all, no one talks that way about staff, especially Ms. Tammy. I mean, she's Brother Bennett's wife. Why the hell would you poke that nest of rattlesnakes? And to talk that way about her in front of her own son? That's too crazy for words!

And words are something we all seem to have forgotten right now.

Amazingly, Alvaro doesn't seem to sense the shift in mood. How the hell can he miss it? It's as blatant as saying you're going to punch someone's mother in the face! To make matters worse for him, he's also unaware that Robbie is now scampering toward Brother Bennett's trailer. But the rest of us aren't. We watch Robbie stumble through the door as he rushes inside, and for a moment all we do is communicate with looks.

"You screwed up big time, dumbass!" Molloy points his finger at Alvaro. "You're about to seriously regret saying that shit."

Alvaro's response is best summarized as "Fuck you! Fuck her! Fuck all of you!"

For a second, Molloy glares at him. His nostrils flare, but he relaxes and a confident smile spreads across his face. Alvaro is the one who's fucked. Everyone here knows that except for him.

We all glance around and share another knowing look. This one says, *Alvaro Pérez, more of a dumbass than a badass. This should be interesting!*

Unfortunately for Alvaro, he's too busy eyeballing Molloy to notice Brother Bennett storm out of his trailer. He flings open the door with so much force that it rattles against the outside wall, and Alvaro swivels toward the sound. His eyes widen as he clocks Brother Bennett marching his way, crimson-faced with rage.

"YOU CALLED MY WIFE A WHORE!?" he screams, pointing toward Alvaro.

Alvaro's bronze complexion pales as he stands frozen in

place. He might be a big dude, but he seems to shrink as Brother Bennett closes in on him.

"ANSWER ME, BOY! DID YOU CALL MY WIFE A WHORE!?"

Trent and Jerry circle behind Alvaro and lunge forward, gripping him by the arms. Brother Bennett charges in and grabs the collar of Alvaro's t-shirt, jabbing a finger in his face.

"Nobody talks about my wife like that!" he snarls. "A dirty raft monkey like you needs to learn his place in this country."

Brother Bennett looks as though he literally might combust. Veins pulse up his neck and along his forehead, and his chest heaves with fury. A wave of fear washes over me, and I start to worry about Alvaro's safety.

Alvaro appears to be thinking the same. All signs of bravado have vanished. His forehead glistens with sweat, and his lips tremble as he tries to stutter out a response. But Brother Bennett isn't interested in listening. He delivers a pummeling punch to Alvaro's stomach, and the big Cuban doubles over, groaning and gasping for air.

The moment he straightens himself up, Brother Bennett reels back his arm again. He connects a vicious slap across the side of Alvaro's face that echoes off the trailer. Trent and Jerry release their grip, and Alvaro slumps to the dirt. By now, everyone has formed a broken circle around the spectacle. Even the Cuban boys who befriended Alvaro as one of their own just stand there, watching on helplessly.

Reaching down, Brother Bennett grabs a fist-full of Alvaro's long, dark hair and yanks it upward. "Stand your ass up!" he growls, and Alvaro lets out a small yelp as he's forced to comply.

Maintaining his grip on Alvaro's hair, Brother Bennett scowls down at him. "First I hear, you're talking big about keeping this faggot hair of yours, and now you're calling my woman a whore. Sounds to me like you had this coming, boy."

Brother Bennett whips out his hand, landing another heavy slap across Alvaro's cheek. Followed by another slap. And another.

Alvaro groans as he's hauled to his feet again. The left side of his face glistens ruby red. Brother Bennett's showing no mercy, however. He draws back his arm once again and aims another hefty slap at Alvaro's swollen face. It connects with a sickening *thwack*, and then the unthinkable happens. Alvaro throws a punch at Brother Bennett!

HOLY SHIT!

His fist merely scuffs across the side of Brother Bennett's head. A weak blow, but it doesn't matter. It still happened. Alvaro Pérez just punched Brother Bennett!

A collective gasp emanates from the crowd of spectators, and the circle widens as we all back away from a fire that's set to blaze into an inferno. My jaw drops open and hangs there like it's stuck. Even Brother Bennett looks shocked, but his fury returns with newfound vigor.

In one fluid movement, he whips out a backhand, striking Alvaro to the ground. He snatches a handful of Alvaro's hair again and starts dragging him towards the trailer. Alvaro screams for help. He reaches back, trying to pry Brother Bennett's hands loose, but he has no choice but to scramble along with him.

"Is this a yucking?" I ask Angelo, as we follow the commotion from as safe a distance as possible.

Angelo doesn't respond. He stares straight ahead, eyes bulging as Brother Bennett heaves up Alvaro like a sack of potatoes and launches him against the outside of the trailer. He clatters against the metal paneling with a reverberating thud. Brother Bennett hauls him up and repeats the process, not seeming to care about the dents he's making on the outside of his home, nor the well-being of the human who's denting it.

As for the rest of us, all we do is watch. That's all we *can* do. Watch, and wait for it all to end. It doesn't appear to be ending anytime soon, though. Brother Bennett's deranged expression triggers memories of my dad's angry face, flushed from bourbon and bitterness.

The present is far more frightening, however. Brother Bennett stalks Alvaro like prey as the poor kid attempts to crawl underneath the trailer for safety.

"I ain't through with you yet, boy," Brother Bennett snarls as he drags him out by his feet and pins him to the ground with one of his huge leather boots. Alvaro falls limp under its weight, whimpering as the fight finally drains out of him.

"Now, let's see about that haircut," Brother Bennett announces for all to hear.

He wants us to witness this sick shit. Of course, he does. What better way to remind us who's in charge? What better motivator than fear?

"TAMMY!" he calls out to his wife.

She stands several feet behind him, wearing a satisfied smirk on her face that turns my stomach.

"TAMMY, BRING ME THE BIG SCISSORS!" Bennett hollers, and she hurries off into the trailer.

A few moments later, Ms. Tammy returns with a pair of scissors and an even more gleeful expression than before. This one chills me, despite the ungodly heat. How could someone enjoy this?

Brother Bennett looms over Alvaro, wearing a twisted grin of his own. He brandishes the scissors while Trent and Jerry hold Alvaro in place, then grips a section of his precious hair, and hacks it off a few inches from his scalp. Alvaro howls as his beautiful, long locks tumble to the ground.

Less than ten minutes later, his flowing mane of hair is reduced to a crop of uneven tufts. And, as if this whole show wasn't humiliating enough, Alvaro Pérez, the badass muscle man from Miami, starts sobbing like a baby. The beating didn't break him, but the haircut sheared away his last ounce of pride.

I turn to Angelo, whose glazed expression mirrors my own sense of disbelief. "If that…" I point back toward the trailer. "If that was a yucking, you never told me it was anything like that, dude. That…That was…"

"That was way more than a yucking." Angelo's voice sounds somewhat distant as though he's reliving what happened in his head. "That was personal, bro, right from the start. That was out of control. Alvaro's lucky he's alive right now."

I shake my head, trying to steady the tremor in my hands. "This place is like living in a nightmare."

"Yeah, except there ain't no waking up. Not yet, anyway." Angelo places his hand on my shoulder and holds my gaze with grave eyes. "Be glad you're only here for a few months, bro. I've been here so long, I've forgotten what it's like to feel safe. I just wanna get the hell out of this place, you know."

A coldness creeps over me as I realize how much I want to get out of here too. After the savagery I just witnessed, I need a way out of the place as soon as possible. I might only be here for a few months, but it only took Brother Bennett a few seconds to make everyone fear for their own lives too.

"Have you ever thought about running off?" I ask him.

"I thought we'd talked about this." Angelo's eyes twitch with suspicion. "You wouldn't be stupid enough to try, would you?"

"No, but it's not like I haven't thought about it. And if I'd been here as long as you, I'm sure I would've seriously considered it."

"Well, I ain't considering it and neither should you." An edge creeps into Angelo's voice. "Running ain't an option, bro. Just keep your head down and do your time. That's how you get out of here, okay?"

I nod, but even though I know Angelo's right, a deep sense of foreboding lurks inside me. It's impossible to ignore the horror I just witnessed. It flashes before my eyes, sending shockwaves through my mind. No matter what Angelo says, I need a way out of here as soon as possible, and today marks the day I start figuring out how. Today marks The Yucking of Alvaro Pérez.

14

A SIGHT FOR SORE EYES

Sunday, April 22, 1990 - Day 22

Metallica Girl. When time for church rolls around, she seems to occupy my mind more and more. I wouldn't say I obsess over her, but seeing her there helps our three services a week feel far less excruciating. There's just something about her. For one, she's super tall — that's the first thing you notice about her — and I kind of have a thing for tall chicks. Her height and looks are just part of the attraction, though. There are things about her I find even more intriguing.

I can't quite explain them all yet, but her taste in music and the person she presents at church are a complete contradiction. Like the way she wears her hair pinched into a tight bun at the top of her head. The way she dresses, always the same plain gray cardigan and an ankle-length navy skirt. And how she always maintains the same reserved and devout demeanor, eyes lowered, clasping her bible. None of that screams of a metal chick who listens to lyrics like *"Lady Justice has been raped."*

More than anything, though, thinking about Metallica Girl is a welcome escape. Not just from church, but from how badly I need to escape Victory Ridge and haven't figured out how yet. Although, to be honest, I started thinking about Metallica Girl from the moment I woke up. She's the reason I asked Angelo to iron my button-down for me, and the reason I stole a spray of Big Dumb Oaf's Drakkar Noir cologne while he was taking his post-breakfast dump. She's the reason I stood in front of the bathroom mirror so long that Molloy threatened to punch me if I didn't get out of his way.

Unfortunately, I haven't spoken a word to Metallica Girl since the day I picked up her cassette sleeve. We haven't even made eye contact. I was taken off Watch nearly two weeks ago, so I could have hung around at the end of the service like the other boys and tried to catch her before she left. I wanted to, but I punked out each and every time.

All of that changes today, though. I have a plan, but first I need to find myself a wingman. Angelo would be my preference, but he's been super-preachy about keeping my head down, so I doubt he'd approve of my idea. Then there's that dimple-cheeked smile of his, which could also work against me. Peaches, however, looks like he was born in a barn, and not in a Jesus kind of way. He's no stranger to a scheme or two himself, which makes him a far better candidate.

The only problem with my plan is that it's about two minutes old, and I haven't had a chance to talk to him yet. I try to catch his eye as we finish breakfast cleanup, but there are too many eyes and ears. Fortunately, Peaches is now our newest roommate after getting off Watch last week, so I plan to pull him aside while we change for church.

Unfortunately, after we finish up and head toward our room, Ms. Tammy's shrill voice freezes us in our tracks.

"KITCHEN CREW, GET BACK TO THE KITCHEN!" she repeats, shrieking down the hallway.

Angelo glances at Oaf, whose face blanches.

"What's going on?" I ask. "Why is she calling us back?"

Oaf turns on me, his large nostrils flaring. "'Cause one of y'all ain't done your job right! And now we're gonna get licks!"

"Oh yeah? How do you know it was one of us?" I fire back. "Could've been you."

As soon as the words leave my mouth, my mind rewinds to my rushed job of cleaning the counters, trying to buy myself some extra primping time before I charm Metallica Girl at church.

"It ain't ever been me," Oaf sneers. "I never mess up. Tell him, Angelo."

"He's right," Angelo says. "But that's only because he's the world's biggest bitch about getting licks. He cleans out of fear. You would too if you had an ass the size of his."

"Go fuck yourself, Angelo!" Oaf flips up his middle finger and shuffles back along the hallway, toward the kitchen.

Angelo chuckles and blows Big Dumb Oaf a kiss. He turns back to Peaches and me with a grin on his face. "C'mon, let's get this shit over with."

We catch up with Oaf and enter the kitchen to find Ms. Tammy waiting for us, arms across her chest. Brother James stands beside her with his paddle, whistling while he watches us walk in. Ms. Tammy clucks her displeasure as she points out a dime-sized stain on the counter, so tiny that I couldn't even see it until I leaned all the way in.

Swallowing my pride, I turn to mumble my apologies to the others. Judging by the murderous glint in Oaf's beady eyes, I'll be lucky if he doesn't smother me in my sleep tonight. The resentment soon floods from his face, however, as Brother James tells us to line up for licks. Each of us will receive three, and all because of my microscopic mistake.

I volunteer to go first out of guilt. Angelo takes his next, and Peaches steps up after him. Brother James doesn't hit nearly as hard as Brother Bennett, but Oaf is a trembling mess as he bends over for his turn. His entire body quivers as he arches his back and yelps through all three licks.

"Sorry, guys. My bad," I apologize once more, as soon as Brother James leaves the kitchen. "It won't happen again."

Oaf shoves past Peaches and grabs the collar of my t-shirt, his eyes damp with tears and wild with rage. "You're damn right it won't happen again, you little punk! I'm gonna make sure of that!"

"Get the hell off me!" I yell, shoving him in his flabby chest as forcefully as I can.

Oaf staggers backward a couple of steps, releasing his grip. He straightens up and starts toward me again, pausing to sniff the air.

"Did you use my cologne?" He wrinkles his nose and scowls at me. "You little shit! You did, didn't you? I really can't wait to give you an ass beating!"

"Oh yeah?" I say, stepping toward him. "Well, I really can't wait to see you try."

An ugly grin stretches across Oaf's face. He leans forward,

pressing his forehead down against mine. I brace myself, standing my ground. He could overpower me with his breath alone, never mind the fact he's a foot taller and a hundred pounds heavier. The best way to bring him down would be to headbutt him on the bridge of his nose, just like Jean-Claude Van Damme in *Bloodsport*. That would mean making the first move, though, and something tells me Oaf would have done that by now if he was going to at all.

Angelo's arm appears in front of my chest, and I take a step back as he slides between Oaf and me. "You guys need to chill," he tells us. "We've gotta go to church soon. If you get banged up from fighting, someone's gonna notice. You know what that means. How many more licks do you wanna take today?"

Oaf sighs and backs off a few steps, glaring at me over Angelo's shoulder. "Good thing you've got your mommy here to protect you, Chuck. Look at you standing behind her like a little bitchass momma's boy."

My skin sears. Accidentally or not, Oaf just landed a bullseye. He can see it painted across my momma's boy face.

"What's the matter, Chuck?" He smiles smugly, reveling in his chance to twist the knife in deeper. "Do you miss your real mommy? Is that what's wrong?"

Big Dumb Oaf cackles with laughter, and I curl my fingers into fists.

"That's enough, Oaf!" Angelo snaps. "It's time to cut this shit out and let it go!"

But Oaf's focus is solely on me. "I think I must be right," he says, with a callous smirk. "You're just a little bitchass momma's boy who misses his mommy. I bet she doesn't miss you, though. I bet she's glad you're gone."

A red mist falls over me. I barge past Angelo, drawing back my arm and swinging a punch toward Oaf's sneering mouth... but it never connects. Oaf's meaty fist reaches me first, socking me right in the eye and knocking me to the floor.

Angelo and Peaches haul me to my feet. My left eye throbs with pain, and my legs wobble for a second as I find my balance. Peaches walks me into the dining hall and sits me on a bench. Angelo returns a moment later and presses something cold against my eye, which is swelling so much I can barely open it.

Brother James shows up a few minutes later. After one glance at my face, he orders Oaf to line up for another three licks. The joy of watching his misery is short-lived, however, when Brother James calls me up for the same as soon as he's done.

So, with a swollen eye and a sore ass, I board The Booger for church. But my plan is ruined. My eye is bulged-shut and purple with bruises. I look like one of the zombies from *Day of the Dead*! There's no way I can talk to Metallica Girl looking like this.

———

FROM THE MOMENT I step into church, I'm drawing glances everywhere I look. Sweat beads on my forehead. This is even worse than I imagined. I can't help thinking about what Metallica Girl told Molloy about not being interested in guys like him. If she sees the state of my face, she'll assume I'm just another thug like he is. So I guess I'll have to make sure she doesn't see me at all.

I convince Angelo to sit with me near the back of the sanctuary, more than a dozen rows behind Metallica Girl's regular spot.

I can see her tall frame sitting down near the front, her dark hair in a tight bun as usual. Taking a deep breath, I try to relax now that I'm safely out-of-sight. The moment service ends, I should be able to slip out unnoticed and hide in the restroom until she clears out.

I spend the next hour gnawing my fingernails, trying to ignore the droning old preacher. I can't ignore the throbbing pain around my black eye, though. I can't stop peering down at Metallica Girl with my good eye either. And as the service rolls to an end, I kick myself into action.

"I need to use the restroom," I whisper to Angelo, and slide out of the pew as the congregation starts to rise.

Hurrying up the aisle, I dart across the lobby straight to the men's restroom. Of the two stalls inside, one is labeled "OUT OF ORDER" but the other is unoccupied. My first stroke of luck for the day. At least I don't have to stand around like a weirdo while I'm hiding out. I step inside and latch the door shut.

Less than a minute later, the restroom door creaks open and someone else steps inside. A pair of brown shoes appear beneath the stall door in front of me. The latch rattles as the person attempts to open it, and they groan with frustration.

"You almost finished up in there, buddy?" a voice that's all-too-familiar asks. "I gotta bus to drive, and I need to shift this turd before it shifts itself."

Great! Brother James is standing outside the stall, quite literally waiting to shit. I take a deep breath and flush my phantom poop down the toilet. When I open the stall door, Brother James's eyes widen with recognition.

"Ol' boy Chuck!" he says, grimacing as he clocks the state of my eye. "Well, move outta the way, son. I gotta take care of business."

I shift aside, and he hurries past me into the stall, tugging the door shut and fumbling with the latch. His belt jingles, and an explosive squelch is followed by a loud groan of relief. I rush over to the sink and turn the faucet to full blast in hope of drowning out the noise. It does nothing for the nauseating stench, however. The instant it hits me, I nearly retch on the floor.

Eyes watering, I hold my breath and bolt for the door. I yank it open and flee for safety, darting out into the lobby and bowling straight into somebody.

"Oh my gosh! I'm so sorry!" I say, gathering myself together. "Are you okay?"

I look up and my face burns with embarrassment as I realize who I collided with. Metallica Girl stares back at me, her blue eyes widening as they focus on my freakshow of a face.

"I'm fine. Don't worry about it," she says, still staring at my swollen eye.

I turn my head to hide it, even though I know it's pointless. Of all the people I could've rammed into, it just had to be her, didn't it?

"Well, I'm sorry I almost knocked you over. That was totally my fault."

To my surprise, Metallica Girl smiles at me. "It totally was," she says. "But I can see why you might have trouble seeing right now, so I guess I'll let you off. See ya!"

And with that, she turns and walks off toward the exit. I stare after her, my pulse racing, wishing I had told her she's a sight for sore eyes.

15

SAINT ANGELO

Sunday, April 29, 1990 - Day 29

It was Wednesday evening when I next saw Metallica Girl. She didn't appear to notice *me*, though, not until after the service. I waved to her in the lobby, and she smiled at me as she walked by with her mother.

I've spent a lot of time thinking since then. And I've put those thoughts into words and those words onto paper. Because I've come to the conclusion that Metallica Girl could be my ticket out of Nowhere. I stare down at the letter I've written her and reread it once again.

Dear Fellow Metalhead,

My name is Will Douglas. I'm the guy who picked up your cassette sleeve when you dropped it in church that day. I'm a huge Metallica fan too, so allow me to compliment you on having such awesome taste! My favorite song on that album is One. I used to listen to it over and over again.

Also, you might remember me as the guy who almost knocked you over last week. Super sorry about that! I'm normally not that clumsy. Honest! I'm sure you noticed my face that day, so it probably won't surprise you that I'm in kind of a rough situation. More than rough actually. I've been sent to a place that's more abusive than I can explain in one letter.

That's why I'm writing to you. I need urgent help, and I'm really hoping you can help me. I need you to call my dad, Frank Douglas, and tell him that the place he's sent me isn't safe. Tell him you saw my face with your own eyes. I'll agree to go anywhere else he chooses, but he needs to get me out of here before anything worse happens to me.

His number is 404-355-4461. If you can, please call on a week-night between 6-7 Mississippi time. That's the best time to reach him. If a woman named Joyce answers, please call back. Please only pass on my message directly to my dad.

I really hope you can help me, and please know that I wouldn't ask this of you if I wasn't totally desperate.

Yours Truly,
Will Douglas

———

"ARE you really stupid enough to go through with this?" Angelo asks, as Brother James steers The Booger into the church parking lot.

"Yep," I say, even though the churning in my stomach is nagging me to reconsider. "Are you really not going to help me?"

Angelo rolls his eyes. "Run me through this plan of yours one more time."

"Why?" I say, rolling my eyes back at him. "You've told me how dumb it is a hundred times already. You just wanna pick holes in it."

"Because it's full of holes, Will!" Angelo makes an "o" shape with his hands to emphasize the point. He shakes his head. "Listen, man, if you're determined to go through with this, fine, I'll help you. I'll be your blocker or something."

A grin stretches across my face. "Seriously?"

Angelo sighs. "Yeah, seriously. Better than you trying this shit by yourself and getting caught."

My heart wells with gratitude, and I have to stop myself from hugging him. "Thanks, man! You're the best!"

He waves me off. "No sweat. Just don't make me regret this. And you'll be paying me back with packages if you get out of here, so know that. Now tell me this plan again."

I delay my explanation until Brother James has parked the bus and we're all filing toward the church.

"We need to find seats near her area," I whisper to Angelo. "Close enough that I can fall in behind her when she's walking out."

"Why do you need to be behind her?" Angelo whispers back.

"Because I'm gonna bend down like..."

"Like you're looking up her skirt?" Angelo cracks up laughing. "This plan is genius, bro!"

"Dude, you said you were gonna help!"

"Sorry, bro, I couldn't resist," Angelo says, trying to pull himself together. "For real, though, why you gotta bend down behind her like a weirdo?"

I bite my bottom lip and glare at him. "I'm bending down so

it looks like I'm picking something up. Then I'll tap her on the shoulder and give her the note like she dropped it."

Angelo bursts out laughing again.

I shake my head in exasperation. "You know what, forget it! I don't want your help anymore. I'll do this by myself."

"Relax, bro. I'm just giving you a hard time." Angelo places his hand on my shoulder. "I get what you're trying to do, but won't she be confused when you try to hand her something that isn't hers? What if she doesn't take it?"

"She'll take it from me," I say. "I *know* she will. Because that's..."

"Because that's what happened before," Angelo interjects. "I know, bro. You told me already, and it still makes no freaking sense to me. But I'm gonna help you, anyway."

"Thanks," I say, grimacing as my stomach spasms.

"You good?" Angelo asks.

"Just a little nervous, I guess. I'll be fine."

He shoots me a look of concern. "Try to relax. You're sweating like crazy, bro."

I nod and wipe off my brow, drawing a deep breath as we enter the church. My heart rate vaults into warp speed the moment I see Metallica Girl, though. I scan the rows behind her for a good space to sit, but the closest pews are already packed with people. The best spot I can find is further back than I would've liked, but Angelo and I snag seats next to the aisle, which should make things a little easier when the time comes.

I try to focus my mind on the next steps of my plan, but my guts keep cramping over and over again. Grimacing through it, I distract myself by gnawing on my fingernails until Angelo elbows me on the arm. I switch to twirling my hair, which he also tells me to stop. Then I keep opening and closing my Bible to check that the letter is still safely inside.

"Yo!" Angelo whispers in my ear. "I know you're tense, bro, but you're driving me nuts with that shit. Cut it out!"

I set my Bible aside and wring my hands to stop myself from touching it. All I can do is watch and wait, glancing back and forth between the preacher and Metallica Girl. But waiting feels impossible. I can't stop tapping my feet, and the sharp twinges in my stomach intensify with every passing moment. When the service finally ends and everyone starts rising to their feet, I reach for my Bible and the world begins to spin and blur.

"You good, bro?" Angelo sounds like I'm submerged in water. "Yo, Will, you okay?" I feel him place a hand on my shoulder, but I shrug him off and charge out of the pew, knocking a stack of pamphlets to the floor along the way.

My feet carry me on instinct, out of the sanctuary and across the lobby. Clutching my stomach, I barge open the restroom door. A spike of nauseating pain doubles me over as I stagger into the stall. I swing the door shut behind me and fumble at the latch, but there's no time to lock it. My insides convulse so violently that I drop to my knees. Scrambling over to the toilet, I heave up my breakfast of powdered milk and cornflakes, and my hopes of escaping Nowhere are spewed out along with it.

I rinse out my mouth at the sink, dowsing my face with water and cursing myself for getting so worked up again. I blew the chance to give Metallica Girl my letter, but that's not my main concern anymore. I'm more worried about where that letter is now. I left my Bible in the pew when I took off running, and I'm hoping Angelo picked it up before someone else did.

As though fate were listening, the restroom door creaks open and Angelo steps inside. He sets my Bible on the counter next to the sink, and I breathe a long sigh of relief.

"Brother James sent me to check on you," he says, looking me over. "You okay, man?"

I glance at my reflection in the mirror. My blond hair is matted with sweat. My eyes are bloodshot and puffy, one with a ring of blue and purple bruises. I shake my head. "No, I'm not okay. You were right. This was a dumb idea."

"Yeah, you ain't wrong about that." Angelo's eyes twinkle as his mouth tweaks into a grin. "Then again, sometimes a dumb idea actually works."

"Well, not this dumb idea," I mutter. "If it worked, she'd have the letter right now."

"What letter?" A smile stretches across Angelo's face until his cheeks dimple.

I stare at him as my brain struggles to grasp what's happening. My eyes dart down toward my Bible and up at Angelo again. He raises his brows, and my heart jolts with hope. I snatch up the Bible and flip through the pages to the place I hid the note. It isn't there.

I gaze over at him, my mouth twitching into a smile. "You gave it to her?"

Angelo holds a finger to his lips. "Let's go," he says. "I can tell you on the ride back. After that, we ain't talking about this again."

I stride forward and wrap him in a hug. "You're a freaking saint, Angelo!"

16

SPLAT!

Wednesday, May 2, 1990 - 32 days

According to Angelo, my antics at the end of church caused more of a scene than I realized. When Brother James saw me take off like that, he thought I was actually running for it. He sent Trent and Jerry chasing after me, jostling past the people walking toward the exit, which caused even more commotion than I did.

Angelo said he had to head them off and explain what was happening. As Trent and Jerry worked their way back down the aisle to tell Brother James, he noticed Metallica Girl walking right past him. He opened my Bible, found the letter, and caught up to her as quickly as he could.

Once he was walking alongside her, Angelo cleared his throat until he drew her attention. She had stared at him curiously, and then her eyes glimpsed the note he discreetly held out toward her.

"What the hell did you say?" I had asked him as we rode The Booger back to Victory Ridge.

"I told her it was from a guy who helped her out once," Angelo explained.

"For real? What did she say to that?"

"She didn't say shit, bro. She just looked at me for a second. Then she took the note from my hand and kept on walking. That was it."

That was three days ago. Three paranoia-inducing days. I don't think I was wrong to trust Metallica Girl, though. Even if she doesn't call my dad, I can't see her calling Brother Bennett to rat me out. Why would she? It's far more likely she would just ignore my request altogether and move on with her life.

However, if she does decide to call him, if she somehow manages to get a hold of him, what will he do? How will Dad react to what she has to tell him? To what I have to tell him. Would he believe me? Would he even care? If he truly gave a shit about my safety and well-being, he wouldn't have sent me to a hellhole like this in the first place, would he?

What's really starting to worry me, though, is what happens if Metallica Girl does manage to convince my dad of the truth. It would take a minor miracle, sure, but I hadn't fully considered this part of the plan. I was too focused on finding the best way to sneak her my note. But when I first came up with the idea, I imagined my dad recognizing that he'd made a huge mistake and flying straight out here to get me.

In reality, however, it wouldn't work like that at all because I now realize my biggest mistake. It doesn't matter whether Dad believes what Metallica Girl tells him or not. If she makes that phone call and delivers him my message, the first thing he's going to do is call up Brother Bennett and demand an explanation. And as soon as my dad explains why he's calling, Brother Bennett is going to learn about everything I've been up to. How will he react after he hears about my letter? What happens to me then?

I shudder as my mind leads me down a rabbit hole of possibilities. I've been here long enough to realize I've broken one of the biggest rules: don't draw attention to Brother Bennett and the things that go on at Victory Ridge. What happens in Nowhere, stays in Nowhere. If news were to spread about all the licks and yuckings he and Brother James dish out, I can't imagine it would be good for business.

BY THE TIME we finish breakfast clean up duty, I've developed a splitting headache from thinking about it all. One thing has become clear, though. It's probably best if Metallica Girl decides not to call my dad. That sounds like the safest outcome at this point. It would feel bitter sweet, but I would definitely take it. The one thing I can't take, however, is all the waiting, wondering, and worrying that seems to consume my every moment.

The only thing worse than that is being unable to tune out Peaches while he prattles on about all the "news" he's heard. Angelo and I are basically a captive audience at this point. Peaches follows along as we pass through the dining room and step outside into radiant sunlight.

He'd overheard Molloy tell Jerry he has a copy of Hustler stashed in the woods, he informs us as we traipse across the lawn toward the schoolhouse. Molloy had "confiscated" it from one of

Alvaro's packages, apparently, not that I'm remotely interested in anything outside of my own shit right now.

When we enter the schoolhouse and Peaches finally shuts up, I release a long sigh of relief and gather up my workbooks. I slump down at my desk and sink back into my own issues. What would I do if I were in Metallica Girl's situation? Think about it. Would I make the call, or wouldn't I?

I probably would, I decide, but likely just the once. If no one answered, I doubt I'd call back, but if someone did pick up, I would do my best to deliver the message. That's what feels most logical to me, anyway. At this point, I can't imagine Metallica Girl feeling any differently.

Opening up my math packet, I flip to my next assignment. *Surface Area and Volume*, how wonderful! I find the matching section in my answer booklet and start filling it out, but too many thoughts tug at my attention. My head throbbing, I set my pencil down and massage my temples.

It might take Metallica Girl a day or two to make up her mind, which would be completely understandable given the circumstances. After that, though, there's no telling how soon she would try to call my dad. Hell, there's a chance she could have called him already. Brother Bennett could be on the phone with him right now, getting ready to grab his paddle and march my way. Chills spike through me at the thought.

Twisting around in my chair, I check the clock on the wall behind me. It's only 9:22. How is it possible for time to drag this slowly? I glance around the room in search of a distraction. All the other guys are either working away or have their heads on their desks. With one exception: our newest inmate, Brian, a skinny, fair-haired kid from Maryland, who arrived in Nowhere just yesterday afternoon.

Brian is standing beside his desk holding his work packet, looking utterly bewildered. He peers over at Brother James, who's buried behind his sports section as usual. I watch on as Brian shuffles nervously over to the desk and clears his throat. Brother James crumples his newspaper shut and glares at him. Brian mumbles something, and Brother James's face twitches with irritation.

"This ain't no rocket science, boy!" he barks at the poor kid. "You finish it, you check it, then you turn it in. It's that dang simple."

"I...I check it myself?" Brian's voice reaches a higher pitch.

"Ain't that exactly what I just said?" Brother James's eyes narrow as he catches sight of me peeking around the divider. "It's good you find this so interesting, Chuck. C'mon on over here and show this dumbass new boy how we get things done."

He leans across his desk toward Brian. "I ain't here to hold your hand, son. We like our boys to figure things out for themselves. It's good for them. So don't go wasting my time with stupid questions from now on."

Brother James waves him away. He takes a sip of coffee and reopens the sports section of *USA Today*, while I lead Brian off to show him the ropes.

Whenever a new kid arrives at Victory Ridge, there's a ritual interrogation that takes place within The Dorm. Everyone is eager to learn about your past transgressions. In other words, what the hell did you do to earn your exile in Nowhere? Learning someone's story helps separate the psychos from the suckers and everything in between. All of which is invaluable information in a place full of pissed-off delinquents.

When I first heard Brian's story, I pegged him as a sucker. All he did was get caught selling pot at junior prom. However, when he was asked what sports he played—the second most-commonly-asked-question—his answer captured everyone's attention, especially Molloy's.

"Hold on a second," he'd said, butting in on the conversation. "You're a *what* kind of a diver?"

"A high diver," Brian patiently repeated, but Molloy just stared at him with a puzzled frown.

"So, let me get this straight. You don't play football or base-ball or basketball or any other team sports, you just dive into a pool over and over again? That's what little kids do every summer. How does that even count as a sport?"

Brian's pale cheeks had reddened. "Seeing how it's in the Olympics and I was state champ in Maryland last year, yeah, I'm pretty sure it counts as a sport."

Molloy's face twisted into its usual sneer. "You know what," he said, with a gleam in his eyes. "I forgot we're going to Leaf River tomorrow. Brother James promised to take us. There's a bridge right there that's perfect for diving. We dive off of there all the time, so it should be a piece of cake for a state champ high diver, like you. Guess you better show us what you've got, new boy."

This was bullshit, of course. Not about the bridge, but the part about us diving off of it. A few of the boys jump now and again, but most of us, myself included, climb up and take one glance down before chickening out. No one dives, though. Never.

I consider explaining this to Brian as I show him how to copy the answers from one work booklet to the other, but I hold my tongue. Telling him wouldn't be worth the backlash I'd receive for ruining everyone else's fun, too. He agreed to Molloy's challenge without the slightest hesitation, and I'm as eager to see what happens as anyone. Besides, the guy is a state champion high diver for God's sake. I'm pretty sure he knows what he's doing.

As soon as school finishes and we're walking back across the lawn to the dining hall, the heckling begins. Molloy and the others amp up their efforts throughout lunch, challenging Brian to see how many flips he can do before he hits the water. Meanwhile, Peaches scurries back and forth between the tables taking bets. A bag of Doritos wagered here, a can of Fanta gambled there.

By the time we board The Booger for a trip to Leaf River, the atmosphere is at a fever pitch. Peaches roams the aisle with his bookie list while the entire bus belts out the chorus to *Take Me to the River* by Talking Heads. And as Brother Bennett cranks up the engine and starts us on our way, we all let out an almighty cheer.

Ten minutes later, he steers us off the road and parks on a dirt track, a short distance from the river. We spill out of the bus into the fiery afternoon heat and head straight for the water, which beckons like a shimmering oasis. Well, one that's murky brown and looks like mud soup, that is. Not that any of us care. It could be purple and yellow, and we'd still get in. We stampede down the embankment, boys stripping off their shirts before they plunge into the river.

Peaches catches up with me and digs me on the arm. "Race

ya!" he says. "Betcha a city licker like you can't beat country-boy quick."

"It's city *slicker*, moron." I tell him, as I lengthen my stride. "Let's go!"

I launch into a full-throttle sprint toward the river, barreling down the last stretch of the embankment. Peaches overtakes me a few yards from the water.

"Hey!" he cries out, as I grab his arm and haul him back. "Quit cheatin'!"

"That's a city licker move right there, country boy!" I run past him in a fit of laughter and dive face first into the cool river. I almost choke on a mouthful of muddy water, but the look on Peaches' face when I resurface is totally worth it.

After a short spell of splashing and horsing around, everyone's attention drifts back to Brian.

"There's your bridge, new boy." Molloy points down the river as he wades into deeper water. Brian stands waist-deep several yards away from him. Tilting his head, he stares appraisingly at the bridge.

"Whatcha think, Mr. State Champ?" Molloy grins as watches Brian for a reaction. "Should be easy for you, right? A piece of cake."

Brian's shrug is as nonchalant as his expression. "I guess," he says. "As long as it's deep enough."

"Oh, it's deep enough," Molloy assures him. "You won't even get close to hitting the bottom. Check it out for yourself if you don't believe me."

Brian eyes Molloy like he's searching for signs of bullshit. After a few seconds, he nods his head and splashes off toward the bridge. When he reaches the shadowy water underneath, he plunges underwater to check the depth and resurfaces a few moments later. He looks back our way, shoots Molloy a thumbs up, and starts swimming for the side of the river.

"NEW BOY'S GOING FOR IT!" Molloy hollers. "NEW BOY'S GONNA DIVE!"

Whoops and cheers ring out around the river, and we all swim forward for a closer view. The cheering turns to jeering, as Brian reaches the shore and starts up the steep embankment toward the top of the bridge. This is actually going to happen!

"He'll chicken out once he's up there," Angelo says, as he treads water next to me. "No way he's dumb enough to go through with it."

The same thought is going through my head. From down here, the bridge doesn't look that intimidating. From up there, though, staring down at the water thirty feet below, it's a whole different story. He might jump, but I doubt he's brave enough to dive. State champ or not.

However, whether from genuine confidence or sheer stupidity, Brian reaches the main road and walks along the edge of the bridge until he reaches the centerpoint of the river. He eases himself up onto the barrier rail and stands upright on the ledge.

"Dive, dive, dive, dive…"

The chant picks up until everyone joins in.

"DIVE, DIVE, DIVE, DIVE…"

We all start slapping our hands against the surface of the water, splashing out a beat. Meanwhile, high above us, Brian adjusts his feet on the ledge, straightening his poise like he's going through some sort of routine.

"DIVE, DIVE, DIVE, DIVE…"

"WHATCHA WAITING FOR, CHICKEN SHIT?" Molloy

screams at him. "THIS AIN'T THE STATE CHAMPIONSHIP. JUST FUCKING DIVE!"

Brian stares down at him for a few moments as though he might be having second thoughts. Then he turns around toward the road again.

"Told you he'd chicken out," Angelo says. "He's gonna climb back down."

But Brian doesn't climb down. He stays right where he is, standing straight and rigid on top of the barrier rail with his back toward the water. He shifts his feet a few times and rolls out his neck. Then in one smooth, flowing motion, he bends his knees and swings his arms upwards, leaping backward off of the bridge.

The taunting gives way to a collective gasp as we watch him twirl and flip through the air with the grace of an olympian, twisting and contorting toward the murky brown water of Leaf River. And then, Brian, the state champ high diver from Maryland, finishes with the most brutal belly flop I have ever witnessed. His body slaps against the surface of the river like a backhand from Brother Bennett.

I shudder as the sound echoes off the underside of the bridge, but an eruption of howling laughter drowns out the noise. Normally I would find this just as hilarious, but something isn't right. Brian floats face-first in the water with no signs of movement.

The laughter tapers off as the others notice, and several of the boys kick themselves into action. Alvaro, the muscle-clad Cuban reaches him first, screaming at Brian as he yanks his limp body upright. Shane and Molloy join him and the three of them start dragging Brian toward the bank. I consider swimming out to help them, but shock freezes me in place.

I glance over at Angelo, whose eyes are transfixed on the scene before him. "This looks bad, man." My voice shakes through every syllable. "This looks really bad. He might be... Do you think he's..."

"Dead?" Angelo meets my gaze, his eyes wide with fright. "I don't know, bro. That fall he took ain't no joke. Look at it this way, though. If he is dead, then that's our ticket out of here." He registers the shock in my face and shrugs. "I know that's messed up, man, but it's the truth."

I open my mouth to respond, but I've no idea what to say. Angelo has spent over three years of his life in this hellhole. Knowing that, it's hard to judge him too harshly. Besides, what sums up desperation more than thoughts like that?

Fortunately for Brian, he isn't dead and is fully conscious again by the time we join the crowd gathered around him on the riverbank. Unfortunately for Brian, however, his entire torso is crimson raw from the impact, to the point it's almost too painful to look at. He slumps back against the sand, groaning and moaning. His face looks sickly pale, and he's clearly too disoriented to care about the barrage insults being fired his way.

As an added insult to Brian's injuries, a discussion breaks out around him while he lies there suffering. A new nickname is in order, and the decision is swift and unanimous. The state champ high diver once known as Brian will now officially be referred to as Splat.

As Splat regains his wits, he insists on returning to Victory Ridge until he's a begging and blubbering mess. Under normal circumstances, in a more civilized place and amongst more compassionate people, that would have been exactly what happened. Rush the kid back and have him checked out as soon as possible.

That's not how it works in Nowhere. Not with this crowd for company. We leave Splat to roast on the river bank for the next couple of hours while we splash around in the cool water and have a good old time.

Most people wouldn't understand how we could do that. Most people would be appalled by that mentality, and I get why. But when you're stuck in a world of constant stress and worry with nothing to comfort or console you, an hour or two in the river feels like a week at the beach.

So, as much as it's hard not to feel sorry for the guy, it's hard to feel too much sympathy for him either, especially after a dumbass stunt like that one. It was our minuscule moment of freedom, and there was no way we were letting Splat ruin it. As for me, I've spent the past few days in a state of constant panic. This was my only escape before heading back to reality, and I made damn sure to enjoy it.

17

THE BOY WHO LIKES TO WRITE

Friday, May 4, 1990 - 35 days

Our adventures at Leaf River may have been short lived, but we sure as hell made the most of our time there. With the exception of Splat, of course, everyone had a blast. It's a good thing we did, too, because a big ass storm rolled through yesterday morning and it's poured nonstop ever since. We've spent so many hours inside the dorm the air is thick with the muggy stench of our own filth. So much so, that it's a relief to step outside into the streaking rain after breakfast.

A mantle of dense, dark clouds hangs overhead as Angelo, Peaches, and I bolt across the lawn toward the schoolhouse, the morning sky as dusky as evening. Thunder rumbles and a few flashes of lightning follow. I push myself into full sprint as the downpour intensifies, but it's like I'm running through a waterfall.

By the time we enter the schoolhouse, we're drenched from

head to toe, and our shoes squeak and squelch as we drip puddles of water across the wooden floor. I gather up my workbooks with wet hands, dump them on my desk, and head to the tiny bathroom at the back of the schoolhouse to dry off.

As I wipe myself down with a wad of paper towels, the thunder rumbles closer until it booms so loudly it sounds like a bomb detonated directly above us. The whole schoolhouse shudders. I quickly finish up and toss the soggy paper towels in the trash. As I reach for the door handle, the heavens unleash another deafening crack, so forceful I can hear the pipes rattle inside the bathroom wall.

The light flickers out, and I stand inside the cramped bathroom in complete darkness. I fumble at the door until I grasp the handle, pulling it open as another thunderclap reverberates through the building. As I step out of the bathroom, a blaze of lightning illuminates the entire schoolhouse for the span of a second, before descending into pitch black again.

My chest tightens. Panic grips me in place. I could only glimpse the scene before me for an instant, but it was long enough to glimpse the towering silhouette of Brother Bennett lurking like a monstrous shadow in the center of the room.

I would like to have imagined it — he's been gone since Tuesday, which has been the one saving grace for me — but three more flashes of lightning confirm my fears. There he is, only ten yards from where I'm standing, dressed in a long, black trench coat that's slick from the rain, water puddling around his brown leather boots.

The lights flicker on again as the power returns. Except for the drumming rain, the schoolhouse is deathly silent. Everyone's eyes are fixed on Brother Bennett. *Please don't be here for me!*

Please don't be here for me! But I know he is. I feel it like a stab wound in my gut as Brother Bennett turns to look my way.

His eyes narrow the moment they lock onto me. "William Douglas," he growls, in a deep, icy drawl. "The boy who likes to write."

My pulse hurtles into a frantic gallop. *He knows what I've done! He knows about the letter!* Memories of Alvaro's yucking flash before my eyes, and a sickening chill sweeps across my skin. I glance around the room until my eyes find Angelo, who watches on with wrinkles of concern across his forehead. I am so dead!

"C'mon over here, William." Brother Bennett beckons me toward him with a wave of his hand. "You've got some answering to do."

Sweat beads on my forehead, and I wipe it off with a trembling hand. My mind screams at me to turn around and lock myself in the bathroom, but my feet are already moving forward. It would only delay the inevitable, anyway, and Brother Bennett looks furious enough as it is. With his arms folded and his jaw clenched, he frowns at me ominously as I shuffle across the schoolhouse and stop a yard or so in front of him.

"I hear you've been writing letters, son. Anything you wanna say about that?"

I consider my response, but my mouth feels too parched to speak. What could I say, anyway? It's obvious that he already knows. He must have spoken to my dad. I hang my head in resignation and stare at the floor.

"How many did you write?" he asks.

"Just one, sir," I croak.

Brother Bennett's eyes study my expression. "You sure about that? This ain't a good time to lie to me, William."

"Yes, sir," I say quickly. "There was only one letter, I swear."

Brother Bennett strokes his chin like he's weighing things up in his head. "And what about the young woman you gave it to? What's her name?"

"I've no idea, sir. I didn't give it to anyone!" I launch into the bullshit story I prepared, one that now seems hopelessly lame. "I was just using it as a bookmark in my Bible. It must've fallen out in church or something. I don't know!"

Brother Bennett's face burns red with fury. He strides forward and grabs hold of my collar, twisting it into a tight grip until I'm unable to move. Flashbacks of Alvaro flicker in my mind: Brother Bennett dragging him by the hair while he howled out for help. Trembling from fear, I try not to piss myself.

"I've heard enough of your lying, boy!" Brother Bennett bares his teeth in a snarl. "It ain't no accident that a girl from our congregation called your daddy, is it now?"

I swallow back my response and answer with a feeble shake of my head.

"Well, let this be a lesson, son." Brother Bennett leans down his head, looking me dead in the eyes. "I find out everything that goes on in my school. Everything. So you can forget about tricking your daddy into coming to save you. Round here, I'm the only help you're gonna get."

He seizes my shoulder with his free hand and digs his fist into my sternum while holding me in place. "I'm gonna help you whether you like it or not, William. I'm gonna teach you how to do what you're told." I wince as he presses harder against my chest like he's trying to break through my ribcage. "Sit down!"

Brother Bennett shoves me backward with his fist, and I slam against the schoolhouse floor. "Get up!" He reaches down and yanks me to my feet. "Sit down!" he growls, and the room tips over as he thrusts me back to the floor.

I'm hauled up again, just like before, and the process repeats until my t-shirt is ripped around the collar, and I'm doubled-over from exhaustion.

"Stand up straight, William," Brother Bennett tells me.

I force myself upright, and he rattles my head with a stinging slap across the cheek.

"You need to listen real good to what I tell you next, son." His hand darts out and lashes my cheek again. "Are you listening?"

My eyes blurry with tears, I sniff and nod my head. "Yes, sir."

"Good," Brother Bennett says, eyeing me coldly. "This little mess you've made needs fixing, and seeing how you like writing letters so much, that's exactly what you're gonna do. You'll write to your daddy and tell him what a filthy little liar you are. Tell him he was right to send you here and that you're getting the help you need. Make it sound good, and we can put this little 'accident' of yours behind us."

Brother Bennett draws back his arm and delivers another slap to my face. "My apologies, William. I guess that was just an 'accident' too." He whips out his hand again, and pain sears across my cheek. "Accidents sure seem to like you, son. I'd get that letter written real quick if I was you."

He pulls a handkerchief out of the back pocket of his jeans and wipes the sweat from his forehead. "Have your letter on my desk before the beginning of lunch. Use the rest of your school time to finish it and make up your lessons tomorrow. Now, get up and face the wall."

After suffering through six of the most painful licks I've ever taken, Brother Bennett sends me off to my desk feeling too sore to sit. I squat with my back against the wall and cry. I don't care who sees or what they might say. I let everything spill out.

Gathering myself together, I collect a pencil and some note paper and return to my desk. I lower my tender ass onto the chair and begin drafting a letter to my dad. It won't take much to convince him I'm a liar, though. Telling him will just validate what he already believes. All the same, writing lies about lying feels like a stiff kick in the nuts after being yucked around the schoolhouse. I grind my teeth as I scrawl out the last line, informing my father that he was right to send me to Victory Ridge, and I'm getting the help I need here.

A half-hour later, I've written out a neat final draft, but I wait until we're dismissed before heading over to Brother Bennett's office. To my relief, he's in the middle of a phone call when I get there and snatches the letter from my hand without uttering a word in my direction. I scurry off to my room, grateful for the tiny shard of luck on such a seriously shitty day.

When I enter, Angelo and Peaches are quick to offer their sympathies. Oaf, however, greets me with a smug, satisfied expression. "That was better than going to the movies," he informs me. "I'd pay some good money to watch that shit again. You've had that coming, Chuck."

His taunts bounce off my brain and disappear into the all-consuming numbness. I collapse onto my bunk and stare up at the ceiling.

"Hey," Angelo says, "I ain't gonna ask if you're okay, bro. I already know the answer. But I'm gonna give you some advice while you remember how this feels."

"Go ahead," I grunt, too beaten to object. "Lecture away."

"The next time I tell you not to do something, you really need to listen, man."

I groan and close my eyes to the world. They snap open again as someone bangs their fist on the doorframe. "Pack your shit, Chuck!"

Shane enters the room and heads straight to my bunk. I stare at him blankly, too dazed to process what's happening.

"Did you hear what I said?" he growls.

"Go easy, bro," Angelo interjects. "Dude just got yucked."

Shane snaps his head around and glares at him. Angelo shrinks back a little, and Shane returns his attention to me. He lifts one of his huge Doc Martens boots onto my mattress, its steel-toe cap inches from my face.

"Here's the deal," he says. "You're back on Watch with me and Molloy until we're told otherwise. If I've gotta tell you to pack your shit again, I'm gonna drag you out of this room and boot you down the hallway. Got it?"

"Got it," I tell him, grimacing as I sit up on my mattress.

Shane watches me as I lower my feet to the floor and start gathering up my things and stuffing them in my suitcase. "You've got two minutes," he informs me. Then he spins around and strides out of the room.

"I'm takin' Will's bunk!" Peaches announces, after Shane disappears into the hallway.

"What!?" I pause my packing and stare at him. "No way! Why the hell do you need my bunk?"

"This mattress sucks ass, dude," Peaches explains as he slides down from his bed. "I'm takin' yours before someone else does."

He skips over to what used to be my bed and hops on,

lounging back with his hands behind his head. A smile spreads to his cheeks, and he lets out a satisfied sigh. "You see," he says. "This is way better!"

"You suck, Peach!" I mutter, snatching my pillow from under his head. "You really, really suck!"

"Yeah, well, you ain't gettin' this bunk back," he hollers as I march out of the room. "It's mines now! Enjoy your time on watch, Chuck."

18

GONE HUNTING

Saturday, May 5, 1990 - 36 days

Much like my first spell on Watch with Shane and Molloy, being confined to their company is far from enjoyable. First off, the bunk they assigned me is even worse than the one Peaches had. Some of the springs are so old and warped they poke through the mattress, so I spent most of the night squirming around, thinking about that little rat all cozied up in the comfort of my bunk, just a few doors down the hallway.

If anything, focusing on a way to pay back Peaches is a welcome distraction from all the other thoughts haunting my mind. The flashbacks of my yucking. Brother Bennett reeling back his arm. Towering over me as I cower on the floor of the schoolhouse. I can still feel the fear slithering through me.

However, if the bed and my bruises hadn't kept me up, Molloy sure as hell would have. He snored like a hog for nearly four straight hours. Even Shane complained when we woke up this morning. Molloy joked about it being his "beauty sleep" and Shane told him he'd need to sleep a lot longer and harder if that was the case, which is funny because it's totally true. Molloy is the type of ugly that wears a smile like a scowl, and he certainly isn't getting any prettier on the inside either, that's for sure.

As if to prove this point, Molloy snatches the biscuit from my plate as I pick up a tray from the kitchen window. This might seem like no big deal, but this is no ordinary biscuit. This is one of Ms. Tammy's special cathead biscuits, golden brown, buttery and delicious, warm and flaky, straight from the oven. She only bakes them on Saturday mornings, enough for each of us to have one and that's it. They're pretty much the only thing I look forward to around here, and I've been salivating about eating mine since the moment I rolled out of bed this morning.

"Hey, what's that for?" I snap at him, not bothering to blunt the sharpness in my tone.

"What's *this* for?" Molloy raises my Saturday morning biscuit toward his ugly mouth and smirks at me. "This is for me, dumbass."

He snickers as he stuffs it into his mouth and bites down into all that golden, fluffy goodness. Crumbs tumble onto the front of his shirt as he chews and chortles at the same time, watching me watch him. I channel all my hatred into a dagger-like glare, hoping karma makes him choke right here in front of me.

"What?" he mumbles, swallowing down the last of his mouthful. "What're you gonna do about it?"

I glare at him some more as though I'm considering my options, and he starts to chuckle. Molloy knows exactly what I'm going to do. Nothing.

By the time evening rolls around, I'm beyond sick of shadowing Shane and Molloy everywhere they go. Molloy, in particular, has grown more and more agitated as the day's worn on. He's an abrasive prick under the best of circumstances, but I've never seen him this riled up before. And I'm stuck in the unenviable position of being his closest target when he decides to lash out. In fact, my presence seems to aggravate him more than anything else.

Right now, however, his attention is on a different responsibility. It's Shane and Molloy's turn on Dorm Duty tonight, which means they have to corral over two-dozen of the most hostile teenagers in the country to their beds by 10 PM. Lights off, no talking. Taking a few licks would be the preferable option, if you ask me, but everyone knows that Shane and Molloy aren't guys to be messed with, especially in moods like this.

I lie on my bunk back in their room, slightly more comfortable now that I've flipped the shitty mattress over and have a moment to myself for the time being. As 10 PM approaches, Shane and Molloy are busy patrolling the hallway, trying to harry everyone into their rooms with a barrage of threats and verbal abuse. Molloy, in particular, is losing his shit in explosive fashion.

"What the hell's your problem, Molloy?" someone yells, after Molloy threatens to shove his head down the toilet. "You on your period again or something?"

"You're the one who's about to start bleeding," I hear Shane respond. "Get your ass to bed before I break your face!"

The Dorm settles down after that, and Shane and Molloy return to the room a few minutes later. Snapping my eyes shut, I lie silent on my bunk as though I'm sound asleep. I listen as they whisper back and forth, too softly to overhear, but there's a buzz of excitement in their voices that snags my attention. I hear the creaks of their bunks as they climb onto their beds. They whisper some more, and a few minutes later, the room falls silent.

Too sore to fall asleep, I toss and turn awaiting the wheezing grunts of Molloy snoring. But as the minutes pass, all I hear is the drone of his fan and the occasional creak as he and Shane shift around on their beds. Both of them are as restless as I am, apparently.

Maybe an hour or so later as my eyelids start to droop, Shane's mattress squeaks and groans like he's sitting himself up. I crack my eyes open and peer across the room. It's too dark to make him out, but I hear the faint thud of his feet against the floor. Soft footsteps patter toward my bed. I clench my eyes shut and steady my breathing, bracing myself for whatever is about to happen. But nothing does.

"Is he asleep?" Molloy whispers, with an urgency that carries his voice.

"Shhh!" Shane hisses, just a few feet away from me. "Keep it down, or he won't be. Get your shoes on. We need to hurry."

Get his shoes on? I peek at the alarm clock: 12:17 AM. Where the hell are they going at this hour of night?

Molloy's mattress creaks as he clambers off of his bunk. A few moments later, shoes scuff against the floor. Turning my head slowly, I squint through the darkness as two silhouettes slip out of the room into the gloomy hallway and disappear from sight.

As silently as possible, I ease myself up and peer toward the doorway, my curiosity fully ignited. Those bastards are clearly up to something, but what the hell could it be? A number of scenarios dance through my mind, but one feels far more likely than the rest. Shane has a key to the pantry. A pantry that stores food for Brother Bennett's family, in addition to the pitiful shit they serve us.

A handful of chips, a cookie, a pack of Ramen, all of these novelties are hard currency in this joint. Free access to a pantry full of snacks is like hitting the jackpot. If it were me, I'd totally take advantage of that scenario. In fact, now that I think about it, maybe there's a way to take advantage of knowing what they're up to.

I could stumble in on them while they're stuffing their faces. Tell them I was worried when I saw they were missing and went looking around for them. It's a better excuse than sleepwalking, anyway. I might earn a punch in the face, but I might get something that actually tastes like food in return for keeping my mouth shut. Some risks are worth taking. Besides, where they go, I go, right? Isn't that what they told me?

My feet hit the floor before I fully think things through. I slip my feet into my sneakers and tiptoe to the doorway. Peeking my head out of the room, I peer down the dark hallway where two shadowy figures disappear into the dining room. Shane and Molloy are heading to the kitchen, just like I thought.

I wait a few moments and slink after them. Reaching the doorway to the dining hall, I pause and listen. A muffled cough. Hushed conversation. A door gently grinds open and groans as it's shut. It's not the kitchen door, though. That's on the opposite side of the hall. The noise came from the door that leads outside. What the hell are they up to?

Stepping into the dining hall, I hurry toward the outside

door. As I reach for the handle, someone turns it from the other side and pushes the door open toward me. I freeze as Shane pokes his shaven head inside the dining hall. His eyes widen and then clench into a scowl.

"Told you I heard something," he says, as I stare back at him in shock.

Shane springs forward and grabs me by the scruff of my neck, squeezing tightly as he forces me outside into the dark, muggy night. He shoves me forward, and I find myself face-to-face with Molloy, whose expression twitches with outrage.

"You little shit!" He smacks me on the side of my head with an open hand. "What the hell do we do now, Shane?"

Shane shoots me a venomous look and sighs. "We take him with us."

Molloy's eyes bulge. "Take him *with* us!?" He rubs his hands through his scruffy brown hair. "You're kidding me, right? You can't actually be serious!"

Shane stares him down. "He comes with us. That way he can't say shit because he came too."

I let out a nervous chuckle. "Sounds like you're kidnapping me."

"You got a problem with that, Chuck?" Shane growls in my ear.

There's really only one answer that works here. I shake my head, wondering where the hell they're going to take me.

"Get moving." Shane shoves me forward. "Keep pace and listen real good to what I tell you. Molloy and me got plans tonight, and you ain't screwing them up, so do exactly what I say exactly when I say it. And if you mention one fucking word about any of this, I'll make sure you limp for the rest of your life. Understand me, Chuck?"

"One hundred percent," I tell him, even though I'm still completely in the dark about what's happening. "I'll keep my mouth shut. Don't worry about that. I'd like to know where we're going, though."

"Tough shit," Shane says. "You'll find out when we get there. Let's go."

He strides off and I follow after him. I glance behind me and realize that Molloy is still standing back where we started, staring our way with his arms across his chest. He shakes his head and hurries after us.

"This is a bad move, Shane!" he mutters, as he catches up. "A really bad fucking move!" He turns on me. "And you! You've got some balls following us like that, you little prick! What the hell were you thinking?"

I shrug. "Figured you guys were sneaking out for some snacks. You know, from the pantry."

Shane snorts out laughter. "That's pretty damn funny, Chuck." He glances at Molloy who looks significantly less amused. "I guess we are sneaking out for some snacks. They ain't from no pantry, though. And they ain't the kind for sharing."

Shane chuckles away, and even Molloy cracks a smile. The joke's lost on me, though. Now I'm even more clueless than before. I follow along in silence as Shane leads us past the schoolhouse toward the backside of the property. But when we reach the edge of the pitch-black woods, my anxiety bubbles to a boil.

"Will you please just tell me where we're going?" I beg them.

"Hunting," Shane replies.

"Okay." I say. "What does that mean?"

A few steps behind me, Molloy chuckles. "It means we're going hunting, Chuck. You hard of hearing?"

I sense they're messing with me, but I swallow my frustration. I'll play along if that's what they want.

"Right, so we're going hunting. Got it. What are we hunting for then?"

"There ain't no 'we' right now, Chuck," Shane tells me. "It's just me and Molloy who's doing the hunting."

I grind my teeth together. "So what are *you guys* hunting for then?"

Shane snaps his head around and glares at me. "We're hunting for some snacks. Now, shut the fuck up and quit asking questions!"

19

MUSIC TO MY EARS

Despite the tightness in my chest, I heed Shane's advice and bite my tongue. I walked myself into this little mishap, and I clearly won't be talking my way out of it. Willingly or not, I'm officially along for the ride no matter how weird this is starting to get.

Shane leads us along the edge of the woods until we leave the school's property entirely. Descending a small ridge, we follow a rutted dirt track that winds between the pine trees until we reach the main road. Submerged in the deep gloom of night, the road looks eerily desolate. Everything is frozen in shadow, and everywhere I turn, I face a wall of impenetrable darkness.

My pulse pounds like a stampede of horses, but we continue on regardless. Shane's Doc Martens clomp upon the asphalt, as he leads us down the middle of the road into the pitch black night. A few steps behind me, Molloy whistles tunelessly while he marches onward. No one talks, but my senses work in overdrive.

Every now and then, the shadows shift in the periphery of my vision, or something rustles the undergrowth. A pair of owls hoot back and forth above the shrill of cicadas, and further along the road, a dog's gruff barking reverberates through the night. We're certainly not alone out here, but it feels like the three of us are the only human beings for miles and miles.

My uneasiness subsides as a forgotten sense of freedom swells inside me. I wonder if Shane and Molloy are having the same experience. That could be the real reason they're sneaking out like this: a chance to wander freely in the outside world again. They might be Trusted Boys, but they're still trapped in Brother Bennett's stranglehold, maybe even more so than the rest of us. Who wouldn't want to escape that for a few hours if they had the chance?

I clutch onto that feeling for as long as I can, but it fades with every passing minute as my feet begin to ache. We must have walked several miles by now, and neither Shane nor Molloy has said a word about how much farther we're going or where. The back of my shirt is drenched with sweat, and my entire body feels heavy with fatigue. I've kept my mouth shut this whole time, but this is beyond a joke.

"How much longer are we going to walk?" I ask, bracing myself for the backlash.

"I'm with Chuck on this, Shane," Molloy chimes in. "My feet are killing me."

"Quit your bitching. We're here." Shane points toward a fenced-in field with a metal cattle gate, off the left side of the road.

Molloy's sour expression disappears. He eyes the field

eagerly, and his mouth curls into a creepy smile that makes my skin prickle. Why does this keep getting weirder?

"Okay, can one of you please tell me what's going on? Seriously, what the hell are we doing out here?"

"You're about to find out," Shane says as he strides toward the field. "Just shut up and keep going."

I stare after him, feeling like the chump in the movies who gets lured into the woods to be murdered.

"Let's get moving, Chuck!" Molloy gives me a hearty smack on the ass as he jogs past and grins back at me enthusiastically. "C'mon, buddy! We ain't waiting on ya!"

What is wrong with him all of a sudden? I'm not sure what weirds me out more, the fact I've no idea they're taking me, or Molloy acting like he's captain of the pep squad. I sigh and tread after them toward the cattle gate.

Molloy reaches it first and clambers up and over, helped on his way with a shove from Shane. I climb over last and scan my murky surroundings. The field looks fairly small, bordered by dark thickets of trees, basically just regular, old farmland. There's no sign of any livestock or crops, though. There's no sign of anything at all.

Shane leads us away from the road through the middle of the pasture. All I can do is keep following along at this point, wondering why we walked all this way to come to some crappy little field. But the field stretches back much further than I realized. It widens into a larger clearing, and as we trudge through the thick grass toward the center, a catcall whistles through the night.

The three of us jolt to stop, our heads swiveling toward the woods. My heart thumping, I strain my eyes for a glimpse of who's out there, scanning the dense darkness of the treeline. The whistle rings out again, and I hone in on its location. A tiny flicker of light draws my attention, as the red glow of a cigarette smolders and fades.

Molloy replies with a whistle of his own, smiling so broadly he looks like an entirely different person. He skips off toward the trees, Shane swaggering behind him. I start after them, keeping a tentative distance. If they came all this way to meet someone, they must have a really good reason for doing so, and I can't think of any reasons that sound good to me. What type of person comes to a spot like this to meet psychos like Shane and Molloy in the middle of the night? Walking into some kind of shady, backwoods drug deal would be just my luck, wouldn't it?

I stare ahead at the wall-like silhouette of the woods, which looms larger and darker as we approach. Several yards in front of me, Shane and Molloy make haste toward whoever's whistling from the shadows. They're still too hidden to see right now, but I catch a whiff of tobacco smoke and notice there are two cigarettes burning in the darkness instead of one.

"Hey!" Molloy calls out, as he and Shane near the edge of the woods.

"Hey!" a female voice answers back. "Who's with you guys?"

I hurry to catch up, and two hourglass-shaped figures emerge into view. Shane and Molloy head straight over to them, and I follow a few steps behind.

"Who's your friend?" one of the girls peers at me, over Shane's shoulder.

"That's ol' boy Chuck," Molloy tells her. "He ain't our friend. He's just a dumbass that followed us out."

As I move in closer, the girl's features meld into focus: big blond bangs and a set of mascara-lined eyes staring out from underneath. I'm not sure why, but something about her feels vaguely familiar. And when Shane slides up next to her and slips his arm around her shoulders, it dawns on me what he meant by "snacks." I glance at the girl beside Molloy, also blond, but with even bigger bangs. And also familiar. I recognize both these chicks from church.

"We brought him with us so he couldn't snitch," Shane explains. "Don't worry about him, though." He shoots me a stern look. "You'll keep yourself entertained. Won't you, Chuck?"

His girl regards me as she drags on her cigarette. She puffs out a plume of swirling gray smoke, and the sweet scent of tobacco wafts up my nostrils. God, I would kill for one of those right now! I chew on an idea while Shane stares at me for a response. If they want me to hang around here while they're fooling around in the woods, then I'm going to milk as much as I can out of the situation.

"Are you deaf, dumbass?" Molloy barks, sounding much more himself. "He asked you a question."

"Okay," I say, holding my nerve. "I can keep myself entertained for a while. All I need is a few of those smokes and some matches."

"Done!" Molloy turns to the blond with the biggest bangs and holds out his hand expectantly.

Big Bangs tuts and rolls her eyes at him. "Fine!" she says, opening her purse with a sigh.

She digs out a pack of cigarettes, which Molloy snatches straight from her grasp.

"What the hell, Donny?" she screeches, as he hurries my way. "I just bought those!"

Molloy stops and stares back at her, bemused. "What's the big deal? You can just buy more tomorrow, right?"

"I don't care!" Big Bangs catches up to him and snatches back her smokes. "I ain't givin' my whole dang pack away. And I ain't stickin' around if you're gonna act like an asshole!"

Oh, he ain't acting, I want to tell her, but she looks my way and flips open her pack of cigarettes. "Here." She pulls out two smokes and offers them to me.

"Thanks!" I tell her, stowing one in my pocket and the other behind my ear.

"You can have a couple of mine too." Shane's girl steps forward with two more smokes and a box of matches in her hand. "I have this as well if you wanna borrow it." She opens up her purse and fishes out a Walkman, which I accept just as eagerly as her smokes, perhaps even more so.

"What're you listening to?" I ask, opening it up to check. "Anything good?"

"I guess that depends on what you think is good. It's just a mixtape. There's some Poison and Bon Jovi on there. Stuff like that."

I try not to cringe, but I guess it's better than listening to nothing. It's also one of the nicest gestures anyone's made in a long, long time, and I thank her with the deepest sincerity.

A few moments later, the two couples split off into the woods in separate directions. I search around for a comfortable spot to chill for a while, and stumble upon a discarded old pickup with a wooden flatbed. It sits wheeless between the trunks of two pine trees, its rusty rims propped up with concrete blocks.

A few shrubs sprout out between the planks of the flatbed, but the wood feels sturdy when I sit down and test it with my weight. I dust off a layer of pine needles, slide myself back against the cab, and slip off my sneakers with a groan of relief. Stretching out my feet, I lay my winnings across my lap and stare at them in a state of foggy exhaustion. Four smokes, a box of matches, and a Walkman. I can see them and touch them, but they don't feel real.

Fighting back a yawn, I pick up one of the smokes and hold it to my nose. I savor its sweet, earthy aroma for a few seconds, and press it between my lips, strike a match, and spark it up. Closing my eyes, I inhale a long, deep draw and cough myself into a fit of hacking laughter. I haven't smoked in over a month, but I wasn't expecting to nearly choke on my first drag.

A haze of lightheadedness sets in and a calmness spreads through me. I take another puff and watch my breath swirl into an ashy cloud drifting upward in the dark. Things could be a lot worse than this right now; that's for sure. I reach for the Walkman and adjust the headphones so they fully cover my ears. Setting aside the other smokes and the matches, I reposition myself until I'm comfortable and press play.

The chorus of *Talk Dirty to Me* by Poison blares into my ears, and my fingers fumble for the stop button. Allowing myself a moment to recover, I fast-forward until I find the next song. A process I repeat through the rest of side A, crappy tune after crappy tune. I open the Walkman and flip the cassette to side B. After the garbage on the first side, my expectations are low, but it's not like I have anything better to do. I light up another smoke and click the play button.

To my surprise, the intro to AC/DC's *Back in Black* kicks into gear, and a smile stretches across my face. "Now we're talking," I say aloud to no one.

As the guitar riff begins, I max out the volume and scoot myself forward until I have enough room to lie down. Clasping my hands behind my head, I lounge all the way back and gaze up at the starry night sky as the music floods through me.

Back in black, I hit the sack

I've been too long, I'm glad to be back

Yes, I'm let loose from the noose

That's kept me hanging about

I'm just looking at the sky 'cause it's getting me high

Forget the hearse, 'cause I'll never die

I got nine lives, cat's eyes

Abusing every one of them and running wild

For a few blissful minutes, the energy of the song carries me off to a different place and time. I'm home again, back in Atlanta, sitting on my own bed, in my own room. All of my CDs are spread out across the covers. I rummage through them and switch from one album to another, sliding out the sleeves to read the lyrics while I sing along.

The memory fades as soon as the song ends, unfortunately, and the rest of side B sucks in comparison. I rewind to the start and listen to *Back in Black* a few more times, but I can't recapture the same levels of nostalgia.

I take off the headphones and wrap its cord neatly around the Walkman. As I stand up and stretch, the faint sound of voices draws my attention to the woods behind me. The voices grow louder as they approach, and Molloy and his girl soon emerge from the darkness.

"Shane back?" he calls out to me.

"Not yet," I reply.

"Shit!" Molloy runs a hand through his scruffy brown hair and checks his watch. "We really need to get going. Seriously."

He bums a smoke from Big Bangs, sparks up, and starts pacing around. She offers me one which I accept even though I still have two stashed in my pocket. I'm taking those babies back to Victory Ridge. A single cigarette is like a solid gold bar in that place, so I guess that makes me rich.

Shane and his girl show up several minutes later. She eyes me as I return her Walkman and thank her again for the favor.

"Shane told me about what happened to you," she says, and my stomach twists. "And I told him nobody deserves a beating just for writing a dang letter to some girl at church. Someone oughta shut that place down."

I couldn't agree more, sister. Even though she's dating a thug like Shane, this chick seems pretty cool.

"Whatever," Shane chimes in. "Chuck knew the rules. He broke them, and he earned the consequence. Move on."

"Whatever." His girl looks at me and rolls her eyes. "I'm Brandi, by the way."

"I'm Will," I tell her. "That's my real name, anyway."

She smiles. "That makes sense. You don't look like a 'Chuck.' My friend's name is Brandy, too." She gestures toward Big Bangs. "But hers ends with a 'y' and my name ends with 'i.'"

I glance from Brandi to Brandy. Just like their names, the pair are far more similar than different. Practically clones.

"So who's this girl of yours?" Brandi asks me. "If she goes to our church, then we probably know her. What's her name?"

"I don't know her name," I mutter. "And she's not my girl."

"Then why did you write her a letter?"

I sigh. "Look, it's a long story, okay?"

"That's right," Molloy interjects. "And we ain't got time to stand here telling stories all night. We gotta…"

"Hush, Donny!" The other Brandy swats him on the arm and turns her attention back to me. "If you just tell us what she looks like, I bet we can figure out who she is."

"Alright," I say, as an image of Metallica Girl blooms in my mind. "She's tall and she's got dark brown hair."

"How tall?" asks Brandi. "Like pretty tall or really tall?"

"Really tall."

"Wait a second!" Molloy's eyes bulge. "Are you talking about that giant lesbian chick?" He bursts out laughing. "I thought I warned you about her. You've got no chance with that one, dumbass."

Brandy swats him for a second time. "She ain't a lesbian, you moron! He's talkin' about Mary Grace."

20

SOMETHING TO DIG WITH

After parting ways with Brandi and Brandy, we begin our trek back to Victory Ridge, back along the road to Nowhere. My body aches from exhaustion, but my mind sprints in circles. Metallica Girl's real name is Mary Grace Baird.

It feels pretty strange at first. To think of her as Mary Grace instead of Metallica Girl, that is. But I guess they're still one and the same. It's like I've discovered her secret identity or something. Metallica Girl is Mary Grace. Mary Grace is Metallica Girl.

Of the three of us, Shane is by far the liveliest as we wander along the road, way more chipper than he normally is. Molloy, on the other hand, yawns as he shuffles along behind us, bitching that we're walking too fast despite him hurrying us along back at the field.

"You know what, Chuck?" Shane asks, breaking off the tune he was whistling. "You really need to learn how to fight."

"No shit," Molloy grunts. "You can't let bitches like Oaf smack you around. That's some weakass shit."

"He's like three times my size," I tell them. "What was I supposed to do?"

"Bust him up," Shane says matter-of-factly. "Make the other guys think twice about messing with you."

"Yeah, well, I'll keep that in mind for when I'm actually in a fair fight."

Molloy snorts a few steps behind me. "There's no such thing as a fair fight, you dumbass."

"He's right," Shane says. "Think about it. This ain't boxing we're talking about. You ain't matched up with someone in your same weight division, and there ain't no referee to make sure you play by the rules. Real fights don't have rules. If you try to fight like they do, you're gonna get flattened. You get what I'm saying?"

I think for a moment and nod. "Makes sense, I guess. If I can't fight fair and there aren't any rules, then I need to find a way to even things up, right?"

"No!" Shane exclaims, with a shake of his head. "If you're trying to even things up, then you're still looking for a fair fight. It's the wrong mentality."

"So what's the right mentality?"

"Fuck fighting fair and fight dirty."

"Got it," I say, though the idea of fighting "dirty" makes me think of my sister trying to kick me in the nuts. "Any tips on how to fight dirty against someone like Oaf?"

"Easy! Oaf might be massive, but he's got the same weak spots as everyone else," Shane explains. "Just target those areas. Whatever he leaves exposed. You see a chance, you take it, and you make damn sure you hurt him. Don't hesitate. That's the number one rule."

"I thought you said there weren't any rules," Molloy chimes in.

Shane jerks his head around and glares at him. "In a fight, asshat. I'm talking about strategy." He turns back to me. "Do not hesitate. Strike as quickly, as violently, and as unexpectedly as possible. Aim for his throat. If he goes down, get on top of him and choke his ass out. Simple."

Shane nods approvingly at his own advice and pauses a moment while he lights a cigarette he bummed from Brandi.

"So," I say, eager to change the subject, "Angelo told me you're a SHARP."

Shane eyes me as he takes a long drag and puffs out an ashy plume. "Yeah, what about it?"

I shrug. "I hadn't heard of that before. You know, skinheads who fight for social justice and stuff like that. I always thought it was the other way round."

"It usually is," Shane mutters.

"Yeah, that's what I figured. I think it's cool that you're different, though. Angelo told me you stuck up for him a few times. He said things got better for him after you showed up."

I glance behind me at Molloy, remembering who it was that Shane stomped out for being a racist dickhead. Molloy, however, doesn't appear to have heard. He's busy grumbling to himself about something else entirely. Shane still eyes me appraisingly, though his expression is now more curious than skeptical.

"So is that the kind of crap you guys talk about when you're sitting on the hill everyday?" he asks. "Why would you waste your time with that instead of playing sports with the rest of us? I get that Angelo's your friend and all, but sports are the only good thing that happen here. Literally."

I frown as I try to formulate an explanation. "Look, I get what you're saying, but I have my reasons, okay?"

"What reasons?" Molloy butts in from behind us. "Either you hate sports, or you really suck at them. Those are the only two reasons I can think of. If the shit in your CD collection is anything to go by, then it's probably both."

This prickles my skin. Molloy wouldn't know good music if it slapped him in his ugly, smirking face, and the memory of my stolen CDs has me itching to do the same.

"You know what? You're a funny guy, Molloy," I tell him. "I guess that's why you're so hilariously bad at baseball."

Shane bursts out laughing, and Molloy's expression darkens. "What would you know about playing baseball, you little metal-head freak?"

"Well, I played six years of travel ball, so enough to know you stink at it," I reply with a smirk, and Shane laughs even harder.

Molloy shuts up after that and broods silently behind us as Shane and I lead the way along the road.

"Six years of travel ball, huh?" Shane says, as a dog's wild barking resounds through the darkness. "I know you've got your reasons, or whatever, but we could use a player like you. Most of these guys can barely hit a meatball, and Brother James always lines up a few games against other schools. Last year we drove down to Biloxi and kicked the crap out of some fancy-pants private school. That was probably the most fun I've ever had here. You should come play with us."

I consider this for a moment, but the dog's gruff barking barges into my thoughts. The poor thing is probably chained to the back of some redneck's trailer. Judging by the depth of its tone, it doesn't sound like a small dog either. Its racket reminds me of our pit mix, Lucy, losing her shit at the squirrels back in Atlanta. There are bigger critters than squirrels around these parts, however.

"Do you guys sneak out like this a lot?" I ask, changing the subject as the din grows louder.

Shane shakes his head. "This is only the second time we've done it. Last weekend was the first. We figured Saturday nights are the safest. Brother James is supposed to be on duty, but he's always passed out drunk before midnight, so we sneak out after that. As long as we're back around four, no one should see us sneaking in again."

Back around four? I hadn't considered how late it was or what hour we'd be returning to Victory Ridge. But now I'm considering something else that failed to cross my mind. We have church in the morning!

"Holy shit!" I yelp. "We have to be up in a few hours!"

Shane glances sideways and grins at me. "Yeah, but it was worth it. Hold on, my lace came undone."

As he crouches down to tie one of his boots, the dog's barks fall silent. A few seconds later, a hoarse, discordant howl echoes out of the woods.

My head swivels toward the sound. "Is it me, or does that dog sound like it's getting closer?"

"It's just you, dumbass," Molloy scoffs. "It's just some stupid yard dog. Someone obviously lives back there. We're the ones getting closer."

The dog howls again, and Molloy answers back with a howl of his own. The dog responds, and Molloy chuckles, cupping his hands to reply.

"Cut that shit out!" Shane tells him.

Molloy lets out one final howl and falls quiet, but the dog does nothing of the sort. Its feral-like barking returns, deeper and raspier and closer by the second. Not the sound of a dog that's chained up. The sound of a dog that's on the move and knows exactly where it's going.

The three of us halt in our tracks, rooted to the asphalt. My heart hammering, I peer into pitch-black night, listening to the barks echo louder and huskier with every breath.

"Guys," I murmur shakily, "I think it's coming down the road."

"Shit!" Shane shoots Molloy a dagger-like look. "Way to go, dickhead!"

Molloy's attention is elsewhere. His head swivels left and right, like he's deciding which way to run. All I can see is darkness in every direction, but running might be our only option. The dog sounds like it's only fifty yards up the road, and closing in fast. And after a few thundering heartbeats, it falls silent.

"Where is it?" Molloy's voice is a quivering whisper. "Where the hell is it?"

I strain my eyes and ears, but I glimpse and hear nothing. Wherever the dog is, it remains shrouded by the black, cavernous night. Watching us.

"Is it still there?" Molloy asks, as a tingling chill scurries up my spine.

A deep, ominous growl answers him, and a short, stocky shape emerges from the darkness like a shadow.

"No one move," Shane mutters. "Stay calm. Don't startle it."

Despite the pounding in my chest, I keep as still as possible as the dog trots down the road and pulls to a stop about ten yards in front of us. It hackles up, its tail raised and rigid. A pitbull:

dark, lean, and muscular, with a set of wide, powerful jaws. It bares its teeth in a snarl and releases a rumbling growl.

My brain screams at me to run, but my legs are locked in place. I glance back at Molloy, who looks as scared shitless as I am. He catches my eye and starts slowly backing away. I'm about to do the same when the dog growls again and bounds forward toward us.

"RUUUUN!" Molloy shrieks.

His sneakers scuff against the asphalt as he takes off in a sprint behind me. My mind screams at me to follow him, to pivot my feet and flee for my life. But fear freezes me in place. I watch in wide-eyed terror as the pitbull charges toward Shane, who stands his ground before me.

Shane shows no signs of panic. He takes two steps forward, deliberate and measured, positioning himself in front of the dog as it bounds closer with every heartbeat.

Only five yards away now.

Shane adjusts his feet.

Three yards away.

Two yards.

One.

As the dog lunges at him, time decelerates. Shane swings his right boot upward, driving its steel-toe cap into the dog's exposed chest. A gut-wrenching yelp rips through the night, slicing right through my heart. The pitbull flips backward in the air and thuds roughly on the road with a whimper. It rolls over and tries to squirm to its feet, growling once again. Shane reaches it in two swift steps. He raises one of his hefty Doc Martens above the dog's head and stomps it down with a nauseating crunch.

I force myself to look away. I force myself not to hear. Not to feel. But it's too late for any of that. I can't unsee the pool of black blood widening around the poor dog's body, nor the trail of Shane's bloody footprints leading away from it. I stumble to the side of the road and vomit violently into the ditch.

A silence follows. Molloy reappears beside me. He stares at the dead dog, his face as pale as moonlight. Shane paces back and forth along the side of the road, muttering to himself and rubbing his hands across his shaven head.

"What the fuck, Shane!?" Molloy finally screeches. "What the fuck have you *done*!? You...you just killed a fucking dog, man!"

His outburst snaps Shane out of his daze. He stares at us like he forgot we were here.

"Do you think I wanted to?" Shane's voice trembles. "What would've happened if I *hadn't*? Would you rather one of us got mauled by a rabid dog? How do we explain that when we show up for breakfast?" He shakes his head and shuts his eyes. "I had to. I had to do it."

The harsh reality of his words sinks in like a chill. He's right, of course. Brother Bennett would yuck the shit out of us. He might even strip Shane and Molloy of their status as Trusted Boys. But to kill a fucking dog!? To stomp its skull in like that? I still can't justify it, no matter the stakes.

Shane's face contorts with anguish, as though he's struggling with the same thoughts and emotions. He slumps down onto the road, buries his head in his hand, and weeps. The kind of weeping that convulses your whole body, that emanates from somewhere deep and raw and permanent.

"Let's just go," Molloy says and starts walking in the direction of Victory Ridge. "Seriously, Shane, get up. We need to get the hell out of here!"

"NO!" Shane screams.

Molloy stops and peers back at him. "Are you fucking kidding me!? What's done is done. We need to get back."

"No!" Shane's eyes remain fixed on the dog. "We need to bury it."

Molloy grits his teeth and curses. "Well, you're on your own for that shit, man," he says. "I'm not the one who killed a fucking dog. C'mon, Chuck, we're getting the hell out of here."

He turns around and begins walking off again, but I make no move to join him. I gaze at Shane, his chest quivering with silent sobs. The burden of what he just did for us begins to sink in.

"I'll help you bury it," I tell him, grimacing as I realize what I'm truly offering. "I don't think I can touch it, though. You'll have to be the one who moves it."

Shane's eyes glisten with teary gratitude. "Thanks, Will," he mutters croakily, and stares up the road toward Molloy, who stands there watching us. "I guess you're walking back alone, you little bitch. Better get used to it."

Molloy ponders this for a moment, glances up the road into the daunting darkness, and comes huffing and stomping back to us.

While Shane stands vigil over the dead dog, Molloy and I search the woods by the side of the road for something to dig with. We stumble across an old wire fence and twist the rusty metal posts until we wrench them from the ground. They aren't all that efficient for digging, but the soil is soft and we manage to hollow out a large enough space for the dog's body.

It looks much smaller in death as Shane carries it over to the grave and lowers it down inside. We cover it as best we can with a loose mound of dirt and stare at it a short, silent moment before we return to the road.

We walk the rest of the way in silence, together, but alone. By the time we arrive back at Victory Ridge, the faint glow of dawn streaks the horizon. We sneak back our way back into The Dorm and drag ourselves into our bunks, exhausted and numb.

Molloy's alarm clock flashes 5:18, but no one sleeps. No one utters a single word. All we can do is lie awake on our mattresses, listening to Shane softly sobbing until it's time for us to rise.

21

BACK IN THE GAME

Saturday, May 12, 1990 - Day 42

Shane broke the news during breakfast, pulling me aside in the dining hall. I'm now officially off Watch again, which means it's time to claim my bunk back from Peaches. I eye the little weasel as I cross the room and sit down opposite him at the table. He glances up at me as he scoops a spoonful of soggy cornflakes from his bowl.

Peaches might look like he bathes in a barn, but he's as sly and savvy as they come. I sense his mind scheming behind the scenes as I inform Angelo and him of my return. He says nothing, but the stiffness of his stare conveys a wordless warning – *You ain't gettin' that bunk back without a fight, city licker.*

During breakfast cleanup, it's Angelo who says nothing. He gives me the cold shoulder, responding to my questions with grunts and shrugs. Outside of Shane and Molloy, he's the only one who knows what happened last weekend. The two of them would kill me if they found out I'd told him, and though I trust

Angelo to keep his trap shut, I wish I hadn't told him quite so much. I saw him watching my conversation with Shane, and he's clearly realized that I'm holding something back.

"What's your deal?" I whisper, handing him a dripping-wet pot to dry.

He shoots me a side-eye glance as he takes it. "What's your deal?"

I roll my eyes. "You're the one who's not talking."

"Yeah, well, you're the one who ain't telling the truth, bro." Angelo turns to face me and I lower my eyes to the murky dishwater. "Why would Shane talk to you privately like that, just to tell you you're off Watch? We both know that's bullshit, man. He's obviously trying to drag you into something, or you wouldn't be trying to hide it."

I gaze blankly at the sink, guilt twinging inside me. "He told me they're sneaking out again tonight," I mumble.

Angelo is quiet for a moment, but I can feel the weight of his stare. "I figured as much," he says. "And I'm guessing he invited you along too."

I answer with a sigh and nod of my head.

"And I'm guessing you said yes." Angelo mutters grimly, and I nod once again. "Are you for real, Will? Even after the shit that happened last time?"

An icy chill prickles my skin as the dog's final moments flicker inside my mind. Shuddering, I choke-back the memory and look up at Angelo. "I don't think there's much chance of that happening again," I tell him, with more conviction than I feel.

"Oh yeah?" he fires back. "What about the chance of falling asleep in church again?"

I have no response to this. Last Sunday was a haze of shellshock and exhaustion. I nodded off on the ride to church, and my eyelids kept drooping during the service until they were too heavy to open. It came as no surprise when Brother James told me and Molloy to line up for licks after we returned to Victory Ridge. Other than that, all I remember is staring at Metallica Girl in a daze and reminding myself that her real name is Mary Grace.

"If I fall asleep, then I fall asleep. It's my problem, not yours," I answer Angelo, feeling a twitch of frustration. "Look, I get you're trying to be a good friend and all, but I can look after myself, okay? I don't need you to lecture me every time I have the balls to do something you wouldn't."

Angelo's frowning eyes narrow into a sharp scowl. "Do whatever you want, bro," he says gruffly. "I hope it's worth it for you."

So do I, quite honestly. I don't tell Angelo this, however. I don't tell him about the deal I struck with Shane in exchange for tagging along tonight, either. But he'll find out soon enough. Because starting this morning, I'll be playing baseball and every other sport at Victory Ridge instead of watching from the hill.

———

"TIME TO PLAY BALL!" Shane slaps me on the back as we jog down to the field. "How's that glove fit?"

I flex my fingers inside the spare mitt he lent me. "It fits fine, but it stinks like ass!"

"Deal with it!" he says. "Unless you wanna use Molloy's extra glove. The one he jerks off in every night."

"Only when I'm thinking about your sister," Molloy jests,

jogging a few steps behind. "I'd rather play with myself than play baseball, anyway. I'm sick of this shitty game!"

Molloy's grumblings have grown more and more frequent since baseball season began. The way he sees it, there's only one sport worth playing and one team worth following. If it's not football or the Dallas Cowboys, then you're damn well going to hear about it.

"You know what?" he says, as we reach the lumpy lot we call a baseball field. "We're playing football this afternoon. I'm calling it right now. No pads, no bitching, and no bullshit. Everybody plays. You hear that, Chuck?"

Shane glances his way with a crooked grin. "Good luck telling Brother James. That should be fun to watch."

"Go ahead and watch me then!" Molloy juts out his jaw. "I'm gonna tell him right now! And he's gonna swear on the good ol' King James that we're playing some football this afternoon!"

Shane and I chuckle as Molloy cracks his knuckles and jogs off toward Brother James and the rest of the boys. My smile sinks when I spy Angelo sitting alone on the ridge above them, but I ignore the pang of guilt. He never asked for my company in the first place; it was my choice to opt out of playing. I don't owe him an explanation just for changing my mind.

Molloy is busy clamoring for afternoon football by the time we join the others. Most of the boys aren't even listening, but the Cuban Crew respond with a barrage of Spanish insults. He continues undeterred until Brother James shuts him up and tells Shane and Benny to start picking teams.

Though it's my first time playing with these guys, I know how this works. The teams are practically pre-picked. Every now and then, whoever wins the toss will throw a wrench in the works – Shane might snag Taz as catcher before Benny does, for example – but that's about it.

On this occasion, however, it's Benny who wins the toss. Taz is his first pick, but Shane watches on with an air of indifference. I've never seen him choose Taz first, anyway. It's always Molloy. But when Shane opens his mouth to speak, it isn't Molloy's name that he utters.

"Are you deaf, dumbass?" Molloy growls in my ear, shoving me forward.

I glance around, wondering if there's another kid called Will, but Shane stares straight at me and nods. The other boys stare at me too, their faces etched with confusion. *Why the hell did he pick him?* I can almost hear them think. *And how come he called him Will instead of Chuck?* I wonder the same as I take my place next to Shane.

Everyone's attention switches to Benny. The Trusted Boy from Miami frowns at me curiously for a second, but he resumes business as usual by selecting his buddy, Lucas. All eyes fall on Shane again, but this time he does choose Molloy, who glares at me sullenly as he stomps over to join us. Benny adds Alvaro after that, and Shane takes Jerry. A few minutes later, the teams are complete, and it's time to play ball!

Having picked second, Shane opts to field first and calls us into a huddle. "Listen up!" His voice is firm and business-like. "You play where I tell you and no bitching about it. If you've gotta problem with that, you can go sit your ass on the hill."

He glances around, but nobody moves. "Good," he says brusquely. "I'll be pitching until I decide otherwise. Molloy's playing catcher."

"Again?" Molloy groans, but Shane stares him down, and he seals his lips.

"Jerry, you're at first," Shane continues. "Peaches starts at second. Trent's at third. Will, you're our shortstop." He pauses to look at me. "You good with that?"

I've only played there a handful of times, but I know the position well enough.

"Works for me," I tell him.

After Shane announces the rest of our lineup, we jog out onto the field to warm up and stretch. Assessing the players around me, our infield seems solid enough, but our outfield looks a little rough around the edges. Stankass Lou slots in nicely at center field, but Splat is like a fish out of water in left field, and our right fielder, Ol' Trippy, keeps staring at the sky and muttering to himself.

The game begins with Taz leading off for Benny's team. Shane strikes him out with three straight fastballs and dishes out the same to Lucas, who curses in Spanish and hammers his bat against the bag. Benny steps up next. I've watched enough games from the hillside to know he's the best player out here after Shane, with a sharp eye and a smooth swing.

He adjusts his grip on his bat and takes a few practice swings before setting his sights on Shane with unblinking focus. Shane stares straight back at him, composing himself with several even breaths. He winds up and fires in a pitch. A tempting slider, breaking sharply to the left of the plate before thudding into Molloy's mitt.

Ball one.

It was a well-executed pitch, disguised as a fastball before swerving off course, but Benny watched it all the way without even twitching his bat toward the ball.

"¡Tíralo más caliente!" he yells toward Shane, and the rest of the Cuban Crew laugh on the side of the field.

Shane ignores them, looking completely unfazed as Molloy tosses the ball back to him. He resets himself and winds up again. A white blur streaks through the air as Shane fizzes a fastball right down the middle. Once again, Benny doesn't even attempt to swing. He stares blankly at the strike zone as if he's still looking for the ball. As comical as he looks, I can understand why. It was thrown so fiercely you could literally blink and miss it.

"Yo!" Benny calls out, now flushed from embarrassment. "Throw that shit again, bro! Throw that shit again. I dare you. ¡Cojones no te metas conmigo!"

Shane stares him down and unleashes another heater toward the plate. Benny swings and manages to get a piece of it, tipping the ball foul. This routine continues for three more pitches until Shane switches to a breaking ball that Benny grounds right toward me.

It's a weak hit at best. On a regular baseball field, it would be a simple play to make. On the cow pasture we're playing on, however, the ball skips and hops over every lump of turf. I watch it all the way and breathe a sigh of relief as I scoop it up. Muscle memory kicks in from there, and I zip the ball into Jerry's outstretched glove while Benny bombs toward first.

The teams trade places, and Shane assigns us the batting order. Peaches is leadoff, Stankass Lou bats second, Shane third, and Jerry at cleanup. I'm to bat fifth, followed by Ol' Trippy, Trent, Molloy, and Splat.

"This is some major bullshit," Molloy mutters. "I batted cleanup last time we played."

"Yeah, and last time you played, you whiffed every single pitch," Shane replies, and Molloy falls into sour-faced silence.

Just like always, it's Lucas who's pitching for Benny's team. Benny is shortstop as usual. Alvaro is at first. A Cuban kid called Homer is at second, and standing out like a sore thumb at third is none other than Big Dumb Oaf, who Benny grudgingly picked last. The final member of the Cuban Crew, Sal, is out in left field, and two of the Texas kids, Ricky and Gordo, complete the outfield.

"Aquí viene la rata," Lucas yells as Peaches enters the batter's box. "Hey, pendejo, you gonna swing today or what?"

I've seen Peaches play enough to know the answer to that question. As has Lucas, who calls for an infield shift. Peaches carries on regardless and puts in a few practice swings before readying himself for the pitch. It's an act that no one is falling for, however. And as Lucas winds up, Peaches shifts his hands along the shaft of the bat, angling it in front of him to bunt the ball, which whizzes by for strike one.

Lucas leads the jeering as Peaches resets himself. I scan the infield and consider where I would put the ball if I were bunting. Yet again, Big Dumb Oaf stands out like a giant, swollen thumb. The only reason he's playing is because Brother James forced him to; it was that or laps for the next hour. And right now, he has the sullen look of someone who wishes they were somewhere else. Knowing Peaches, this won't have gone unnoticed.

Sure enough, as the second pitch whizzes in, Peaches angles his bat toward Oaf. He times the bunt perfectly, directing the ball down the third-base line. Big Dumb Oaf reacts like a slow motion replay. His eyes widen as the ball bounces on the turf a few yards in front of him. He glances toward Lucas, who screams at him to make the play. Oaf shifts his ogre-sized feet into action, lumbering forward like a bear on its hind legs. By the time he stoops down to pick up the ball, Peaches is already safe at first base.

Lucas scowls at Oaf with outright disdain. Muttering a curse, he turns to face the next batter as Stankass Lou steps up to the plate.

"Better not get hit on by a Roach!" Molloy calls out.

Lucas pretends to ignore him, but his tanned cheeks tinge red as he attempts to focus. This isn't your average Roach he's up against, and he's well aware of that. Stankass Lou might be useless with a bar of soap, but he's got the cleanest swing here after Shane.

"Throw the ball, Miami Vice!" Molloy heckles Lucas again. "Whatcha waiting for?"

Jutting his jaw, Lucas winds up a pitch, unleashing a wild fastball that Taz scrambles to collect. Our team cheers triumphantly as Peaches scampers to second base. Lucas stomps on the turf in disgust, but matters only get worse for him. Peaches steals third on his next pitch, and Stankass Lou hits a single to bring him home. Then Shane steps up and bombs a two-run homer deep into left field.

Lucas fumes on the mound, crimson-faced and chest heaving. The dude looks like he's about to implode, but he inhales several deep breaths to calm himself while Jerry approaches the plate. I'm up next, I realize. I grab the first bat I see and hurry to the on-deck circle.

Working through my practice swings, I watch the two of

them square off. Lucas gets behind in the count, but Jerry bails him out by whiffing at a couple of crappy curveballs. I won't make the same mistake when I get up there, I decide. And after Jerry strikes-out swinging, my time has arrived.

I can hear the yells of encouragement behind me as I make my way to the plate, but the words sound muffled and distant. My mind flashes back to the last time I faced down a pitcher. My mom was there watching, sitting in the bleachers. She was the one who was cheering me on. *Was.*

But that was a different me, in a different life. Reaching the batter's box, I pull myself back to the present. I set my feet in the dirt, adjust my grip around the bat, and assume my stance. I lock eyes with Lucas, who snarls something in rapid-fire Spanish that makes Taz snicker behind me.

"What's so funny?" I ask.

Taz peers up at me and smirks. "He says you look like you're lost, bro. You should go back to the hill with your mulatto boyfriend."

He chuckles, and I turn my face before he sees me flush with anger. Flexing my fingers, I tighten my grip on the bat and face down Lucas with a surge of determination. Whatever this fucker throws me, I'm going to absolutely crush it!

Lucas glares back at me and winds up a pitch. I shift my feet, eyes on the ball as it bullets through the air toward...*me*! I try to twist my body away, but it's too late. The ball clobbers against my leg like a sledgehammer. I collapse on the ground with a yelp of pain, hoots of laughter ringing out around me.

Welcome back to baseball, buddy!

22

NO SWEAT

My left thigh throbs furiously for the remainder of the game, which ends prematurely in the middle of the sixth inning, with the score 5 - 5. Brother James calls it, after a scuffle between Taz and Molloy nearly escalates into a mass brawl between both teams. Apparently, Molloy saw Taz spit inside the one-and-only catcher's mitt before he handed it to him. Taz didn't exactly deny this, but he took offense to the accusation, anyway, and it all kicked off from there.

Once a reasonable level of peace is established, Brother James dismisses us and threatens a lineup of licks should any issue spark up again. The shit-talking continues into the dorm, however, with Molloy stoking things up along the way. By the time lunch rolls round, a deal is struck to play a game of tackle football this afternoon. Same exact teams. Losers shower last.

I haven't played football since my sixth grade PE class, and that was just flag football. We were never allowed to hit one another. The only time I've played tackle football was at some summer camp my dad shipped me off to, but those were some of the best games ever. I imagine plowing through Lucas and slamming him to the ground, revenge for hitting me with that bitchass pitch. Despite the aching stiffness in my thigh, I'm more than feeling up for it.

There's another score to settle first, however. I swing by Shane and Molloy's room after lunch to collect my pillow and suitcase and head along the hallway to my room. Peaches is already inside, stretched out on my bed in nothing but a pair of Bart Simpson boxer shorts.

His eyes narrow the instant he sees me. "That's your bunk over there, Chuck." He points at his crappy, old bed in the corner of the room.

"You sure about that, Peach?" I step toward him, trying not to smirk.

Peaches swings his legs off the edge of the bunk and sits upright on the mattress. "I sure am, Chuck," he snaps, tensing his jaw. "Got somethin' to say about it?"

He sits there watching me, coiled like a spring in case I'm looking to scrap, which I'm not. I don't need to. Instead, I check the doorway to make sure no one's snooping in, reach my hand inside my pillow case, and pull out one of the smokes I stashed away from last weekend. I hold it out in front of me and wave it in the air, like I'm dangling a carrot.

The animosity melts from Peaches' face as he gazes greedily at the cigarette. After all of five seconds, he hops down from my bunk, grabs his pillow, snatches his prize from my hand, tosses his pillow on his old bunk, and walks straight out of the room without saying a word.

Angelo shows up about ten minutes later and does a double take when he sees me lounging on my bunk feeling thoroughly satisfied with myself.

"We struck a deal," I say as he stares at me quizzically.

I'm about to explain when Peaches walks into the room with his hand deep in a bag of Cool Ranch Doritos. He stuffs a handful in his mouth and crunches away, not sparing me the slightest glance as he passes by my bunk and hops onto his. Peaches doesn't smoke, you see; he dips. I knew this, of course. But I also knew the value of what I was offering him. Smokes are currency in this place. Cold, hard cash. Just like a bag of chips.

Angelo sniffs the air, ogling Peaches as he digs his hand inside his prize again.

"How about one chip for me, Peach?" he asks.

Peaches shakes his head. "No way," he mumbles through a mouthful of chewed-up Doritos. "These are mines."

About an hour later, the call goes out. It's time to settle the feud from earlier, with a civil game of good ol' tackle football.

"TO THE BATTLEFIELD!" Molloy hollers as we file along the dorm hallway.

I consider how this will play out. Given that we couldn't get through six innings of baseball without wanting to kill one another, I can't imagine a game of football lasting more than a few downs. In fact, the more I think about it, the more it sounds like some kind of twisted social experiment. Take thirty of the country's most unstable teenagers, stick them in a field, and let them knock the shit of one another without any protective gear whatsoever. It's a Molotov Cocktail of a disaster just waiting to happen, and I cannot wait!

As it turns out, I can wait. We all have to. Benny pulls Shane aside as soon as we reach the field, and now the two captains are in deep discussion.

"I knew they'd do this," Molloy grumbles, pacing back and forth as our team waits on the opposite side of the field from Benny's. "They always agree to the terms and try to weasel out of them later, like a bunch of bitches. I'm sick of this bullshit!"

After a minute or so, the captains shake hands and jog back to their teams.

"Peaches plays with them," Shane informs us. "We're taking Oaf."

"You're kidding?" Molloy glares at him as Peaches grudgingly heads toward the other side of the field. "You traded the fastest kid on our team for a fat ass who can't even run."

Shane stares him down. "And Benny and his boys cover our lights-out duty for the rest of the month. But maybe you'd prefer we played baseball again instead because that's what Benny was gunning for."

Molloy shuts his mouth and fumes silently while Oaf waddles over to join us. I'm hardly Oaf's biggest fan — being detestable is by far his strongest quality — but I'm not sorry to see him trade places with Peaches. I may have won my bunk back, but I owe the little runt a couple of hard hits for taking it in the first place.

It's clear as soon as the game begins that it's basically a free-for-all. I start off at tight end, but the first few possessions are a blur of blocking and barging, being slammed to the ground and getting back up again. When we're finally forced to punt, I yell over at Splat and switch positions with him to play cornerback, so I can match up against Peaches at wide receiver. He eyes me opposite him, and his mouth twitches into a grin. I smile back as

I imagine building up a head of steam and plowing right through him.

After the first couple of downs, however, I still haven't had an opportunity. Thanks to Molloy, that is. As it turns out, he's a beast of a linebacker. A one-man defense machine. The way he cannons into tackles makes me glad I'm not playing against him.

He sacks Alvaro on third down for another loss, and it looks like I'll have to wait until next time for a shot at Peaches. However, despite it being fourth and close to thirty yards, Benny's team sets up to throw instead of punt when they return from their huddle. I keep my eyes fixed on Peaches, mirroring his movements as he switches positions. As soon as the ball is hiked to Alvaro, he takes off in my direction.

I resist the urge to break forward and match him stride-for-stride. That's exactly what he would want me to do. Peaches knows he would burn me. Besides, it's not an interception I'm after; I want to absolutely pummel the sneaky, little prick. All I have to do is keep him right there in front of me. The rest is all timing.

I backpedal a few yards as Peaches sprints closer. Down the field behind him, Alvaro drops deep in the pocket, weighing up his options. Peaches glances back at him and curls his run inside. Alvaro spots him and heaves the ball down the field. My moment has arrived!

I steam forward, closing in on Peaches as the ball spirals through the air. He catches it in his stride and cuts toward the end zone. His eyes widen as he sees me in his path, charging at him full speed, just a couple of yards away. All he can do is clutch the ball and brace himself.

Adrenaline spikes through me as I launch myself into the

tackle. I bulldoze Peaches clean off his feet and slam his scrawny frame to the ground. He winces as my weight crashes down on top of him. I roll off, worried I may have seriously hurt the little, shit-licking hick. But Peaches hops to his feet before I have the chance to check on him.

"No sweat," he says, standing over me, and then jogs off like he just flattened *me*.

My thirst for vengeance boils into a murderous rage, and I make a vow to utterly destroy him. But as I soon learn, Peaches isn't your average little, shit-licking hick. Even though he burns me for a touchdown the next time, I manage to clobber him on four more occasions. And all four times it's the same. He's the first one up. "No sweat," he'll say, even when he looks too dazed to mean it. It's infuriating!

What's equally infuriating is how we're reffing the game. It's basically Molloy and Benny arguing every call, and they seem to be making up the rules as they go. The two of them are stuck in a heated debate as to whether it's first down or second, arguing for so long that a couple of guys leave. No one is even certain what the score is anymore. And, eventually, after failing to reach an agreement on anything, the game ends with both teams claiming victory, which presents a whole new conflict back at the dorms.

"Losers shower last, dumbass," Molloy says as Benny leads the Cuban Crew toward the front of the shower line.

"That's what I came to tell you, bro," Benny fires back. "You guys are in the wrong spot."

Molloy and Benny stare one another down, neither of them budging. Shane stands at the head of the line in front of Molloy, watching on. I'm a few places down the line behind Jerry and Trenton. I don't have the seniority for a spot like this, but Molloy insisted, which means he knew it would rile up Benny and his gang.

Taz glares at me and whispers something to Alvaro as Benny and Molloy start arguing about the game again. One claiming they won by a touchdown, the other claiming the opposite. I'm quite certain it was a tie, to be honest, but I refrain from sharing this. Both of them are intent on being right. Meanwhile, Alvaro and Taz are having a hushed conversation with Sal, Homer, and Lucas, and now all five of them keep looking over at me.

After a few moments, Lucas steps forward and nudges Benny, who breaks off his argument with Molloy.

"Yo, how about we settle this with a fight?" Lucas says, looking first at Shane, and then at Molloy. "Our boy, Taz, against him." He turns and points right at me.

I glance over at Shane who looks at me and raises his eyebrows. I nod and turn toward Lucas.

"Sounds good," I say, ignoring the knot in my stomach. "Where and when?"

"Right here, right now, pendejo!" Taz says, stepping up to me. "We gonna do this or what?"

I size him up. The two of us are practically the same height, although Taz probably outweighs me by a few pounds. I shake this out of my head. It doesn't matter. There are no fair fights, right?

I hand my towel to Jerry, and the rest of the boys form a tight circle around Taz and me. The Cuban kids cheer Taz on in Spanish, and he raises his fists in a fighting stance. We're both half naked, in nothing but a pair of shorts, but then so is everyone else in the bathroom. I try to ignore the awkwardness of it all and focus on the advice Shane gave me about targeting the weak spots.

Whatever he leaves exposed. You see a chance, you take it, and you make damn sure you hurt him.

Raising my fists, I step toward Taz, searching for the chinks in his armor. He dances on his toes in front of me and feints a punch in my direction. I flinch back a little, and the Cubans howl with laughter. But Taz just showed me exactly what I was looking for. I smile through my blushes and edge closer to him, waiting for him to try the same shit again. Waiting for my chance.

Do not hesitate. Strike as quickly, as violently, and as unexpectedly as possible.

A few heartbeats later, Taz lurches forward like before, only this time he doesn't fake a punch; he throws one. Not that it matters, though. My plan is already in motion as I dive downward and tackle him by the knees. I'm up and on him the moment he thuds to the floor, aiming a punch at his throat that he deflects onto his own face with a flailing arm. My fist connects with the side of his nose with a sickening crack.

Blood floods from Taz's nostrils, streaming down his mouth and chin and onto his chest. I draw back my arm to hit him again, but Benny and Lucas swoop in to end it on his behalf. I hop off of him, and they haul him to his feet. He moans and clutches his nose, dripping crimson splotches on the floor as he's led out of the bathroom.

I look over at Shane, who beams at me and nods his

approval. "Will gets the first shower," he announces, and Jerry tosses me my towel. I catch it with shaking hands, trying to ignore the small puddles of blood upon the white tiles. Trying to ignore Angelo's reproachful frown as he watches from the doorway.

23

LIFE IS AWKWARD

Sunday, May 13 - Day 43

Shane and Molloy are waiting outside when I slip out the back door of the dining hall and step into the silent, muggy night.

"You're four minutes late," Molloy grumbles.

"I had to take a piss," I lie, avoiding his gaze as the three of us set off into the darkness.

"Anybody see you?" Shane asks, his long strides setting the pace.

"Nope," I lie again, with a shake of my head.

It's not like the truth is all that bad, but I'll spare them from it, anyway. It's better for everyone that way. Especially me. They'd send me straight back to the dorm if they knew Angelo was still awake when I snuck out. If they knew he knew what we were up to.

"Good luck," he mumbled sullenly as I tiptoed out of the

room. It was the first thing he'd said to me since breakfast cleanup duty. I paused at the doorway for a moment, thinking of something to say. An excuse. A lie. I could tell him my stomach was acting up again, that I was heading to the bathroom. But what was the point?

"Thanks," I whispered, though I doubt he wished me any luck at all, and then I slunk into the hallway.

I'm hoping for some good luck now, however, as we begin our trek along the pitch black road toward the meeting place. The three of us walk side-by-side in silent apprehension, the grim weight of last weekend hanging heavy in the air. That feeling thickens like an invisible fog as we draw closer to where it happened. I shudder at the thought of seeing those bloodstains on the asphalt again, but I focus my eyes on the darkness ahead and keep moving forward.

The sight of a familiar-looking cattlegate soon lifts our moods. We clamber over it and trudge across the field to the same thicket of woods where we met Brandy and Brandi the last time. However, as we draw closer to the trees and the abandoned, old pickup, something is clearly amiss. There are three female figures waiting for us instead of two. And one of them is considerably taller than the others.

My heart fires around my chest like a pinball. Holy fucking hell! They brought Mary Grace along!

I halt in my tracks, staring at the sight ahead of me. Shane and Molloy howl with laughter. These assholes knew the whole time and never said anything!

"You alright there, Chuck?" Molloy digs me on the arm with his elbow. "This ain't a good time to spew your guts up."

An awkward chuckle escapes me, which splutters into a fit of coughing as I inhale a noseful of his cheap cologne. Molloy smacks me on the back, too hard to be helpful. He leans in close, and I try to wrinkle my nostrils shut.

"Get it together, dumbass! You don't wanna embarrass yourself in front of Big Bird, do you?"

I suppress an urge to scream in his face. Maybe if someone had given me a heads up, I wouldn't be acting like such an idiot right now. I planned to kick back with some smokes and hopefully listen to some better tunes than last time, but alone, not with company, and certainly not with Mary Grace.

"C'mon." Shane shoves forward. "The clock's ticking."

My legs tremble with each step, but I manage to match Shane and Molloy's eager pace as they hurry toward the girls. It's not until we're a few yards away that I can see Mary Grace clearly. She leans against the side of the rusty truck, watching us approach. Our eyes meet for a moment, and my insides flutter.

Whenever I've seen her in church, she's always worn a plain skirt, shirt, and cardigan, with her hair tied in a tight bun. Tonight, her brown hair hangs straight and free past her pale neck, down to her shoulders. She wears checkered Vans, denim shorts, and a dark t-shirt with something written in cursive that's illegible in the dark. And then there are her eyes, silvery blue and glinting with moonlight.

"Well, good luck to you, Chuck." Molloy strolls up beside his girl, Brandy, and drapes his arm across her shoulders. "Need any advice before I go? Looks like you're a little too short for that one." He glances from me to Mary Grace and snickers. "That should make things interesting."

"Knock it off, Donny!" Brandy smacks him on the arm.

"That's not why she's here. She came to talk. Nothing more. I told you that."

"Okay, okay!" Molloy raises his hands in surrender. "Didn't mean nothing by it. Just messing with ol' boy Chuck for a minute." He winks at me and chuckles. "Y'all have fun...talking. Let's go, Brandy."

As he leads her off by the hand, Shane steps forward and tosses me something. I catch it instinctively and stare down at my hands. My eyes widen. It's a pack of Marlboro with the wrapper still sealed.

"The smokes are on me tonight," Shane tells me. "But don't even think about getting greedy. If you take more than three, I'm gonna boot your ass back down the road. Understand?"

"Got it," I say, as he hands me a lighter. "Thanks, Shane!"

He nods, and then he and Brandi venture off into the night. I steel myself with a couple of deep breaths and turn toward Mary Grace. Arms folded across her chest, she watches me curiously as she leans against the old pickup. I clear my throat, pulling my gaze away from her long, slender legs.

"Well, that was awkward," I say, and force out a laugh that sounds as uncomfortable as I feel.

Mary Grace shrugs his shoulders. "Life is awkward."

Grasping for a response, I come up empty. *Life is awkward.* Yeah, she couldn't be more right.

I steal a few glances at her. To describe her as tall isn't accurate enough. I mean, she's definitely tall — a little over six feet by my estimate — but she's also long-limbed and gangly. She's her own kind of awkward, in her own kind of way. Just like me, I suppose. Just like life.

"I thought your name was Will," she says, and I realize I'm

staring at her legs again. I jerk my head upright, hoping the darkness will hide my blushes. "That's what you told me in your letter. So, why did the dipshit that Brandy's dating call you Chuck?"

I grin at her. She's already the most interesting person I've met here, and calling Molloy a "dipshit" makes her all the more appealing.

"It's just a dumb nickname I get called sometimes," I tell her.

Mary Grace cocks an eyebrow. "Are you going to tell me why, or am I supposed to guess?"

She smiles at me, and I chuckle nervously. No dancing around things with this chick, huh?

"Sorry," I say, "I've just never had to explain it before, I guess. The other guys came up with it my first night at Victory Ridge. I puked my guts up on the way to church. It was so bad we had to turn the bus around." I laugh a little, but Mary Grace looks more concerned than amused. "Anyway, that's why they started calling me Chuck. It's not a great story."

"Well, it doesn't sound like a place where great things happen," Mary Grace says, her eyes solemn as she watches me.

I nod in silent agreement, and ease myself down onto the wooden flatbed of the pickup. To my surprise, Mary Grace moves to join me, and I shift over to give her more room.

I stare down at the pack of smokes Shane gave and peel off the wrapper.

"Want one?" I ask, as I open the top.

"No thanks. I don't smoke."

"Mind if I do?"

She shakes her head. "Go ahead and kill yourself, but thanks for asking, at least."

I chuckle. "You're welcome."

I slip a cigarette between my lips, spark up the lighter, and lean the tip into the flame. I draw deep and exhale, slow and steady.

"I'm guessing you were surprised to see me tonight," Mary Grace says. "Your friends seemed to enjoy your reaction."

"Yeah," I say, puffing out an ashy cloud of smoke. "But I wouldn't call them my friends. Not really, anyway."

"I'm not really friends with those girls either. We hang out occasionally, but we've got nothing in common when it comes to anything interesting. Anyway, here we both are, tagging along with people we don't like."

The two of us fall silent as though we're chewing over our next words. Like usual, my mind is clogged with too many questions. Choosing the right one feels overwhelming. By asking Mary Grace something personal, I open the door for her to do the same. And there are plenty of other doors I don't want her knocking on.

As wary as I am, though, there are a few things I have to know. I clear my throat to break the silence between us.

"So, I know this is a charming spot and all, but I don't get why you'd want to...How do I say this?" I pause to consider.

"Are you wondering why I came here," Mary Grace picks up, "in the middle of the night with a couple of Debbie-Gibson-wannabes I don't really like?"

We both laugh. "Exactly!" I say. "Especially when the Debbie-Gibson-wannabes are meeting up with two maniacs from the world's worst reform school. I know Brandy said you came here to talk, but you didn't need to come all the way out here to do that. I mean, I'm glad you did, don't get me wrong, but it would've been easier to talk after church."

Mary Grace chews on her bottom lip for a moment. "I suppose that's true, but it wouldn't be the same. For you or for me. I'm not myself when I'm at church. I'm just pretending to be someone I'm not if you know what I mean."

"I sure do," I say. "I don't go there three times a week out of choice."

She pauses and looks at me for her moment with heavy eyes. "I'm really sorry I couldn't help you get out of that place, Will. I tried, but your dad...he blew up at me before I had a chance to finish telling him everything. He started yelling and cursing at me. Calling me a liar. Calling you a liar. I didn't know what to do, so I just hung up the phone. I'm sorry, Will. I thought he would at least care a little...but he didn't."

Deep down I had known he wouldn't, but I was so desperate I deceived myself into hoping he might. I puff the last of my cigarette and stub it out.

"Don't be sorry," I tell her, pulling a fresh one out of the pack. "It's me who should apologize. I'm sorry I put you in that situation. I should never have asked that of you."

Mary Grace shifts around to face me. "But you did, and that's okay, Will. Asking someone for help is always okay. I made the choice to help you, so quit feeling bad about it. I must admit, though, I'm still curious to know why you chose me. We'd never exactly talked before. I mean, you nearly knocked me over in the lobby that one time. Then there's the Metallica thing, obviously. No one else listens to them around here, and you just happened to be the one who picked up the cassette sleeve I dropped. But I was still a complete stranger to you, just as you were to me. No offense, but it's kind of a big leap of faith to think I would help you."

"So why did you?" I ask, eager to deflect the conversation.

Mary Graces gazes off in thought. "Because I know how it feels to be stuck somewhere you don't want to be," she says. "Brandy told me you're from Atlanta."

I nod my head, noting her own diversion off topic. "Born and raised," I tell her. "Lived there all my life until I got shipped off to paradise."

"I'm guessing your dad is the one who shipped you off."

I nod again. I sense where this is leading.

"Why?" she asks, confirming my suspicions. "What happened?"

I turn away for a moment and spark up my fresh smoke. It feels like the thousandth time someone has asked me this question. Drawing on my cigarette, I ponder my response. Up until now, I've given the same stripped-down version of the truth. A highlight reel of my misdeeds: the switchblade at school, getting expelled, sneaking out to see Metallica and being arrested for stealing a t-shirt.

Over the past month or so, I have fine-tuned this story down to perfection. Whenever one of the guys at Victory Ridge asked, that's what I would tell them. That's all they wanted to hear. The crazy shit I did to earn my sentence alongside them. Anything else was considered inconsequential.

I can sense that won't be the case for Mary Grace, though. There was no judgment or accusation attached to her question, unlike the way the other guys ask, which basically means "What did you do?" After her phone call with my loving father, she already knows there's more to it than that. So how much of the truth do I tell her? Despite the cries of protest in my head, I decide to take another leap of faith.

"Would you prefer the short version of what happened or the long one?" I ask, though I'm certain of her response.

"I would prefer to know more than less," Mary Grace says. "I'll take the long version, please, and you can take however long you want. But if you skimp on details, just know I'll have questions."

She grins at me, and I smile back half-heartedly, already regretting my decision. There is no turning back now, though. I take another deep drag on my cigarette and force my mind to lower its guard. Doors I've kept closed creak open. And the past comes flooding out.

"The last two years have been...really tough," I begin, trying to think without feeling and instantly failing. "I lost my mom in a car crash. After that it was just me, Dad, and Candace, my little sister. Things had never been great between me and my dad. It was my mom I was closest to. She was always there for me. There for everything. With Dad, I kind of felt like the kid he didn't want. They adopted me as a newborn after a doctor told my mom she couldn't have kids. A year later, she gave birth to my sister. From that point on, it was Candace and Dad, and me and Mom. Until the accident."

I pause to steady my breathing. I can feel Mary Grace watching me, but I can't look her way.

"I'm so sorry, Will," she says tenderly. "I can't imagine losing my mom. It would feel like losing my entire world."

"Then you can imagine," I say, fighting back another wave of tears. "That's exactly how it felt. Like all my worst fears came true. I didn't have anyone to turn to either. My dad just completely shutdown as a parent. All he did was work. When he was home, he wasn't really present if you know what I mean."

I picture Dad during the months following Mom's accident. Every evening was the same. He would sit alone at the kitchen table, still dressed in his dentist uniform: a pair of tan slacks, a pale blue button-down with a red tie, and his signature white coat, which highlighted the silver waves in his brown hair. For the next few hours, my dad would refill his glass with bourbon until the bottle was more empty than full. By the time I woke up in the morning, he was gone again.

"So who looked after you and your sister?" Mary Grace asks.

I stare at her for a moment. "No one, at first. We were basically left to run wild. After a few months of that, Dad moved Grandma into the spare bedroom to keep an eye on us. But she's practically senile. I would just sit on the couch next to her watching reruns of The Golden Girls until she nodded off. Then I was free to do whatever."

I used to swipe a few bucks from her purse to buy smokes before I left, but I leave that part unsaid.

"So how did being 'free to do whatever' work out for you, Will?" Mary Grace smiles at me knowingly.

I laugh. "You're looking at it," I say. "But you probably figured that out already. You probably want to know what the hell I did."

Mary Grace frowns a little. "Do I? Hmm, let me think about that," she says, and curls a strand of dark hair around her pale finger.

I watch her, feeling more mesmerized by the second, and equally as mystified. She, on the other hand, seems to be figuring me out rather quickly. For the most part, anyway.

"Did you hurt somebody?" Mary Grace asks after a few moments.

"No," I tell her. "I mean, I got into fights and stuff like that, but nothing major. Just the normal crap."

"Were you dealing drugs?"

"What? Hell no! Never have and never will. I smoked pot a few times. That's about it."

Mary Grace smiles at me. "Well, I think that's all I need to know then."

"Really?"

"Yep."

I squint at her. "I don't get it. You wanted to know why my dad shipped me off here. You asked what happened."

"And you told me," she says. "There's nothing more to explain. You lost your mother, Will. That's what happened. In a way you lost your father, as well, but it doesn't sound like he was much of one to begin with. It sounds like he would've shipped you off no matter what you did. And none of that is any of your fault."

Is that true? I gaze at Mary Grace and wish I could believe her. What she said makes sense, but nothing feels that way when I think back about it. Compassion for the child who lost his mother dried up a long time ago. It's hard to care about a kid who has stopped caring about anything. Teachers started looking at me differently. Other kids' parents wouldn't let them hang out with me. They saw me as a bad seed, a lost cause. A troubled teen who didn't give a shit about anything or anyone.

And I *was*. I was all of those things. But that's not all I was, and it's certainly not all I am. Being around Mary Grace is a reminder of that.

"You okay, Will?" she asks softly.

"Yeah," I say, wiping my eyes before the tears spill out. "No one's ever said that to me before. Everyone kept telling me I'd brought this on myself. I guess I started to believe them."

"Well, now sounds like a good time to stop, don't you think?" Mary Grace says, arching one of her thin dark eyebrows and making a goofy face that makes me chuckle.

"Sure," I say. "I'll give it a shot."

"Good!" She claps her hands together and smiles at me. "From now on, you should only blame yourself for your actions and not your circumstances. Sound good?"

"Sounds good," I say, grinning back at her.

Mary Grace twirls a finger through her hair again as she watches me. "I'm sure you made some stupid mistakes before you got here, Will, but I'm not going to judge you for that, okay? Not with what you were going through. But I still need to know that I can trust you if we're going to be...friends. Sometimes that's hard for me, so..."

Mary Grace breaks off as a high-pitched scream punctuates the night. Yelps of panic echo through the woods behind us. We exchange a worried glance and hop to our feet, peering through the dark mass of trees.

"That sounds like Molloy," I say, tilting my head to listen. The cries subside and two voices yell back and forth in a frantic exchange. "That's definitely Molloy. What the hell's going on?"

"Something tells me we're about to find out," Mary Grace says, staring toward the woods as voices grow louder and closer. She turns and looks at me, her pale skin like white marble in the moonlight. "I wish we had more time to talk tonight, but it sounds like we're going to have to wait until next time."

"So you're going to come and hang out with me again?" I ask, feeling a giddy smile spread across my face. I gaze at her, trying to ignore Molloy's crude grumblings as he and Brandy make their way toward us. Mary Grace tilts her head and stares at me thoughtfully.

"Are you a good guy, Will?" she asks. "You seem like one, but I don't know many good guys, so it's hard to tell."

Am I? Am I a good guy?

"I want to be," I tell her.

Mary Grace considers this for a moment, and one corner of her mouth tweaks into a crooked smile.

"Good answer," she says.

Our attention shifts back to the woods as two gloomy figures emerge from the darkness. Molloy is moving strangely, muttering irately to Brandy who walks alongside him. He keeps clawing at himself and wiggling around like he's doing some weird dance.

"What the hell's wrong with you?" I call out to him. "What was all the screaming about?"

Molloy grimaces and reaches down to scratch the back of his legs.

"Fucking hell!" he growls.

"Seriously, what happened to you?"

Molloy and Brandy glance at one another.

"You tell him," Molloy says.

Brandy rolls her eyes and sighs. "We were...you know," she says. "And he didn't realize he was standin' in an ant pile, and so..."

"They were everywhere!" Molloy blurts out. "Hundreds of

them. All over me. Everywhere. On my legs, my ass, my dick! Stop laughing, you asshole!"

But I can't. It's impossible. Mary Grace covers her mouth with her hands, and even Brandy giggles away next to him. Molloy's face darkens.

"Fuck all of y'all!" he yells. "I'm going."

He turns and strides away towards the road. Brandy starts after him and manages to stop him a short way off. The pair of them engage in an animated discussion, Molloy scratching away at himself.

A few minutes later, Shane emerges from the woods with Brandi.

"What the hell is going on?" he asks.

After a brief explanation, everyone hoots with laughter again. Well, everyone except Molloy, who storms off like he's heading back to the road.

This time, after hurried farewells to the ladies, it's Shane and me who catch up with him.

"Don't fucking talk to me!" Molloy snaps as we pull up alongside him. "Not a fucking word."

"Fine," says Shane. "If you're feeling too sensitive, I'll just talk to Chuck." He turns to me and flashes a mischievous grin. "I guess he's feeling a bit sensitive about the whole thing. We probably shouldn't mention anything about it."

"Fuck off, Shane. I'm not feeling sensitive. I feel like I have a thousand fucking ant bites, and I've only got two fucking hands to scratch them!"

"Well, don't look at us for help," Shane says. "I'm not scratching your sweaty ass for you. You do seem sensitive, though. Doesn't he?"

"Maybe a bit." I chuckle. "We probably shouldn't antagonize him."

We crack up, but the pun flies right over Molloy's thick head, most likely because he has no idea what that word even means.

I consider explaining it, but distant barking silences our laughter, transporting my mind back to the last time we walked along this road. I don't pray often, but after what happened here a week ago, I'll try anything to avoid a repeat.

I glance up at the star-littered sky. "No dogs tonight, please. For the love of Jesus, no dogs tonight," I whisper to the heavens.

24

WORTH IT

It's 3:24 in the morning when my head hits my pillow. My body aches from exhaustion, but my mind is still abuzz. Every thought and feeling circles back to Mary Grace. Her pale skin, radiant in the moonlight. Her gleaming eyes as she smiled at me. The carefree way she played with her hair. The way she listened without judgment as I opened up to her. Always attentive. Always honest and empathetic.

My eyelids soon droop until they are too heavy to keep open. When I awake a few hours later, a shaft of morning light beams through the window. I blink until my eyes adjust and grudgingly rise from my bunk. Aside from me, the room is empty. My three roommates have already joined the scramble for first dibs on a morning dump or a pre-breakfast shower.

Judging by the clamor outside my room, everyone else has as well. Boys clomp along the dorm hallway in a wild stampede, yelling over one another, whistling, singing, and talking shit.

Bleary-eyed, I slip down from my bunk. I throw on some pants and a t-shirt, and venture out into the morning mayhem.

I catch up with Angelo and Peaches in the dining hall. Angelo throws me a few disapproving looks during breakfast, but he doesn't say shit about me sneaking out. He gives me the cold shoulder during clean up duty, too, which is fine by me. I'll take the silent treatment over one of his lectures any day of the week.

By the time we're boarding The Booger for church, though, I'm done with being ignored. I plop down in the spare seat next to him. Angelo's eyes twitch toward me, and then he turns to stare out the window.

"So, was your adventure worth it?" he mumbles, without bothering to look at me.

"Would you believe me if I said yes?" I ask him.

Angelo snorts and continues to gaze out the window in silence. Yeah, that's what I thought.

"Okay," I say, "time to spit it out. Why are you acting so pissed at me?"

Angelo turns and scowls at me. "Because you're pissing me off, obviously."

I roll my eyes. "Okay, why am I pissing you off so much then?"

"I could tell you, bro, but you ain't gonna listen because you ain't gonna like what you hear."

Now he's pissing me off! "I asked, didn't I? Why the hell would I ask if I wasn't going to listen? Just tell me!"

"Fine!" he snaps. "I thought we were tight, okay? I thought we trusted one another. But all that's changed since you started hanging with Shane and Molloy. You've changed. You're becoming just like them."

"Ah, I see," I say, with a smirk. "This is because I stopped sitting on my ass like you everyday. Well, I'm sorry that I like playing sports again. I didn't realize you'd take it so personally."

"Don't be a dick, Will!" Angelo glares at me. "I never made you sit with me, and it never bothered me when you stopped. I was actually glad you started playing again. I could tell you wanted to, even from the start. But that's not what I'm talking about, man."

Angelo's expression softens a little, and he sighs. "I'm talking about the way you've been acting, bro. The lies and shit. How you're desperate for Shane's approval. Even Molloy's. Any chance to impress them, and you jump." He lowers his eyes and shakes his head. "You should have seen yourself after you busted Taz's nose. Grinning at Shane and high-fiving Molloy while Taz was slipping on his own blood. Is that who you wanna be, Will?"

Resentment simmers inside me as I consider his question. Angelo watches me, awaiting my response. I stare straight ahead at the seat in front of me, my cheeks tingling. *Is that who you wanna be?* He's just trying to make me feel ashamed of myself. Good ol' Saint Angelo trying to shepherd me along the right path. His path. Not my path.

"What's it to you?" I say. "Why do you care so much?"

Angelo's brow furrows. "Why do I care? Because I'm your fucking friend, bro! At least, that's what I'm trying to be. I've been trying to keep you straight since day one, but you don't wanna listen, just like I said. If you wanna be like Shane and Molloy, go ahead. It's your life. But trust me, they don't give two shits if they drag you down with them. I'm the only person who actually cares about you in this place, Will, maybe even anywhere. I wish you'd see that."

I lower my gaze from Angelo's wounded expression and stare at my hands in sullen silence. There are too many truths in what he just said, but he's wrong about one thing. He's not the only one who cares about me. Not anymore, anyway.

I realize Shane and Molloy aren't going to guide me down the path to salvation. I'm not stupid. But they do have my back, so they care in their own way, I guess. In a place like Nowhere, that's nothing to sniff at. And then there's Mary Grace. In the short time we spent together, she showed me more kindness and compassion than I could have possibly imagined. So I'm sick of Angelo acting like he's the only person I should trust.

When we arrive at church, I ditch him the moment my feet hit the parking lot and catch up to Peaches. The instant we enter the sanctuary, my eyes seek out Mary Grace. There she is on the right side of the room, sitting next to her mother a few rows from the front. Her hair, which fell so freely several hours ago, is now restrained in its usual tight bun again. Back to pretending she's someone else. Metallica Girl in disguise.

We never had a chance to talk about music last night, unfortunately. That's something to look forward to next time, I guess. I run through a list of questions I might ask, trying to fend off sleep as the old preacher drones on about miracles and the Holy Ghost. Miraculously, I manage to stay awake through the remainder of the service. But when we all get back to The Booger, we learn that one of the other boys was not as fortunate.

"This is too good to be true!" I say, sitting next to Peaches on our way back to Nowhere. "Seriously, it's like Christmas came early."

I haven't stopped grinning since I heard the news. I couldn't if I wanted to. The entire bus buzzes with the same feverish anticipation. Hoots of laughter ring out as everyone clamors to be heard. Boys kneel backward on their seats to joke with the guys behind them. Others lean across the aisle, yelling back and forth in lively conversation while The Booger jolts along the road. Everyone brims with infectious enthusiasm.

Well, almost everyone. Big Dumb Oaf sits alone at the front of the bus, sullen and silent in the row nearest Brother James. I picture him quivering with fear while we revel in his misery like we're tailgating a football game. The dumbass thoroughly lived up to his nickname this morning.

You see, it's one thing to fall asleep in church. That happens to pretty much everyone at some point. You just take the standard three licks and move on. But Oaf didn't just doze off during the service. He slumped over on the person next to him and started snoring like a feral hog, with his head on their shoulder. Unfortunately for Oaf, that shoulder belonged to Brother James.

"I've never been so excited to watch someone get licks before," I say to Peaches, my exhaustion muted for the time being. "How many do you think he'll get?"

Peaches is too engrossed to answer. He scrawls on the back page of his Bible with the broken tip of a pencil, his tongue poking out the side of his mouth as he concentrates. I glance down at what he's writing. Other than some numbers the rest is illegible, but I know exactly what he's doing.

An idea forms in my head: two birds with one stone. Definitely risky, but more than worthwhile if I'm able to pull it off.

"Wanna make a bet, Peach?" I ask.

Peaches stops writing and looks up at me. Mischief glints in his eyes. "Depends," he says. "I ain't done with the odds yet."

I smile. Peaches can play it cool all he wants, but he never passes up a chance to scheme, especially when it comes to a bet. "Keep your odds for the other guys," I tell him. "This is just a bet between…roommates."

The word "friends" almost slips out, but I catch myself just in time. I've already hooked Peaches' interest, referring to us as best buds might make him suspicious.

"Alright then," he drawls. "What we bettin' on?"

I shrug. My turn to play it cool. "I guess we could bet on how many licks Oaf gets. I mean, there's no way he's only getting three for this. Brother James was pissed! It's going to be double that at least, right?"

Peaches stays poker faced. "Maybe," he says. "Is that your bet?"

"Nope," I say, deciding to up the risk. "I bet you Oaf doesn't make it past five."

"Huh?" Peaches squints at me. "How come?"

"Do I have to give a reason?" I ask. "He either makes it past five licks or he doesn't. It seems like a pretty straightforward bet to me, but you're the bookie around here."

Peaches still eyes me suspiciously but I can tell he's scheming behind the scenes.

"What's your wager?" he asks, rubbing his chin.

"Hmm. Good question." I stare off, wrinkling my forehead as though I'm mulling things over. "Okay," I say, after a few seconds. "If you win, I'll give you another smoke. How about that?"

For a split second, Peaches' eyes widen. He quickly blinks out of it and restores his deadpan expression. "That works for me," he says, trying to sound indifferent. "If you win, I'll make your bed for a week. Deal?"

He reaches out his hand to shake on it. I stare at his grubby fingers and shake my head instead. "No deal. I could pay someone half a smoke to do that for a whole month."

Peaches frowns. He knows that's true. "Alright then," he says. "I'll give you my breakfast biscuit next Saturday. If that ain't a fair deal, I ain't sure what is."

I shake my head again. Nope, not today, Peach. This time you're the one getting scammed. "Make that the next two Saturdays," I tell him. "Then we have ourselves a deal."

The crafty, little shitbag has the audacity to look offended. Peaches knows full well the odds are heavily in his favor. After all, why would Oaf be unable to make it through six licks? He might be the world's biggest bitch when it comes to being hit on the ass with a paddle, but why on earth would Brother James allow him to stop? This deal is a no-brainer, and Peaches knows it.

Well, it's a no-brainer on paper, anyway. The odds are certainly against me, but Peaches has no idea how I plan to tip the scale in my direction. I still have no idea if I can pull it off, but I'm going to swing for the fences regardless.

I clear my throat, and raise my eyebrows as Peaches looks my way. "Do we have a deal or not?" I ask, reaching out my hand.

Peaches regards my outstretched hand for a moment and reaches out his own. "Works for me!" he says, flashing a stained-yellow smile as we shake and make the deal.

With step one accomplished, I turn my focus to step two. I've waited for a moment like this ever since Oaf socked me in the eye. But this is more perfect than I could have imagined. When we return to school, Oaf will be marched into the dining hall and stand alone in the middle of the room. Everyone's eyes will be on him while Brother James paddles him into a whimpering mess.

As I learned early on, the number one rule when taking licks is to make sure you don't flinch. If you do, there's a good chance the paddle will miss the fleshy parts of your ass and strike your lower back or the backs of your legs. Much more painful.

Fortunately for me, though unfortunately for Oaf, this is a rule he can't seem to grasp. He flinches every single time. Whenever the paddle is about to connect, his reflexes kick in. Oaf arches backward like he's trying to thrust his enormous asscheeks out of the way and lessen the impact. Straight up rookie shit!

It's ridiculous, really, but it also presents a unique opportunity. Another chance to put Shane's advice on fighting into action. You see, when Oaf arches away from the paddle, his gut lifts upward. This leaves him perfectly exposed for exactly what I have in mind. I'll earn myself a few licks of my own, but vengeance against the biggest asshole in Nowhere, Mississippi, is more than worth it.

When we arrive back at Victory Ridge, Oaf is marched into the dining hall by Brother James. A group of us follow behind, all equally eager to watch him suffer. Brother James could charge for this. It would be worth every penny. But he seems perfectly happy to have an audience.

Brother James strolls up to Oaf, twirling his paddle in his hand. "Three licks for sleepin' in church," he announces, "and three more for fallin' asleep on yours truly."

Oaf's ruddy cheeks turn sickly pale, and the dining hall

echoes with laughter. I catch Peaches' eye and he nods at me. Six licks, as expected. Game on!

"Turn your fat ass around," Brother James growls at Oaf, who grudgingly lumbers into position. Shifting his feet apart, he leans forward and places his shaky hands on his knees. I run through my plan, fine-tuning my strategy. Weaving through the onlookers, I edge my way around the dining hall until I'm directly in front of Oaf, roughly several yards away.

Behind him, Brother James adjusts his grip on the paddle. Oaf squeezes his eyes shut, bracing himself for the first lick. His entire body quivers. A sickly grin twitches on Brother James's face as he draws back his arm and swings the paddle forward. Oaf flinches like he always does, his gut flopping upward.

Thwack!

The paddle clouts him across the small of his back, and he howls with pain. The hall echoes with laughter as Oaf hops in circles, clutching his lower back while he grimaces and groans. He certainly makes a show of it; I'll give him that.

"C'mon now, boy!" Brother James barks. "Quit jiggin' around and let's get this done!"

Still whimpering, Oaf reluctantly assumes the same position. The second swing connects, and he flinches just like before. I pay close attention to the next two licks, focusing on the timing. The moment he's most vulnerable. Each time it's the same. Oaf arching backward to protect his rear, leaving everything else open and exposed.

With the count now at four licks, my moment is here. It's now or never. Time to make sure the fifth lick is the last one Oaf takes. That might sound like a small mercy, but if all goes to plan, he'll be wishing he could have taken the sixth lick instead.

"Last two," Brother James calls out. He points his paddle at Oaf, whose eyes are puffy red and his cheeks drenched with tears. "Don't worry, boy. I always save my best two licks for the grand finale. Now bend that big ass over again."

Oaf sniffles as he places his hands on his knees for the fifth time. I glance over at Peaches and find him already watching me. He smirks and raises his eyebrows up and down. I'd think the same if I were him. Just one lick away from winning the easiest bet ever.

I smile back at him and wink. Peaches' smug grin fades from his face. He tilts his head and squints at me, like he's just figured out I'm up to something. Well, you'll find out soon enough, Peach. It's about to happen!

Ignoring a few muttered threats, I force my way to the front of the crowd before Brother James sets himself for the fifth lick. I shift my weight to my toes and lean forward in preparation. My heart pounds like a bass drum. My eyes stay glued on Brother James, trying to gauge my timing as he steps up behind Oaf. The moment he draws back his paddle, I rush forward.

Oaf has no idea. His eyes are squeezed shut as the paddle whistles toward his ass. He flinches right on cue, arching his back as another *thwack* echoes off the walls, and leaving his groin fully exposed as I drive my foot into his testicles, soccer style. A kick timed to perfection!

Big dumb Oaf squeals like a wild hog. His hands shoot straight to his crotch as he doubles over and slumps to the floor in a giant heap. I stand over him as he writhes in agony, sobbing like a small child. Finally, sweet, sweet revenge!

The dining hall erupts with manic laughter. I glance around. Everyone is in hysterics, hooting and hollering as they scramble forward for a closer view of Oaf's misery. Alvaro slaps me on the back, tears trickling down his cheeks as he congratulates me in Spanish. Benny and Lucas both high five me. Even Brother James wipes his eyes while he chuckles away.

He catches me looking at him, and I smile and shrug my shoulders. "How many?" I ask him, as he walks my way.

Brother James grins and glances down at Oaf. "I'll give you two," he says. "Plus the one he never got."

Three licks? Beyond worth it! I take all three without complaint. No flinching. No yelping. Like a lick-taking pro! The moment Brother James leaves the dining room, I march over to Oaf and point my finger in his big, dumb face.

"I'll take three licks everyday for kicking you in the nuts. Three licks is a fucking bargain!"

Oaf says nothing, but the rest of the guys are in full-on party mode. My fellow inmates thoroughly approve. I walk away feeling six inches taller, pausing for fist bumps and high fives along the way.

I know that I probably shouldn't feel proud about this, but I do. And I don't feel the slightest bit bad about it either. Oaf is by far the biggest piece of shit in this place. Just ask anyone. And seeing as he punched me in the face, it was time to send him a message of my own.

Well, message delivered, and everyone was there to witness it. I also won my bet with Peaches in the process. Revenge topped with a sprinkle of sweet victory. A feeling I'm going to savor for as long as I can.

25

MIDNIGHT WITH METALLICA GIRL

Saturday, May 19, 1990 - Day 49

I t feels like the past week dragged on for an eternity. A trail of storms rolled in during school on Monday morning, thundering nonstop through Thursday evening. This meant no sports, of course—even today the fields are far too flooded. My only option is to stay cooped up in The Dorm, counting the minutes until I can hang out with Mary Grace again.

I don't have much longer to wait now, but it feels as if the past few hours have moved as slowly as the last seven days. Whenever I check the alarm clock, it seems stuck at the same time. I could swear those red lights have flashed 11:57 for nearly five minutes now!

At least tonight I don't have to pretend to be asleep. I used my feud with Oaf as an excuse to bunk with Shane and Molloy for a few nights, which should help me avoid Angelo's disapproval for the time being as well. The three of us sit silently on our beds, waiting in the darkness of the dorm. After what feels like hours instead of minutes, Shane finally signals it's time to go.

Before long, we're trekking along the pitch-black road again. Shane and Molloy chat back and forth, but I'm too deep in my own head to talk right now. I fall a few steps behind them and follow in silence. Every thought and emotion revolves around Mary Grace. Each stride leads me closer to her company.

My insides tingle as I imagine her waiting by the discarded, old pickup: tall, pale, and slender, her dark hair flowing freely as she curls a strand around her finger. I must have reflected on last weekend a thousand times since we parted ways. Our encounter was far too brief. We mostly talked about me, which was fine and all. I completely get why she would be curious. But I realize I'm now ravenously curious about her, too.

My head swarms with questions I'm desperate to ask her. She said she knew how it felt to be stuck where you don't want to be. What did she mean by that? Where is she from and how come she can't be there anymore? Why does a badass metalhead like her have to pretend to be something she's not? And that's just the tip of the iceberg.

As we draw closer to our meeting place, the questions yield way to worrying she won't show up. I saw Mary Grace at church on Sunday and Wednesday, but we never spoke. She never even looked at me. So there was no way to confirm if she's coming or not. I considered slipping her a note again to ask, but I'm bound to have eyes on me after what happened before.

By the time we reach the field and climb the cattle gate, I'm grimacing from the sheer suspense of it all. But when the old pickup emerges into view, there she is. Mary Grace sits on the wooden flatbed beside Brandy and Brandi, awaiting our arrival.

My arrival. My heart prances wildly in my chest. Keep it together, Will. Keep it together.

"Hey!" I call out to her, waving awkwardly as I approach. "Good to see you again." Did that sound lame? It felt lame. Molloy's smirking at me, so it was definitely lame. Shit! I wait until we're closer and clear my throat to try again.

"Good thing it finally stopped raining, huh?" Dammit! That sounded equally as lame. Lamer even. I wish Shane and Molloy would just hurry off into the woods and quit staring at me with those stupid grins on their faces.

"Will's already whipped," Molloy mutters, nudging Shane on the arm with his elbow. He winks at me. "That didn't take long. You must have a thing for tall chicks."

"It's good to see you too, Will," Mary Grace intervenes, as I fight back my blushes. She stands up and folds her arms across her chest. Shane and Molloy seem to take this as their cue to get on with their own business and join up with Brandy and Brandi before slipping away.

Mary Grace smiles at me, those pale eyes of hers sparkling in the moonlight. "It's kind of hilarious how awkward you are around those guys. What's up with that?"

I smile back and shrug. "Life is awkward, right? I think someone once told me that. Happy to entertain you, though."

Her face lights up, and she giggles. "Well, at least you pay attention to the things I tell you. You definitely win points for that."

Score! "Speaking of which, though," I say, grasping at the opportunity. "You didn't really tell me much before we ran out of time. I think I did most of the talking."

"Ah, so it's my turn tonight." Mary Grace shoots me a teasing look. "Is that where you're going with this?"

"Well, you had your questions, and I have mine, so..." I raise my brows, and Mary Grace chews on her bottom lip.

"Fair enough," she says, and exaggerates a sigh. "Let's sit down, though. My feet hurt from walking here."

My feet ache as well. I join her by the truck, and lower myself onto the wooden flatbed next to her. Mary Grace shifts around to face me, crossing one long leg over the other in the process.

"Okay," she says, sporting another playful grin. "What are you itching to know about plain, old me?"

I resist telling her she's neither plain nor old. I've sounded like an awkward idiot quite enough for one night. As to what I'm "itching" to ask her, those questions have melted from my mind for the time being. All I can do is gaze at Mary Grace and inhale the sight of her. Tall and slender. Dark hair and alabaster skin. The vibrant gleam of her pale-blue eyes. Her pink lips curved into a smile.

As I lower my eyes, her t-shirt snags my attention. It looks eerily familiar. I lean forward to peer at it, and my eyes spring wide open.

"Holy shit!" I exclaim, followed by a splutter of laughter.

Mary Grace's eyes dart from mine to her shirt. "What?" she asks, squinting down at it.

I shake my head in disbelief. I would recognize that t-shirt anywhere. A black concert tee with *Metallica* in purple script above a huge skull that has a fist punching out of its forehead. Beneath that, in smaller purple font, it reads *Damaged Justice*. The name of the tour they were on when I snuck out to see them last August. The very same t-shirt I was arrested for trying to steal.

"What?" Mary Grace repeats.

"Nothing," I say. "Just checking out your badass shirt. Is there anything on the back?"

"Thanks," she says, twisting around to show me. Sure enough, there is the tour list. The exact same t-shirt. Crazy!

"You saw them on that tour?" I ask.

Mary Grace frowns and shakes her head. "I wish! My brother, Sam, bought me this shirt. He saw them three times last year. Once in New Orleans, once in Shreveport, and then he saw them again in Biloxi because The Cult was opening."

Memories flood back to me. "That was their second US tour that year," I say. "That's when I saw them back in Atlanta."

Mary Grace's eyes widen. "You've seen them? I am so stinking jealous! Was it amazing?"

I laugh nervously, thinking about how that evening ended. "Well, I had to sneak out of the house to go, but, yeah, both sets were awesome. The Cult were killer, but Metallica tore the place down."

Mary Grace sighs. "I doubt I would've had the guts to sneak out like you, but I wish I could have been there. Someday maybe."

"Your brother wouldn't take you with him?"

"Sam? Oh no, it was my mom who wouldn't let me go. Well, my stepdad really. Sam was hellbent on smuggling me out the house so I could go."

"Sounds like a cool brother," I say.

"He's the best," Mary Grace mutters solemnly. "But I don't get to see him much anymore. Not since we moved here."

She fingers the pendant on her necklace for a moment and her eyes brighten up again. "I bet you would love Sam, though. He has his own metal band back home in New Orleans. Sam's the bass player, but he writes a bunch of their songs too. They're really good, and Sam says they've been talking to a couple of labels about a record deal. I think they might actually make it!"

"That's badass!" This chick just keeps getting cooler. "What's the name of his band?"

"They're called Executive Anarchy." Mary Grace beams with pride. "Their songs are pretty political, but they hit hard. Sam says they're trying to call attention to all of the corrupt shit the government does around the world. He and the other guys get riled up about that stuff."

"Sounds good to me," I say. "Cool name, too. Definitely metal. Do you have a tape of their songs? I would love to check them out sometime."

"Sure! I have a copy of their demo tape at home. I'll bring it with me next time. Oh, that reminds me." Mary Grace unfolds her long legs and hops to her feet. She walks up to the driver-side door of the truck and yanks at the handle. The door screeches open and she leans inside to grab something. A bag of some kind. She loops the strap over her shoulder and shoves the door shut.

"I brought you some gifts," she says, flashing a mischievous smile as walks back and settles next to me on the flatbed again. Removing the strap from her shoulder, Mary Grace places a brown leather handbag on her lap and unfastens the flap. Her eyes sparkle with excitement as she reaches inside and pulls out a sealed pack of Camel Filters.

My eyes bulge. "You got these for me?"

Her pale cheeks tinge with color. "Of course." She hands me the pack of smokes, which I gratefully accept. "I hope they're the right kind. I asked Brandy what to get, so it's her fault if not."

"Any kind is the right kind," I tell her. "Being picky isn't a luxury I have anymore. But, seriously, this means a lot. Thank you, Mary Grace."

Mary Grace curls a finger through her hair. "You're welcome, Will."

For a few thumping heartbeats, we lock eyes and everything else ceases to exist. My skin tingles and my heartbeat quickens. A thousand thoughts and urges swarm my head. Most of all, though, I feel an overwhelming sense of gratitude. A part of me wants to embrace Mary Grace with a kiss. The rest of me wants to wrap my arms around her and cry.

I do neither, and after a few seconds, Mary Grace lowers her eyes from mine and opens her bag again. "I really am being forgetful today," she mutters, rummaging right down to the bottom. "There they are." She produces a small box of matches and hands it over. "You'll probably be needing those. And I brought you this, as well."

Mary Grace removes a Walkman and headphones out of her handbag and sets them between us on the wooden flatbed. "It's my old one," she says. "You can keep it for now if you like. I just changed out the batteries, but I'll bring you more next time in case they run out. There's a mixtape I made inside. Metallica mostly, of course, but there's some Slayer and some Anthrax on there too."

Once again, all I can do is stare at her incredulously. Smokes, matches, and music. How can she like me this much? And a mixtape with Metallica, Slayer, and Anthrax? How can she possibly be real?

Mary Grace looks like she might be wondering the same. "You okay?" she asks.

"Yeah, I'm just..." I stare at the Walkman and the pack of Camel Filters, and shake my head. "I don't know what to say. This is...this is the nicest thing anyone's done for me in a hell of a long time. It probably doesn't seem like much to you, but it means a whole lot more than you can imagine, trust me."

Mary Grace's cheeks darken a shade, but she manages a bashful smile before breaking her gaze from mine again. An awkward silence follows. I tear open the pack of smokes and pop one between my lips. I'm about to strike a match when Mary Grace shifts a couple of inches closer to me on the flatbed of the truck.

"Could I have one of those, too?" she asks, as I turn her way.

"Sure!" I say, swallowing my surprise. "You're the one who paid for them. Have as many as you want."

I only add the last part because I'm certain she won't want another, but I still feel a snag of irritation as I slide one from the pack and pass it to Mary Grace. She presses the cigarette between her lips, and I spark a match and hold out the flame. Her face illuminates as she leans forward to light it. The moment she draws a breath, she hacks it out again in a series of smoky coughs.

"Holy shit! You okay?" I pat her on the back, trying not to laugh while she coughs her lungs up.

After a minute or so, Mary Grace appears to have shaken it off. She wipes the water from her eyes and releases a long sigh. "Well, that was embarrassing."

"Was that your first time smoking?" I ask, before taking a drag of my own cigarette.

She nods. "I guess that was obvious, huh? Well, it's even more disgusting than I imagined. I feel a little lightheaded, actually."

"That's pretty normal," I tell her. "It'll wear off in a minute or so. Do you still want this?" I pick up her cigarette, which she dropped on the ground when she started coughing. It's basically whole.

She raises her brows and shakes her head. "Absolutely not! Sorry for wasting it, though."

"Oh, it's not wasted," I tell her. "Don't you worry about that." I stub it out and slot it back inside the pack.

Mary Grace slides off a hairband from around her wrist. Gripping it between her teeth, she pulls her hair into a ponytail and ties it tightly into place. My mind wanders as I watch her. Wandering and wondering. She is certainly a puzzle, nothing like the girls I know back home. Nothing like anyone I know.

As if on cue, Mary Grace shifts back against the truck's cab and pulls her long legs to her chest. I haven't asked her what I intended to yet, but I realize she's given me more than enough to work with so far. She referred to New Orleans as "home." Her big brother, Sam, still lives there. He's obviously special to Mary Grace. She never said this outright, but her adoration radiated through every mention of him and his band. It was obviously Sam who introduced Mary Grace to metal and inspired her love of music.

"So," I say, breaking the silence, "how come you're having Mardi Gras here instead of back home?"

Mary Grace clenches her jaw and sighs. "Two words," she says. "Douchebag Dave."

"What?" I chuckle. "You sure that's not three?"

Mary Grace snickers. "Yes, I'm perfectly sure. It's the name I secretly christened my stepdad. His real name is David Goode, but Douchebag Dave is a way better fit. Even if it does feel too nice for him sometimes."

I stub out my cigarette and spark up the one Mary Grace took a drag on. "So what's his deal, other than being a douchebag that is? Did he grow up around here or something and that's why you moved?"

"No, he's from somewhere in Indiana, originally. Someplace small and shitty where they raise douchebags, I suppose."

I crack up. "Sounds like Nowhere, Mississippi to me! No wonder he wanted to move here."

"Well, technically we live in Petal, but they're one and the same if you ask me." Mary Grace pauses, a frown creasing her forehead. "We moved here because Douchebag Dave decided to transfer to Fort Shelby. And when I say he decided, that's exactly what I mean. He came home from the Naval base one day and told us we were leaving New Orleans, just like that. No conversation with my mom, his wife. No consideration about how I might feel, a teenage girl who'd lived there her entire life, leaving everyone but her mother behind."

Mary Grace's eyes well with tears, but she sets her jaw and wipes them dry. "But that's Douchebag Dave for you. He lives his life by the word of the King James Bible. The husband leads his family, the wife serves her husband, and all that shit. From the moment my mom married that asshole, he's controlled every part of our lives."

I nod solemnly. "I'm guessing he's the reason I see you at church."

"Yep! And you know what the crazy part is? He doesn't even go with us. He preaches at the base on Sundays and sleeps there Monday through Thursday. The fact he's hardly around is the one saving grace I have."

"Why did your mom marry this guy if he's such a prick?"

Mary Grace sighs, a small frown upon her face. "I ask myself the same thing all the time. Sam thinks it's because Dad and Dave are total opposites. Dad is pretty much everything Dave despises and vice versa, which makes sense because Dave hates New Orleans for the same reasons Dad loves it. I guess Mom felt like trying something different, but she wound up getting a different type of shitty. Being bad husbands is pretty much the only thing they've got in common."

She pauses to swat a mosquito on her leg and twirls a finger through her hair again. "It's not like my dad's a terrible person or anything like that," she explains. "He's not manipulative and controlling like Dave is. He never tries to control anything. Mom says that was his biggest problem. No self control whatsoever. She calls him a wanderer. Says that's just how he's made, and he wasn't made for marriage. Dave calls him a hedonist, which isn't entirely inaccurate. But Dave also says he's plagued with demons and a slave to sin, so it's hard to take the guy seriously."

"Sounds like Douchebag Dave needs a job at Victory Ridge," I say. "Do you talk to your dad much?"

"Every now and again." Mary Grace forces a melancholy smile. "He's a jazz musician in New Orleans, so he works late and sleeps late. He calls from time to time. Whenever he stops wandering for a moment."

I stand up to stretch and lower myself down again. "Sounds like music runs in the family," I say, tapping the ash from my cigarette. "What instrument does he play?"

"The French horn." Mary Grace stifles a yawn. "But he isn't in a band like Sam. He's more like a freelance musician. Other bands will hire him for studio work or gigs around New Orleans. He's worked with a bunch of famous musicians and singers over the years, like Charles Lloyd, Art Blakeley, Irma Thomas, Pete Fountain. He even got to play a few shows with James Booker before he passed away."

I squint at her. "I've never heard of them. My dad isn't into jazz. He used to play Juice Newton records around the house, so you can see why I turned to metal."

"*Juice Newton*!?" Mary Grace snorts out laughter. "Who the hell is *he*?"

I chuckle along with her. "I think you mean who the hell is *she*?"

"What!?" Mary Grace's eyes widen, and she rolls onto her side in hysterics. "Please tell me you're kidding?"

"I'm not," I tell her, trying to stay straight-faced even though I'm speaking the truth. "Juice Newton is actually quite a famous country singer. My dad loves her."

"I don't believe you. You're totally making this up."

"Nope. I wish I was, though. Her songs sound like ass! But I bet you've heard at least one of them before."

"Okay, then." Mary Grace narrows her eyes mischievously. "How about you sing it to me and I'll tell you if you're right?"

"You're kidding?"

"No, no, no! If you weren't kidding, then I'm not either. Let's hear it."

"This is pointless. You know this song already. Everyone does. It's called Angel of the Morning." I start humming the melody of the chorus.

"Hmm, it doesn't sound familiar at all." A smile twitches at the corners of Mary Grace's mouth. "Looks like you're going to have to sing it for me."

"No way. I'm a lousy singer. You don't wanna hear it, trust me."

"Oh yes, I do! C'mon, Will." Mary Grace leans closer as she speaks, her tone playfully imploring. "Look at all this stuff I brought you. It's just one song."

"Fine," I huff, "but I'm only singing the chorus." I clear my throat and draw a breath. *"Don't call me angel in the morning, angel."* Mary Grace covers her mouth with her hands, muffling her laughter. *"Just touch my cheek before you lea*....Okay, that's enough. You totally know that song."

"I totally do," Mary Grace says, her face bright red from laughing. "I had no idea who sang it, though, I swear. You were right about that. I doubt I'll ever forget who Juice Newton is, thanks to you."

"You are very welcome," I say, sarcastically. "Now, how about you sing me some James Booger or whatever he's called."

"James Booker." Mary Grace shakes her head at me. "Not going to happen, but maybe I'll make you a mixtape one day. He's probably the most talented piano player to ever come out of New Orleans. When I was younger, my dad made me listen to his records before he took me to my piano lessons. Yes, I used to play piano. Not very metal, I know.

"So music really does run in the family, huh?"

"Not with me," she says, with a chuckle. "I never had much

of a talent for it. Anyway, I haven't played in years. Not since Dad left us."

"Left you?" I say, thinking of my mother and the way she left us. Lost forever.

"Yes, left us. As in he walked out on my mom and me to be with another woman. A lounge singer named Ariel. Yes, like the fucking mermaid! Can you believe that? And now here I am, three years later, stuck in the sphincter of Mississippi with Douchebag Dave and all of his Bible-bashing bullshit. Life really sucks sometimes, doesn't it?"

Sometimes? "More than it should," I say, feeling a heaviness in my heart. "I'm sorry things turned out the way they did for you, Mary Grace. I'm sorry for both of us. This might sound like a dumb thing to say, but at least you still have music. As long as you have that, you have a way to escape. Something that connects you to where you want to be. To your dad and Sam. Music was all I had after my mom's accident. I don't know what I would've done without it."

Empathy radiates from Mary Grace's expression. "That doesn't sound dumb at all, Will. In fact, that's probably the sweetest thing anyone's said to me in a long time. And I promise you, for however long we're friends, I'll make sure you have music too. I mean, didn't I already? We should listen to some before someone gets mauled by ants again."

"Sounds good to me," I say, picking up the Walkman. "So, I've been meaning to ask. Is *And Justice for All* your favorite album, or do you hide other cassette sleeves in your Bible?"

Mary Grace giggles. "*And Justice for All* isn't even my favorite Metallica album. I mean, it's a great record and all, and *Harvester of Sorrow* is a killer song, but there's no way it's their best album."

I nod, genuinely impressed. "*One*, might be my favorite Metallica song right now, but I agree with you. What would you say is their best album then?"

"What do you think I would say?" Mary Grace fires back. "I'll give you one guess."

So now we're both testing one another, huh? "Okay, I'll go with *Master of Puppets*."

She grins at me. "Nice try, but for me it's *Ride the Lightning* all the way."

"I can't argue with that choice," I say, losing myself in her eyes for a moment. I shake it off and hold out the headphones. "Want to share?"

"Of course!" Mary Grace nods enthusiastically, and shifts closer until we're sitting side-by-side, our shoulders touching. "I'm exhausted," she says. "Do you mind if we lie back while we listen?"

"Sure," I say, with more composure than I feel.

My pulse gallops as we stretch back on the wooden flatbed of the old pickup. Mary Grace yawns next to me, which sets me off as well. After a few moments of shifting around to get comfortable, I feel fatigue set in as the adrenaline drains out. For the remainder of our time together, we gaze up at the starry night sky and listen to Metallica. Together, we escape into our music.

26

RUNNING NOWHERE

Friday, May 25 - Day 55

We've just returned to the dorm after dinner when Trenton sprints along the hallway voicing the alarm.

"RUNNER! WE'VE GOT A RUNNER!"

Heads poke out of doorways on all sides of the hallway.

"Who?" someone calls out. "Who ran?"

Their question is passed up the line, and the answer sent back is loud and clear.

"Mooney!"

Carl Mooney, the new kid. He's not your average new kid, though. Mooney arrived on Wednesday, attempted to set the dorm on fire on Thursday, and was placed on watch this morning by Brother Bennett. It's safe to say he's made quite the entrance for himself, and now he's making quite a show of his exit as well. His attempted one, anyway.

"I knew he was gonna run," says Peaches, pushing me

forward so that we're following the pack. "That new boy's about as country as they get. You never know, he might just get away."

"Wanna bet on that, Peach?" I ask.

Peaches shakes his head. "I ain't bettin' on that."

No one loves a bet more than him, but he's heard the same stories I have. Try to run away, and Brother Bennett will hunt you down.

Outside the main building, the chase is on. Boys scatter in all directions across the property, calling out to one another, their voices amped with adrenaline. It looks as though Peaches and I are the last to join the hunt.

"That way!" Peaches points towards a group of guys running into the woods behind the schoolhouse.

We start off in their direction, but come to halt as Brother Bennett's truck roars up the gravel road and grinds to a halt behind us.

"Which way did that boy run?" Brother Bennett yells, leaning his head out the driver side window.

"We don't know, sir," I say. "We didn't see. But most of the other boys ran that way." I point toward the woods on the far side of the property.

Brother Bennett locks me in a cold, unyielding stare. "Get up on the back." He gestures to the bed of his truck. "NOW!"

"Yes, sir," we say at once, jolting into action at his command.

I place my foot on the bumper and hop over the tailgate into the bed of the truck. Peaches clambers in after me, and Brother Bennett stomps on the gas. The tires spin up a cloud of dust and the truck lurches forward and accelerates down the driveway. Brother Bennett shifts through the gears, taking a hard right onto the main road that sends Peaches and me slamming into one another.

"YELL IF Y'ALL SEE SOMETHING!" he hollers back at us.

I try to keep an eye on each side of the road, fields to my left and woods to my right. But we speed by so quickly that everything is a blur. Suddenly, Brother Bennett slams on the brakes, and Peaches and I pitch forward into the back of the cab. He swerves onto the narrow dirt road that runs behind our property. The very one Shane, Molloy, and I use when we sneak out. The truck shudders along the rutted surface, flinging Peaches and me around like we're being yucked.

"HOLD ON TIGHT!" Brother Bennett yells back at us.

Yeah, no shit!

Sliding my hands up the back of the truck's cabin, I grip the top edge and adjust my feet until I'm facing forward. Feeling a sudden surge of boldness, I steady myself and stand all the way up. Wind whips through my hair, and I smile at the thrill of it. For a few seconds, I almost forget why we're out here. And then something darts across the road up ahead. No, not something. *Someone.*

Carl Mooney!

"THERE!" I scream, but Brother Bennett is already stomping on the brakes as we skid to a stop.

Peaches vaults over the side, and I follow after him. The two of us take off in the direction Mooney ran. We charge into the woods, hurdling roots and ducking under branches. I peer between columns of trees for another glimpse of him, but he's nowhere to be seen. I can hear voices behind us; the others are in pursuit as well. All of us are hot on Mooney's trail, hunting him down.

Peaches and I venture further into the woods. Crossing a small stream, adrenaline spikes through me as I spy movement up ahead. A silhouette darts across the top of a small ridge and disappears behind a tree.

"OVER THERE!" I shriek, pointing as I rush forward.

Cresting the ridge, we spot Mooney again, up ahead, zipping between the trees like a deer. But before I can open my mouth to alert the others, he's gone again. I pause to catch my breath, clasping my hands behind my head.

"That boy can run!" Peaches jogs up, panting. "Which way did he go?"

"That way." I point towards the sector of trees where I last glimpsed Mooney. "He's heading that way."

Peaches peers up ahead, squinting. "Well, I don't know what you're stoppin' for. This here is *fun!* Let's go!"

He takes off again, and I hurry to catch up, pulling past him and leading the charge. We reach the area I last saw him and tear on through. There are no signs of movement up ahead, but the woods are thinning out. As we advance further, we pass a red sign nailed to a tree. Bold white letters inform us that we're on "PRIVATE PROPERTY" with "NO TRESPASSING" written underneath.

We glance at one another and continue on, picking our way through more cautiously. But the woods lead us to a clearing and towards a tall, wooden fence. The flattened roofs of two mobile homes rise up behind it. And there is Carl Mooney, leaping up to grab the top of the fence and scrambling up the side.

"THERE HE IS!" I yell.

Mooney pauses near the top and jerks his head around to look at us. My pulse drumming, I thrust myself into action. So too does Mooney, swinging his legs over the fence and dropping out of sight.

His disappearance triggers an outbreak of savage barking from beyond the fence that sounds like Mooney is being ripped apart by a pack of wolves. I pull up short, frozen in place as Peaches rushes past me.

"C'mon!" he yells. "We're gonna lose him!"

"I can't," I mutter, but my words are swallowed by the feral frenzy of barking and growling. How many dogs are behind that fence? Three? Five? What does it matter? Even one dog is one too many for me. But Peaches is already halfway up the fence.

"C'mon, Will. He's gettin' away!"

My feet feel too heavy to budge. All I can do is watch as Peaches reaches the top of the fence and peers over the other side. And listen as the barking shifts in his direction.

"Shit!" Peaches yelps, and leaps back down. A second later, the fence shudders in front of him as the snarling mob of dogs claw at it from the other side, their growls reverberating through the wooden planks.

"There's no fucking way I'm going in there!" I inform Peaches.

"No shit!" he replies. "I ain't messin' with no rabbit dogs."

"I think you mean 'rabid', Peach. Come on, let's get the hell out of here."

He nods, and we turn back toward the woods.

"I knew I shoulda took that bet," Peaches says, as we retrace our path between the trees. "Told ya he'd get away."

"I'm pretty sure you said he 'might'. And just because he got away from us, doesn't mean someone else won't catch him. Either way, we should get our stories straight before we show up empty-handed. If Brother Bennett asks, we never saw Mooney again after he crossed the road. We searched everywhere we could, but we couldn't find him. That's the safest story to tell."

Peaches nods in agreement, and we wind our way through the woods towards the dirt road where Brother Bennett stopped his truck. When we reach it, however, his truck is nowhere in sight.

Peaches glances around. "You sure this is the right spot?"

I nod. "Yep."

"Well, shit!" Peaches peers up and down the road. "Did everyone go back already, or are they still out lookin'? Should we just go back? I don't even know where the hell we are, and it's gonna get dark before long."

I gaze down the dirt path towards the main road.

"Relax, Peach," I tell him. "I know the way back."

———

SHADES OF PINK and purple mingle above the horizon, darkening into an indigo sky as we march up the driveway towards the dorm. We're not the first to arrive back at Victory Ridge. In fact, most of the boys have already returned. According to Shane, Trent and Jerry, the two Trusted Boys who were in charge of watching Carl Mooney, are still out on the hunt with Brother Bennett.

Everyone else is hanging around outside the dorm, watching for the flash of headlights that will signal their return. Wagers are being exchanged as to whether or not Mooney will be with them, and a confident Peaches is making full use of his insider knowledge. That scheming little fucker is going to clean house with these fools, but I'll make sure he pays for my silence.

About an hour later, a set of headlights emerge from the darkness, weaving along the driveway towards us. Brother Bennett's truck rumbles up and grinds to a stop on the gravel next to the porch. The driver side door flings open, and Brother Bennett steps out. He slams it shut with so much force the entire vehicle shudders. Judging by that, and the somber expressions Trent and Jerry wear when they emerge from the back, things did not go so well. And Carl Mooney's absence is glaring.

Angelo appears next to me, his eyes on the scene before us.

"I thought Bounty Hunter Bennett always gets his guy," I mutter.

Angelo glances at me. "Not yet," he says dryly. "But we were the ones out hunting, bro. Now he's gotta handle it himself. He'll make a few calls and get eyes on the lookout. Mooney won't get far before Bennett drags his ass back here. You'll see."

"EVERYONE INSIDE" Brother Bennett hollers as the crowd parts to make way for him. "NOW!"

Everyone jumps into action, bumping into one another as we try to file inside at the same time. We pack into the dining hall and fill the benches along the tables. Brother Bennett paces between them, the room silent but for the thudding of his boots. Trent and Jerry are the only others standing. Their eyes shift uneasily around the room.

Brother Bennett stops a few yards in front of them and adjusts his black cowboy hat. He eyes them coldly. "I gave y'all an important job this morning." His deep drawl resounds throughout the dining hall. "And I remember being crystal clear about what I expected y'all to do, am I right?"

"Yes, sir," Trent and Jerry swiftly respond.

"And what did I tell you, Jeremy?"

"T-to...to not let the new boy out of our sights," Jerry stammers in response. "In case...in case he tries to run."

Brother Bennett clenches his jaw and nods slowly. "That's right. And I said y'all better keep a real good eye on this one. 'Cause that ain't just any ol' new boy, son. That little son-of-a-bitch tried to burn down my school! And now he's out there running wild because of y'all!"

Brother Bennett strides forward and grabs Jerry by the front of his shirt, twisting it in his grip as he yanks Jerry towards him.

"So how about you explain something to me now, son?" he growls as Jerry trembles in his clutches. "If it was y'all's job to watch that boy like a hawk, how come he got away like that? How come he had enough time to get away from every single one of y'all in here?"

"He was using the bathroom," Jerry hurriedly explains. "We...we were waiting outside the door. He must've gone out the window."

Smack!

The slap echoes out, and Jerry staggers backwards, his shirt still gripped by Brother Bennett, who reels back his hand and delivers another. Jerry groans as he's pulled upright, his left cheek crimson red.

"Of course he did!" Brother Bennett snarls at him. "If y'all can't see him, then y'all ain't watching him. He can do what he likes!"

He yanks Jerry towards him by his shirt and shoves him to the floor, where he collapses in a heap.

"Get up, boy!"

Jerry scrambles to his feet and is sent crashing back down again.

"Get up!"

Jerry complies, and Brother Bennett grabs him and dishes out another round of knee-buckling slaps before turning his attention to Trent.

"So, how long did y'all wait outside that bathroom before going to check on him?"

Quivering, Trent clears his throat. "Five minutes, sir. Maybe ten. I ain't sure."

"You *ain't sure*!?" Brother Bennett grabs him by the collar and connects a vicious slap.

A minute later, Trent joins Jerry on the floor, red-cheeked and slumped with defeat. Both of them well and truly yucked. Brother Bennett pulls a handkerchief from his pocket, lifts up his hat, and wipes a layer of sweat from his forehead.

"As for the rest of y'all," he says, addressing the room. "Seems y'all could use some help getting in shape for the next time this happens. We had over twenty-five boys in those woods and not one of y'all could catch him. Looks like all my boys are gonna be runners tonight. Get outside and line up on the driveway. Now!"

For the next hour, we run up and down the long, steep driveway to the main road, over and over again. Everyone is out to supervise: Brother Bennett, Brother James, Robbie, even Miss Tammy waddles out of her trailer to watch us toil through our punishment. When Brother Bennett finally calls it a night, we're all sent straight to our rooms sore and sweaty. No showers, just lights out.

"I just can't believe it," Peaches says lying in bed, after

Brother James and Robbie finish checking the rooms one last time.

"Believe what?" Angelo asks.

"That Mooney actually got away. It's kind of cool."

"You're wrong about that, Peach," Angelo says. "Actually, you're wrong about both those things."

"Oh, yeah!" Peaches fires back. "How do you figure?"

"Well, for one, Mooney might have gotten away from *us*, but that doesn't mean he's getting away from Bennett. He'll have people on the lookout, trust me. He doesn't mess around with this shit. What happened isn't cool at all. Bennett will call a lockdown tomorrow. I guarantee it. Wanna bet against me, Peach?"

Peaches stays silent. Angelo's been here longer than Peaches, Oaf, and me combined. He never makes bets unless he knows he's going to win.

"What's a lockdown?" I ask.

"You'll see."

27

LOCKDOWN

Wednesday, May 30 - Day 60

Just as Angelo predicted, a lockdown was announced during breakfast last Saturday, and it doesn't appear to be ending anytime soon. For the past five days, this place has functioned like a prison instead of the miserable madhouse I've grown to know and despise. And right now everyone misses the madhouse because a lockdown is like turning the heat up in Hell.

As I've come to learn, the purpose of a lockdown is to strip away the few pitiful privileges we have left. No passes into town for the older boys, no phone calls for anyone, no visits into town, no free time, no sports, but lots of random running. To top it off, trips to church are now suspended until further notice.

Under normal circumstances, this would have felt like a perk, not a punishment. But it means my access to Mary Grace is now completely cut off. I can't even smuggle her a note to tell her what's going on, and Shane pulled the plug on sneaking out again as soon as the lockdown was announced. He and Molloy both agreed that it would be far too risky, which is saying a lot. Better to wait it out than to throw it all away by getting caught when the spotlights are on us.

So it's now been a week and a half since I last saw Mary Grace. For the past week and a half, all I've thought about was the way her fingers grazed against mine while we laid on the bed of the truck listening to Metallica. I've spent hours overanalyzing this moment ever since that night, and I think I've finally reached a conclusion. Mary Grace wanted to hold my hand, but she wasn't sure if I wanted to hold hers, even though I did. And all the while, I was wondering the exact same thing about her. Next time will be different. Whenever there finally is one.

———

"GOOD NEWS OR BAD NEWS?" Shane asks, after pulling me aside during lunch.

I shrug. "Good news?"

"I'm going to church tonight," Shane says. "Molloy is too."

My hopes lift ever so slightly. This could mean the lockdown is coming to an end.

"Okay. So what's the bad news?"

"You'll be staying right fucking here tonight." Shane burst out laughing as my shoulders slump. I should have seen that coming, but I can't seem to stop myself from hoping.

"C'mon, Will!" Shane slaps me on the shoulder. "Quit your Eeyore shit and lighten the hell up! I'm just giving you a heads up in case you wanna pass a note along to you-know-who. I can give it to Brandi tonight if you get it to me before the end of dinner."

As soon as I finish cleanup duty, I hurry back to the schoolhouse to finish up my workbooks, but I end up scrawling out several drafts of a letter until I feel satisfied with the results.

Dear Mary Grace,

Sorry I wasn't able to hang last weekend. I wanted to drop you a note to let you know what's going on because shit got kind of nuts over here. Basically, this new kid showed up last week and tried to burn down the dorm with a lighter and a can of hairspray! He managed to set part of the ceiling on fire, but it didn't do much damage. Anyway, Brother Bennett put him on watch, but he snuck away from the two guys who were watching him and ran off into the woods. All of us were sent out to chase after him, but he ended up getting away, and we all got in trouble for not catching him. Crazy, right? Such bullshit!

Brother Bennett went psycho after that and banned pretty much everything, even though he found the kid two days later and brought him back. Anyway, that's why I couldn't sneak out last Saturday and why none of us have been to church. Shane and Molloy just found out they can go tonight, so hopefully things are starting to settle down, and I can sneak out again on Saturday. I hope I can, and I hope you're doing well.

See you soon,

Will

P.S. Thanks again for the Walkman and the tape you made. You are seriously the best! I haven't had a chance to listen to it since we hung out, but Shane got me some Tupperware from the kitchen pantry, and we put everything inside then buried it in the woods. I'll dig it up whenever we sneak out again, but it's safe for now.

Good enough, and at this point, it will have to do. I fold the letter several times, slide it into the back pocket of my jeans, and finish filling in the answers to my math packet. I'm halfway through my English work when Robbie runs into the schoolhouse and straight over to Brother James. Robbie leans in to tell him something, and Brother James's eyebrows jump upwards. He hops to his feet and clears his throat.

"Y'all stop workin' an' listen up." He paces around the center of the schoolhouse, shoulders set back, chest puffed outward. "Hey! I said listen up! Angelo, put your shit down and pay attention. Eyes on me, son!"

I glance across the room at the other boys. Their expressions reflect my own thoughts. *Who is this guy, and what happened to Brother James?* He prowls the room with an intensity that snares my attention, a complete contrast to his usual attitude of indifference.

"Seems we've got ourselves a baseball game." Brother James eyeballs us as he swaggers into the center of the room. "Friday the 8th against Calvary Christian."

"Those bitches from Biloxi?" Molloy yells out. "Those guys sucked ass last year! We beat them by eight runs. We're gonna absolutely destroy..."

"Different team, different year, son," Brother James hollers over him. "And for all y'all too stupid to figure it out, Friday the 8th is right round the corner. We've only got nine days to get ourselves ready, so we ain't got time to talk about last year's game. We ain't got time to think about it, neither. We gotta make good use of the time we've got and make sure we whoop their asses again when they show up at the ballfield in Petal. That's our fuckin' house! Y'all hear me?"

"Yes, sir!" I say, in unison with everyone else.

"Good!" Brother James nods and claps his hands together. "Make sure y'all remember that. 'Cause when we step on that field, every single one of y'all is gonna be more primed and ready than any of those chumps from Biloxi. I'm gonna make sure of that. I've been here four years and ain't never lost a game. And that ain't changing next Friday, neither. No, sir, it ain't. Y'all best make sure of that."

Brother James claps his hands again, and points to the schoolhouse door. "School's out. Go get changed and get your asses straight down to the field. Practice starts in fifteen minutes."

Conversations fly back and forth as we rush back to the dorm. *Who should start? Who should play short? Who's the best catcher, Taz or Molloy? Who wants to bet that Shane throws a no-hitter?* I tune the noise out until it's a wordless buzz in the background. My mind is focused on the game in an entirely different way. And on one detail in particular.

Brother James said the ballfield we're playing at is in Petal, a town we pass through on our way to church in Hattiesburg. The exact same town where Mary Grace lives. Should I invite her to the game? She doesn't seem like the sporty-type, but something tells me she'd want to come.

If I'm honest, though, I'm not sure what the right thing to do is when it comes to Mary Grace. I know we've only hung out twice, but it's obvious that we both want to be more than just friends. I've let myself get lost in the fantasy of that, but I can't keep ignoring the fact I'm leaving in a month. I need to find a way to tell her before things get more serious, and inviting her to my game isn't going to help with that, right?

I slyly stash the letter when I get back to my room, and quickly change. I'm still debating with myself when I reach the field, but an ear-piercing whistle soon severs my thoughts.

"JOG IT IN!"

The man before us looks like Brother James. He sounds like Brother James. He even wears the same Cincinnati Reds hat as Brother James. But he walks with a straight-backed swagger, and his voice carries a confident authority. With his arms folded across his chest and a whistle between his lips, Coach James eyes us as we gather in front of him. He wears a pair of cleats, white pants, a red t-shirt that matches his hat, and an expression that says "I'm not here to fuck around." All of us settle into silence.

We begin with a series of running drills, all of which are Coach James's own creation. Designed "to clear your dumb fucking heads of distractions," was how he explained it to us. Basically, we sprint back and forth a bunch of times between random distances. It's far from revolutionary, but it is effective at eliminating distractions. All I can focus on is how much I don't want to run anymore.

Pretty soon we're begging for a water break. Coach James allows us two minutes. Enough to wet your lips if you're near the back of the line. I'm lucky enough to squeeze in behind Shane and Molloy near the front, but a few of the boys are still waiting for their turn at the water hose when Coach James calls them back. To my delight, Oaf is one of them. I chuckle to myself as I watch him lumbering back to the field, his face crimson red and his oversized t-shirt drenched front and back with sweat.

Unfortunately for Oaf and the rest of us, running remains the theme for the remainder of practice. Coach James decides to time our laps and sprints, jotting down our stats on a clipboard.

He paces between us while we catch our breath, preaching about the benefits we'll feel while we're wilting like weeds in the heat. What about dehydration and heatstroke, you maniac?

I receive an answer to this question sooner than expected as Oaf stumbles to the side of the field and hurls up the contents of his stomach. The sour stench of bile taints the air.

"Uuuugh!" I pull the collar of my t-shirt over my nose, but it's like the smell is stuck inside my nostrils.

Everyone around me is doing the same. Lucas, who's only a few yards from Oaf's pile of puke, starts gagging until he throws up too. This triggers Sal, which sends the rest of us sprinting for the safety of fresh air. And that's how our first practice ends, without us throwing a single ball.

28

A LONG, HARD LOOK IN THE MIRROR

"I ain't sure which one's worse," Peaches grumbles, while Angelo and I are scrubbing pots after dinner. "The old one or the new one."

"You need to quit talking in riddles, bro," Angelo tells him, and nudges me on the arm. "Is this how you Georgia boys talk back home? Did any of that make sense to you?"

I chuckle. "That's a negative. What the hell are you talking about, Peach?"

"I'm talkin' about Brother James," he says, with a huff of exasperation. "He ain't given two shits since the day I got here, and now he's actin' like the fuckin' Terminator, all of a sudden."

I shrug and scrub another pot. "Who the hell cares?" I say, turning on the faucet to rinse it off. "We get to play in an actual baseball game at the end of this."

"I ain't bitchin' about that," Peaches says. "I just don't get this place sometimes. That's all I'm sayin'. We're in the middle of a dang lockdown, and now we're fixin' to play baseball against another school? How does that make sense?"

"Just think of it as a sign that the lockdown's ending," Angelo tells him. "We'll all be back at church again on Sunday, is my guess. Everything else should settle back to normal after that."

For my own selfish reasons, I hope to hell he's right. "Good!" I say. "I know church sucks ass, but at least we get to escape this shithole for a couple of hours. I miss seeing the outside world."

"I bet that's not all you miss seeing," Angelo mumbles, so only I can hear.

"What's that supposed to mean?" I ask, jerking my head around to face him. My cheeks flush as he flashes me a knowing smile. I flick my wet fingers at him, spattering soapy water on his shirt. Angelo laughs and splashes me back.

"Hey, I just mopped right there!" Peaches points at the puddles on the floor, scowling at us.

"Don't worry about it, Peach," Angelo says, still chuckling. "You and Oaf can head to the dorm. We'll finish things up."

Peaches eyes him for a second, like he's waiting for the catch, and then sets the mop in the bucket and scampers out of the kitchen. Oaf follows behind him, shooting Angelo and me a cold, suspicious stare as he exits.

The moment we're alone, Angelo turns my way. The humor drains from his face, replaced by a pensive frown. A look I know all too well. I brace myself for another life-altering lesson from good ol' Saint Angelo. Here we go again! What will it be this time?

"Look, man," he begins, "I'm just gonna come out and say it. I walked right behind you in the schoolhouse this morning. I saw you writing another letter to that chick, okay? And I saw you pass it to Shane when you picked up your dinner tray. Please tell me you're not trying to..."

"No!" I snap, my cheeks burning once again. This is not the lecture I was expecting. "It's not like last time, okay? That's not what's going on. I'm out of here in a month, Angelo. Why would I try to escape *now*? Why would I risk it?"

"Yeah, that's what I was wondering." Angelo frowns at me skeptically. "But that hasn't stopped you sneaking out in the middle of the night. I still don't get how that's worth the risk. Unless..." His eyes widen, and he smirks at me. "You little... You've been meeting up with her, haven't you? That's why it's been worth the risk!"

Angelo bursts out laughing as a sheepish grin creeps across my face. It was worth the risk when it was just for some smokes, music, and a few hours of freedom. But the time I've spent with Mary Grace transcends all of those things. Would it still feel worth it without her there? I'm not so sure.

"I've only met up with her a couple of times," I explain. "She's cool and all, and we're into the same music and stuff, but it's nothing serious or anything. We just like hanging out with each other."

"You know what?" Angelo says. "This is gonna sound weird, but I'm actually kinda relieved. I still don't think it's worth the risk, but I thought the only reason you were sneaking out was because of Shane and Molloy. No offense, but that's how it's looked lately. But now I know the real reason is really tall and makes Will's cheeks turn red when he talks about her."

My face burns right on cue, and I grab Angelo in a half-hearted headlock. "Okay, okay!" He raises his hands in surrender, still chortling as I release my hold. "So what's her name, this 'reason' of yours?"

"Mary Grace." My heart lurches as her name leaves my lips.

"Sounds like a girl you'd meet in church, alright." Angelo picks up his towel and starts wiping down the pots I just washed.

"Yeah, well, she's about as churchy as we are." I reach into the sink and pull the plug out from the bottom. "She's not like you'd expect," I say, watching the filthy water drain through the hole. "She's...she's just really cool to hang out with."

Angelo stops working and stares at me. "I get why you wanna play it down and all, but it's obvious you really like this chick." I let my silence confirm his suspicions. "That's tough, man," he says, his big brown eyes solemn and sincere. "It's easy to leave a shitty place when the people you're leaving behind are just as shitty. It's different when you're leaving someone you actually like and care about. Trust me, I know."

Bitterness reels up inside me. "Oh yeah? What makes you so sure about that?"

Angelo meets my gaze with a melancholy smile. "Because I'm going home, Will. And I'm gonna miss you, bro."

It takes a second for what I heard to sink in, and the gravity of his words yucks me back to reality. Angelo watches my reaction with an air of concern. I know I should say something. *Congratulations! Amazing news!* But those words feel wedged in my throat right now. "When?" is all I manage to mumble.

"I'm going home on Friday, June 15th." Angelo's face lights up, a broad smile dimpling his cheeks. "Not soon enough, but what's sixteen days when you've waited three years, right? It still doesn't feel real, man! Can you believe it? I finally get to meet my baby sister!"

No, I can't believe it. I'm not sure I want to. Sixteen days and no more Angelo. I never imagined that he'd leave before me. It was supposed to be me leaving him behind, and now I'm losing him instead. I glance at Angelo, whose eyes well with tears of joy and relief. One spills as he blinks them back. I watch it trickle down the dimple on his cheek and try to silence my bitter thoughts.

"Your baby sister is going to love having a big brother like you," I tell him. "I'm happy for you, man."

"Thanks, man! That means a lot." Angelo claps me on the shoulder. "I'm happy for me, too. I'm happy for both of us. You're getting out of here only two weeks after I do. We're both going home, remember?"

"Right," I say, ignoring the whispers of doubt in my head. *Ninety days*, said the judge. *Ninety days*, promised my dad. Only thirty remain, but Brother Bennett hasn't said shit about me going home. Not yet, anyway.

"So how did you find out?" I ask him. "Did Bennett call you into his office or something?"

Angelo nods. "A couple of weeks ago. The best conversation I ever had with that racist motherfucker. Sixteen more days, and he can kiss my black ass goodbye."

"Wait..." I say, frowning at him. "You've known you were leaving for two weeks, and you're just now telling me? You're kidding me, right?"

Angelo's smile fades. "I'm sorry, man. I guess I was waiting for the right time."

"And that took you *two whole weeks*!? That's messed up, man! I thought I was your friend!"

"You are my friend, Will!" Angelo scowls at me. "You're the

only person I've told about this! And what about *your* friend, huh?" He points a finger at my chest. "Have you told that chick when you're leaving? Does she even know?"

The fight drains straight out of me, and I drop my gaze to the floor.

"Yeah, that's what I thought," Angelo mutters. "Sounds like you need to take a long, hard look in the mirror, bro."

29

LONG LIVE THE BOOGER!

Sunday, June 3 - Day 64

Yet again, Angelo gets it spot on. Brother Bennett makes the announcement during breakfast. The lockdown is officially over. Regular service resumes at the boys home. This means back to church, of course, which makes it impossible to ignore something else Angelo was right about. I still haven't told Mary Grace I'll soon be heading home to Atlanta.

The two weeks since I last saw her has felt like several months, thanks to being locked-down in the dorm the whole time. We've gone outside to practice each day, but that's pretty much it. Even that's been a drag. Coach James has every drill so absurdly regimented it feels more like bootcamp than baseball. It's given me plenty of time to think, though. More time than I would have liked.

It's not like Angelo was wrong to call me out the other day. I was a total hypocrite for popping off at him like that. I know what he means about waiting for the right time to tell me he's going home. With Mary Grace, it's a bit more complicated. I've spent the last couple of weeks thinking about *how* to tell her. I know it's the right thing to do, but that doesn't make it an easy thing to do. Or even an easy choice to make. I can feel something happening between us that I don't want to end. If I tell her it has to, then that makes it all the more real.

I consider writing Mary Grace another note before we leave for church. I could be straight with her about everything. Apologize for not telling her sooner. Let her know I understand if she doesn't want to hang out anymore. But the thoughts stay in my head. There's a chance I'll get her response to my last letter today. I may as well wait and see.

———

A MANTLE OF DARK, pregnant clouds looms overhead as I hurry across the gravel lot to The Booger. The old girl's engine clatters and creaks while she idles beneath the stormy sky. Gusts of wind whisk through the pines on the far side of the field, their tall masts swaying back and forth. It doesn't take a meteorologist to forecast the weather this morning. By the time I plant myself on the seat next to Angelo, a crack of thunder reverberates through the sky, and fat raindrops splatter upon the windows.

A moment later, the heavens empty. Benny and the rest of the Cuban Crew are last to arrive. Everyone on board hoots with laughter, watching them streak across the gravel lot as the rain lashes down. A huge cheer erupts as they scamper inside the bus for safety, drenched and out of breath. With a grunt and a sigh, Brother James wedges himself behind the steering wheel. He sets the windshield wipers on full blast and steers us into the storm.

Rain torrents down with rapid intensity, hammering on the roof as we rumble along the road to Hattiesburg. The downpour shows no signs of letting up either. Streams of brown water submerge both sides of the road, and the flooding soon becomes so hazardous that Brother James has to slow the bus to a crawl.

We arrive at church several minutes late, but we're not the only ones delayed by the weather. The moment we hop off the bus, we dart through the deluge and trickle inside along with the other soaked stragglers. The pastor is already standing at the pulpit, prattling through his opening remarks. I search for Mary Grace as I drip my way down the aisle. There she is, just like always.

My heart rate triples. I slide into an open pew behind Angelo, and stare past the rows of people in front of me. All I can see is the back of her head, and the tight Baptist bun staring right at me. I bet she hates wearing her hair like that. I mean, presumably, it's not by choice.

I picture the way she looked the last time I saw her, the *real* Mary Grace. Her dark hair falling free and easy to her shoulders. Checkered Vans, jean shorts, and the same badass Metallica shirt I once tried to steal. It's such a stark contrast to the soulless costume she's wearing now. I watch her tug at the shoulders of the navy blue cardigan like it doesn't quite fit. And she's right. It doesn't fit because it isn't *her*. None of this is.

Thankfully, the storm has passed through by the time we leave church. Steam rises from the sidewalk as we empty outside into the thick, sticky heat. I try to catch Shane's eye as we walk back to The Booger, eager for a sign that he has something for me. A wink or a nod would do, but he's too busy talking shit to Benny to notice. If he was given Mary Grace's reply to my letter, I'll have to wait until we're back at school to find out.

Around twenty minutes later, Brother James pulls in the driveway at Victory Ridge. The moment he parks the bus, Coach James appears in his place. To everyone's bemusement, we're told to get changed for practice and head straight down to the field. "Sundays ain't just for church no more," he informs us, as we file out of the bus.

"This is a total waste of time," I hear Shane complaining to Molloy on our way into the dorm. I hurry to catch up with them. "Seriously, how are we supposed to practice when our field looks like a fucking swimming pool!? Does he not remember driving to church in that shit? What the hell's wrong with him?"

"More than a few things," I say, pulling up alongside them. "But I'm sick of this Jekyll and Hyde bullshit!"

Molloy squints at me. "What the hell does that mean?"

"Don't worry about it," I say, turning my attention to Shane. "So...did Brandi happen to give you anything for me, by any chance?"

"Oh yeah! I'd forgotten." Shane's hand darts to the front pocket of his pants. He pulls out a folded white envelope and hands it to me. I check it's still sealed and slide it discreetly in my pocket. It will be later before I'm able to read it, but I'll still have plenty of time to write a reply. I can ask Shane to pass it along tonight during evening service.

Unsurprisingly to anyone but Coach James, baseball practice lasts less than an hour before he finally abandons it. This was more than enough time for us all to get soaking wet and caked with mud, of course. Scrubbing yourself clean in a freezing cold shower is neither easy nor ideal, but I shiver my way through it as quickly as I can.

Angelo, Peaches, and Oaf are all still showering when I return to the room. I throw on some clothes, retrieve the envelope from my hiding spot, and hurry outside to find a private place to read. The moment I reach the far side of the school house, I tear open the envelope and unfold the sheet of paper inside.

Dear Will,

Thanks for writing me another letter! It's definitely different from the first one you wrote to me, but it's still pretty crazy! The more I hear about this Victory Ridge place, the worse it sounds. I asked the Debbie Gibson Twins what they knew about this Brother Bennett guy, which wasn't a whole lot. Apparently, those two douchebags they're dating don't talk about much, not that I'm surprised. Anyhow, it sounds like he stepped straight out of a nightmare. No wonder you were so desperate to get away from him! I still feel bad I couldn't help you with that, but I'm glad you're still here from a selfish perspective.

I assume it was Brother Bennett who sent you guys into the woods to chase after that crazy kid. This is seriously blowing my mind, by the way! If he was worried about one kid running wild, why the heck would he want the rest of you doing the same? It doesn't make sense. Surely that just ups the risk of other kids trying to escape. It seems like the perfect opportunity while everyone is looking for someone else. I'm sure you were tempted. Atlanta is a long way to run, though.

On a different note, I have some amazing news from New Orleans to share! It's officially official. Executive Anarchy is going on tour! Sam called last week to tell me. It's just a few gigs at some dive bars in Alabama, but I'm so excited for him! Their first one is in Mobile in a couple of weeks. Then they play in Montgomery, Birmingham, and finish up in Tuscaloosa on the 22nd. And the best part is, they'll be stopping in Hattiesburg on their way back to New Orleans. Can you believe it? I haven't seen Sam in over three months, and now I get to see him in just a few weeks! I really want you to meet him. Maybe we can figure out a way.

One last thing before I wrap things up. When I was talking to the DG twins the other day, they said you guys are playing a baseball game against another school on Friday. You never mentioned it, so I'm not sure if you'll be playing or not. If you are, I would totally come watch. As long as you're cool with that, of course.

Well, that's all my news. School is finally done for the summer, so I'm just going to kick back with my headphones on, blare some music, and count the days until Sam comes to town. Other than that, I'm just looking forward to hanging out again. Hopefully we'll see one another soon.

Take care, Will.

MG

P.S. If you are cool with me coming to the game, please reply tonight because I won't be there on Wednesday. My mom's choir is singing at a different church, so I'm going with her.

P.S.S. I was talking to Sam about you, so now he's convinced you're my boyfriend. Just letting you know in case you do get to meet him.

As my eyes linger on the last two lines, reality slaps me fully awake. I've allowed things to escalate to a whole new level. Shame swells inside me as I reread Mary Grace's letter. She didn't write this to me, I realize. Not really. This was meant for a different Will. One she assumes will be in her life beyond the next month. That's who she talked to Sam about. That's who she's looking forward to hanging out with again. That's why she wants to watch me play baseball on Friday.

I hang my head as I tear the letter into shreds, scattering them across the sodden ground. It was never my intention to deceive her. Truly, it wasn't. Mary Grace never asked how long I'd be here, and it never came up while we were together. It's all excuses now, of course, but it's not like I was trying to avoid telling her. It was like our conversations took on a life of their own. I was just swept up in the flow of it all. That's the only way I can explain it.

None of that matters much now, though. There's only one way to make this right. There's no way to avoid hurting Mary Grace, however. That ship has sailed and now it's heading straight for the rocks.

My head in a haze, I circle around to the front of the school-house and pull open the door. It's gloomy inside and eerily empty, but enough daylight creeps in for me to find what I need. I grab a pencil and a few sheets of notepaper, and sit down at my usual desk. I stare at the blank page in front of me, willing the right words to come.

What if they don't, though? What if the right words don't exist? What if it's just about doing the right thing in the best way I can? So what's the best way to tell someone you're leaving forever and neglected to mention it? Dropping a bomb like that in a letter sounds like the coward's way out to me. No matter how much the prospect terrifies me, no matter how torturous it will be, I need to tell Mary Grace in person. I owe her that much, at the very least.

But what to tell her about the baseball game? She'll be

expecting a response. If I say yes and invite her along, I'm only leading her on more, right? And I can't say I'm cool with her coming and then blindside her with the truth, either. Maybe I should tell her I'd be too nervous if she showed up, and that I'll see her the following night when I sneak out. That's when I plan on telling her the truth, anyway.

I'm still staring at the blank sheet of notepaper when I hear the call for lunch. The afternoon proves equally unproductive, and I spend dinner poking at my plate of bland noodles, wondering what the hell I'm going to write. But when the time arrives to leave for evening service, it doesn't matter that I haven't written a single word. We're not going to church anymore. We're not going anywhere. There's been a death at the boys home.

———

TODAY, Sunday, June 3rd, The Booger passed into eternity. It happened a short while after dinner. Brother James had heard a loud bang when he cranked the old girl up for our trip back to Hattiesburg. The engine started hissing and black smoke billowed out from under the hood. By the time I arrived on the scene, several flames flickered from the front of the bus. Brother James was scrambling around yelling for someone to fetch the hose.

After half an hour of chaos, The Booger sits charred and smoldering at the top of the driveway. A crowd of us stand vigil on the gravel lot. In classic boy's home fashion, we try to make the best out of a shit situation. We hold an off-the-cuff funeral for our faithful, old bus.

"The Booger sailed us safely through her last storm today," Jerry says, stepping forward to lead the sermon. "She was a good bus. She was a strong bus. She was *our* bus. But the Lord has called her home to the big parking lot in the sky."

"Tell it, pastor!" someone calls out, and several others echo his sentiments with an "amen."

Jerry nods solemnly. "Her time with us has come to an end, but she will never be forgotten. We all remain. We all suffer on. But The Booger is free forever. Long live The Booger!"

"Long live The Booger!" we all echo back.

30

GAMEDAY!

Friday, June 8 - Day 69

I'd forgotten what it was like to feel nervous and excited all at once. The pregame jitters jolt through me like spikes of electricity as everyone piles into the dining hall for breakfast. The room buzzes with restless energy, every comment and conversation centered around our game at 4:30. It's no surprise when Coach James orders us straight down to the field after we're done. Extra fielding drills to "iron out the last of y'all's fuck ups," he so eloquently informs us.

Much to our frustration, however, he refuses to reveal any information about our starting lineup. "Does this look like the pregame meetin', boy?" is his response whenever someone asks. "Shut the fuck up and focus on the drill!"

Our pregame meeting is scheduled after lunch in the schoolhouse at 1 PM, a full three and a half hours before the game starts. Brother Bennett is in attendance, sitting on Brother

James's desk with his thick arms folded across his chest. His dark eyes watch everything and everyone in forbidding silence. Talk about a buzz kill!

Coach James holds court in the center of the room. He sports a fresh haircut, a pair of cream khakis, a crisp white shirt, and a navy blue tie with white polka dots. Wait, no! Those aren't polka dots at all. He's wearing a tie covered in tiny baseballs! What in the actual fuck?

"We're as ready as we can be to win this game today, y'all," Coach James begins, nodding approvingly as he glances around the room at us. "But we ain't won nothin' yet, 'cause we ain't earned nothin' yet. We got some real good baseball players on this team. And we know we've got the fight inside us. But unless we unite as a team under God's glory, that ain't gonna be enough. We gotta use His light to visualize our victory. Always remember that."

As Coach James steals a glance at Brother Bennett, I realize this speech is more about pandering to *him* than mentally preparing us for the game. We've heard this spiel all week, but with way more cursing and far less Jesus.

After a few more minutes of spiritually-infused inspiration, Coach James concludes his speech. Much to the relief of everyone in the room, this also concludes Brother Bennett's visit. The change in atmosphere is palpable the moment he departs, like everyone was holding their breath the entire time and finally exhaled. Even Coach James puffs out a sigh as he loosens his tragedy of a tie.

"Tell us who's starting, sir," Benny yells out.

"Yeah," Jerry chimes in, "like you promised."

The rest of the room joins them, myself included. Our

protests amplify until our voices become a wall of noise echoing throughout the schoolhouse. Coach James holds a hand up to quiet us, but he could be holding his paddle right now and that still wouldn't stop us.

"Quiet down!" he hollers, but our din drowns him out. We've waited long enough, and the waiting has made us mutinous. Coach James knows he's defeated, and we know it too. If he wants us to shut up, he better drag Brother Bennett back here or give us what we want.

Coach James's face turns Cincinnati red. "FINE!" he screams, throwing his hands into the air. Our voices trail into silence as he stomps over to his desk and drags a large cardboard box out from behind it. A few of the boys mutter with excitement. We all know what's inside. Uniforms!

As Coach James reaches down to lift open the box, we all lean forward for a glimpse. A murmur of *oohs* spreads throughout the room as he pulls out a pristine white shirt, holding it on either side of the collar so that it dangles open. It's nothing fancy, just a plain white tee with a red "VR" on the front upper left corner. At least it looks official, though. Now we're going to look the part while we beat this team's ass.

"Listen up," Coach James says, and we all fall silent again. "We only got one set of jerseys, so if you get one, that means you're startin'. The rest of y'all need to wear a plain white t-shirt for the game. That's just the way it is."

Shit! I glance around the room. Everyone stares anxiously at the cardboard box. The stakes were just raised even higher. Those jerseys might be low budget, but anything beats sitting on the bench wearing a white undershirt with yellow pit stains.

To no one's surprise, Shane is first to receive a uniform.

Benny is second and then Lucas. Molloy and Jerry after that. I almost sigh with relief when I hear my name called next. Coach James balls up a jersey and tosses it my way. I catch it and straighten it out to discover which number will be mine.

"Five?" I mutter, more to myself than anyone else.

"You gotta problem with that, Chuck?" Coach James snaps. "Johnny Bench wore number five, and he's a Redleg's legend! He won the World Series back-to-back and was an All-Star fourteen fuckin' times! So if you gotta problem with number five, I'll just take that jersey back and find someone else to play your spot."

"No, sir!" I say quickly. "No problem here. Number five is great."

This softens Coach James's expression. He resumes handing out uniforms to the lucky few, and our starting lineup is soon complete. Shane will start on the mound, Jerry at first base, Peaches at second, Alavaro at third, with yours truly playing shortstop. Benny, Ricky, and Stankass Lou will make up the outfield.

———

A COUPLE OF HOURS LATER, we're dressed for the game, lining up to board our new bus. Much like The Booger, she isn't much to look at, just a beat-up old school bus that's been given a coat of pale blue paint. Brother Bennett brought her home yesterday and we Christened her The Smurf Turd shortly after. She's not much of an upgrade, though. Her seats are slightly less tattered, but that's about it.

The ride to the ballfields in Petal bubbles with tension. The usual loudmouths and shit-talkers sit in silent focus. All except Molloy, of course. He's in rare form and feeling creative.

"Okay, how about to the tune of *Time After Time*?" he calls out. He receives a few groans and a cry of "shut the hell up" in response, but Molloy looks undeterred. "I'm taking that as a 'yes.' Okay, here we go." He clears his throat. "*Sitting on the bus again, I play with my dick and think of you.*"

A few heads turn and laughter trickles out around us.

"C'mon, guys," Molloy says. "I can't do this alone. Will, you're a writer." He winks at me. "Help me out, man."

As he's being a dick, I feign disinterest for a second, but only for a second. I started thinking of lines the moment he began singing. I clear my throat, draw a deep breath, and begin with Molloy's line.

"*Sitting on the bus again, I play with my dick and think of you. You're driving from Biloxi, with no idea what waits for you.*

"*Baseball, bloodshed, that's what you'll find.*"

A few boys start clapping in rhythm, and it spreads throughout the bus.

"*Feeling like, you're dead, 'cause we kicked your...*"

We manage to come up with two whole verses by the time we reach the ball field. The moment we pull into the parking lot, however, we all fall silent. A shiny white bus is parked behind the bleachers. It has a neat navy trim with *Calvary Christian* written along the side, the "T" rising up like a cross. Our opponents are already on the field warming up.

The moment Coach James parks our shitbox of a bus, we're up and ready. We gather up our gear and crowd the aisle, pressing forward as the doors open.

"Holy shit! They're wearing pinstripes," Shane remarks as we march towards the home dugout. "Can you believe that? These pansies think they're the fucking Yankees. I hate the fucking Yankees!"

Sure enough, the opposition is decked out in gray uniforms with navy blue pinstripes. These little shits have *actual* jerseys that button down the center, matching the pants, socks, and even their cleats. Proper uniforms! We, on the other hand, look like we rolled out of the trailer park in our pajamas. Most of our bench is wearing shorts and sneakers instead of baseball pants and spikes, looking like some *Bad News Bears* kind of shit!

As 4:30 approaches, a small crowd of spectators spreads across the bleachers. My focus begins to drift that direction more frequently than I would like. The hype leading up to this game was a helpful distraction, but now Mary Grace is back in my thoughts. I can't ignore that she had wanted to be here, that she asked if I was cool with her coming and never received a response. There's still a good chance she might decide to show up, of course. I consider how that would feel, knowing what I plan to tell her tomorrow. Knowing that will change everything between us.

I try to shake myself out of it as we jog onto the field. Shane takes to the mound and strikes out Calvary's leadoff hitter to open the game. He ends up walking the next guy, and works their third hitter to a full count. With a runner on first, Shane fires in his pitch. The batter swings, driving the ball towards me. It skips across the dirt, and I scoop it up on the run, flipping it to Peaches at second. He pivots and throws the ball to Jerry at first base for a double play. Inning over.

I steal another glance at the bleachers as we jog back to the dugout. There's still no sign of Mary Grace, which is probably for the best. I would be far more distracted if she was over there watching me. Even so, I find myself wishing she could have seen that play. Coach James saw it, though. He greets me with a brown-stained smile and a hearty slap on the ass when I return to the dugout.

As Calvary takes to the field, we all stand up and holler encouragement to Peaches, our leadoff hitter. On his way to the on-deck circle, he turns around and flashes us a mischievous grin.

"Y'all need to pay attention and see how a leadoff hitter does it right!" he yells, and gives us a final nod before swinging at the first three pitches and striking out.

Coach James curses in exasperation, fuming at Peaches as he shuffles back into the dugout.

"That was some textbook shit, Peach," I say, slapping him on the back. "Like straight out of the How to Be a Dumbass textbook. I'm impressed."

"I got dirt in my eye," he mumbles glumly, and I burst out laughing.

The first inning ends scoreless, and still no Mary Grace. She isn't there for the second one either, nor for the third or fourth. By the end of the sixth inning, I've stopped checking the bleachers. The game remains a stalemate, and Coach James grows tenser with every pitch. His voice is hoarse from screaming so much, and his white shirt is drenched with sweat. The blowout win we were hoping for isn't going as planned, and the tension is starting to creep into our play.

Shane opens up the 7th inning with a series of sloppy pitches, but manages to get a couple of lucky outs to keep us going. The Calvary shortstop steps up next. He's fielded solidly all game, but Shane has struck him out twice already. Not this time, though. He crushes the first pitch deep into the corner of right field and ends up sliding into third for a triple.

Up steps their second baseman, a kid who looks like a scrawnier version of Peaches, if that's even possible. He's whiffed at every pitch the whole game, and I'm anticipating the same as Shane stares him down and launches in a heater. Like the batter before him, he swings at the first pitch.

Crack!

The ball bloops over Alvaro at third base. For a second, the kid looks as shocked as I am. Hearing the screams from his dugout, he drops what remains of his bat and bolts for first base. A moment later, the shortstop stomps on home plate to give them a one-run lead.

I glance toward our dugout, fully expecting to see Coach James combusting with rage. He just stands in front of the dugout, loosening his special tie while he watches on in silence. By the time we close out the inning and jog to the dugout, he's all business again, speaking animatedly to Shane, who is next up to bat. When he steps up to the plate, Shane instantly responds. He drives the first pitch toward the left-field wall for a stand-up double.

Our bench goes wild, and we amp up our rowdiness as Jerry makes his way to the plate. He fouls off the first four pitches before slamming one through the infield. Shane strides home to tie up the game, but we're not done yet. The momentum just shifted our way. I can feel it. All of us can. Finally, we've got them right where we want them.

With one on and zero out, Benny steps up to bat. As I'm next in the order, I move to the on-deck circle, but I'm not there for long. The second pitch pegs Benny on the shoulder. He tosses aside his bat, hurling Spanish insults at the Calvary pitcher as he jogs to first base.

I channel all of my focus as I make my way to the plate, but the Calvary coach delays my opportunity, walking out to the mound for a pitching change. I resist the urge to look for Mary Grace while I stand there waiting. If she's here right now, I would rather not know.

The new pitcher is a beanpole of a boy, the kind who looks out of place in his own body. I step back and watch him throw a few warm-up pitches. His throws are awkward but accurate, all of them straight down the strike zone. I know a junk pitcher when I see one, and from the way he keeps twitching, I can tell that he's nervous. He's nothing more than a coddled little church boy, of course, not some battle-hardened boy's home kid like me.

After a few more pitches, the ump calls me to the plate. I dig in and set my feet, eyeballing the beanpole pitcher in hope of unsettling him even more. *Come on, church boy. Let's see what you've got. Show me!* He winds up his first pitch, and a white blur whizzes right by me, smacking into the catcher's glove.

"Strike one," the umpire grunts.

Okay, that was more than a decent fastball, but if he throws me one of those again, I know I can crush it. His next pitch is a curveball, however, which goes nowhere near the strike zone, and his catcher has to scramble to snatch it up. *Where's that fastball, chump?* This time he obliges, but it's way too low to swing at.

"Ball two."

The pitcher winds up again and throws me another crappy curve to make the count three and one. *You're gonna have to give me that fastball, kid. Come on!* I reset, and channel my focus as he winds up once more. Here comes the pitch, a white blur like before. A fastball right down the middle. Eyes glued to the ball, I swing with all my strength.

Crack!

The impact reverberates through the bat and up my forearms. A solid connection! Tossing aside my bat, I charge toward first base, watching the ball rise into the air until it disappears in the glaring sunlight. Rounding first, I spy Benny coasting his way to third, raising his arms in the air. What the hell is he doing? I glance towards our dugout to find everyone jumping around in celebration. Hold on a second. Did I just...? Holy shit, I did! I just knocked the ball out of the fucking park!

The dugout cheers me home, hands slapping my back, helmet, arms, and ass as I high-five my way back to the bench. It took us a while to get going, but now there's no stopping us. We start raining runs on them like a Mississippi thunderstorm. By the top of the 9th, we're winning 11 -1.

Coach James pulls Shane for the final inning, and Lucas steps in to seal the slaughter. But by now, it doesn't matter. Calvary Christian Academy has tapped out. They basically just slap at the remaining pitches. I should probably have given up, too, by now, but I just can't help scanning the bleachers for Mary Grace one last time as the game fizzles to an end. There's no sign of her, of course, but as we're lining up to high-five the Biloxi losers, I spy the Debbie Gibson Twins waiting near the car park.

I catch up to Shane as we walk back to the dugout. "Hell of a game, man!" I tell him.

"Hell of a homerun!" he says, high-fiving me. "Those guys didn't suck as much as last year, but they're lucky it took us seven innings to shake off the rust. We still destroyed them in the end, though. I'll see if Brandi can bring some booze tomorrow night, so we can celebrate the right way."

"Sounds good to me," I say. "Can you ask her to bring Mary Grace along too?"

Shane cocks an eyebrow and grins at me. "Only if I get to tell her how desperate you looked when you asked me that."

I chuckle. "Fair deal, I suppose."

Coach James calls us over, and we all jog in and huddle up in front of the dugout. He drones through a surprisingly brief victory speech, and makes way for Brother Bennett to say a few words. He wears a broad smile that looks alien on his face. He is pleased, he tells us. He is proud of us. We are good Christian boys. For now, at least.

31

———

THE TRUTH

Sunday, June 10 - Day 71

Tonight's the night. No more delays. I adjust the strap of my wristwatch, newly acquired from Peaches for the price of five smokes, and press the sides to illuminate its face.

12:09 AM. Nearly time.

Rubbing my eyes, I try to clear my head. I've spent the past few hours lying on my bunk in the darkness, with nothing to do but grapple with my own anxiety. *How do I tell Mary Grace? What should I say? How will she react?*

For what feels like the thousandth time, I run through all the potential outcomes. None of them are particularly great. I just hope she can accept my apology. That's ultimately the best-case scenario. She'll feel hurt and disappointed, obviously, but maybe we can try to stay friends and write to one another or something.

Of course, her reaction could be far more extreme. I can't imagine Mary Grace going psycho and clawing my eyes out, but the idea of seeing her break down and cry frightens the shit out of me. I'd take being slapped and cursed out over sobs and silence. However, now that I think about it. Of all the possible reactions Mary Grace might have, the worst would be indifference. If I tell her I'm leaving and she doesn't care, that will hurt me far more than anything.

One thing is certain, however. I'm going to lose whatever this is I have with Mary Grace. That's just the way it has to be, right? Three weeks from now, she'll be here, and I'll be back in Atlanta. No matter what I want or how I feel, this is how it has to be, I guess.

In addition to telling Mary Grace, I've also made another decision. No matter the outcome tonight, this will also be my last time sneaking out. With only a few weeks left, there really is too much to risk. Angelo would be proud.

I glance down at his bunk across the room. Just a mound of covers in the darkness, I can hear the soft, rhythmic rasp of his snoring. *You've been a good friend, Angelo. But I'm going out tonight. One last time, because I have to.*

When I sneak outside and meet up with the other two, Shane insists we make a pit stop at our cache in the woods before we head off. He gives no particular reason why, but he was bitching about being out of smokes and knows I have a fresh pack stashed away, so I'm under no illusions about his motivations. I'm glad he brought it up, though. I keep forgetting it's there, like it's buried out of sight, but also out of mind. Plus, I should probably take along the Walkman Mary Grace gave me. She might decide she wants it back when all is said and done.

We reach our stash in the woods a few minutes later. Shane brushes away the leaves that camouflage our hiding spot and removes the stack of branches covering the hole. He reaches in and hands me my Tupperware container. I open it and take out the Walkman.

"Should I bring anything else?" I ask, catching Shane's eye.

He arches an eyebrow. "You know what to bring. Quit fucking around!"

I chuckle, grab the pack of smokes, and hand him back the container, which he returns to its home in the ground. Before long, we're walking along the dark country road toward Petal. Three figures enveloped in blackness and three amber dots smoldering from the ends of our cigarettes. Well, *my* cigarettes.

With the other two contentedly puffing away, I slip on my headphones and push play. The unmistakable intro of *For Whom the Bell Tolls* chimes into my ears, the peal of church bells blasted away by that badass guitar riff. The music drowns out my thoughts for a few minutes, but the moment the song ends, they start creeping back in. I'm beginning to doubt I can go through with this. I don't want to tell her I'm leaving and watch that news completely change the way she feels about me.

"Are you a good guy, Will?" she once asked me.

"I want to be," was my reply.

I meant it then, and it's still true now. Only now I can't prove I am a good guy without showing her that I'm not one. To be a good guy, I have to be the bearer of bad news. News that makes me a bad guy. Jesus Christ in a manger, I've dug a major shithole for myself this time!

My mind cycles through this every step of the way to our meeting spot. Right up until the moment I see Mary Grace standing in the shadows, leaning against the rusty pickup. My thoughts fall silent, all except for one voice inside my head, screaming for me to turn around and run away. I do my best to ignore it and carry on toward her.

As we approach the truck, the Debbie Gibson Twins part from Mary Grace's side. They gesture for Shane and Molloy to follow them, and the pair scurry after them. Within a few moments, the two of us are completely alone. Mary Grace wears her usual checkered Vans and jean shorts, but instead of that infamous Metallica concert tee, it's an Exodus t-shirt she has on tonight. Still a fine choice.

It's not just her shirt that's different about her tonight, though. Is it her hair, maybe? No, something else. I peer into her pale blue eyes, their upper lids a darker shade than normal. Makeup! Mystery solved. Her lips are darker and glossier as well. Standing before me in the twilight, she looks truly radiant.

"Hey!" Mary Grace says, with a hint of giddiness. "We finally get to hang out again! I thought I'd have a chance to see you yesterday. I was planning to come to your game, but Douchebag Dave came home from the base, so we had to go out for dinner as 'family.' Ugh!" She makes a grossed out face, and her smile instantly returns. "I heard you guys won, though. Brandy said you hit a homerun. That's awesome! I wish I could've been there to see it! Anyhow, I bet you're glad that lockdown thing is over. How've you been?"

What the hell's going on with her? I've never seen her all chatty and peppy like this before.

"I'm okay," I tell her. "The game was fun, but you didn't miss much other than the last few innings. Sorry I couldn't get back to you last Sunday, by the way. Our bus died, so we couldn't make it. Anyway, what's going on with you? You look like you're in a majorly good mood tonight."

Mary Grace beams like a kid on Christmas morning. "Well, that's because I had a majorly good day today. I got some really amazing news earlier that I've been dying to share with you!"

"Wow!" I try to keep a smile fixed on my face. Why is my timing always so terrible? "Sounds exciting. I...I have some news to share as well, actually."

"Well," she says, "I think your news is going to have to wait because *I* can't. Plus, I really don't want to. I'm way too excited!"

I let out a half-hearted chuckle. "I guess you better go first then."

Mary Grace stands in front of me, hands clasped in front of her, and her lips pursed in a smile.

"Okay," she begins, "so you remember what I told you in my letter about Sam's tour, right? And how they're stopping in Hattiesburg on their way back from Alabama?"

I nod my head. "Of course."

"Well, there's been a teeny tiny change to those plans. Here, sit down." She lowers herself onto the flatbed and pats the spot next to her.

"So what's the change?" I ask, sitting down beside her. "I assume they're still coming here or you wouldn't be so happy about it."

"Oh, they're still coming alright. But instead of just staying for a couple of hours, they'll be in Hattiesburg for two whole nights!"

"That's great!" I say. "Now you'll have way more time with Sam. When is he getting here again?"

"He'll be here Friday the 22nd. Less than two weeks from now!" Mary Grace radiates with joy. "But that's not all I was going to tell you. Aren't you curious why he and the band are staying longer?"

"Well, sure, but I assumed it was to see you."

"Nope." Mary Grace shakes her head, wearing a mischievous grin. " It's because they scored another gig. Only this one isn't in Alabama. It's going to be just down the road in Hattiesburg."

"No way! That's too fucking cool!" I smile at her. "You're going, right? You have to! This is your chance to finally see him play."

Mary Grace laughs. "Of course I am, silly! And you're going with me."

Wait. What?

Mary Grace's smile falters as she notes my reaction. "What's wrong, Will? You do want to go with me, right?"

Sweat pours out of me. "No, it's not that. I would love to go," I say, and I truly mean it. "I'm just not sure that I can."

Her smile reignites. "Oh, don't worry about any of that. I've got it all figured out already. The show isn't until eleven-thirty on a Saturday night, so you'll just have to sneak out a little earlier is all. Sam's girlfriend is driving up from New Orleans with a couple of her friends, so she can take us to the concert. We just have to figure out a place to pick you up."

My lips part, but I stay silent. I came here to tell her the truth, and now I'm forced to let her down in a whole new way.

"What's going on, Will?" Mary Grace's eyes search mine imploringly. "I thought you'd be excited about this. Instead of hanging out in some stupid field, we can go to a concert together, on an actual date. And it's not just any concert, it's Sam's band that's playing. He even told me to bring you along. We can figure out a better plan if that's what it is. We can find a way to make this work. Just talk to me."

The desperation in her voice stabs at my heart. I open my mouth to respond, but the words evade me yet again. "I'm sorry," is all I'm able to mumble.

"You're *sorry?*" An edge creeps into Mary Grace's tone. "Sorry for *what*, Will? What the hell's going on?"

I inhale a deep breath and sigh. She deserves the truth. That's what I came here to give her. "I'm sorry, Mary Grace, but I can't go with you."

Mary Grace stares at me, her pale-blue eyes heavy with hurt and confusion. "Why not?" she snaps. "You just said you'd love to go, so why the hell can't you?"

I gaze at the ground, wishing the world would swallow me up. "It's too risky," I mutter, rubbing a hand through my hair.

"*Too risky?*" Mary Grace frowns at me. "What are you talking about, Will? How is it any more risky than sneaking out tonight? All you have to do is make it to the main road. We'll find a spot near the school to pick you up."

"Look, you don't get how things work there, okay?" I say, feeling a spike of frustration. "It's a matter of logistics. We wait until midnight before we sneak out. It's too risky before then. Our lights go out at ten, but no one goes straight to sleep. They chat for a while. They're up using the bathroom, or they stay up reading with a flashlight. It's way too risky to sneak out until everyone's asleep."

Mary Grace's shoulders slump. "So you're not even going to try? You're just saying you can't, and that's it? You have two weeks to figure out a plan. I can help you. We'll figure one out together."

Tell her, you pussy! Look her in the eyes and tell her the truth!

"I'm leaving in three weeks."

The words seem to hang in the air. Mary Grace squints at me for a second, and then her mouth hangs open.

"You're leaving?" she mumbles, her eyes glistening wetly. "Where are you going?"

"Home." My voice is hollow. The word "home" has never sounded so empty.

A tear spills onto Mary Grace's pale cheek. "In three weeks?"

I nod solemnly. "That's why it's too much of a risk. If Brother Bennett catches me sneaking off to Hattiesburg, he could tell the judge back in Atlanta, and that could really mess things up for me. I need to be a lot more careful from here on."

Mary Grace sniffs and wipes her cheeks with the back of her hand. "When did you find out about this?"

Shit! "A while ago."

Her eyes narrow. "How long is 'a while ago?'"

Fuck! I wipe the sweat from my brow.

"When did you find out you were leaving, Will?"

I clear my throat. "Far enough back that I should have told you already. I'm sorry."

An owl hoots through the silence.

"Why didn't you tell me?" Mary Grace asks, after a few moments.

"I don't know," I mumble, with a shake of my head. "I thought about telling you in the last letter I wrote, but that didn't seem right. I worried if I told you like that, I might never get to see you again. I didn't want that to happen."

"Interesting." Mary Grace frowns at me. "This makes me

wonder what you *did* want then. I mean, if you knew you were leaving so soon, why would you 'risk' sneaking out here to meet me?"

"Because I like you."

"Oh, you *like* me? What do you like about me, Will?"

"Everything. You dig the same music as me. You're smart. You're funny. You're...you're pretty."

"Blah, blah, blah! How very original of you! Don't try to flatter me with generic bullshit, okay? It's insulting and you're wasting your time!"

"I'm not trying to flatter you. It's the truth. I'm not good at saying these things, but I want you to know that you're someone I care about and respect..."

"*Respect*!?" Mary Grace lurches to her feet, towering above me. "If you respected me, Will, you would have told me the truth as soon as you knew it. But you didn't. You hid it. So what did you hope to gain from hiding it, huh? Did you want to fool around in the woods with me and then run off home once you'd had your fun?"

"No!" I cry out, hopping up from the flatbed to face her. "That's not how it was. I swear to you."

Mary Grace's chest heaves, and she buries her head in her hands.

"I'm sorry, Mary Grace. I don't know what else to say."

Sobbing softly, she peers at me with mascara-stained eyes. "Then say goodbye, Will. It sounds like that's all you came to do anyway." She squats down by the front of the pickup, reaches her hand underneath the rusty bumper, and pulls out a Tupperware box. "Here!" she says, thrusting it towards me. "I brought this for you."

I take it from her, and she holds my gaze with puffy, red eyes, streaks of makeup smearing her cheeks. "Goodbye, Will," she sniffles, and then turns and strides off toward the main road.

"Wait!" I call out, and start jogging after her. "Mary Grace!"

"Don't, Will. Just leave me alone, okay?"

"Can you please hold on a second? I really am sorry!"

"You've said that already. Please just let me go."

"Where are you going?"

"Home," she says, and the word sounds just as empty.

32

ONE TO GROW ON

Wednesday, June 13 - 74 days in

"You are so busted!" Shane and Molloy corner me in the kitchen at the end of breakfast cleanup. They each grab one of my arms and start leading me toward the exit. Angelo and Peaches stare at me in confusion, and I shrug as I'm ushered past them.

"Nice try, you sneaky little fucker," Shane says, with a wide, devious grin. "You almost got away with it."

I force a dry smile. There's no point in pretending I don't know what he's talking about. He's right; I was so close to getting away with it. It looked like I was going to. So how did they find out?

"I can't believe you tried to rob us of our boy's home rights, Will," Molloy says, looking genuinely affronted. "Birthday licks are a rule around here! You can't bitch out by not telling us when your birthday is. That's some messed up shit!"

"Don't worry about it," Shane tells him. "The bigger the bitch, the harder the licks, remember? Now we get to wish him a proper happy birthday."

Shit! Back when I first arrived, I used to think licks were no big deal. It was usually just a couple, rarely more than four or five. The most I saw anyone receive was ten. Until the day of Peaches' birthday, that is. Fifteen licks and 'one to grow on'.

The dumbass ran his mouth off the whole week leading up, telling anyone who would listen about his damn birthday, and exactly when it was. No one said shit about any birthday licks, not to him, me, or anyone else who didn't know. On the morning of Peaches' big day, I was surprised when they grabbed him during breakfast, but it was a shock when they brought out the paddle. The rest was too brutal to watch. Keeping my mouth shut was an easy decision after that.

As Shane and Molloy march me into the dining hall, I'm greeted with a mixture of jeers and applause.

"There he is!" Benny shouts. "The man of the moment!"

Everyone is crammed inside like it's time for lunch. On the menu today, Will Douglas, the birthday boy. The kid who tried to weasel out of a boy's home tradition. All around me, everyone is hungry for a slice.

"We should give him extra for trying to hide it," Oaf calls out. "No mercy licks either." A chorus of agreement echoes around the room. "I'm calling first shot," he yells again, and is promptly told to "fuck off" by a dozen different people. Taz steps up next to state his claim, and sits his ass down again when he receives the same response.

"Friends first." Angelo steps out of the crowd and grabs the end of the paddle Molloy is holding. Molloy grips the other end and stares him down. "That's the rule, right?" Angelo says, holding his gaze.

Molloy shoves the paddle into his hands. "Go ahead. Bitches hit first."

Angelo stares down at the paddle and turns to face me. "Happy birthday," he says, arching a brow. "Wish I could have gotten you something better than this, but it is what it is, man."

"No mercy licks, Angelo," Molloy yells. "Just smack him hard and pass it along. Let's get this shit going."

I nod at Angelo. "What he said. Let's get this over with." Steeling myself with a sigh, I turn around, grip the edge of the dining table, and bend over.

Smack!

A more forceful impact than I expected, but half-hearted enough that the sting subsides within a few seconds. Peaches steps up next, and Angelo hands him the paddle. His lick connects with an extra dose of love, and the heat of it still lingers as the next person steps up.

I glance back. To my surprise, it's Oaf who's holding the paddle, his fat cheeks puffed out in a grin of delight. I guess he's managed to claim "friend" status for being my roommate. I'm not worried, though. I've watched him at batting practice plenty of times. The effort required to swing those flabby arms doesn't translate into power. Just as I predicted, the paddle connects with less force than Angelo's.

After Oaf, it's a free-for-all. By the time the lick count reaches double figures, my ass is raw and numb. As is the custom, however, the last round of licks belongs to the Trusted Boys. Benny, Jerry, Shane, Molloy, and Trent are still arguing over who gets to deliver the extra lick, the final blow I'll receive. The 'one to grow on', as it's known, is supposed to be the most vicious of the lot. It matters little to me who dishes it out, though. Either way, they're all going to paddle me as hard as they possibly can, Molloy and Shane included.

With the bartering over, Trent leads off with a hit that burns an extra layer of heat upon the throbbing numbness. Jerry thumps me just as hard. As does Benny. I expect Molloy to hit next, but up steps Shane. After brandishing the paddle with a practice swing. He flexes his fingers around the grip and takes aim.

Smack!

I grunt and stumble forward, adjusting my feet to maintain my balance. My ass sears like it's on fire, and my eyes blur with tears. I clench them shut as laughter echoes throughout the dining hall. Only one more lick. One to grow on, and then all of this is over.

"My turn." I hear Molloy say behind me. I glance back and glimpse his smug satisfied smirk as he steps forward with the paddle. "To my good friend, Will," he announces. "It is my honor to give you your final birthday lick. We call it 'one to grow on' and I'm gonna make sure you always remember it."

"All I can remember is Shane's, right now," I spit, knowing it will rile him. "If this is 'one to grow on' I'm growing bored of waiting for it."

Laughter rings out around us, and Molloy swings before I can properly reset. Although I'm too numb and swollen to properly tell, this works to my advantage. The paddle slides off my ass instead of smacking it full on.

I ease myself upright, wincing through the pain. After all the mayhem, the room is strangely silent. As I glance around, I realize why. Arms folded across his broad chest, Brother Bennett stands in front of the dining room door, his face masked in shadow below the rim of his black cowboy hat.

"Time for school," he announces, and everyone jumps into action. "Not you, William. You stay with me." Brother Bennett's deep drawl booms above the trample of footsteps, and my heart lurches into a gallop.

"Follow me to my office, William," Brother Bennett instructs me as the dining hall empties. He motions me ahead of him, so I've no choice but to lead the way.

"Is everything okay, sir?" I ask, trying to keep my voice from trembling.

"No reason why it shouldn't be, son," Brother Bennett replies. "It's your birthday, isn't it?

"Yes, sir."

"Congratulations," he drawls, without a hint of sincerity. "It's good to see that the boys wished you well. That's a strong tradition here at Victory Ridge. A small reminder of how Jesus suffered for our sins. No one should be allowed to forget that, William. You understand?"

"Yes, sir."

We head down the hallway to Brother Bennett's office, and I stand aside as he unlocks the door. The cool air hits me the moment he swings it open. I follow him inside, savoring the soothing breeze as it sweeps across my skin. Brother Bennett sits down behind his desk.

Leaning back in his seat, he removes his cowboy hat and places it on the shelf behind him.

"Sit down." He gestures to the empty chair in front of his desk.

My asscheeks throb as I move toward it. The idea of sitting right now makes me want to wince. The chair looks far less comfortable than the one he's sitting on, but at least it's cushioned. Easing myself down, I grimace. Not cushioned enough, though!

"Would you mind if I just stand, sir?" I ask. "It's just...well, it's a bit too painful to sit, sir."

A sneer curls on Brother Bennett's lips. "Your comfort is not my priority, William. Take a seat."

The pain intensifies as I lower myself down on the chair again. I try to angle my ass to shift my weight around, but nothing eases the discomfort. I take a deep breath and try to cast it from my mind. Brother Bennett props his elbows on the arms of his chair and clasps his hands.

"So today is your sixteenth birthday. Is that right, William?"

"Yes, sir."

His dark eyes bore into me. "That's an important milestone for a young man, but the only milestones that truly matter are on your path to salvation. Your path to becoming a good Christian man, who puts the Lord above himself. Brother James and I are both pleased with your progress along that path. You've been doing much better around here, lately. As a reward, I've decided to bend the rules this one time."

I'm being rewarded? I shudder as my skin prickles. Why does this feel so icky?

"As you know," Brother Bennett continues, "phone calls are strictly prohibited for new boys during their first ninety days. However, given the improvements in your behavior and attitude, you will be allowed one phone call with your daddy. Today, after lunch."

Holy shit! "Thank you, sir." Thank you very much indeed. I have a long list of questions for that asshole, and asking about my flight home on the 30th is right at the top.

Brother Bennett leans forward and places his elbows on the desk. "Be thankful for all the Lord has given you, William. Remember that. Brother Robbie will be supervising the call with your daddy. You'll have ten minutes, not a second longer. He'll collect you after lunch and explain the rest of our rules, which you will be expected to follow exactly."

"Yes, sir, and thank you again!"

33

HOTDOGS IN HELL

I'm met by Shane and Molloy on my way to the schoolhouse, both of whom are on a "break."

"What did Bennett want?" Shane asks, lounging casually beneath a tree like he didn't just destroy my ass with a paddle. I resist the urge to ignore them and keep on walking. I'm curious about something, and I have a feeling they'll have answers.

"I'll tell you, but first you need to tell me how you found out it was my birthday."

"He's the one who found out." Shane nods towards Molloy, who grins at me devilishly. "He can tell you."

Molloy rubs his hands together enthusiastically. "I've been waiting for this moment."

"I bet you have!" I glare at him. "Just like you were waiting for the chance to hit me last."

Molloy fakes a pouty face and pokes out his bottom lip. "Aww, poor little baby," he says, mockingly. "That was boy's home justice, Chuck. You're the dumbass who was trying to cheat the rules, so don't get all pissy that you got a spanking to set you straight."

"Whatever," I mutter. "Just tell me how you found out."

"You sure you wanna know?" Molloy smirks at me, and I jut my jaw and glare at him. "Don't sweat it," he says, with a chuckle. "I'm telling you whether you wanna know or not. I found out while I was in the middle of making breakfast this morning. I was by myself when Miss Tammy showed up because Shane was away jacking off somewhere."

"I had to run to the shitter," Shane chimes in.

"Right," Molloy continues. "Shane was away jacking off in the shitter, and I was left to deal with Miss Tammy. Anyway, she comes in all pissed off and starts making a fuss about things as usual. But then she tells me we're gonna be changing the lunch menu for today. We're all having hotdogs for William Douglas's birthday."

"What!?" I've seen enough birthday licks to know they're never followed by a birthday lunch. "Why?"

"This is the best part," Molloy says, on the verge of cracking up. "She said your daddy called and talked to Brother Bennett. Told him he'd sent extra money on this month's check so everyone could have hotdogs to celebrate. That's the reason you got busted. Because of your own dad!"

Shane and Molloy hoot with laughter as I roll my head back and groan. Thanks again, Dad! You just keep screwing me over. *Hotdogs!?Really!?* You ship me off to hell and *that's* how you wish me a happy birthday?

"So what happened with Bennett then?" Shane asks me.

I let out a deflated sigh. "He told me I have a phone call with my dad after lunch." Shane and Molloy crack up again.

"Yeah, yeah, have fun laughing at me, assholes! I'm out of here."

"Hey, Will!" Molloy calls after me as I storm toward the schoolhouse. "Tell your dad we said thanks for the hotdogs!" I flip him off without glancing back.

All in all, this is typical of my dad. Whenever he bothers to make a halfhearted effort of some kind, it always backfires in my face instead of his. It's been this way ever since I can remember. Like the day he came home with a football signed by the Georgia Bulldogs 1980 National Championship winning team. I was maybe eight or nine; it was a couple of years or so after they won. I remember Dad showing it to Mom in the living room, and walking up to join them. When I reached out to touch the ball, he batted my hand away.

"This is not for touching," he said, even though he was holding it, which didn't make any sense.

"It does look like something he would be able to play with, though, honey," my mom had said, pulling me onto her lap. "Maybe you could buy one that he could play with. You could show him how."

I had no interest in learning how to throw, and I'm sure my dad had even less interest in teaching me. When Mom asked for something, though, we both had a habit of saying yes. We had that in common, at least.

A few weeks later, maybe, my dad came home with another ball. I'd completely forgotten about the whole thing by then, but Mom hadn't. "Your daddy wants to throw the ball with you," she said, though I could tell by Dad's grimace that he'd rather head back to the office.

I followed him out into the backyard in silence. "Stand over there." He pointed to a spot on the lawn several yards away. I moved over to it and turned around to face him. "Put your hands up ready. Watch the ball. And don't close your eyes."

Then he threw it. He didn't even ask if I was ready. He just launched the ball towards me. I remember it wobbling through the air toward me. I stuck out my hands and squeezed my eyes shut. The next thing I remember I'm howling in pain and clutching my thumb, which took the full force of the ball.

I ran inside to my mom, screaming, "Dad hurt me! Dad broke my hand!"

After that, no more playing catch with Dad. No more anything, really. But that's just the way it was with my old man and me, and the way it will always be. Mom and I shared a bond. With him, there's nothing. There never has been.

———

BY LUNCHTIME, everyone knows about my dad's menu request for his special birthday boy. The moment I enter the dining hall, the heckling begins. Every single one of these guys would take a hotdog over the dogshit we normally have to eat, but that doesn't stop them. They're all just as eager to kick me while I'm down, peppering me with put-downs as we line ourselves up.

I endure the abuse as we wait for the birthday lunch to begin, but commotion in the kitchen soon draws everyone's attention away from me. Everyone falls silent to listen.

"You better be yanking my chain, boy!" Brother Bennett's voice booms out. "You bought all these hotdogs and forgot about the buns?"

"I-I'm sorry, Daddy!" Robbie's voice quivers in response.

"The Good Lord must have sent you to test the strength of my faith, son. You're slower than a fly in molasses. Now get out of my sight! I can't stand to look at you!"

Robbie bursts out of the kitchen in tears and breaks into a run through the crowded dining room. No one laughs. No one dares. Besides, witnessing Brother Bennett rip apart anyone, even one of the other "adults", is never comical or entertaining. It fills my entire being with dread.

With the interruption now concluded, the lunch line resumes order, and each of us shuffles forward to pick up a paper plate with one pathetic, bunless hotdog, no condiments, and half a handful of stale chips. Happy fucking birthday to me!

Gingerly, I lower my tender ass on the bench across from Angelo, Peaches to my right, and stare at my miserable excuse for a birthday treat. What would Dad say if he knew his phone call earned me 17 licks; all for the gift of this depressing pink weiner staring back at me? He'd likely lecture me about being honest, as if he's ever honest with himself.

"Lies will always catch up with you, Will." How many times have I heard that crock of shit leave his lips? Lies live with us whether we want them to or not, but Dad chooses to live in them. He only sent me here so he wouldn't have to deal with me. He didn't know how to, and he didn't care enough to try. If this birthday lunch is an example of him trying, I wish he wouldn't bother.

Near the end of clean up duty, a puffy-eyed Robbie enters the kitchen and approaches me. Considerably shorter and slighter than the other men at Victory Ridge, particularly his giant of a daddy, Robbie Bennett looks even more withered than usual after his public berating. It's hard not to feel sympathetic.

"W-what you starin' at, Chuck? You g...you gonna puke or something?" Robbie smirks and glances around the kitchen in hope of laughs.

All sympathy for him vanishes.

I shake my head. "I just assumed you were here about my phone call. Your dad said you'll be supervising it."

Robbie scowls. "That's why I'm here, dummy. Daddy said t-to take you to his office. Gave me his keys." His front pocket jingles as he pats it.

"Okay," I say, waiting for him to lead the way, but Robbie Bennett looks permanently lost. Just a fellow broken boy. "So, should we go *now*?" I ask him.

He stares at me vacantly. "That's why I'm here."

"I'll finish the rest of the pots, Will," Angelo says. "Go take your phone call."

This seems to prompt Robbie into action, and he turns to leave. I give Angelo a nod of appreciation and follow after him.

"Daddy said I gotta tell you the rules about ph-phone calls," Robbie says, as we head along the hallway toward the front section of the main building, where the offices are located. "Number one rule is no cussin'. Daddy don't stand for no cussin'. That's why I gotta listen on the other ph-phone."

"Wait..." I squint at him. "You're going to be listening to my call?"

"That's right," Robbie nods, with an air of self-importance. "Daddy said I gotta make sure you ain't cussin' or tellin' lies and stuff."

Telling the truth, more like. What the hell is this, the USSR?

We reach Brother Bennett's office, and Robbie digs out the

key and unlocks it. Again, I'm hit by the rush of cool air as we walk inside.

"Daddy said the number's on his desk." Robbie points at a yellow Post-it note. I walk over and glance at it. Dad's office number.

"I know his number, but does *he* know I'm calling?"

"Th-that's what Daddy said."

"Okay," I say. "Any other rules I need to know, other than no cussing or lying?" I'm stalling, but I need a few more seconds to steel myself.

Robbie furrows his brow. "Well, Daddy don't like no arguin' neither. And you ain't supposed to say nothin' n-negative. Only good stuff."

"Good stuff? Like what?"

Robbie darkens a shade. "Like God and baseball and hot dogs and stuff. Just d-don't say nothin' bad, g-got it?"

"Aye, aye, comrade," I raise a hand in mock salute. "Ready when you are!"

"Wait till I'm across the hall and d-dial the number. Holler when it starts ringin'."

The moment Robbie exits the room, I take a long, deep breath and lift up the phone. I dial the 404 area code, followed by the rest of my dad's office number. The dial tone switches to a resonant chime.

"It's ringing," I call out, and hear a click as Robbie picks up the other receiver.

"Good afternoon, this is Douglas Family Dental. How can I help you?" a woman answers. The sickening familiarity of her nasal voice feels like needles being shoved in my ears. Fucking

Joyce! The moment I saw the number, I should have prepared myself.

"Hello?"

I clear my throat. "I'd like to speak to Dr. Douglas, please."

"Will?"

Shit!

"Will, is that you?"

Shit, shit, shit!

"It's you, isn't it? I know it is. Your father said you'd be call-ing. How are you, sweetie pie? Everything going good?"

Fuck off, Joyce!

"Is my dad there?"

"Of course, sweetie. He's in his office eating lunch right now. You know, it's just so nice hearing your voice after all this..."

"Look," I say, cutting her off, "I need to speak to my dad. Can you just go tell him I'm on the phone?" Silence. "Please. I don't have much time to talk."

"Well, in that case, let me just put you on hold for a second, and I'll go interrupt your father's lunch for you. How about that?"

The line falls silent, and I'm left to marvel at how well she can leave me feeling like an asshole. How can I impose upon my dad's lunch when he's expecting me to call during it?

A half-minute later the phone crackles to life. "Will?" my dad's gruff voice speaks into my ear.

"Hey," is all I manage to utter back.

"Happy birthday, buddy. Sweet sixteen, huh? Did you enjoy the hotdogs?"

I swallow back the words pressing against my lips. No cussing. No arguing. Nothing negative. None of that will help, anyway. Only one thing matters about this conversation, and I'm not interested in dancing around it for the sake of formalities, whether Robbie's listening or not.

"Yeah, the hotdogs caused quite a stir. Definitely a surprise. So, what's the plan for the 30th, Dad? I'm hitting ninety days in a couple of weeks, and no one's told me how I'm getting home yet. Don't worry about sending Joyce out, though. I'll be fine flying by myself."

Silence.

"Dad?"

"I'm here, Will."

"Did you hear what I just said?"

"I did."

Then why the hell isn't he answering me? "Well?"

"Well what, Will?"

"Well, aren't you going to tell me what the plan is?"

"How are you doing, son? How are you feeling?"

Sweat beads on my forehead. This conversation is not going as planned. He wants to know that I've changed. That I'm some newly improved version of myself. Well, if that's what he wants, I'm more than happy to give it to him. Only talk about good things, right? This one's for you, Robbie.

I draw a deep breath and blast into bullshit mode. "It's funny you should ask, Dad, because I'm actually doing better than ever. I know you probably won't believe me, but I've tried really hard to change since I got here. In fact, Brother Bennett was just telling me how pleased he is with my progress. He's helped me realize how selfish I was acting, and how I took out my anger on everyone. You were right about me needing help. I'm ready to come home and be a better person now."

"Well, that's great to hear, Will."

"Yup, pretty great. So are you picking me up on the 30th or am I flying by myself?"

Silence.

"Dad?"

Still no response. My heart thumps faster.

"Listen, if you've not booked me a flight yet, no problem. Just give me some idea of what the plan is, okay? That's all I'm looking for. Dad?"

"Will, can we please talk about this later?"

Is he kidding me? Sweat trickles down my forehead.

"No, Dad, let's talk about this now. I don't have another phone call between now and then. You need to tell me what the plan is!"

He clears his throat. "The plan has changed, Will."

My heart spasms wildly in my chest.

"What do you mean?" My voice sounds distant and slurred.

"Everything's already decided. I spoke with the courts and the Bennett family. We all agree it's best if you stay until graduation."

The room blurs. My mind falls numb and silent, and for a moment I feel nothing but the achy sting of my battered backside.

"I know this may not be the news you wanted to hear on your birthday, which is why I was reluctant to discuss it. But hearing that you're doing so well there certainly backs up this decision. I hope you understand that I'm only trying to do what's best for you."

"What's best for me? Dad, I'm already a year behind. You're talking about leaving me in this place for three years!"

"And why are you a year behind, Will? Whose fault is that? I'm not the reason you were expelled from school, young man. I'm not the one who..."

"You lied to me!" I say, cutting him off. "The judge said ninety days. That was all. You agreed. That's what you promised me!"

He sighs. "It's already been decided, Will. I signed the paperwork last week."

I slam the phone down and crumple into tears. Robbie pokes his head inside the office. He stares vacantly at my sobbing, snotty mess of a face, and closes the door. For the next few minutes, I let everything pour out of me until there's nothing left but emptiness.

34

GOODBYE, ANGELO

Friday, June 15 - 76 days in

"Will?"

A hand presses against my shoulder and shakes me. I crack my eyes open, blinking rapidly as light floods my retinas.

"Will, wake up, man."

It's Angelo. His face phases into focus. A friendly smile. His large brown eyes laden with worry. I rub the sleep from my eyes and glance around.

"What time is it?"

Angelo checks his watch. "Nearly two o'clock in the afternoon. And it's Friday, in case you're wondering what day it is." He walks over and sits on the end of my bunk. "I was hoping you might drag your ass out of bed before I leave, bro. But it looks like that ain't happening, huh?"

I spy his suitcase and backpack on the floor beneath his

bunk. I pretended to be asleep while he was packing last night. Maybe I should feel more ashamed about that, but I've only got enough pity for myself right now. Mr. Three Years is heading home, and I'm stuck here to pick up his legacy.

"What time are you leaving?"

Angelo shifts around to face me. "My flight's at 5:30 in New Orleans, so…"

"So this is it."

He nods solemnly. "This is it."

A silence settles between us.

"Well, are you ready?" I ask, after several awkward seconds pass.

"Of course, man! I've been ready for over three years…" He pauses and lowers his gaze. "I've been waiting for this day for way too long, bro. It just sucks that I'm leaving you in such a shitty spot right now."

"Don't worry about me. Just focus on what you're going back to. That's what got you through the last three years, right?"

Angelo nods. "If it worked for me, it can work for you, too, man."

"Oh really?" I scoff at him. "Do you think it's that fucking simple for me, Angelo? Maybe you haven't figured this out yet, but I don't have a family like yours waiting for me! I don't have a mom who mails me packages, or a cute baby sister I'm dying to meet! I've got a dad who wishes I didn't exist, and a mom who's…she's…" Tears spill out and I bury my face in my pillow.

Angelo places his hand on my back. "I'm sorry, bro. I know it ain't the same for you. I know about your mom. I didn't mean to…"

"No, you don't!" I snap, and Angelo flinches back his hand. I turn around and sit up on my mattress. "You don't know shit about my mom, okay? You're just like everyone else around here. You only know what I've told you."

Angelo furrows his brow with confusion. "You said she died in a car crash."

"No, I said I *lost* her in one. It would have been easier if she had, though." I cringe after saying it, but I know it's the truth.

I knew it two years ago, as well. I didn't really understand what a coma was back then, but the doctor sat me down to explain. *"Your mom is missing a softball-sized part of her brain, Will. She's breathing, but that's all she'll be able to do anymore."*

My dad and Candy were convinced Mom would wake up. They would feed one another's delusions about some Hallmark-movie ending that was never going to happen. It made me sick to my stomach and still does! Nothing would prepare me for what happened next, though.

It still feels like a cruel nightmare: coming home from school and seeing the ambulance parked in our drive. I sprinted inside the house in a panic. A nurse milled around our kitchen talking to Dad.

"What's going on?" I asked him.

He smiled and sipped a mug of coffee. "Your mother's home."

I remember the surge of hope inside me, but also a nagging sense that something was amiss. Three medical assistants were moving the furniture around in the study. The next thing I knew, they wheeled out the grand piano and wheeled Mom inside the room on her hospital bed.

"She's back where she belongs now," Dad said to me as we stood staring at her motionless body. "Aren't you glad to have her back?

Now you'll be able to see her everyday. It's better that way. Better for everyone."

"Will?" Angelo sits there staring at me. "I don't understand, man. What are you trying to tell me?"

I wipe my eyes with the back of my hands. "My mom's been in a coma ever since the accident," I tell him. "The doctors say she's never coming out of it, but my dad refuses to accept that she's gone. He keeps her at home and pays a nurse to look after her. She just lies in bed, day after day, hooked up to a feeding tube. But she's not really alive anymore. She's not actually living."

"Shit..." Angelo shakes his head. "I don't even know what to say. I'm sorry, bro. I had no idea."

The pity in his eyes infuriates me. "I don't need your fucking sympathies, okay? I need you to understand why *your* way doesn't work for me. Everytime I think about home, I'm reminded of her. She wouldn't want to be kept alive like that! She would be heartbroken if she knew! She would be furious! So fuck you for telling me to focus on what I'm going back to, Angelo! I'm better off staying here than watching my mom rot away in a bed!"

My own words shock me. I would never have admitted that before, but now, more than ever, I know that it's true. I flop back on my mattress and stare up at the ceiling, wishing he would just hurry up and go.

"Listen, man," Angelo says, "I really don't want to leave this way."

"Tough shit! I guess you don't have a choice, do you?" I roll over and turn my back to him. "Safe travels, Angelo. Enjoy being home with your family again."

"C'mon, Will. Please don't act like this."

"Act like what? Like it's time to say goodbye?"

Angelo sighs. "Alright, I guess this is how it's gotta be right now." He slides down off my bunk and walks over to his luggage. "Hey, Will?"

"What?" I grunt.

"I'm gonna miss you, man."

Tears leak from my eyes, but I say nothing in response.

"I know you ain't in a place to hear this right now," Angelo continues, "but there are still people in your life who truly care about you. Don't push them all away, okay? If you close your eyes for too long, you'll forget how to open them."

"Okay then," I snort. Typical preachy Angelo! "Thanks for the advice."

I hear him pick up his bags. "I guess I should probably get going."

"Yeah, I guess you should."

"I'll be in touch soon, okay? I'm not just saying that either."

I roll my eyes. "Sure, sounds good. Goodbye, Angelo."

"Goodbye, Will."

35

HOLY ROLLERS

Sunday, June 17 - Day 78

I jolt upright, gasping, ice-cold water streaming from my face to my chest.

"Enough of this shit, Will. Get up!"

Shane looms over my bunk, arms folded across his chest. Molloy grins devilishly behind him, waving an empty cup in his hand.

"What did you do that for, you fucking asshole!?" Shivering, I wipe my face with my covers and glare at him. "I'm sick, remember? How am I supposed to get better if you throw cold water on me when I'm trying to rest? Do you have any idea how that feels?"

"Wet!" Molloy smirks at me. "Now get out of bed!"

I shake my head. "Brother James gave me permission. He said I..."

"Brother James just sent us up here to get you," Shane interjects, matter-of-factly. "He said to tell you that 'your get-out-of-jail-free card has officially expired'. So I guess you better get your ass out of bed and get dressed."

"Fine!" I say, throwing my covers aside. "Leave me alone to change, and I'll head down to breakfast."

Molloy snorts out a laugh. "You slept through breakfast, dumbass. It's time for church."

———

EVERYONE ELSE IS ALREADY SITTING NEXT to their usual bus buddy by the time I board The Smurf Turd. Finding a seat isn't a problem, though. My usual row is empty. I settle into my seat on the aisle, leaving Angelo's window seat vacant. For the first time, his absence feels real.

I acted like a total ass the day he left. It wasn't him I was angry at. Something tells me he knows that, but I still wish he was here so I could tell him and apologize. Right now, though, he's back where he wants to be. Home with his family again.

So where the hell do I want to be? Not here, that's for sure. Not back home either. There's no family for me there. Not really, anyway. Just the depressing sight of my mother withering away in a hospital bed and a depressed, drunken father who resents my existence.

His voice slithers through my mind, harsh and mocking and thick with liquor. I clench my eyes shut, but it's impossible to shift. *"There's no place for you here, you selfish little shit!"* the voice slurs. *"You don't care about anybody but yourself."*

I open my eyes to find Peaches standing in the aisle, squinting down at me.

"Scoot over," he says, nudging me on the shoulder.

Too caught off guard to object, I slide over to the window seat, and Peaches plops down beside me.

"What's up?" I say, in a tone implying "what do you want?".

"Oh, I'm just seein' how my buddy Will's holdin' up." He gives me a sideways glance as he lounges back in the seat.

"Oh yeah? Just checking on me, huh?" I raise an eyebrow. "That's why you came over?"

"Yup," he says. "Just saw you sittin' here alone and thought I'd come keep you company."

"Bullshit. You want something."

Peaches has the audacity to look offended. "What? Why would you say somethin' like that? I'm just tryna be a good friend, Will!"

"Were you trying to be a good friend when you offered odds on whether I'd go home after ninety days or not? Yeah, I heard about that shit, Peach! You exploited all the private shit I told you just to rig a few bets."

Peaches' cheeks turn pink. "Don't know 'bout no exploitin'. I just bet against your dad. So what? Ain't like I was bettin' against you or nothin'."

"You're kidding, right?" I swivel toward him so abruptly that he flinches away. "You totally bet against me, Peach. Let's be real. But that's not the point. The shit I told you guys about my dad was personal, man. I didn't think you'd trade it around like fucking smokes."

"Relax, buddy!" Peaches lifts his hands in surrender. "I'm gonna cut you in on all the profits. Don't you worry. I ain't the type of dude that screws over his friends to make a buck, okay? That ain't the way I do business."

I turn away and stare toward the front of the bus. "Okay, Peach. If you say so."

"You know what," Peaches says after a few seconds of silence, "I've been thinkin' we'd make a pretty good team. What would you say to bein' business partners? I've got a damn good idea to discuss. It's my best one yet."

Finally, he gets to the point of his visit. I roll my eyes. "This isn't the time, Peach, and I'm not interested, okay?"

"You see, that's where you're wrong, buddy." Peaches leans in closer. "This is exactly the right time. You gotta hear me out to know if you're interested or not. And trust me, you're gonna be interested."

I sigh. Peaches might be as red as roadkill, but he has some big, shiny brass balls. There's no denying that.

"If I hear you out, will you leave me the hell alone?"

Peaches nods enthusiastically. "For the rest of the day."

I shake my head. "Fine. Make it quick and make sure it's interesting."

"How 'bout both?" he says, and leans in even closer. "I'm callin' it Holy Rollers. A boy's home brand of custom-made smokes." He watches me as though waiting for the genius of his words to sink in.

"Very clever," I tell him. "Please carry on."

He nods and clears his throat. "So, a few weeks ago, I started collectin' cigarette butts. They ain't hard to find when you're lookin'. There's always some down by the trailers and plenty in the parkin' lot at church. There was a bunch at the ballfield the other day. I even found 'em over there by the woods behind the schoolhouse. Figure the older boys must be sneakin' out there, but I ain't found a stash or nothin'."

Shit!

"Peach, can you please get to the point?"

"Anyways, figured I'd use what tobacco was left to roll my own smokes. Worked pretty good, I guess, but it took two dang weeks till I had enough to roll more than one. Which got me to thinkin'. If I had my buddy Will as my partner, maybe he could bring me a whole pack every week. Then I could turn twenty smokes into forty, maybe even sixty. I could control the whole dang market. *We* could run this fuckin' place, buddy!"

I look at Peaches and see him in a whole new light. His eyes scour my expression expectantly.

"I'll pass," I tell him.

His smug smile withers. "Huh?"

"Listen, Peach, it's a clever idea. I'll give you that. But that's some nasty ass shit, man! You're literally picking trash off the ground and selling it as something else."

Peaches frowns. "Not if *you're* on my side. You can get me the real deal! Do you even know how much one smoke is worth in the dorm?"

I shrug. "A bag of Doritos?"

Peaches chortles, shaking his head. "See, you don't know shit about shit. That's why we gotta be partners. You can get the smokes, and I know what to do with 'em and exactly how to do it. It's a match made in Nowhere, Will. Let's make this shit happen!"

I chuckle. "I'll think about it, Peach."

"Do that!" Peaches says, his confidence reignited. "We ain't gettin' out of here anytime soon, buddy. Why not get away with as much as we can, right?"

Right. Peaches might be a ruthless little shit, but he's far from stupid. That's why he's not prying into how or why I have access to cigarettes. He knows I'll view that as a threat, and he needs me more than I need him.

"I'll take it all under consideration, Peach," I say, as he rises to leave. "But I have one more question."

"Shoot," he says.

"Holy Rollers? That's a pretty dope name. You came up with that?"

"Sure did! You see, we at Holy Rollers take pride in our cigarettes. That's why each one is hand-rolled in holy scripture. We ain't got no rollin' papers round here, but there's a whole lotta pages in the King James Bible. And we've gotta whole lotta Bibles, buddy!"

36

I WAS WONDERING WHERE THIS WAS

A short while later, as Brother James steers us into the church parking lot, I'm reminded of one Bible in particular. One with Metallica lyrics hidden inside. The guilt of hurting Mary Grace stabs at my heart, twisting its blade with every thrust. All that was numbed after the phone call with my dad. I was far too engulfed in my own misery to care about anyone else. It all comes flooding back now, though, as I return to the place I first laid eyes on her. Back to where it all began.

She was so full of exuberance when I first showed up last week, and then so deflated and heartbroken as she stormed off into the night. I doubt it would matter that my circumstances have changed now. Even if there's a chance Mary Grace doesn't hate me, I doubt she would trust me or want to hang out again. I can't say I blame her. We'll always see one another at church, I guess, not that she would ever talk to me when she's with her mom. She never even looks at me. I'm sure she'd prefer that I leave her the hell alone. Maybe that's the best thing for both of us.

Entering church, I force myself not to search for her and manage my way to the pew without lifting my eyes from the carpet. I slide along next to Peaches and open my King James Bible on my lap. Staring blankly at the pages, even the reminder of his Holy Rollers scheme fails to oust Mary Grace from my mind. Whether I can see her or not, I know where she is. Like the warmth of a nearby fire, I can feel her.

A notion dawns on me. Within the last week, I've lost my two best friends. However, as strongly as I feel Angelo's absence, I can sense Mary Grace's presence. I'm not sure what that means, exactly, but it has to mean something. Angelo said I still have people in my life who truly care about me, and he's right. I couldn't see it at the time. Maybe I didn't want to. But I can see it now as bold as black on white.

I might not have anyone back home who truly cares about me, but that doesn't mean I have no one. Angelo cares, and I care about him. Right from the beginning, he was a kind and empathetic friend. He was more of a brother to me than anyone. And I'll always love him for that. I lost him before I could tell him that or properly show him. That's not a mistake I want to repeat, especially not with Mary Grace.

With her I never had to be anyone but myself. She reminded me how it felt to feel affection again, both for someone and from them. Reciprocal. Genuine. Soulful. I could tell her things I wouldn't dare reveal to anyone else, and she shared as deeply with me. She made me tapes and bought me cigarettes. She even made a plan to bust me out and take me to her brother's concert. She showed she cared in more ways than everyone else in my life combined. I can't afford to lose Mary Grace, too.

I straighten up and scan the area she normally sits, searching the pews for the back of her head and that tight, brown bun. Instead I find her staring back at me over her shoulder. My heart lurches as our eyes lock. What is she doing? She never looks back at me like this.

Mary Grace's pale eyes hold mine in a sympathetic gaze. She smiles softly, and I force one back. Her smile widens, and she turns back around to face the front. My pulse thumps wildly. What in the hell was that all about? One minute she's storming off into the night, and the next time I see her she's turning around to grin at me in church! She never even looked back at me before she got pissed off and didn't want to see me again. And I've no idea how I'm supposed to know what any of this means.

I'm about to lose myself in a maze of overanalyzing when my attention is drawn to a soft ripping sound to my left.

"What the hell are you doing?" I whisper to Peaches, who is in the semi-discrete process of folding up pages of scripture and stuffing them in his pockets.

"Supplies," he whispers back and rubs his thumb across his first two fingertips. "Ka-ching, ka-ching, buddy. Got me a business to run."

"If you get caught doing that *here*, you're going to get a yucking, you moron! Cut that shit out!"

Peaches hangs his head a little, and shuts his Bible. I like him, but sometimes he's as stupid as he is clever. Something he said on the bus keeps tugging at my attention, though. *"We ain't gettin' out of here anytime soon, buddy. Why not get away with as much as we can, right?"* I know he was just trying to convince me to team up with him, but there's a bitter truth to what he said. It's given me a glimpse of the bigger picture.

The next few years of my life are now set. No matter how good or bad I am, I don't have the power to change that. I'm here until I graduate. There's no time off for good behavior. No early release. 90 days will pass by, and that number will keep on rising. No matter how much I resent all of that, I just have to accept it.

On the flipside, though, I can't stay any longer than I already am, which means the risk just plummeted. So why not get away with as much as I can? There's nothing holding me back anymore. I can give Mary Grace exactly what she wants now. I can try to win her back. All I need is something to write with.

My eyes dart to the shelved compartment on the back of the pew in front of me. Brother James always gathers up the pens and pencils from the backs of the pews before any of us are permitted to sit. Apparently, someone was stabbed with a pen at the church we used to attend in Petal, which is why we now drive to Hattiesburg.

This time I'm in luck, though. I spy the broken tip of a pencil tucked beneath a pamphlet. Picking up the booklet with one hand, I palm the piece with the other. I open the pamphlet on my lap and examine my find. The lead point is practically intact, but there's barely enough wood remaining to grip with the edge of my fingertips. Far from ideal, but it will have to do.

I nudge Peaches. "Give me one of those pages in your pocket," I tell him.

He squints at me. "No way," he whispers back. "Those are my business supplies."

"Fine," I say, "Give me one of those pages, and I'll partner up with you on Holy Rollers. Deal?"

His eyes light up. "That's a deal!" he says, digging in his pocket and pulling out a wad of torn Bible pages. "Which one do you want?"

"Whichever has the most blank space. The less writing the better."

He stares at them. "They've all got writin' on 'em, Will. They're from the dang Bible!" Peaches' voice elevates beyond a whisper, and Brother James's head swivels in our direction. He scowls and holds a finger to his pursed lips.

"Here," Peaches slips me a page that's only partially covered in text.

"Thanks," I say, slipping it into my pocket. "Listen, now that we're partners, I'm going to need your help with something, Peach. No questions asked, okay?"

His eyes dart around like he's trying to settle on a decision. "What do you need me to do?"

"I'll tell you when I get back," I say, waving my hand until I catch Brother James's attention. He scowls at me from the end of the pew and mouths something as he shakes his head. I mouth back the words "I need to go to the bathroom" and grimace as I clutch my stomach. His frown of frustration fades, and he hurriedly waves me his way.

I stand up and start shuffling along the pew toward the aisle, boys tucking in their legs to make room. I can feel the attention shift my way, heads turning around to look. None of that bothers me. Making a scene works far better for me anyway. I pause as I pass Brother James and cover my mouth, pretending to gag.

He flinches away from me. "Go!" he whispers frantically and shoves me out of the pew.

I hurry up the aisle into the lobby and straight to the men's restroom. Relieved to find the stall empty, I lock myself inside and remove the paper and the pencil tip from my pocket. Gripping the tiny piece proves even trickier than I expected, but I don't need high-quality handwriting right now. As quickly and as legibly as I can, I scrawl out a message on the blank space of the page.

Dear MG,

I'm sorry I was such an idiot. I understand if I messed things up between us. I wish I could change what happened, but all I can do is change what happens next. I'm no longer leaving. My dad told me I'm staying until I graduate. As much as that sucks, it would be a million times worse without you in my life. I know I need to earn back your trust, but there is nothing I want more than to sneak out next Saturday and go with you to Sam's concert. You are more than worth the risk. I hate that I ever made you question that. If you can forgive me and still want me to go, please let me know.

Will

Satisfied, I head back to my seat, moving as gingerly as possible as I slide past a wary Brother James again and back along the pew to my spot.

"What was that all about?" Peaches asks, as I settle in beside him.

I glance at my watch. "You'll find out soon," I whisper. "I still need your help with something. No questions asked, remember?" He nods, and I lean in closer. "I need you to distract

Brother James at the end of the service. I'll tell you when the time is right."

"Distract him how?"

"However you can! It's not rocket science, Peach, just keep him distracted. You're the craftiest, little shit I know, so figure it out. Show me why I partnered up with you."

Peaches chews his bottom lip. "Okay, just tell me when you need me."

As service draws to a close and everyone files into the aisle, that's exactly what I do.

"Now! Let's move!"

I drag Peaches in front of me as we slide along the pew, nudging him forward. Brother James is waiting at the end of the pew, supervising us as we exit into the aisle. I glance down several rows and spot Mary Grace shuffling along in line. Her eyes find mine, but a sudden commotion in front of me seizes my attention.

Peaches has one of the new kids gripped in a headlock. The pair of them flail around the pew while Brother James gawks at them in disbelief. He snaps out of it and into action, grabbing Peaches by the back of his shirt as I scoot past him into the aisle.

The pew across ours has already emptied. I duck inside for cover as everyone slows down to watch the scuffle, like cars braking as they pass by an accident. I peer down the aisle and find the tall figure of Mary Grace just a couple of pews away. I slip the note out of my pocket and wait until she steps right next to me.

"Excuse me," I say, and she gasps as I appear. "You dropped something."

I reach my hand out toward her, the note between my fingertips. Her pale eyes sparkle, and a smile spreads across her face, tingeing her pale cheeks pink.

"Thank you," she says, her fingers grazing mine as she takes it from me. "I was wondering where this was."

She turns and merges back into the crowd, leaving my skin tingling and my heart reeling.

37

ONE FINGER SALUTE

Peaches now refers to our partnership as "The Alliance" even though we haven't exactly made it official yet. After taking licks for the stunt he pulled to help me, he can call it whatever he wants. Keeping my own self-interests aligned with his is probably the wisest move at this point, anyway. So here's to The Alliance!

In fact, Peaches and our new partnership is the reason I'm risking a trip to my stash in the middle of the afternoon. Peaches knew he'd earn licks, but he helped me anyway. So, even though he hasn't asked for anything in return yet, rewarding him with a couple of smokes for having my back seems the right thing to do. It should also buy me some leverage if I need it.

I reach the edge of the woods and weave my way through some shrubbery. I find my spot near the base of a tall pine, on which I scraped off the bark in the shape of a crude *M* for Metallica. Setting aside the branches I placed over the top of the hole, I reach in and remove two boxes of Tupperware. One contains my pack of Camel Lights and the Walkman Mary Grace gave me; the other I've never opened. In fact, this is the first time I've seen it since I stowed it here, the night I told her I was leaving.

I peel back the plastic lid and rummage through the tapes inside, all six of them. When was the last time someone made me one tape, never mind six? I pick out *...And Justice For All*, retrieve the Walkman from the other box, and pop it inside. I fix my headphones and press play.

This album has always helped me escape. It's all I listened to after Mom's accident. I even run it on repeat through my head when I'm in church. Every word. Every verse. Every chord on every crunchy riff. I know this album better than I know myself.

I slump down and lean back against the trunk of the pine. Closing my eyes, I let the music flush everything out of my mind. Well, not quite everything. Metallica Girl is right here next to me, the two of us sprawled back on the hood of the pink pickup, listening together. Her hand clasped in mine.

The opener, *Blackened*.

...And Justice For All, the title track.

Up next, *Eye of the Beholder*.

Followed by *One*, my favorite.

I open my eyes and press stop. Mary Grace copied her brother's demo tape on one of these cassettes. I remove *...And Justice For All*, slot it back in its case, and sort through the others until I find one with "Executive Anarchy" written in Mary Grace's neat cursive.

Five songs are listed on the insert.

One Finger Salute

Message in a B-2 Bomber

Silent Sabotage

Bye-Bye, Bundy

Nudely Rude

If I was intrigued before, the titles certainly amp up the hype. They sound like metal songs to me, but what do they actually sound like? I insert the cassette and click play. Guitars, bass, and drums sputter to life, interchanging intermittently. The sound quality pales in comparison to what I just listened to, but the energy and rhythm weave and build until all the instruments unite, and the music pulsates through me.

I focus on the bass, Sam's voice in all of this. Its deep resonance pounds like a heartbeat amid the rasping blare of guitars and tribal thumping of drums. This is really solid shit! Sam's no Cliff Burton or anything, but he's definitely talented! The songs are also way better than I expected. The singer underwhelms me a little bit, but he totally makes up for mumbling through the verse when he screams out the chorus.

"Come join the call, and raise das boot.

Brick walls can't shoot! One finger salute!

Spoils and oil from Berlin to Beirut.

Fight for the truth! One finger salute!"

———

THE LYRICS REVERBERATE through my head as I sit aboard The Smurf Turd on our way to evening service. My new bus buddy and business partner, Peaches, sits beside me. He's worn the same triumphant grin ever since I thanked him with those smokes, and it shows no signs of wearing off anytime soon. He shows no signs of shutting up about our new business plan, either.

"We need a scheduled system," he says. "How many smokes can you get each week? Five? Ten? If you could get a whole pack of twenty, that would be..."

"I've no idea, Peach. I've told you that." I straighten up in my seat and rub my eyes. "I'm done talking about this right now, man. I'm done listening to it. When I know, I'll tell you. Until then, please just stop."

"Can't just stop thinkin' about our baby, Will."

I groan. "Think about it all you want, just stop talking about it. And stop calling it our baby! I'm sick of hearing you go on and on about it, so just take a break for now. Got it?"

Peaches juts out his jaw and falls silent. He folds his arms and glares at the seat in front of him. Good! Let him pout. There's no room in my head for this shit right now. The desperate need for Mary Grace's response consumes every ounce of my energy and focus. I'm so anxious I have to clasp my hands on my lap to stop them shaking.

By the time we're walking into church, I feel like I'm on the verge of a nervous breakdown. Last Sunday, she turned around and smiled at me. That certainly gives me hope, but one smile doesn't guarantee forgiveness. Sliding into an empty pew, I spot her near the front beside her mother. My insides jitter as she turns and glances over her shoulder, scanning the rows behind her until her eyes land on me.

A smile lights up her face again, even wider and brighter than last time. I smile back at her, feeling the tension ease from my mind and body. She holds my gaze for a few seconds and turns around to face the front. I inhale a deep breath and blow it out gently. Everything is okay, Will. Everything just might work out.

As my worries drain away, I grow all the more eager to read Mary Grace's reply to my note. But my eagerness swells into impatience when the service crawls to an end, and by the time I'm on The Smurf Turd as it rumbles back to Nowhere, I'm on the verge of ripping out my hair. The moment we're off the bus at Victory Ridge, I follow Shane and Molloy to their room. I thank Shane as I snatch the folded envelope from his hand and hurry to the bathroom where I shut myself in a stall.

Dear Will,

Yes, I forgive you and still want you to go with me! I accept your apology for being an idiot, but I'll give you a pass on being selfish because your sucky news just made me super happy! As for the concert, I'm excited beyond words! Sam's girlfriend is driving up from New Orleans. I've never met her, but Sam says she'll pick me up and take me to the concert. That's all I know right now, other than it's on Saturday at The King James Tavern and they'll be on stage around 11 o'clock. I'll make arrangements to get you too, and I'll have the plan laid out by Wednesday. It will be like breaking you out of jail!

See you soon, Will!

MG

P.S. Just so you know, things would be worse without you in my life too.

Silent tears trickle down my cheeks. One drips from my chin and splats on the page, blotting the paper with a damp circle. My heart twinges with an overwhelming sense of relief and gratitude. I can't remember the last time I was forgiven instead of demonized, or when someone felt happy I was staying instead of trying to get rid of me. When was the last time someone told me that I made their life better?

If someone as amazing as Mary Grace likes me this much, then maybe I'm not that shitty of a person, after all. Like never before, I want to show her she's right.

38

DESPERATE DEALS

Wednesday, June 20 - Day 81

Dear Mary Grace,

I've made a plan for Saturday and Shane and Molloy have agreed to help. This means I need to ask you for more help too, unfortunately. They both want a pack of cigarettes as payment for keeping watch while I sneak out. I really hate to ask, but would you be able to get those for me? I have nothing to pay you back with except my company, but I promise to keep you safe from any mosh pits!

As you can see, this really is like breaking me out of jail. You were right about that! I know you said you'd give me the full plan at church this evening, but the safest place to pick me up is a dirt road that runs behind the property. It might be hard to find in the dark, but it's about a quarter of a mile before you reach the school driveway. I'll read your letter tonight and whatever time you say you're coming, that's where I'll meet you.

Take care until then, Mary Grace. I can't wait to give this dump the One Finger Salute and watch Executive Anarchy tear up Hattiesburg with you!

Will

I fold my note twice and slip it to Shane on our way out to The Smurf Turd. He and Molloy drove a harder bargain than I anticipated, but I guess the risk is higher than usual. I'm just fortunate they're both on Dorm Duty this Saturday, otherwise I would be shit out of luck. Peaches would be my only other option, given our new alliance. I'm not sure how much help he'd be with this, though.

My safest bet is to bunk with Shane and Molloy and pony up for their services. Well, I'm mostly asking Mary Grace to pony up, but I still have to make their beds for the next month on top of the smokes they demanded. I can't complain too much, though. No one else can keep the hallways clear after 10 PM like those two. They're my best and only chance at pulling this off without fucking things up.

In a rare display of efficiency, the bus departs for evening service ahead of schedule. We arrive at church over ten minutes early. This is a first for me. I'm used to hurrying inside as the service is about to start and seeing Mary Grace already seated beside her mother. It's strange to find her absent and the sanctuary so empty.

With so many vacant pews to choose from, I find one a couple of rows behind her usual spot, and I settle in next to Peaches and wait. As the beginning of service approaches, however, there's still no sign of Mary Grace or her mother. I spy Shane and Molloy sitting with the Debbie Gibson Twins across the aisle. At least I know my message will get passed along, but what about hers?

She was supposed to have the plan laid out tonight. That's what she told me in her last letter. I held onto it in case I needed the details, but it only tells me where and when the concert is. How am I supposed to know when she's picking me up? How am I supposed to know if she's still coming for me at all?

I run through dead-end plan after dead-end plan on our drive back to school. By the time we arrive, I'm on the verge of conceding defeat. My head pounding, I drag my feet to the dorm. I'm about to enter my room when I hear Shane and Molloy's voices behind me. I stop, and turn around.

"There he is!" Shane points at me as he walks up the hallway. "Come here. I got something for you." He nods toward the doorway of his room and disappears inside with Molloy.

Hope sparks inside me as I start after them. Did Mary Grace manage to pass a note along even though she wasn't there? It's definitely possible. If she knew she wasn't going, she could've given it to the Debbie Gibson Twins.

As I enter their room, waves of relief roll through me. Shane holds a white envelope in an outstretched hand.

"From Big Bird," he says.

I thank him as I take it, and immediately tear it open. Normally, I'd scurry off to find privacy, but I'm too exhausted to care right now. I hop onto their spare bunk and unfold Mary Grace's letter.

Dear Will,

As you no doubt know already, you won't see me at church tonight. Nothing to worry about. My mom had a bad migraine and wanted to stay home. She's fine now, but she's been having them more often lately. Probably a symptom of being married to Douchebag Dave. Speaking of which, everything is falling perfectly into place for the concert on Saturday night! Dave will be in town when Sam arrives on Friday, so we'll go to dinner and stuff, but he's got to be back at the base by Saturday afternoon, so that's my main obstacle out of the way.

The rest of the night should be simple. Sam's girlfriend, Nat, is going to pick me up at 10:15 and then we'll head straight over to get you. Just try to be down by the main road around 10:30, I guess. We'll flash our headlights so you know it's us. Other than that, I'll keep my fingers crossed that everything goes smoothly for you. I can't believe it's only three days from now! This is going to be the best night ever! Thank you so much for spending it with me!

Love,

MG

I finish reading and slide Mary Grace's letter in the back pocket of my pants. The plan sounds pretty straightforward for the most part, as long as everything runs on time, of course. I'll need to get rid of this letter once I've memorized the details, along with her note from last Sunday. Time to get rid of the evidence.

"How about I kick your ass at Uno again?" Molloy asks as I slide off the bunk.

"Maybe later," I say, heading toward the doorway. "I need to get something from my room."

A surge of panic grips me as I exit into the hallway. Where did I hide the other letter? I remember reading it in the bath-room last Sunday, and then what? I run through my list of hiding spots: my pillow case, my Bible, the open seam on the underside of my mattress. I can't recall stashing it in any of those places. It must be in one of them, though.

As I enter my room to check, I do a double take and halt in my tracks. I don't have to look far to find what I'm looking for. Big Dumb Oaf sits on his bunk clutching the other letter in his hands. He's not the only one reading it, though. My loyal business partner, Peaches, leans in next to him.

My anxiety boils into a seething rage. "What the fuck do you think you're doing!?"

They jerk their heads up, eyes widening as they see me standing by the doorway.

"I tried to stop him!" Peaches flushes with shame, flinching back as I stride forward and snatch the letter from Oaf's hands.

Oaf rises to his full height in front of me. His mouth twists into a sick smile as his beady brown eyes flicker with satisfaction. "What's wrong, Chuck? You look worried."

I clench my hands into fists, my chest heaving with rage. All I can do is bite my tongue and glare at him. Oaf might be a lowlife cretin, but he's still boy's-home smart. He just caught me with my pants down. Now he's got me right where he wants me.

"What are you all worried about, Chuck?" Oaf steps toward me, snickering sadistically. "You worried I'm gonna ruin your big night? I guess I could if I wanted to, right?"

My skin sears. "Tell me what you want, Oaf."

He takes a few steps forward and gets right up in my face. My forehead is just a few inches from the bridge of his nose, which I'm itching to break.

"I wanna get you where it hurts the most," he says, and I

wrinkle my nose at the sour stench of his breath. "Let's see if your girlfriend forgives you again when you're a no-show on Saturday, huh? Or what Brother Bennett says when she comes to break you out of jail. He's gonna yuck your ass like Alvaro, once I tell him what you're up to. I can't fucking wait!"

Peaches squeezes his scrawny frame in front of me. "You ain't tellin' him nothin'!" he says, trying to shove Oaf back. "This stays between us, got it? Snitchin' ain't right! We can work out a deal."

Under normal circumstances, I would feel grateful for his support. It comes a bit late, however. Where was his loyalty when the two of them were reading my letter? He's only intervening now because he'll fail to benefit if he doesn't. If Oaf rats me out to Bennett, then Holy Rollers is dead in the water.

"You're just as bad as he is, Peach!" I tell him. "You read it too! Where did you find it, and why were you messing with my shit?"

His shoulders slump. "It was in this pocket." He pats the rear of his khaki pants, which are cuffed at the bottom like they're too big for him.

"Why the hell was it in your..." I break off my sentence as the realization hits me. Those are my fucking pants! The same pair I wore to church last Sunday.

Peaches swallows and clears his throat. "You were already wearing those pants, so I figured you wouldn't notice if I borrowed these. I only got one pair, and the zipper broke. I didn't know there was a note until I came back here and emptied the pockets." He points to a stack of torn-out Bible pages on his bunk. "Sorry, Will! Oaf snatched it up when he saw what I had."

I shake my head and sigh. "Let's just get this figured out, okay? Are you gonna snitch or keep your mouth stitched, Oaf? What's it gonna be?"

Oaf curls his lips into a sneer. "What's it worth to you?"

I clench my jaw until my teeth grind together. The bastard is going to milk every ounce he can out of this.

"I tell you what," I say. "I'll give you my Saturday morning biscuit and make your bed for a week. All that just for keeping your mouth shut. How does that sound?"

Oaf eyes me dubiously. "That's a start," he says. "I'll take next Saturday's biscuit as well."

"Deal!" I say, sticking out my hand to shake on it. There's no way I'm giving him a single thing after this weekend, but he doesn't need to know that.

Oaf glances at my outstretched hand and shakes his head. "I'm not done."

I drop my arm to my side and scowl at him. "What else?"

"I want you to get me chips and a soda," he says, brimming with self-satisfaction.

"Fine," I tell him. "I'll get them on Saturday and bring them back to you."

"No!" Oaf frowns at me suspiciously. "I want the chips tomorrow and the soda on Friday."

"You're kidding me, right? How am I supposed to do that?"

Oaf shrugs his huge shoulders. "Not my problem. Figure it out, or I'm talking to Bennett."

I glance over at Peaches and raise my eyebrows. "I'm going to need you to take care of this," I tell him.

The little shit has the nerve to look hurt. "You don't mean..."

"Yep," I say, cutting him off. "That's exactly what I mean."

"But I've only got one left…"

"I don't give a shit, Peach! This is your fault! If you want more smokes, you need to help me out here."

"Fine," he says glumly, "I'll take care of it."

39

THE KING JAMES TAVERN

Saturday, June 23 - Day 84

"Nervous?" Molloy pokes his head inside the room and smirks at me. Shane is still out in the hallway marshaling the rest of the guys to bed.

"What do you think?" I glance at my watch: 10:12 PM. Sam's girlfriend should be picking up Mary Grace in just a few minutes. I need to get on the move as soon as possible. "Is everyone in their rooms yet?"

Molloy leans back to look. "I think so. Let me check with Shane."

He disappears into the hallway again, and I tap my feet restlessly as I sit waiting on the spare bunk. My heart thumps inside my chest like a bass drum. Sneaking out of the dorm is the hard part, I remind myself. After that, it should be a little less stressful and a lot more exciting. Hopefully!

"Psst!" I jerk my head toward the doorway. Molloy leans inside the room again. "Shane says you're good to go."

Adrenaline surges through me. I nod and slide down from the bunk, slip on my sneakers and tread warily toward the doorway. Molloy steps aside and watches the hallway while I slip out of the room. I'm used to everything being still and silent when I sneak out, but The Dorm still stirs with life. A cough here and there, muffled voices, and a snort of laughter. I leave all of it behind me as I tiptoe down the hall.

When I reach the outside doors, I pause and listen. Nothing. I've made it past the main gauntlet. As far as nearly everyone else is concerned, I'm tucked away in bed like they are. Drawing a deep breath, I reach for the handle. I know I had help, but that was way easier than I expected.

Easing the door open, I peer out into the pitch-black night. Nothing moves. No signs of life except for the raspy shrill of cicadas. Yesterday was a new moon. Tonight, it's the merest sliver of a crescent, just a threadlike silver curve etched into the inky sky.

I slip outside and guide the door shut behind me. Cloaked in darkness, I skulk across the yard, past the schoolhouse to the edge of the woods. I follow the treeline toward the back of the property, the pines rustling softly above me.

By the time I stumble upon the dirt road, my eyes have adjusted to the gloomy surroundings. I check my watch again: 10:28. They should be here any minute, but there's no sign of any headlights yet. I trudge onward, peering into the darkness as I follow the rutted tracks toward the main road. As the tracks curve around a small ridge, though, two blinding bright circles appear in front of me.

My pulse racing, I raise a hand to shield my eyes from the glare. Peeking between my fingers, I glimpse the outline of a small car. Its headlights flash off and on again. She's here! This is actually going to happen!

I jog forward as the back-passenger-side-door swings open. A long leg stretches out and plants itself on the road. The other leg follows, and Mary Grace emerges from the car.

"Will!" she calls out as she rises to her full height. She waves at me excitedly. "This is so crazy! I can't believe we're actually doing this!"

I breathe her in the moment I reach her: Metallica Girl in a black *Kill 'Em All* tee that's cropped above the navel. Good God Almighty! My gaze lingers on the smooth porcelain skin of her stomach, the narrowness of her waist. I force my eyes down, but that stirs me up even more. A denim skirt, the hem frayed midway down her long, slender legs. Black boots laced below her knees.

"Will?"

I look up and let her pale-blue eyes pull me in. They gleam with a vibrancy I've never seen before, brimming with exhilaration.

"Hey," I mumble, sounding as dazed as I feel.

"I'm so happy you're here!" Mary Grace flashes a smile that's even more dazzling than the headlights. "This is going to be the best night ever!"

She hugs me so abruptly it takes me a heart-jolting second to react. I reach around to hug her back, but she's already releasing me. We step apart, and she reaches down to clasp my hand. My pulse rockets into warp speed. Static sparks up my arm, sweeping across my skin.

Mary Grace beams at me. "Come on," she says, dragging me toward the car. "We need to hurry or we'll miss the start of the show." She lets go of my hand as she reaches the open door. "It's going to be a little bit cramped in here, but it's not a long drive."

Cramped? I thought it was just her and Sam's girlfriend. Who else is in there? I peer past Mary Grace as she stoops to squeeze inside and inhale a waft of cigarette smoke. It swirls in a haze beneath the roof of the car, hanging over the faces of three other chicks like a cloudy veil.

Mary Grace squints at me curiously from the middle seat. "Get in," she says, patting the spot next to her. The way she has her long legs tucked up in front of her looks awfully uncomfortable. Her expression says otherwise, though. She beams at me blissfully, and I climb in beside her.

"Alright, let's get this show on the road!" the driver calls out as she starts the car into gear.

"Will, this is Nat, by the way." Mary Grace tells me. "Sam's girlfriend."

"Hey, Will. Nice to meet you." Nat peers back at me as she maneuvers a three-point turn to take us back to the main road. She's pretty, with large brown eyes and olive skin. Her chestnut hair falls to her shoulders in a teased-out perm.

"This is my best friend, Steph." Nat tilts her head toward the blonde who's sitting shotgun. Steph looks at me like she just smelled a fart, and turns back around. "And that's my little sister, Dana, sitting across from you. She's a royal pain in the ass, so sorry in advance."

Steph grumbles something in agreement, and Dana smirks and rolls her eyes. She looks about the same age as Mary Grace and me, with the same olive skin and large brown eyes as her older sister.

"Good to meet you, Will," she says, swiping a stray strand of brown hair away from her face. "Feel free to ignore my big sister. She's just cranky because she starves herself."

Woah! I stifle a laugh. Well, this chick isn't boring!

"What the hell, Dana!?" Nat shrieks. "I'm on a liquid protein diet. How many times do I have to explain that to you? I *do not* starve myself!"

Dana snorts dismissively. "If you say so. But I don't think drinking one of those Oprah-fast shakes for breakfast everyday qualifies as eating. It's just powder in a glass of milk for goodness sake!"

"It's called Optifast, you moron!" Nat snaps at her. She huffs and shakes her head. "I swear, this is the last time I'm taking you anywhere!"

The car falls silent, and I clear my throat to break the tension. "Well, as long it's real milk you're drinking, that sounds a hell of a lot better than what I get for breakfast."

"Oh yeah?" Dana says. "No milk for the prisoners?"

"Just the powdered kind."

She scrunches up her face in disgust. "On your cereal?" I nod my head, and Dana shakes hers. "That's just wrong! What the heck do they serve you for lunch?"

"Depends," I say. "Yesterday, it was what we call a Mississippi Brunch, which is basically two slices of bologna served on the palm of your hand."

"You're kidding?" Mary Grace frowns at me. "You've never told me this before."

I shrug. "It didn't seem important."

Dana chuckles and nudges Mary Grace. "I think we need to get your boyfriend a Whopper before the night's over."

We all laugh, but I hope she isn't kidding.

"So tell us about this crazy place we just rescued you from, Will." Nat peers at me through the rearview mirror. "Is it as bad as Mary Grace says? She told us there's a guy in there who's actually shot somebody. Sounds more like a prison than a school."

"That's what Brandi said, anyway," Mary Grace adds. "Is that true?"

I can't help but chuckle. "Yeah, I guess that's *kind of* true. There's this kid named Homer who held-up an ice-cream truck with a BB gun back in Miami."

"Wait, his name is Homer? Like Homer Simpson?" Steph's blond head swivels around to look at me. "I love that show!"

"Right," I say. "Haven't seen it in a few months, but, yeah, great show. Anyway, I think his full name is Homero. Not that it matters."

"That's it?" Dana asks. "He sounds like a proper assassin!"

"I guess this other kid called Ricky could qualify too," I say, with a chuckle. "He claims he shot his step-dad in the face with a stapler gun."

"Sounds like my kind of guy!" Mary Grace nudges my arm and shoots me a teasing smile.

"Hey!" I nudge her back. "Just get me a stapler gun, and I'll take care of Douchebag Dave, okay?"

She laughs loudly, and I wrap my arm around her shoulders.

A short while later, the telltale lights of civilization punctuate the night. If we're calling Hattiesburg civilization, that is. It might feel like a sprawling metropolis compared to where I was just picked up, but everything looks dead and dormant as we turn off the highway. We cruise along a gloomy service street past rows of shuttered storefronts.

Mary Grace squeezes my hand. "We're almost there!" she whispers in my ear. I smile, squeezing her hand back as we cross a shadowy set of railway tracks.

After a few turns, we cut through a sleepy, silent neighborhood and enter a more industrial part of the city. A ghost town of warehouses and storage lots with barbed-wire fences passes by the windows. Nat takes a left at the next stop sign, turning onto a narrow street with a liquor store on the corner. A couple of rough-looking dudes loiter outside. They yell something as we drive past, and Nat steps on the gas.

As we approach the end of the road, she rolls to a stop before we reach the intersection. The resonant thump of live music shudders through the open windows of the car.

"Is this it?" Mary Grace grips my hand even tighter. "Are we here?"

"This looks like the right place," Nat says. "Sam said to park around back."

As she starts the car forward again, I lean sideways to peer between the front seats. Facing us across the street, The King James Tavern looks about as royal as a rat in the rain. It's just a small, brick building with blacked-out windows, yet it feels more alive than anything else in the city.

A white sign hangs above the entrance, with *King James* inscribed beneath the face of a small brown dog with a crooked ear. Manning the doors below, a fridge-sized bouncer eyes our car as we roll past and drive around the side of the building. The music pumps louder, vibrating through the frame of the car and shuddering through me. Nat pulls into a small lot with maybe a dozen other vehicles and parks next to a dented, old van.

"Okay, so here's the deal." She twists around in her seat to look at us. "The three of you are underage, so we're sneaking you in through the side door. Sam spoke with the manager already, but I'll need to tip the bouncer before we can let you in. Just wait outside for a few minutes and stay out of trouble, okay?" Her eyes settle on me. "Same goes for when you get inside."

"I'll be good," I tell her. "I promise."

The moment we exit the car, Mary Grace practically drags me forward by the hand. "What time is it?" she asks, glancing at her watch. "Shit! It's nearly eleven already!"

"I wouldn't worry about it," I assure her. "Some other band is still playing. They'll have to clear their gear off the stage when they finish, and Sam and his crew will need to set up theirs. So you're not going to miss anything. I doubt this is the type of place that gives a shit if things run on time or not, anyway."

Mary Grace chuckles alongside me. "That's a very good point, Will," she says, hugging my arm as we step into the alley by the side of the building.

While Nat and Steph head around front to pay their way in and pay off the bouncer, Mary Grace, Dana, and I wait near the side entrance. A couple of minutes later, the door swings open and music blares out, echoing through the alleyway. Nat emerges from the building and waves us inside.

Mary Grace pulls me with her, releasing my hand as we step into a cramped hallway. A thumping bassline reverberates through the walls, and the smell of stale sweat, booze, and smoke wafts up my nostrils. Nat leads us along the corridor until she reaches a door at the far end. She knocks twice and enters.

Mary Grace looks back and beams at me. She says something, but the music drowns it out too much.

"WHAT?" I call out to her, leaning in closer to listen.

"I SAID ARE YOU READY TO MEET SAM?"

Shit! Here we go! I force myself to smile. "HELL YEAH! LET'S DO IT!" I say, and follow her through the doorway.

I enter a small room crammed with people and filled with smoke. "SHUT THE FUCKING DOOR!" someone yells, and I realize they're yelling at me. I reach back and swing it shut. The door slams harder than I intended, and the music muffles into the background.

I face the room again, expecting everyone to be staring at me. Everyone's attention is on Nat, who's in the middle of recounting my jailbreak like it was some high speed getaway. Mary Grace stands in front of me, Dana next to her. Everyone else except Nat is lounging back on one of the couches. Four dudes and a few other chicks. The coffee table in front of them is littered with beer bottles. I spy a small bag of pot and a pipe amongst the mess, and the ashtrays are stacked so high with butts I can imagine the money signs in Peaches' eyes.

I scan the other guys' faces for a likeness to Mary Grace. Sam isn't hard to find. Pale-blue eyes stare back at me from the couch. He wears a black sleeveless t-shirt, and tight acid-wash jeans, his long legs stretching out and under the coffee table. His hair, dark brown like Mary Grace's, falls past his shoulders.

"So you're my little sister's boyfriend, huh?" Sam smiles, but his eyes narrow skeptically.

"Really, Sam? That's how you're going to introduce yourself?" Mary Grace smiles and shakes her head. "Will, this is Sam.

Sam, this is *Will*. And we aren't anything official yet, like I told you already."

I clear my throat. "Nice to meet you, Sam. Mary Grace gave me a copy of your demo tape. You guys are pretty damn sick!"

"You think so?" Sam asks, still squinting at me suspiciously.

"Definitely!" I tell him. "I know it's just a demo, but I like to think I know good music when I hear it."

"Yo, I like this kid." The guy next to Sam nudges him.

His hair is dark, long, and wavy, and he wears a thick layer of black eyeliner. He takes a hit on the pipe and offers it to me. I wave it off, and he sets it down on the coffee table again.

"It's dope that you dig our music, lil' man," he says. "My name's AJ. I'm the singer."

"Good to meet you, AJ," I tell him. "The way you scream out the chorus on *One Finger Salute* is killer. That's probably my favorite song. The lyrics are badass! Did *you* write them?"

"*I* wrote them," Sam says. He smiles at me and chuckles. "I guess you're alright, Will."

He lifts his long frame off the couch and stretches to his full height. Standing several inches taller than Mary Grace, Sam has to be at least six feet four. He reaches into his pocket and pulls out a handful of one dollar bills.

"Here you go." He hands a few to Mary Grace. "Buy yourselves a Coke or something. The other band's about to finish their set, so you should probably head out there. We'll hang out after the show, okay?"

Mary Grace gives her brother a hug, and we head back out into the hallway, along with Nat, Steph, and Dana.

40

THE SHOW MUST GO ON

The main floor of The King James Tavern is as tiny and dingy as I imagined. The floorboards are warped and sticky underfoot, and all the cigarette smoke has stained the ceiling yellow. It hovers in the air like gray fog, and it dawns on me how badly I'm going to stink when I get back. If anyone takes one whiff, they'll know I've been up to something. I'm not sure what to do about that right now, though.

The five of us hang near the edge of the small stage while the band jams through their last song. An audience of roughly twenty people cluster in front of them, and several others mingle at the bar on the opposite side of the room. Not much of a crowd, but enough to make a tiny place like this feel bustling. They whoop and applaud as the band finishes their set.

"Let's get a drink!" Mary Grace grabs my hand, practically hopping with excitement. "Come on! Before the show starts!"

She leads me toward the bar, weaving through a cluster of

leather-clad metalheads and dodging an old, bleary-eyed biker as he staggers by.

"Are you sure they'll serve you?" I ask, as she hops on a barstool and leans on the counter.

After nearly three months in Nowhere, the idea of buying a Coke feels somewhat alien to me. Ordering one at a bar feels like living in a different dimension. Not for Mary Grace, though. She flashes me a radiant smile, and all doubt disappears.

"Of course they'll serve me," she says, with the air of a woman several years her senior. "You should probably hang back behind me, though, and try not to be noticed."

As Mary Grace attempts to catch the bartender's eye, I notice she's already caught the eye of three preppy-looking frat boys at the end of the bar. They slide a few stools closer, and to my disgust I realize they're dressed almost identically, except for the color of their polo shirts. They're obviously here for the first band who were playing Southern rock covers.

The one wearing a white polo keeps ogling Mary Grace drunkenly. He has a mop of fair hair, flushed rosy cheeks, and appears oblivious of how douchey he looks with his collar up. Still leering at Mary Grace, he hops onto a stool a few spots down from us. His cronies follow his lead and sit next to him. One is short and scrawny in a pale pink polo shirt. The other is taller than the first two, wearing a striped blue polo that bulges over his gut.

When Mary Grace finally catches the bartender's attention, he tells her he needs to change a keg and will be right back.

"Hey...Hey, tall girl," White Collar Boy calls over to her while we wait. "Whatcha drinkin'?"

Mary Grace's shoulders stiffen. She glances his way from the corner of her eye but pretends not to have heard him. I'm trying my best to avoid eye contact too, but I'm itching to turn around and glare at him. He mutters something to his simpleton side-kicks and they laugh like idiots. My cheeks burn, and I flex my fingers into fists.

"Come on," I say, patting her on the shoulder. "Let's just go. We promised Nat we'd stay out of trouble."

"No," she says. "I want my Coke, and you're getting one too. We're not causing any trouble."

Shit! When did I become the voice of reason? I glance over at White Collar Boy and find his glazed eyes staring back at me.

"Who's the kid?" he slurs, but Mary Grace continues to ignore him. "Hey...Hey, you!" This time I know he's talking to me. "Are you her little brother or somethin'? Did your babysitter bring you to the bar?"

His lackwit friends crack up again, but I follow Mary Grace's lead and pay him no attention, a task made easier by the bartender's timely return. He takes her order, fishes two icy bottles of Coke out of a cooler, and pops off the tops. Mary Grace pays and picks up both of them, but as she turns away from the bar, a hand darts out and seizes her arm.

"Why're you runnin' off so fast, tall girl?" White Collar says. "I ain't done lookin' at those sexy, long legs of yours."

"Let go of me right now!" Mary Grace shouts, but I'm already lunging between them. I grab White Collar's wrist and wrench his grip loose from her arm. Mary Grace yelps and stumbles back against the bar.

"What the fuck do you think you're doin', boy?" Spit sprays from White Collar's mouth as he reels around to face me. Pink Shrimp and Big Blue flank him, fists at their sides. I'd take my chances one-on-one with any of these guys, but three against one is a beating waiting to happen.

"Hey!" White Collar steps closer to striking distance. "I asked you a question, shithead! You ain't got nothin' to say?"

He stares me down, puffing out his chest, and I can tell he's psyching himself up to hit me. I consider swinging first, but his focus shifts to something behind me and his eyes widen. He backs away as the hulking frame of the bouncer steps in front of me, blocking him from view.

"That's him! That's the one!" Nat strides up to the bouncer, her perm bobbing as she points at White Collar Boy. "I just saw him grab her. It's the same creep who grabbed my ass when I came out of the restroom."

"What!?" White Collar's eyes widen. "That ain't true! I never...I ain't even seen her before!"

The bouncer turns his huge shaved head toward Mary Grace, who's wiping down the front of her shirt with a wad of napkins. The Cokes she was carrying a few moments ago now stand half-empty on the bar behind her. She looks at me and frowns. Shit! Did *I* do that?

"Did any of these guys put their hands on you?" the bouncer asks her, his voice like a bulldozer grinding rocks.

"That one did." Mary Grace points at White Collar Boy, and the bouncer turns his attention back to the polo triplets.

"That was just an accident." White Collar backs up a step, raising his hands to plead his innocence. "I was just tryin' to talk. I didn't mean no disrespect."

The bouncer holds a meaty finger to his lips, and the dumbass falls silent. "Fun's over tonight, boys," he growls. "Y'all had best get goin' before we do things my way."

White Collar and his cronies scurry off without so much as glance. The bouncer follows several paces behind them and returns to his post at the doors.

Feeling a pang of guilt, I turn toward Mary Grace. "Are you okay? I'm really sorry if I…if I, uh…"

"It's fine, Will. *I'm* fine. I mean, I'm damp and a little sticky, but at least I smell sweet." She sighs softly and smiles at me. "I know you were just trying to be gallant and all, but you really gave me a fright just now. One second you're behind me, and then you're barging right past me. I managed to save most of our drinks, though."

"I'm really sorry, Mary Grace. I just couldn't let him grab you like that."

"Well, didn't let him grab me for long, did you?" She chuckles and passes me a half-full bottle of Coke. "Come on, walk me to the restroom. Let's see if I can clean myself up a bit better before the show starts."

With Nat accompanying us, we cross the crowded floor with what remains of our Cokes. Sam and his bandmates are out on stage setting up, shifting equipment and unraveling chords. AJ stands at the mic, running a quick sound check.

"Come with me." Nat takes Mary Grace by the hand as we reach Dana and Steph by the edge of the stage. "Let's get you cleaned up." She leads her off toward the restroom and Steph follows after them.

"What happened to her?" Dana asks, pulling a pack of Winston Lights out of her handbag.

"Can I get one of those?" I ask.

"Sure!" She lights up her own and hands me a smoke and her lighter. "Is she okay?"

I spark up and fill her in on what happened between sips of my Coke. As the sugar rushes to my head, I'm struck by how surreal it feels to stand here like a normal person in the real world. I know the illusion won't last, though. At the end of the night, I'll have to return to my regular, shitty life like some kind of boy's home Cinderella.

None of that matters the moment Mary Grace reappears, however. My worries drift away, and all I want to do is savor every second I have with her tonight. The lights dim as she reaches me, and the members of Executive Anarchy take to the stage.

"Come on!" Mary Grace's eyes gleam with exhilaration. She grabs me by the arm and drags me into the crowd. Sam straps on his bass and slaps a few warmup chords. The lead guitarist does the same and makes a couple of final tuning adjustments. As AJ grips the mic and pulls it free from the stand, the drummer taps his sticks together to count off the first song.

A crunchy wall of sound blasts out of the speakers, and AJ growls into the microphone. The sound quality is pretty shitty, which is to be expected in a place like this. The King James is a far cry from the Omni Center in Atlanta, and Executive Anarchy is a million miles from being Metallica. Even so, there's nowhere else I'd rather be right now, and there's no one else I'd rather be with.

I watch Mary Grace as she gazes at the stage, radiant with delight. She doesn't give a shit how it sounds. She doesn't give a shit how she dances either. She flails her long limbs around like she's having a seizure of some kind. Glancing my way, she flashes a smile that's only for me. I smile back at her and bob my head to the music. Nothing has ever felt as real and pure as she is right now. She's intoxicating.

I join in the applause as the song ends, cheering and whooping as loudly as I can. I recognize the next one as *One Finger Salute*, which is my favorite from the demo tape. Even so, I pay little attention to what's happening on the stage. Mary Grace is the only show I'm interested in watching. I need to find a way to kiss her tonight. When she drops me off, maybe. Just a short moment alone.

Someone bumps me in the back, and I spin around to find a couple of drunk dudes trying to start a mosh pit. I'm about to turn around again when something catches my eye behind them. A tall, broad-shouldered man in a cowboy hat stands by the front doors talking to the bouncer. I gasp the air from my lungs, panic streaking through me, as Brother Bennett turns and stares toward the small crowd.

I jerk my head around, my heart thumping wildly. What the fuck!? This can't be happening! This shouldn't be happening! Why is he...How the hell did he...What the fuck do I do?

A tap on the shoulder jolts me out of it. Mary Grace beams at me, but her expression wilts and her eyes flicker with concern. I stare back at her, gulping short, shallow breaths, my entire body trembling.

"What's wrong?" she mouths.

I glance over my shoulder and spy Bennett walking onto the floor. There's no time to explain. I grab Mary Grace's hand and pull her with me, shouldering my way toward the backstage door. Wrenching it open, I release her hand and nudge her ahead of me. I slip in behind her, holding the door ajar to peer through the crack. Brother Bennett wades through the crowd in front of the stage, searching around for me.

"WILL, WHAT'S GOING ON?" Mary Grace hollers above the music.

I pull the door shut and take her by the hand again. The last thing I wanted to do was fuck this night up for her. It's too loud to explain anything right here, though, and I'm not hanging around this hallway waiting for Bennett to catch me. I lead her back to the room where we met Sam before the show.

"He's here for me!" I say the moment we're inside. "Brother Bennett! He's out there right now!" Mary Grace gasps, and covers her mouth with her hands. "I've got to get the hell out of here! I can't let him find me here!"

"Are you sure it's him?" she asks. "How does he know you're here?"

"It's definitely him, okay?" I pace the room, tugging at my hair. "The only way he could know is if someone fucked me over." Oaf, of course! Who else would be low enough to rat me out like that? "It doesn't matter right now, though. I need to hide until he's gone."

"And then what, Will? You still have to go back there. You can't hide from him then."

She's right. I am so fucking screwed! My stomach twists into a tight knot.

"I guess I can't go back then," I say. "I don't know what else to do."

Mary Grace moves toward the door. "I do," she says, gripping the handle. "I'm getting Nat, and we're driving you back right now. You'll be in less trouble if he finds you there instead of here, right?"

There's logic to what she's saying, but... "I can't let you miss Sam's show, Mary Grace."

She raises a hand to cut me off. "Yes, you can. He wouldn't be here looking for you if it wasn't for me. It's my turn to be gallant, Will. I care more about what happens to you than missing a few songs, okay?" She peeks her head into the hallway and turns back to me. "Alright, here's the plan. You go out the side door and wait by Nat's car. I'll run and get her, and we'll meet you there as quickly as we can, yeah?"

I draw a deep breath and wipe a layer of sweat from my forehead. "Okay," I say, joining her by the door. She opens it and we step into the hall.

"Ready?" she asks.

I nod. "Ready."

Mary Grace squeezes my hand and sets off toward the backstage door. Adrenaline surges through me as I turn and dash the opposite direction down the hallway. I shove the side door open and burst into the pitch-black alleyway, almost barreling into a truck that's parked outside the entrance. Brother Bennett's truck!

I side-step around it and dart down the alley toward the parking lot. Reaching the safety of Nat's car, I lean on the hood to catch my breath.

A bottle clinks behind me. I jolt upright and wheel around. Three shadowy figures hang out beside the tailgate of a nearby truck, parked just across the lot. Their conversation breaks off the moment they notice me.

"Holy shit!" one of them blurts. He takes a few steps toward me, peering through darkness. "It's that little punk from inside!"

Fuck! It's those douchebags from the bar again! This is exactly what I don't need right now! I back up around the side of

Nat's car as White Collar Boy swaggers my way, swigging back a bottle of beer. Big Blue and Pink Shrimp follow behind him.

"I'm not looking for any trouble," I tell them.

White Collar snorts at me. "Y'all hear that?" he glances at his cronies. "This little punk says he ain't lookin' for no trouble." He swigs his beer again and glares at me. "I'd say it's a little late for that, boy."

I back up some more, trying to keep the car between us, but Pink Shrimp and Big Blue flank around to block me off. I glance over my shoulder, back toward the side entrance. Brother Bennett's truck is still there, but there's no sign of Mary Grace and Nat yet.

White Collar laughs. "I guess you're shit out of luck tonight, boy."

Ain't that the fucking truth! Big Blue starts to circle behind me as the three of them close in. I swivel left and right, searching for an opening, but they quickly block me off. I turn to face White Collar and ball my hands into fists.

"WILL!"

I twirl around toward the alley, and my mind reels. Molloy stands outside the open door of Bennett's truck, staring right at me. The sight of him stuns me stock-still. What is he doing here? Was he the one who…No, that doesn't make sense. It must have been Oaf.

"WILL!" Molloy screams again, pointing my way. "BEHIND YOU!"

I shift my feet to turn around and stagger forward as something hard clobbers me on the back of the head. My vision swirls as I stumble to my knees. I lean one hand against the ground to keep from falling, and reach the other around the back of my head. My fingers come away wet with blood, and the world begins to spin even faster.

Slumping limply to my side, I lie on the hot concrete and groan. My head throbs with intense, stabbing pain, and my eyelids feel too heavy to hold open. I let them fall shut and feel myself sinking below the surface. The world above me comes through in fragments of muffled noise.

Raised voices and Molloy cursing...

Feet scuffling around me and a deep, drawling voice booming out...

A slapping sound like the crack of a whip, followed by a sharp yelp of pain...

The slam of car doors. The growl of an engine. Tires screeching as a vehicle speeds off.

Hands grip me under the arms and sit me up. I can hear Brother Bennett talking to me, but he sounds several miles away. I reach a hand down to steady myself and try to open my eyes, but it's like trying to peek under a closed door. I can only part my eyelids enough to see a thin, blurry strip of what's in front of me. But then I hear a familiar voice calling out my name.

Mary Grace! Her appearance reignites my senses. Forcing my eyes open, I try to push myself up. My legs wobble under my weight, and Molloy grips my shoulders to keep me steady.

"Will!"

I gaze up the alley toward the sound of Mary Grace's voice. The streetlight near the entrance swirls with golden halos, but I can see the silhouette of her tall, thin frame standing within its glow. My legs buckle as I try to walk toward her. I stagger off balance, but Molloy catches me before I fall. He straightens me up, and hoists my arm across his shoulder. Wrapping his arm around my back, he helps me forward.

Mary Grace watches on helplessly as I'm led up the alley to Brother Bennett's truck. She stands outside the entrance, with Nat, Steph, and Dana just behind her. The despair in her eyes slices through my heart. This is what happens when you run around with the likes of Will Douglas. He can't fuck things up for himself without ruining it for everyone. He's never going to change. As soon as she sees that, she'll realize she's too fucking good for someone like me.

"Are you okay?" she calls out as we reach the truck. "You're bleeding!"

I try to tell her I'm fine, but my voice croaks and the words stick in my throat. I'm light years away from feeling fine right now. Molloy leans me against the side of the truck as he opens the back door.

"What did you do to him!?" Mary Grace yells, pointing her finger at Brother Bennett. "Look at him! He needs to go to a hospital!" She turns around to Nat. "Run inside and tell someone to call an ambulance!"

"NO!" Brother Bennett's voice lashes out like a whip, startling the girls to silence. "Y'all ain't calling anybody. That boy right there belongs to me, and I'll decide how he's taken care of." He turns to Mary Grace, towering several inches above her. "And I can assure you, young lady, none of what happened to William was done by my hand. Troubled boys make a habit of finding trouble. I suggest you keep better company from now on."

Brother Bennett whips around, pulling out his keys as he strides away from the four girls.

"Get him in!" he barks, heading for the driver-side door of his truck.

Molloy lurches into action, using his shoulder for leverage as he helps me up onto the backseat. He slams it shut and runs around the other side to get in. I stare at Mary Grace through the window, my head foggy and pounding with pain. Tears flood her eyes as she stares back at me. As Brother Bennett revs the engine into gear, I mouth the words "I'm sorry." And then she's gone.

"Well, I hope you had your fun tonight, William." Brother Bennett sounds more weary than enraged. "You can count yourself lucky. If we hadn't shown up when we did, this could've ended up a whole lot worse for both of us."

Lucky!? Is he fucking serious? If he hadn't shown up when he did, I wouldn't have run into those pricks again! I touch the back of my throbbing head again. My hair is matted with sticky blood, and a golf ball-sized lump has swollen up around the wound.

"What in God's name were you thinking, boy?" Brother Bennett's dark eyes glare at me in the rearview mirror. "You think you can just sneak out to some bar and meet your girl? Was it worth getting a bottle slammed across your head? You could've been killed!"

My mind flashes back to White Collar Boy swigging his beer before I turned around. No wonder it felt like being struck by a hammer.

"Neither of y'all breathes a word about this," Bennett continues. "Not to anyone. Is that understood?"

He'd get better odds on Hell freezing over than the pair of us keeping this quiet. I'm more than happy to tell him what he wants to hear, though. I exchange a subtle glance with Molloy.

"Yes, sir," we both reply.

"We'll discuss this further in the morning," Bennett tells me. "Right now, you should thank the Lord for that concussion, son. It just saved you from getting the yucking you deserve!"

I lean back against the headrest and grimace. Maybe it's just the concussion, but a yucking doesn't sound so terrible compared to how I feel right now. I'm sure he'll find other ways to make me suffer. So be it. I'm already in a world of hurt, so what's the point in fearing a little more pain?

41

A BRIEF ENCOUNTER

Saturday, June 30 - Day 90...+1

"You gotta run again after this?" Peaches mutters as we clean up the dinnertime mess in the kitchen.

"Yep," I say. "Every day after breakfast and dinner for the next month, remember?"

Peaches shakes his head. "I still can't believe how light you got off!"

Neither can I, quite honestly. Brother Bennett wasn't kidding when he said I should thank the Lord for my concussion. He worked himself into such a fury on the way back, I was sure he would change his mind and yuck the shit out of me. Instead he stuck me on watch with Shane and Molloy again and told me to report to Brother James for my running punishment.

Seeing as I returned from my night out empty-handed, however, I'm still in debt to both of them, as well as Peaches. I've already told Oaf he can go fuck himself, but the other three keep

369

hounding me and threatening to add interest. And as Molloy enters the kitchen, that's exactly what I'm expecting him to do.

"Hey, Will," he says, as Shane follows behind him, cradling a medium-sized cardboard box in his arms. "You got a package from your boyfriend."

Shane dumps it on the countertop next to me, and I snort dismissively.

"Nice try, assholes! I don't get packages, remember?"

"Well, you did today, dumbass!" Molloy fires back. "Open it up!"

I lean over the box, and stare at the shipping label. The name *Will Douglas* is printed above the school's address. Who the hell sent me this? My eyes glaze with tears as they find the sender's name and address.

Angelo Ramos

2234 165th Street

Los Angeles, California 90260

"Hey!" Shane prods me on the shoulder. "Are you gonna open it or stare at it?"

I blink back my tears as the others gather around, closing in with interest. Not Oaf, though. He slips out of the kitchen, his ugly mug all bitter and twisted. Peaches hands me a kitchen knife, and I shift the box around as I cut the taped edges. It's a good bit heavier than it looks. What the hell have you sent me, Angelo?

"Did Chuck get a package?" I hear a voice call from the door. "What's he got? Is he trading?"

The boys here are savages when it comes to packages. As soon as the news leaks out, it's like a drop of blood in the ocean and all the sharks come circling. I can feel the crowd pressing in as I flip open the top of the box.

My eyes bulge! Holy shit! It's like opening a treasure chest and being blinded by the gold. The boys behind me are already listing the items off.

"A pack of chicken-flavored Ramen!"

"A couple of Hershey bars!"

"A bag of Doritos!"

"What kind?"

"Nacho Cheese, baby!"

"Hell yeah! Those are the best!"

"Oh Shit! There's a six-pack of Dr. Pepper in there, too!"

Gasps!

The jealousy around me is thick enough to slice. Angelo's package is stacked! I can't believe he did this! Sending packages is just something guys say they'll do before they leave. No one ever does, though. But I guess it shouldn't surprise me that much. Angelo was always different from everybody else here, and in the best of ways.

Rummaging through my bounty, I spy an envelope at the bottom of the box. A letter! I won't be opening that here, though. I pick up the box and push my way through the small crowd, ignoring the audible dismay around me.

"Listen up!" Peaches yells above the clamor. "All trades are now suspended until further notice, but y'all can negotiate through me in the meantime."

I make my way to Shane and Molloy's room and plop my package on one of their spare bunks. The pair of them follow behind me.

"Piss off, Roaches!" Molloy yells as a couple of heads peek through the doorway.

"What else did you get?" Shane asks. "Because you still owe us big time for last weekend, remember?"

"Trust me, I know. You've been reminding me all week. I'm gonna make sure we're squared up. Don't worry." I open the box and remove the envelope. "Look all you want," I tell him as he peers inside. "Just don't take anything."

I hop on the bunk as Shane and Molloy descend on the box like vultures. Lounging back, I tear open the envelope. I remove the letter, unfolding it as I read.

Dear Will,

I hope you're feeling better by the time you get this package, and I hope it helps some if you're not. I feel bad about the way we left things. You're like a brother to me. I hope you know that. I hate that I kept telling you to stay focused on what you're going home to. I never would have said that if I knew what that actually meant to you. That was wrong of me, anyway. It doesn't matter how you get through things. All that matters is being strong enough, and something tells me you're even stronger than I am.

As I unfold the bottom half of the letter, something falls onto my lap. A photograph. Angelo's face stares up at me. His big brown eyes are alight with elation and dimples etch his cheeks. His arms are wrapped around a toddler-sized girl with a head of thick black curls, beaming up at him instead of posing for the camera.

I'm still getting used to being home again. It feels weird sometimes, but in a good way I guess. I've mostly been hanging at my mom's apartment and trying to help her out as much as I can. She's working two jobs right now, but I'm going to get a job as soon as I can so she won't have to be so busy. I'm just trying to make up time with my baby sister. She's the cutest thing ever, and I'm going to make sure she grows up safe and happy. I'm adding a picture to the package, so you can see how perfect she is.

I really hope you write back to me, man. I want us to stay in touch. I feel like I can be a better friend now that I'm in a better place. There's a better place out there for you as well.

Stay safe, brother,

• *Angelo*

There's a better place for me too, huh? Whatever you say, Angelo. It's hard to feel bitter at him after seeing that package, though. There's at least a dozen different treats in there! I watch Shane and Molloy lay out the contents on the mattress beside me.

"See anything you like?" I ask, and their heads whirl my direction.

Molloy looks like he might actually be drooling. "Everything!" he says.

I chuckle. Exactly as I suspected. "Okay then. I'll give you one-fourth of everything to clear off our debt. That's one-fourth for each of you. The other half gets split between me and Peaches."

Their eyes widen, and they glance at one another and nod. "Deal!" Shane says. "But how're you gonna split all of that four ways?"

A wide smile spreads on my face. "We're going to have ourselves a little party tonight, boys! VIPs only!"

Shane grins and nods his head. "Good thinking! I could use a good party." He turns to Molloy. "I think it's time we made that phone call." Molloy gapes at him quizzically. "The one we talked about earlier, dipshit."

"Oh yeah!" Molloy smirks at me.

"What are you guys talking about?" I ask.

"Don't worry about it," Shane says, as he turns toward the doorway. "You'll find out soon enough."

———

SEVERAL HOURS and over a dozen Uno games later, we gorge ourselves on the goodies from Angelo's package. The four of us lounge on the bunks in Shane and Molloy's room, sipping our Dr. Peppers and trying to out-burp one another.

"Tell us the story about Oaf again, Peach!" I tear open a bag of Doritos, scoop out a handful, and pass him the bag.

"Nah, I'm too tuckered out for tellin' stories," he complains. "I think I ate too much!" He digs his hand in the bag and shovels a stack of chips into his mouth.

As miserable as I felt the day after the concert, I nearly pissed myself laughing when I heard what happened while I was gone. It came as no surprise to learn it was Oaf who ratted me out. I suspected as much the moment I saw Bennett in The King James. Seeing as I had every intention of screwing him over too, I guess I shouldn't complain too much.

It was the way Oaf went about it, though. That's the part that really pisses me off! The bastard waited until the exact time of the concert before he squealed to Brother Bennett. He could have chosen to tell him earlier — Bennett could have caught me on the way out and avoided a late-night trip to Hattiesburg — but he didn't. Oaf waited until he was certain I would get into the most possible trouble. That's where his genius plan backfired in his face.

Peaches spied him sneaking out of the room around 11 o'clock and followed him out of the dorm. He intercepted him on his way down to Brother Bennett's trailer and tried to coax him back in. But Oaf was hellbent on hurting me and shoved him aside, marching up to the trailer and knocking on the door. Bennett was furious when he opened it and all the more livid when Oaf explained why he was there.

When Bennett asked him how he knew about the concert, Oaf had beamed with pride as he told him about the letter he read a few days before. His smile faded a second later when he was told to turn his ass around, and Bennett gave him six brutal licks for not telling him sooner.

Justice. At least, that's what it feels like.

"Hey, Will," Shane says, rising from his bunk. "I need you to run to my stash for me while I take a shit."

"No way, man! I'm done running tonight. Send Peach or Molloy."

"Peach doesn't know where it is, and Molloy can't barely find his own dick when it's dark. Just go get my smokes for me. I'll make it worth your while."

"Dude, that's all the way over by the back road. I'm in my fucking boxers!"

"Who cares? No one's out there to see you. Just hurry up and go!"

"Fine!" I slip my feet into my sneakers. "But nobody touches those Hershey bars until I'm back."

The night is oddly cool and quiet outside, like the aftermath of a storm as the skies settle. A silver half-moon gleams above me as I retrace my steps from a week ago to the dirt road. I was so amped with adrenaline that night. I picture Mary Grace stepping out of Nat's car, looking more radiant than ever before, her face lighting up as she sees me. It all happened just a stone's throw away.

I find Shane's stash and remove the ferns he used to cover the hole. As I'm about to reach in, a light flashes in the corner of my vision, and I lurch to my feet. The soft rumble of a car draws closer, its tires grinding against the dirt tracks. I dart behind the trunk of a pine tree, and peek my head around. Two headlights beam through the darkness. The car rolls to a stop and idles nearby. A door opens.

"Will?"

My heart hammers. What the hell? No way!

"Will, are you out here? It's me."

I step out from behind the tree. Like a ghost in the Mississippi night, Mary Grace stands in front of me on the moonlit road. This can't be real!

"How?" I gasp. "What are you doing here?"

I drink her in. Her pale skin and slender frame. Her dark hair pulled back in a ponytail. She's not dressed up for a metal concert, but she's even more beautiful than I remember.

"Shane's the one who arranged it," she tells me. "He called Brandi and asked her to pick me up. She just got her license a couple of weeks ago."

Ah, so that's what Shane and Molloy were acting all shady about!

"I've been so worried about you!" Mary Grace steps toward me and takes my hand. "The last time I saw you…"

"I know." I link my fingers between hers. "Everything's okay, though. I'm fine now. I'm always fine when I'm with you."

Jesus! Why do I always sound so damn awkward? Whatever the reason, Mary Grace doesn't seem to care. She smiles at me bashfully.

"I'm really sorry that I ruined your night last week," I tell her. "I know how important it..."

Mary Grace leans down and silences me with a kiss. My mind reels as I part my lips and kiss her back. After ten seconds or so, she pulls away and locks eyes with me. My heart rate spikes out of control, and I'm self-conscious about being in my boxer shorts for a whole other reason.

Mary Grace glances at the car behind her. "I have to go in a minute," she says. "Brandi borrowed her brother's car, and he needs it back. I'm sorry I can't stay long. I just wanted to come see you for a few minutes. To make sure you're okay."

"I'm really glad you did," I tell her, my lips still tingling.

Mary Grace smiles. "Me, too. We'll hang out again soon, though, okay? We've got some catching up to do." She winks at me as she backs away, and then she turns and walks toward the car. When she reaches the passenger-side door, she looks back at me and waves. "See you later, Will! Take care of yourself, okay?"

"I'll try," I say, waving back at her. "Have a good night, Mary Grace!

———

HOURS LATER, my mind still lingers on our kiss as I lie awake in the darkness of The Dorm. Shane and Molloy snore soundly, and Peaches has passed out in a food coma on the other spare bunk. I stare up at the dark ceiling above me, reliving my brief encounter with Mary Grace. I've only kissed a girl once before, but that was just a game of spin the bottle at some stupid party. This was the first time I've kissed someone I really like and who really likes me back. So that makes it my first *real* kiss, I guess.

It blows my mind how much I seem to matter to Mary Grace. It's like she truly believes I'm worth it, which even makes me start to believe it. I feel this burning need to show her how much she matters to me, too. How she matters more than anyone now.

I understand why Angelo kept telling me to focus on what I was going home to. For him it felt true. Home is where he can be with the people who matter most to him. That certainly isn't true for me. My mom meant the world to me, but that frail, withered body that rests on the hospital bed isn't her. Not anymore.

When you think about it, though, Angelo was right about a lot of things. There is a better place for me out there. A better someone, that is. Mary Grace might not be a home where I can live each day of my life, but I feel most at home when I'm with her. Who could have imagined I would find someone like her in the middle of Nowhere, Mississippi?

I yawn widely. Sleep tugs at my eyelids, but I sit myself up and slide down off the bunk. There's one last thing I need to do tonight. I tiptoe across the room to the desk beside Shane's bed, grab what I need, and return to my bunk. I click on the flashlight to illuminate the notepad on my lap, and I begin what may take me a while to finish. As the tip of my pen touches the paper, I write *Dear Angelo...*

AFTERWORD

JEFF FRANTAL

The more you tell a personal story, the more it becomes just that: a story. For me, recalling memories about experiences I preferred to forget, somehow distanced me from them. Tell your story often enough, and it starts to feel like you're talking about someone else. Eventually, you recite it without reliving it.

The people and experiences from my six years in Victory Ranch left me with an abundance of two things: mental baggage and stories. When I finally emerged from Eastabuchie, Mississippi, I managed to tolerate the former by sharing the latter. I had some crazy-ass tales to tell, and would have one ready for any occasion. I shared funny stories when I wanted laughs, and sad ones when I needed pity, but the horror stories were always reserved to prove that I suffered and still survived...and this was the full extent of my life's accomplishments.

After hearing a story or two, people would sometimes say, "You should write a book!" But, that's just something people say. *Right?* Either way, I had no interest in that idea. Far too many unresolved issues stood in the way, too much trauma to sort through. So I stuck to hand-picking tales to share over pints, road trips, early morning runs, meals, and anywhere else they would fit. That was good enough. Writing about my time in Mississippi would mean going back and picking at old wounds. It would mean revisiting the issues, not to entertain friends between pints, but to understand them better myself. To understand myself better too.

Eventually, I started playing with the idea of a book. Sure, write a book, but how?

I went about this the same way I've survived every day since 1996...I asked for help.

That's where Paul Munro came into the picture. A middle-school English teacher and avid YA reader, I met him at a school where we both taught and were soon good friends. For several reasons, I did not want to go at this alone. When finally deciding to push forward with this book, I asked Paul to be my co-author.

The bastard passed, but, after some convincing, Paul joined this project. Thank God! Paul took the real events and people from my time in Mississippi and was instrumental in turning those things into what you just read.

As for the people, the places, and the events in this story, there's far too much reality and not nearly enough fiction. We were abused by the adults. We abused one another. We deserved better. By now, you have a pretty good idea of what some of my experiences were like, a crash course in boys home life.

Paul and I based Will on my personal boys home experiences, but Will is far cleverer than I ever was. Will's backstory is mine too: lost mom, absent dad, and strings of bad decisions that eventually landed me in the last place I wanted to be. I learned quickly, but Will learned quicker. I made friends, but Will made them far more easily. Our mindsets are basically the same, but using a fictionalized character allowed me to distance myself from it all. Will is the kid I was and the kid I wish I could have been.

While fictionalized, adding Mary Grace made sense to both the story and my experiences, but I came to realize that Mary Grace represents what I was missing in life. How could Will ever get to a good place mentally by the end of this story? Not possible!

Paul had to fight tooth and nail to get me to see otherwise. Mary Grace was the only way. What she offers, what the hope of love offers, can go a long way. Most of these characters and events come from my memories; Mary Grace came from Paul Munro's creativity and persistence. I couldn't imagine this story without her.

Boys home life taught me how to create my own family. There, my friends filled that role and provided all the things a person needs: support, trust, love, companionship, and acceptance. I somehow found those things in the castoffs of Eastabuchie, Mississippi, the middle of Nowhere. They became my family.

Once free, I found mother-types, dad-types, and countless brothers and sisters along the way. I am lucky to be surrounded by these people still. They are my family too. Getting married to my amazing wife and adding our two children completed the circle. Family redefined.

The bizarre, troubling, humorous, and shocking events and people of Victory Ranch haunted me. Looking back, I see how telling those stories and writing this book has been deeply cathartic. There is value in the years I believed to be worthless. Who would have thought?

Six years to live it, thirty years and counting to process it, and two years to write about it, but it has all worked out well enough somehow. You can't find Nowhere, Mississippi on a map, but places and problems like Nowhere tend to find you. What then? If nothing else, I hope this book proves that not only can you survive the worst life throws at you, you can rise far, far above it.

ACKNOWLEDGMENTS

Jeff and Paul would like to thank the following for their support.

- Our wives, Laura and Terri, for their constant love and encouragement.
- Our children: Ally and Katie Frantal; Eileigh, Callum, and Mairi Munro.
- The Bairds of Griffin, Georgia: Allyne, Jon, Joan, Kathy, Lisa, and wee King James.
- Paul's parents: Irene and Robert Munro, for providing moral support from across the pond.
- Our guinea pig readers: Dena, Sami, Andy, Al, Branton, and Margaret.
- Variant Brewing Company of Roswell, Georgia, for fuel and refuge!
- And to all of the friends who cheered us on along the way.

ABOUT THE AUTHORS

Jeff Frantal lives in Roswell, Georgia, with his wife and two daughters. He works as a tutor and has been an educator for over 20 years. *Nowhere, Mississippi* is his first novel and is inspired by his time in a boys home, from 1990 to 1996.

———

Born in Edinburgh, Scotland, Paul Munro is a former middle school English teacher who lives in Marietta, Georgia, with his wife and three children. He is a member of the Atlanta Writers Club, and *Nowhere, Mississippi* is his first novel.